1 MONTH OF
FREE
READING

at

www.ForgottenBooks.com

By purchasing this book you are eligible for one month membership to ForgottenBooks.com, giving you unlimited access to our entire collection of over 1,000,000 titles via our web site and mobile apps.

To claim your free month visit:

www.forgottenbooks.com/free792762

ISBN 978-0-656-33827-6
PIBN 10792762

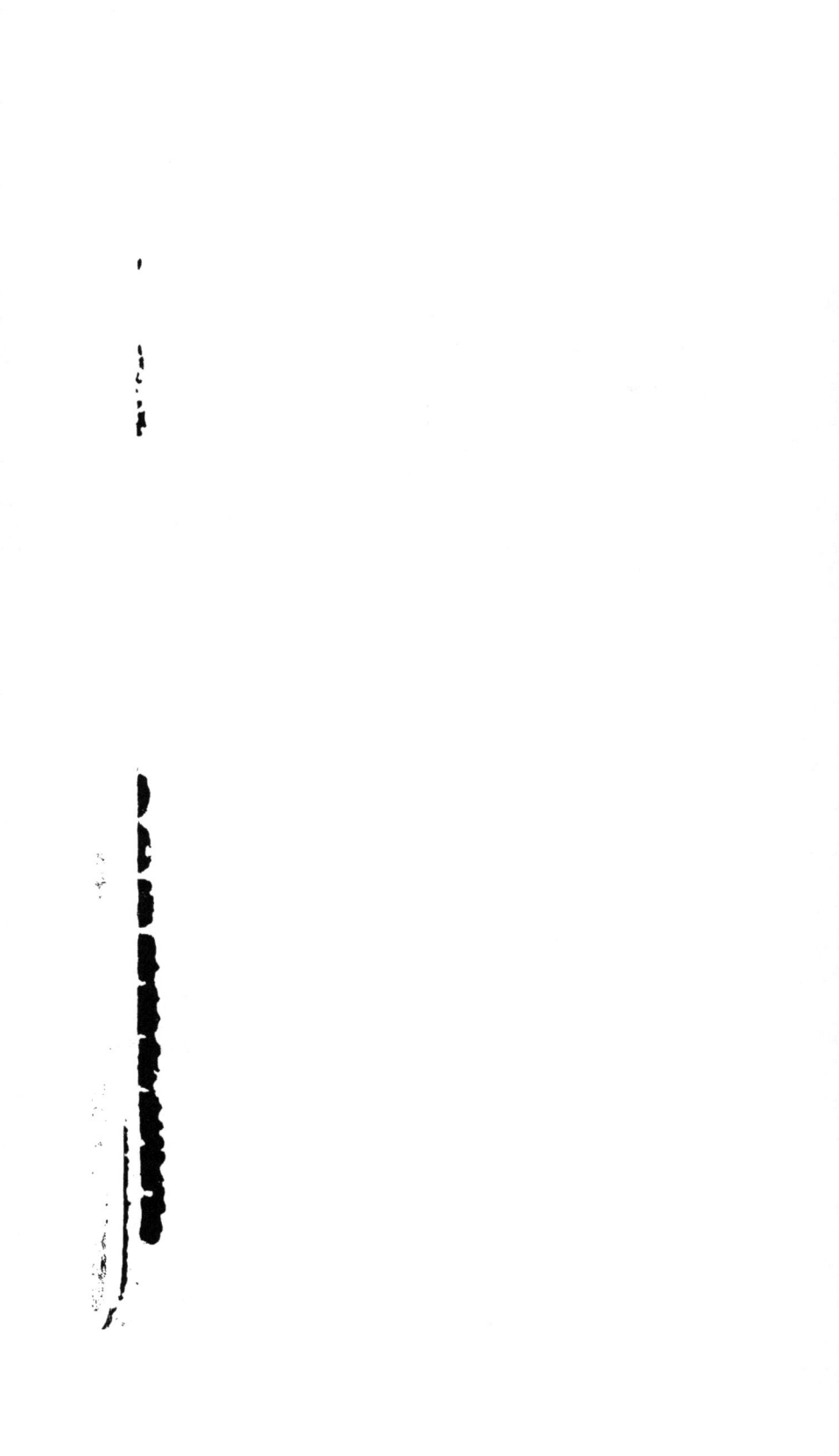

1ˢᵀ Thro

FAUCIT OF BALLIOL

A Story in Two Parts.

BY

HERMAN CHARLES MERIVALE.

New Edition.

LONDON:

CHAPMAN & HALL, Limited, 11, HENRIETTA ST.
COVENT GARDEN.

1882.

Bungay:

CLAY AND TAYLOR, PRINTERS.

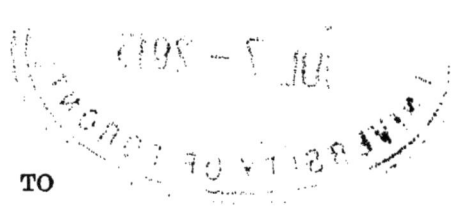

TO

Virginia and Isabel Bateman,

IN KINDLY MEMORY OF THEIR MOTHER, MRS. S. F. BATEMAN,

TO WHOSE FIRST SUGGESTION AND FAVOURITE IDEA

THE ORIGIN OF THIS STORY IS DUE,

THE BOOK WHICH GREW GRADUALLY OUT OF IT INTO ITS PRESENT

PROPORTIONS, IS DEDICATED BY THEIR ATTACHED FRIEND

THE AUTHOR.

HAZARD SIDE,
    EASTBOURNE,
September, 1881.

CONTENTS.

PART I.
The Prologue.

viii CONTENTS.

PART II.

𝕿𝖍𝖊 𝕯𝖗𝖆𝖒𝖆.

CONTENTS.

PREFACE.

SOME words now omitted from the dedication and title-page of this story have been so much misunderstood by certain of my critics, that I take privilege of preface to assure my readers that such as it is this story is entirely my own, and is no more "on the lines of Goethe's 'Faust'" than of Homer's 'Iliad,' which it is indeed open to anybody to discover for himself. It is indebted for nothing but the starting-point all stories need. I could give many proofs of this, whereof to the candid soul one will suffice: namely, that, to my discredit be it said, I am so poor a German scholar and so little addicted to translations, that when I wrote this story I had never read one line of Goethe's 'Faust.' I am afraid it is too clear that the critics in question hadn't either.

One of them, writing of the play which I based upon the same story (and the modern dramatic critic of a certain type is of all men the most fearfully and wonderfully made), produced a column and a half of disquisition on the philosophy of Goethe (having no bearing on my work whatever), which deserves to be remembered beyond its passing hour for the profundity of its conceptions. The writer even addressed to me language of severe reprobation for having ventured to produce, in the man-servant Chaffers, a *shadow of Mephistopheles' poodle!* I only meant him for a man-servant, and startled at the charge, I inquired what it might mean. Now in Goethe's poem Mephisto is first introduced into the laboratory of Faust under the guise of a dog; and I fear me that the writer in question having somewhere heard of this, had evolved from his consciousness the peculiar theory that Goethe's devil kept a lap-dog.

Is it necessary to add that the journal responsible for this amazing feat of scholarship and candour says that it has "the largest circulation in the world"? It ought.

H. C. M.

June 15, 1882.

FAUCIT OF BALLIOL.

PART I.

The Prologue.

CHAPTER I.

GUY AND DAISY.

TIME was made for slaves, not chroniclers; and I will not undertake to give an exact date, but say that it might have been some fifteen or twenty years ago, when there met for the first time, among all the gaieties and forgetfulnesses of an Oxford commemoration, a young fellow of Balliol and a prosperous city merchant's pretty daughter, to make up their minds respectively in about ten minutes, and to know they had made them up in about as many days, that there never could have been such a Balliol fellow, or such a merchant's daughter, in existence before. They saw each other first "on the banks," dear on a summer evening to the heart of every Oxford man, where Guy Faucit of Balliol, who in taking to the lecture-room had not forgotten his victorious captaincy of the Oxford eight, was engaged in the mysteries and delight of coaching the present crew

/₵/   B

of his college for a forthcoming struggle with Third
Trinity for the cup at Henley. Guy Faucit was a
household word among the mariners of Isis : for for
three consecutive years he had left Cambridge in the
lurch at the historic goal of Mortlake, first with the
matchless stroke which kept such a clean and even
swing for the whole length of the course, steady and
strong as a pendulum, and never quickening up through
loss of nerve or want of reserve of power, till just the
critical moment of the finish, when he launched out
in the sharp, strong spurt which set all the ranks of
Oxford cheering from the steamboats, and defied all
the pluck and skill of the Light Blue to redress the
balance or to score a victory. The "Faucit spurt" was
a proverb, like the "botte Nevers" of the "Duke's
Motto." Then, as the bones grew stronger-fleshed
and the muscles harder, he subsided into the less
conspicuous place of number seven, and there, too, with
his eyes fixed between the shoulders of his stroke-oar,
kept him up to the tradition of the conquering stroke.
The stroke would row with an energy not his own when
he felt that he had Faucit behind him, and it was not
till Guy, as strong and original at his books as at his
oar, had come out as the best first-class man of his
year,—repute in this instance being too strong for the
alphabetical precedence which at Oxford shrouds the
senior classic in a becoming mystery (even before that
he was *facile princeps* for the last vacant fellowship of
his college),—and taken his place among the instructors
of youth while yet as young a man as many of them,.
that the sister-university could get a chance of her share
in the birthright again. Guy Faucit's was the stalwart
six-foot figure which at a round swing-trot kept pace
on the shore with the swing of the Balliol eight, as she
shot through the narrows of "the gut" as straight as
an arrow, under the cunning hand of the Honourable
James Gosling, who was cut out by nature for a "cox,"
and regarded the post as the height of athletic distinction. On Faucit he depended with a filial interest, and

implicitly trusted him both to marshal him to victory
at Henley, and to "pull him through" his divinity in
the schools. James was very much exercised about his
"divinity;" but a close examination, on his side, of
the ways and customs of examiners, having convinced
him that to their minds the word conveyed no theo-
logical or doctrinal meaning whatever, but resolved
itself into a question of dates and hard names, he
was growing easier about the future. He had learned
both to spell and to pronounce Mahershalalhashbaz and
Cushanrethashaim, having satisfied himself that, as
names of eighteen and sixteen letters respectively, they
were the two longest-winded monarchs in the Old Testament, and good enough to floor any examiner withal.
He carried an abstract of the list of the kings of Israel
about on his shirt-cuffs in the form of a *memória
technica*, while the kings of Judah occupied the crown
of his hat. And at the foot of his bed, so that it might
meet his eyes the first thing in the morning, and
preside over the extinction of his candle at night, was
a table inscribed with some mysterious hexameters,
beginning—

Crof Deletoff Abaneb Exafna Tembybe Cyruts.

Years afterwards, when his hairs were turning grey,
would the Honourable James remember that hexameter,
and wonder what on earth it could have meant.

Stowed away among cushions in a punt, in the
charge of two happy and envied undergraduates who
had the fortune of the acquaintance of Mr. Fairfield of
the City, merchant, a certain Miss Daisy Fairfield
watched the advance of the Balliol eight, and of the
figure on the opposite bank, from a lair among the
grasses on the Oxford side, somewhere below the point
where the lazy little Cherwell tumbles into the arms
of Isis, just in time to see many a good ship "bumped"
into a lower place.

The "'Varsity" barge, and the lesser barges
clustered about it, were gay with innumerable buntings

and bands of uncompromising brass (for the most
part limited in their repertory to the "Hardy Norse-
man"), and butterfly toilettes of the most fascinating kind and the most tempting variety, setting
off the pretty and wholesome faces of the sweet girl
wearers, deeply intent upon the results of this near
glimpse into the inner life and youth of the mysterious
and more favoured animal called man. He, on his
side, divided himself even at that early age into the
two classes of the susceptible and the hardened, the
duck and the brute, and either hung entranced on
Beauty's notes, and tethered in her ribands, or walked
the banks apart, a thing of misogyny, in a suit of
flannel even more decided than usual, or with a face
jaundiced with an extra dose of the midnight oil,
and contracted into that expression of inward pain so
commonly consequent upon a debauch of Aristotle.
Gosling always maintained that, until the birth of
Aldrich, no one man had ever caused so much suffering
"off his own bat" as the classical monster whom he
always described as the "Staggerist."

Close by where Daisy sate was the punt of the
champion punter of the world, hanging out for a
motto the rather lugubrious legend, innocent of a
personal pronoun, "Saved the lives of many gentlemen." And, dressed in all the bright and daring
combinations of colour which Young Summer rejoices
in, to the encouragement of healthy-minded people
who believe in colours and combinations, the beautiful
Christchurch meadows, with dainty little Merton set
like a gem in the centre background, looked their
pleasantest upon the scene. Not without reason does
the Oxonian cherish in his heart a placid conviction
that he may set his Christchurch meadows against the
famous "backs of the colleges" in the Light-Blue
land, and not be afraid of the comparison.

There then sate Daisy Fairfield, revelling in the
beauty and interest of the scene, and in the comfort
of her situation, as she nestled among her cushions,

trusting herself to the adroitness of her youthful punters, whose control over their cumbrous instrument occasionally suggested that under more hazardous conditions they might be more likely to destroy the lives of many gentlemen than to save them.

Except, perhaps, the paddle of a canoe, nothing is more capricious than a punt-pole in the ambitious hands of youth, possessed as it is of all the malignity of inanimate objects to a degree not emulated till the invention of the bicycle, that iron fiend, which, when running away with a man down-hill, produces in his mind a sense of helplessness surpassing show. Jem Gosling's first appearance in a punt was never forgotten by his friends, when he embarked upon a race, without having tried his hand before, impressed by the obvious easiness of the thing. He got his bark, or had it propelled for him, into the mid-current, swung it round slowly twice on its own axis, something receding in the process, then walked straight over the side after his punt-pole into the water, and wallowed. Daisy's guides, however, were a little more skilled than that, and at this moment were resting on their poles, cradled by the waving grasses under the shore.

"It's a splendid sight," said Daisy, with enthusiasm, as she saw the Balliol crew coming up with a will, the eight broad and red-striped backs working together like a machine. "Splendid!" she exclaimed, her eyes lighting up as she watched the men.

Daisy Fairfield was one of those who move and speak as goddesses among women, with a girlhood promising a very majesty of maturity. Hers was the veined-marble complexion, with the paleness of statue-land, not of ill-health, touched with a tender rose by exercise or excitement; the tall and free and supple figure which matches such complexions best; the violet eyes with the black bull's eye, and the wealth of wavy hair, of chestnut toned with gold, in all the pride and glory of eighteen. No touch of hardness was in the look or in the voice then, to mar the picture with a thought of ill. It was a picture of happiness and goodness undefiled.

Oh ye men and women, oh ye women and men, who from selfishness, vindictiveness, perversity, love of gain, any of the paltry and self-avenging motives which grow so fast by what they feed on, and spring up like brambles round the strait gate and the narrow way, to choke the access further, — ye who, in despite of love's simplest message, seem to delight in working your neighbour harm, to the baffling of the comprehension of more single-purposed hearts, do you never think, I wonder, when you see the outward and visible traces of your doings on the faces and lives of those, at whose expense you did them? do the terrible warnings of the olden law carry with them no fear, no starting of the conscience that will not die in you, by whatever name you call it—evolution, or indigestion, or what not? Under those outward and visible signs, too often, lies an inward and invisible scar beyond your healing, though it was not beyond your making; a scar of the heart or of the mind, or maybe of the soul. Go down on those straightened knees of yours, even at the eleventh hour of the night, and pray, though it be but in the name of the poor modern clay-god called Humanity, that you may yet do unto others as ye would that they should do unto you. If you have wronged your neighbour, ask him to forgive you, and if he humbly holds a better faith than yours, remember this—his creed teaches him to ask for pardon, even as he is ready to give it freely when he is freely asked. But I cannot so read the Divine and loving command as to see that it enjoins the impossible, and asks of man what he cannot do, to forgive unasked. As with the Divine pardon, so with the human, the one condition precedent of forgiveness would seem to be this—let the wrongdoer come, and ask to be forgiven. The Lord "forgave that servant" because he asked Him.

But I am anticipating here, and would not mar my

own memory further, of Daisy Fairfield as she was in those Oxford days.

Up the river then came the Balliol eight, cheered by an indiscriminate band of admirers racing up the Berkshire bank, and heralded by the "long stern swell" of Faucit's steady and musical lungs.

A pleasant companion-picture was he to the eye, the English athlete of some eight-and-twenty, with the big forehead and the clear blue eyes, which shall explain themselves later.

"Put your back into it, three." And three, conscience-stricken, put in his back.

"Put his back into what?" asked Daisy, maliciously or in good faith. "Where else is it to go? It's big enough, certainly."

Tompkins of Trinity explained how backs were put in.

"Oh! And who is the director-general of backs on the other bank, who runs so fast and shouts so loud?"

"You don't mean to say you don't know?" cried Bones of Balliol, scandalized. "Why that's Faucit; not P. W.,—the other."

"Not P. W.,—the other," repeated Daisy, reflectively. "Indeed! This becomes really interesting, and will take time. Forgive me my ignorance, and tell me first, who is P. W.? I want to reduce the situation to its primitive elements."

"P. W.'s Faucit of Exeter, the mathematical fellow, a long thin man in goggles, who was proctor last year, and got it hot in the theatre. I wish you'd heard it. The men all let out like mad, for he'd proctorized half the place."

"How did he do that, and what is it when it's done? I'm learning, you know."

"Well, proctorizing means having a man up for something—going about in mufti, or having a spread at the Mitre, or that sort of thing."

"It sounds very bad, and should be punished. What does the proctor do for it?"

"Generally gets a man gated, you know," said Bones. "It's an awful nuisance in the summer term." "It would be. Proctorizing seems to be what the police call taking up." "Something in the same line. But the proctor's the peeler and the beak all in one—first runs you in and then sits on you. That's not fair any way." "As far as I understand it, it isn't. Why don't you apply for a Habeas Corpus when you're gated, and bring an action for false imprisonment?" "Oh," commented Tompkins, "that's law. We haven't got any law here, except the Vice-Chancellor's Court. He's dead the other way." "No law?" said Daisy. "What a delightful place! How one lives and learns. I never knew that the University was a sort of modern Alsatia." "What's that?" enquired Bones. "Don't you know? They ought to teach you." "Don't teach us much later down than Rome. It's not the form." "How odd the difference of form is," remarked Daisy. "They don't teach us girls much higher up than the piano. And my education has been so neglected that I never heard of P. W., or of the other. And now I want to know all about him too. You have given me such a description of P. W.'s moral and physical qualities in a few words, Mr. Bones, that I believe I should know him if I met him. Now tell me about the other."

"Ah! that's another sort altogether. That's Faucit of our place, commonly called 'The Clipper,' and familiarly loved as old Guy. He was the best stroke the 'Varsity eight ever had, and he's a crack tennis·player besides."

"He might have been one of the best men in the eleven too," chimed in Tompkins, "only he said he couldn't do everything, and hadn't the time to get out to Cowley Marsh often enough."

"But he can do everything for all that," added

Bones. "Just look at what he did in the brains line—got the Balliol before he came up, and the Hertford in his first year, and the Ireland in his second, and a double-first in Mods. before you knew where you were."

"And only didn't do the same in Greats," said Tompkins, "because he liked classics best, and said he didn't believe in a man trying too much, just like the cricket."

"Besides, he wanted to have time for his own reading, which he's very fond of," chorussed Bones. "And he got a fellowship at the old place before he went in for his degree, and the dons said they wouldn't have it done again."

"Because it wouldn't be fair on the others," quoth Tompkins. "And now he's the best lecturer and the jolliest don in the place, and as good a fellow with the men of other colleges as he is with his own."

"And still coaches the eight as nobody else can coach it, and puts on half-fifteen a year at tennis. Ran old Barre himself hard the other day, at the fair odds of side-walls and openings."

"Putting on half-fifteen and running old Barre must be wonderfully exciting," smiled Daisy, inwardly delighted with the honest and lovable enthusiasm of her young squires. "You all seem quite fond of 'the other.'"

"I should think we were," said Bones.

"Grand old trump," added Tompkins. And so "The Works of Guy Faucit," as they would have been called in Homer, were sung in the true epic style by his two chroniclers.

Daisy Fairfield felt really interested and attracted by the history, as she had been at once by the striking appearance of the man with the strong rather than handsome features, the curly crisp brown hair, the fair Saxon complexion, and the look of power upon the face. Daisy was a student in heads, and a foe to the commonplace. She might have asked and heard more of Faucit, had not the inevitable chaperon—for let not

my readers believe that this scene had passed without
one—at this moment woke from a refreshing slumber.
She was a nice, pleasant-looking specimen of portly
middle-age, brooding over the youthful three like a
mature duck.

"I think, my dear, I should like to go ome to tea,"
said Mrs. Pepperharrow. "There's the ball to-night,
and you mustn't overeat yourself."

"Overeat herself, Mrs. Pepperharrow!" said the
astonished Bones.

"The eat of the sun, Mr Bones, is great upon the·
river."

"Oh! quite so. I beg your pardon."

CHAPTER II.

THE BALLIOL ROOMS.

MIDNIGHT! yet not an eye in the academic city closed
in sleep. No eye, at least, belonging to any one with a
proper measure of self-respect; for all the world and his
sweetheart were at that year's Christchurch Ball. It
was what is called a grand commemoration in the year
I write of, and beautiful Alma Mater was in her
blandest mood of motherhood, favoured by weather
which showed her everywhere at her best. Foliage
and sward looked their softest and greenest in the fair
gardens of Worcester and St. John; and the leaves of
Magdalen Walks, with their belt of trees girdling the
old enclosure, whispered their confidences to young
undergraduate lovers and their goddesses for the hour,
and discreetly kept the secret of those they listened to
in return. The fantastic figures perched on their
pedestals in Magdalen quadrangle grinned sympa-
thetically at the young people who came in and went
out in a more advanced stage of the world's most

chronic malady. It was a fine time for pairing, and
the opportunity was not lost. Many a young and
ambitious fellow of his college, vowed only the week
before to celibacy and the comfortable selfishness of the
Common Room, began to count the cost of deserting
academic life for the bar or the press, winning name
and fame by persuasive orations at Westminster, or
trenchant witticisms in the 'Saturday Review,' and
leaving the dead languages to bury their dead, for the
sake of some pair of bright eyes which had suddenly
flashed in upon his solitude, and burned decided holes
in his trencher-cap and gown.

On the evening before Show Sunday he had been
proudly looking forward into a distant future, to the
day when he might stand before the world of his
measuring-rod as the Provost or Principal of his college,
after serving all the stages of tutor and bursar in due
course. Then, perhaps, he would take unto himself a
helpmeet upon proper prudential and academic principles, suitable to him in years and views of life, to sit
at his feet and the bottom of his table, and shine with
the reflected radiance of his scholastic glory. To him,
perhaps, as the old stage-directions say, entered on that
Show Sunday some gracious young vision in flowers
and lace, entirely frivolous and illogically sweet, with
no special charm for many but the bloom of English
girlhood, suddenly to upset all his calculations through
the open sesame of an "introduction," under the broad
interlacing branches which span the Broad Walk of
Christchurch in the earliest order of architecture, to
the silver Sunday music of Oxford's innumerable bells.
Without rhyme or reason would young Suckling of
Oriel change his theories of existence at this touch of
harlequin Fortune's motley wand, and contemplate
"das irdische Glück" from an altogether different
point of view. After all, was he not born to get it
"genossen" in the time-honoured fashion of the
majority of healthy-hearted mankind?

Is it possible that some such spirit as this, summoned

in His inscrutable purpose from the vasty deeps of
life by the great Enchanter's voice, overshadowed Guy
Faucit's strong will and sober nature with a warning, on that afternoon by the river? Even as he
was swinging steadily up the bank, intent as usual
just upon what he was doing and no more, keenly
marking the merits and defects of the young athletes
working their best under his experienced eye, and
inwardly resolving the possible results of effecting a
change in the boat between numbers six and seven,
he caught a rapid glimpse, in passing, of a girl's
figure propped up among the cushions of a punt,
in an attitude of genuine interest in the doings of
his crew. He just marked her in passing, and as he
was crossing to the Balliol barge with a boatful of
other men, after the cruise was finished, he saw her
again, closer and more at his leisure, springing ashore
from her little bark under the emulous guardianship
of Bones and Tompkins. They passed him close by,
and as Bones saluted him with the proper sign of
respect due to his tutor, mingled with an obvious
dash of pride in his own new duties, Faucit instinctively raised his hat in answer, and bestowed a very
honest and respectful look of admiration upon Daisy
Fairfield. Whether she looked at him or not at the
same moment I cannot undertake to say; but certainly
she saw him. And when a rapid little Parthian glance
shot back at him over her shoulder when she had
gone a little further with Bones (Tompkins, the sly
dog, was sedulously paying court to good Mrs. Pepperharrow), it fell upon a responsive place; for the fact
is, that Faucit of Balliol was looking after her with all
his might and main.

"Good Heavens!" he thought to himself, "what
a lovely girl!" But the vision passed; and Guy
Faucit, his hands in his pockets in attitude profound,
whistling to himself a few rather thoughtful bars,
strolled homewards through the busy corn-market to
his rooms in Balliol.

The rooms in Balliol, which he had tenanted ever since he took his first class five years before, and had gradually furnished and improved with every evidence of scholarship and taste, making a hobby of them, seemed that evening, he couldn't imagine why, to want something he couldn't conceive what. The pictures were few and grave and good, carefully chosen and paid for at a good round price, for the most part the most careful reproductions that the engraver or his kindred artists could furnish of the solid masterpieces of an olden day. There Titian's daughter carried her fruit and flowers, with the fair head thrown back in the attitude as perfect in its audacity of pose as in its nature and its grace; there the pretty chocolate-girl, whom Dresden loves through the eyes of Liotard, proffered her dish of sober drink with the slightly contemptuous air of a young person something above her work, and apt to dream of the marble halls which a posse of Saxon admirers had no doubt placed at her disposal; there Rembrandt's bonnie wife sat perched upon the knee of her painter-husband, her head and his twisted round, the one festively and the other coquett-ishly, over the brimming glass of honest German beer; and there, in its deep unfathomable awe, the despair of painters past, present, and to come, not all lost or wanting even through the medium of the copyist, above the watching reverence of the upturned baby-faces, the strange, ineffable, thrilling mystery of God-head upon earth looked down upon the gazer, out of the eyes of the mother and child of Our Lady of San Sisto.

The books which lined the walls were kindred to the pictures: so that nothing seemed wanting in the two classes of home-companions, which, with a com-fortable dog curled up on the hearth-rug, make the most loving and responsive company for the $\mu\acute{\epsilon}\rho\omega\psi$ $\grave{\alpha}\nu\grave{\eta}\rho$ of a worthy mould, who lives, from choice or destiny, alone. They were chosen for reading, and looked all read, gradually gathered with a gradual patience, so that they were still small in bulk though great in matter. Bindings and editions were not neglected, though not essential: a clear, readable type being the only definite condition grafted upon the contents of the book. The Catholic taste of the reader was evident from the various nature of the subject-matters, and evidently had chosen for its province the masterpieces of style and thought rather than any special line of study. English literature was the staple of the collection, though French and German had their proper part in the arrangements, and Latin and Greek, as became a classical tutor, were respectfully, but not overpoweringly, represented.

The little inner sanctum—for in the larger room the pupils were received—told a tale of another kind. Stags' heads spoke of long-vacation stalkings in the North; an amazing collection of miscellaneous and polyglottic pipes recorded wanderings over half the tobacco-smoking world; and silver oars and silver racquets, and tankards whose very sight suggested the Elysian pleasures of a "long drink," sang of many victories in the athletic field. In such a little bachelor's paradise, what was it of which Faucit, who had grown into his life and his rooms, can suddenly have felt an unrealized want that evening? Did he miss the serpent, or the serpent's inducement?

He had ordered a quiet and solitary dinner in his rooms, and in due course his servant appeared with it. The college cook, a discriminating artist, who was quite as capable of catering for the cultivated taste of a travelled fellow, as for satisfying the zoological appetites of undergraduates with hunkiform beeves and mutton, provided Faucit with a dainty, but not the less solid, repast, of which Guy, whatever the nature of his reflections, ate with an irreproachable zest and a generous capacity, mixing his liquors in defiance of the modern science of Dyspepticism, and correcting bitter beer with his favourite Burgundy. The meal over, he had installed himself in his leathern chair, with a pet pipe and a cup of black coffee, slippered and magazined, when a knock at the door interrupted his occupations.

"Come in," he said, not altogether sorry to be interrupted, for, hard-worker as he was, he was gregarious of soul; and the figure of the youthful Bones presented itself.

"Hallo, Bones; what do you want?"

"Well, sir, I came to ask if you'd excuse me from reading essay to-morrow. The fact is, I've been about all day with friends, and haven't got it done."

"In which state you certainly can't read it," said Faucit. "But why don't you go to your rooms now, and work away till you've done it?"

"It would take me a good long time, sir. I'm always slow over my essay-work. And I've got to go, at least I want to go, to the Christchurch Ball to-night."

"Well, we mustn't be too particular at Commemoration time. But remember, the schools ain't very far off, my boy, and you want a good deal of brushing up."

"I know I do, sir; and you're so kind in working with me, that I'd even give the ball up and get through the grind if you wished it."

"I don't wish it," answered the other. "You'll have a day or two after the balls and flower-shows before you go down, and you can finish off the essay easily enough. I suppose it'll be a good ball?"

"First-rate, sir. The thing's to be really well done. Ain't you thinking of going?"

"I?" said Faucit. "No; I've some work of my own on hand, and there's nobody up this time I know much about. You seem better off. Are you going with the ladies I saw you with by the river to-day?"

"I'm going to meet them there, sir. Did you see them?"

"Just in passing. The girl looked very pretty."

"That's just what she is," said Bones, "and no mistake about that. And she's as nice as she's pretty, too. My governor knows hers in business in London, so they asked me to call when they came on Saturday, and I've been doing the right thing for them all the week. I had some waltzes with her at the Masonic Ball last night which I shan't forget in a hurry, and I'm going to repeat the dose to-night. I wish you'd come, sir. I should like to introduce you to Miss Fairfield."

"That's her name, is it?" said Guy. "I don't do much in the ball way now, and haven't since I took my degree: so I'm afraid I shouldn't be much addition to the party. Dance away, and good luck to you."

"Thank you, sir. I'll be sure to have the essay done before we go down. I wish you'd come; but if you won't, good night."

"Good night, Bones." And the youngster took his departure.

Guy Faucit smoked on awhile, drank his coffee, and meditated over his magazine. Then he sat down at a well-covered writing-table, and plunged into pen and ink. He had made himself a good name already among the Saturday Reviewers, then a band of keen and ardent spirits, who had given a new impulse to journalism by their fresh and powerful and witty work, and attracted many a young college ambition to their ranks. Strong sense and scholarship were Faucit's best points in the contribution, and even at that age he was not fond of the practice of anonymous vivisection. He did his work carefully that evening, and rather slowly, more than once travelling away from it; but the power of concentration, which was his in a marked degree, existed then as afterwards, and he had a habit of mastering any stray access of wilfulness in an uncompromising way. *Age quod agis* stood him in good stead as his motto in everything; and he had once distinguished himself by entering under the head of his "favourite occupation," in one of those senseless feminine albums which record a series of imaginary preferences improvised under pressure of invention, "whatever I happen to be doing."

So he finished his article at the cost of some increase in the tax on his time, smoked another pipe and turned over the pages of a new novel, and then began to meditate on bed. He looked at his bed and he looked at his watch, *plurima mente revolvens;* and he began to undress, and he walked up and down his room, and again he sat and meditated. Then he contemplated his night-gown comfortably folded on his pillow, while only the sounds of night came up to him from the quiet quadrangle. Then he took a sudden excursion to his wardrobe, and surveyed his evening clothes, submitting them evidently to a mental test of comparison. Then he visited his snuggery again, and from the glass behind the mantel-piece took down a ticket. Then he made that indescribable but definite sound to himself, which appears in the play-books under the form of "Humph"; and finally, as with a mind suddenly made up at the price of some self-disapproval, he put himself into those evening clothes of his rapidly enough, and after a placid exit through the porter's lodge—that official regarding him with some respectful astonishment—he swung down the street at a steady pace, and as the clock was on the stroke of twelve he found himself among the guests at the Christchurch Ball.

CHAPTER III.

THE CHRISTCHURCH BALL.

DAISY FAIRFIELD was in the full flush of a young girl's triumph. If I could choose my experiences of the raptures of life, I should like to be a great statesman for a season, a victorious soldier for another, a

C

successful author for a third, and a reigning beauty
for a fourth. In the absolute intoxication of effect
I imagine that the last of the four may have the
best of us all. There must be something in that
spontaneous homage, not called out as the result of
labour or of years, but offered without reserve at the
shrine of youth in its most winning natural guise, by
statesman and soldier and author and everybody else,
which has no parallel in the grosser experiences of
man.

Daisy Fairfield tasted the cup to the full in this
her year of grace. Her father was prominent among
the sober race of London merchants, becoming fast
less well represented than it used to be, who built
solid fortunes by solid and honourable work, and without attempting to vie with the magnificent palaces of
Belgravian and Kensington districts, which with all
their size look as if they were meant to be sold to
a company at an early date, contented themselves
with strong and comfortable houses on the slopes of
Bloomsbury, or, under the influence of the westward-ho
movement which seems to be the history of all big
towns, in the regions of Portland Place.

In those broad and airy latitudes our Daisy bloomed.
Her father's friends were of that large and varied class
which probably, amongst a good deal of dulness, supplies about the pleasantest varieties of London society,
I do not say of social life. I suppose that the socio-
geographer would map it out as part of the "upper
middle," whatever that dissective formula may imply.
Lawyers rising and risen make perhaps the chief staple
of it, and a pleasant staple too. Notwithstanding the
fabled preference of the sex for soldiers and curates,
the barristers hold their ground very well, by right,
I suppose, of the power of talk which is presumed
by privilege and practice to belong to them, though
in too many cases on slight ground enough. The
"chambers" which are supposed to receive them daily
seem to have a very doubtful existence in some cases,

and to leave them free for dinners and balls and junketings innumerable, even sometimes for those two haunts of the acknowledged idlers, which stamp imprudent youth as "no good to anybody" in the working world—the Park and the five o'clock tea. But others, and, as a rule, it must be admitted pleasanter ones, fight their wig-armed battle of life to a purpose under the god-like discipline of patience, and mean business, as soon as they can get it, very emphatically. In the same set are their successful seniors to encourage them; and the ambitious junior who has just been getting perhaps snubbed in court, much to an inward moving of the spirit and a conviction that till you become a Q.C., and can command success, justice is but a name, is consoled by dining at the same table with the kindly old judge who inserted that flea in his ear, and makes up for it by bestowing on him words of friendly counsel, and the results of his own full life and experience.

And the while, and perhaps better still, young Tyro is consoled by a flirtation with his lordship's pretty daughter, whose bright eyes beam upon him with unprofessional encouragement, while her lips assure him that there was a time, and a very long time, when papa despaired of ever getting any business whatever.

"Of course he says he never had any connection at all, Mr. Tyro, and got into a big practice at once by his own merits, dear old thing. And his merits were always splendid, you know. But mamma told me that it was nothing of the kind, and that when I was born she didn't know how they were ever going to get on. And if it hadn't been for a first cousin down in the north who was a big attorney, and wanted to do him a good turn, I don't believe papa would ever have done anything at the bar at all." So the young. counsellor lives on hope, and retails pleasant circuit-stories in a very cheery and attractive way.

Rising and working journalists and writers, doing

mysterious somethings in unconfessed anonyme, and
reputed to be dreadfully clever, with here and there
a lawless dramatist, the subject of much shaking of
the head and evil omen, as of one hurrying downwards
on the broad path of self-destruction, but nevertheless
of some secret admiration and envy, as the privileged
denizen of a mysterious world not open to everybody
—these and other waifs and strays of the many-minded
ocean of labour, generally thrown high and dry to
begin with, by the inhospitable wave of the Bar—with
distinguished professional physicians to give the talk
another savour no less pleasant in its way, city-toilers
to bring their quota of experience, and rose-buttoned
government clerks to give an airy jauntiness to the
whole, make up the society which has a distinctive life
of its own, and provides busy-hearted London with a
second and a winter season, full of welcome associations
and attractions which belong to it, rather than to the
crush and hurry of the spring and summer. In this
society Daisy came to grown-up life, to become at
once the first prize in the garden. Her mother was
a chronic invalid who lived retired; so she was the
pride and charge of various chaperons, but most of the
good-natured Mrs. Pepperharrow, who was a general
favourite for her known possession of that attribute, and
devoted to Daisy. Her husband, Mr. Pepperharrow,
was a great success in soap-boiling, and through city
matters first had been brought into intimate relations
with the Fairfields, who were near neighbours of his
in the house in Portland Place.

Like Scott's imaginary June-rose, Daisy had first
"budded fain" in winter's snow, during this preliminary season, with a large and-wide-spreading result
upon her segment of the circle I have described.
The most opposite effects were created in the most
opposite minds. The young barrister hitherto devoted
to his work grew suddenly neglectful, and appeared
at five o'clock teas, a rare and welcome animal, to
the delight of the world of womanhood, which at

these entertainments is so unfairly in the majority. He shared the masculine honours, probably, with the last and most depressing product of the new civilization, the comic-singer of the drawing-room, who "entertains" in the evening in those epicene public resorts which mainly supply the theatric wants of the large class of people who still look upon theatres as something vaguely wrong, and express approval or emotion in nothing louder than a gentle sibillant sound, as thus—s-s-s. When Lambkin of the Colonial Office first took up this semi-public line, he was much disconcerted by these sounds, which he thought meant hissing. But after a time he found they were simply what reached his ear of the confidential and admiring criticism of one fair Philistine to her neighbour, and meant—"How s-silly!" Then he was consoled, and persevered in the path of glory. In the afternoon Lambkin was the stay of five o'clock teas, and was never so glad as when he met some wandering solitary male, to whom to confide "what an awful audience" this was.

The idle barrister, meanwhile, took an opposite cause, deserted his usual haunts except in the evening, appeared in court regularly at ten o'clock and in chambers afterwards, and dreamed of some un-imagined income to lay at Daisy Fairfield's feet. Her singular charm exercised its power upon nearly all who came across her, and made her a prime favourite with young and old, for of the society of the last she showed herself provokingly fond. She liked somebody who had done something, she would tell her distracted adorers, and was always ready to throw over the best waltzer among them, if he had nothing better than his youth and his waltzing to boast of, for a chat with some older and more travelled mariner on the seas of time. Something grave and deep looked out of the clear blue eyes, more akin, as by some forecast of a troubled future, with the trials and struggles of this life of ours, than with its sunnier and more thoughtless day. A deep reader in her quiet hours at home, loving to steep her mind in the thoughts and the wisdom of the wise and thoughtful, she took enjoyments as they came frankly and happily; but even while she seemed most thoroughly a part of the world of mere pleasure, she was yet more deeply a careful watcher of the "divine tragi-comedy" of life. She was so happy and frank withal, however, that she never frightened her young worshippers away—many as may have been the mortal quarrels which rose on her account between Damon and Pythias, or Orestes and Pylades—though she would often find an opportunity, by some quiet word of timely but seemingly careless counsel, to strengthen some waverer for the world of work, some trifler for the life of earnest. There was no fate for her among them, though; and through the first half-year of her queenly life in her world's eye, she moved like Queen Elizabeth through her own spacious times, in worthy maiden meditation, fancy-free. So her young life passed on through its opening stage, and through the first months of the London season proper, during which she made but small incursion into the more fashionable regions of society's latitudes and longitudes, until, through the persuasion of some young Oxonian whom she had met and fraternized with at her father's table, she added an Oxford Commemoration to the scene of her growing experience.

Her card was full from a very early date, at that Christchurch ball; but, truth to tell, some of the names that filled it were rather hard to decipher, and occupied some occasional blanks with mysterious pencil-marks of her own. She did not quite know what Oxford might bring forth worth talking to or sitting out with, and wisely reserved herself for emergencies. The scene was very bright and very gay, and Daisy Fairfield was well pleased and happy. She liked her unsophisticated cavaliers thoroughly, had picked up an amazing amount of miscellaneous information on university politics in general, and even mastered something of the secrets of half-fifteen and old Barre, by a careful cross-examination of Tompkins of Trinity between the figures of a quadrille. Never was anybody, some people said, who so much wanted to know everything, or was so nice to tell everything to. The music of Godfrey's "Guards," or "Mabel," whatever was the tarantula-dance of the day, was just over; and the enraptured Bones had just led his partner to Mrs. Pepperharrow's side. He had been perplexing himself over the old problem, what was the most delicate form in which to ask a young lady whether she would like anything to drink, when she solved it by saying that she would like to sit down. And just as he was handing her over to her chaperon, who was confiding to Tompkins that she oped the supper would soon begin, he saw an unexpected figure standing quietly at his side. Daisy Fairfield saw it too, and her heart gave the most unwarrantable jump for no reason whatever. She had been speculating on "not P. W.—the other" half the evening, without the least knowing why.

"You here, sir, after all?" said Bones. "Oh, I am glad!" And without further prelude, and with all the confident ingenuousness of youth, he added: "Oh, Miss Fairfield, do let me introduce you to our fellow, Faucit, whom we were talking of this afternoon. Miss Fairfield—Mrs. Pepperharrow—Mr. Faucit. Mrs. Pepperharrow—Miss Fairfield."

"May I have the pleasure of a dance, Miss Fairfield?" said Guy.

How many of the world's lightest or most serious chapters have opened in those familiar words?

"I am afraid that you're rather late in the field, Mr. Faucit," she answered, consulting her card.

The charm of her voice, which was very great, caught Faucit's sensitive ear at once. There are women to whom one can shut one's eyes and listen for the sheer pleasure of sound, half inclined to laugh with the pleasure, without even the need of heeding what it is they say, as one listens to the conversation of a piano under a sympathetic hand. Daisy Fairfield had a voice of this kind, and Faucit felt at once that he was in the presence of a masterpiece, one of those few and far-between women, in whom nothing has been left out, as it were.

"Have I no chance of anything?" he asked. "Not even of an odd quadrille?"

"I am afraid the quadrilles are all— Do you care for a waltz, Mr. Faucit?"

"Very much. But I hardly liked to ask for that."

"I can give you this one, which is just beginning. I think," she added demurely, "that my partner won't come."

"He must be very blind to his own interests," said Guy, "if I may judge from seeing you waltz with Bones just now. I am lucky in his mistake." And then, with the long, free, preliminary glide which launches a well-matched pair into one of the greatest of harmless enjoyments, Guy Faucit and Daisy Fairfield made their first step together.

I who chronicle these things, remember well once, when I had worked myself—I was younger than I am now—into a very æsthetic and well-informed phase of mind, having a profound talk with an eminent American blue-stocking in a public room at Newport or at Narragansett, no matter where. We had got into very deep waters indeed, and I was boldly but gravely propounding some astounding theories of biology which had never occurred to me in my life till that moment, much to my companion's edification and approval.

"Now tell me, Mr. Balbus," she said, half-shutting her eyes and throwing back her head, as evidently expecting something from the answer to enlarge her experience, "tell me what you consider the most even sensation of momentary content to which the human soul is capable of rising?"

I reflected for a brief space, and replied—

"I can tell you, Mrs. Pozzy, without hesitation. It is a perfect waltz with a perfect partner, to perfect music, on a perfect floor."

The shock told, for Mrs. Pozzy sat bolt upright and looked at me.

"Do you mean to say, Mr. Balbus, that you waltz?"

"I do indeed; I delight in it."

"Then," she said, with that instant appreciation of a situation given to a quick woman, "let me introduce you to my daughter."

The very next week I was a guest at Mrs. Pozzy's country cottage, and had an elegant time. In the intervals of those ambrosial nights of philosophic disquisition, I found Miss Wilhelmina M. Pozzy a very charming partner.

Guy and Daisy settled down in earnest to their stride. He was a past master in the art, thanks to a perfect development of the time-ear. Tune-ear, oddly enough, he had none, and could never hum "God save the Queen" with a proximate approach to correctness, though he knew what music he liked to hear, and understood it in that sense very well. But the time-ear is a different thing, and made his appreciation of a false step in a waltz as keen as of a halting verse. The best singer of his day will often be unable to take one turn in the waltz correctly. Guy had perfected his waltzing during a long vacation in the States, where they understand it better than anywhere. He knew the difference between the Portland glide and the Boston dip, and quick or slow, forward or reverse, he steered his deft course through the whirling and converging couples without a bump or a halt, till he could land his partner safely in a quiet corner. He could send her half to sleep in a slow and dreamy measure, or send the young blood coursing through her veins by a swing like a steady racer's.

As for Daisy Fairfield, he found her one of those partners in a thousand, who learn in a moment the sort of dancer they have to deal with—whether they have to nurse him tenderly through the performance, get as little kicked as possible, and do all the steering themselves, or can trust entirely to their cavalier in charge, and give themselves up without afterthought to the pleasure of the whirl. They adapt themselves at once, after the first minute, to the step of their partner, who, on his side, meets them half-way, and fall into "two step or three" at short notice. Two or three *time* is a misnomer, by the way; for whatever the step, all true waltzing is in three time. Such a heaven-born waltzer as Daisy Fairfield was no weight for Guy Faucit to carry; his arm circled her waist and scarcely felt it, as the lithe and gracious figure sailed on its royal round. They enjoyed their first turn with never a word on either side, and it was a long one, and the breathing of both was but slightly quickened when they stopped.

"You waltz very well, Mr. Faucit," was all she said.

"I need not tell you the same, Miss Fairfield."

After a short pause she smiled.

"Are you ready again?"

"Quite. It's a pity to lose any of it."

To do them justice, they lost very little.

To how many couples of the modern day, I wonder, has their first waltz been their opening adventure, their first dallying with the fruits of fairyland? It is on that ground, I suppose, that some good people still object to it, and that its original sin at first raised a decorous outcry even from such a pattern of propriety as Lord Byron. Why that should be I know not. The roads to that fairyland are many, and it is a country none the worse for the opening up of such a poetic way as this. But a way it is, past denial. To awkward dancers the waltz is a very ordeal, a gymnastic exercise of a trying and often painful kind. But it is a magic

key for others, which opens out a vista of possible
sympathies. Between two kindred natures, it is apt
to establish at once an electric communication. Why
not? Are all possible magnetisms wrong? As I once
heard a hardworking clergyman say, in a capital speech
on the supposed wickedness of going to the theatre,
" Is a young man or woman to be ticketed for the
journey of life like a package, and labelled, ' this side
up, with care'?" Faith, such a package is apt to
be compact of very brittle glass indeed.

The waltz was over and the music ceased. A few
quiet words of commonplace were all that then passed
between the two, as they wandered up and down the
rooms.

" The supper-rooms will be open directly, Miss
Fairfield; so I suppose you will not care for a cup
of tea now?"

" Not now, thank you. Is your crew likely to win
at Henley?"

" I hope so; but I don't feel sure. The Cambridge
boat is very strong. You saw us this afternoon,
then?"

" Oh yes; and you were pointed out to me on the
bank as a sure guide to victory. Both Mr. Bones and
Mr. Tompkins, who were with me, seemed to look
upon defeat under your banners as impossible."

Guy laughed.

" There are no such believers as young believers,
Miss Fairfield; and it is something to have established
a name. But I don't think the Trinity men will run
away from mine, for all that. Is there any chance of
your being at Henley, and seeing the result?"

" I expect so. This is only my first season, Mr.
Faucit, and, as you see, I am being taken to everything.
A boat-race will be new to me, and from what I saw
to-day, it must be wonderfully exciting. I suppose
that to rowing men it is something glorious, very
different from—a waltz." A very slight hesitation
here.

"Different certainly," he answered, "but not better in its way; at least not always." Daisy inhaled a long sweet breath from the flowers she carried. Guy was one of those partners with whom it is not necessary to set them down. "The great charm of life, I think," he went on, "lies in its infinite variety."

"So I think too," she answered, "woman as I am. I wonder if we shall think so as we grow older."

"I expect so, if we go the right way to work. Did you ever hear of a saying of Count Cavour's, Miss Fairfield, that to a sensible man two things should be impossible—rancour and boredom?"

"I never heard it. It sounds very good and very true. Where did you pick it up?"

"In a memoir I have just been reading of him. A very great and interesting life, over, one would think, just at the wrong time. I wonder what such deaths mean. But I ought to beg your pardon for bringing such matters into a ball-room, just after a first waltz!"

"Why? Are you one of the men who always think it necessary to apologise to a partner for supposing that she can care about anything but the musical glasses?"

"If you say that," he answered, "I shall have to beg pardon again. But perhaps I am the sinner, for really I can think of very little except that waltz of ours. I wonder if I have any chance of another."

"Well, I'll see."

They were close to Mrs. Pepperharrow as Daisy examined her card. That lady was just leaving her seat on the arm of a dignitary who had taken possession of her, and left the emancipated Tompkins free to devote himself to a young person in a white frock with red ribbons, of the primitive order of youthful English millinery. But she looked happy and amused enough to wear anything.

"Daisy dear," said Mrs. Pepperharrow, "I'm going to 'ave something to eat. The supper-rooms are open, and Dr. Parley has been kind enough to ask me.. Won't you ave something too?"

"May I take you in to supper, Miss Fairfield?" said Guy.

A young and beaming undergraduate was making his way towards Daisy as the first bars of the "Lancers" struck up.

"Well, I shouldn't be sorry. And—a little of these very young men does go a long way." Daisy was a full year younger than the object of her description. "Oh, Mr. Billington," she said, "I feel very much ashamed of myself; but will you excuse me for this dance? I have been dancing every round dance on the card, and want to go in to supper. I will find something later for you if I can."

Billington of Brasenose submitted with the best grace he could, and Guy and Daisy went in to supper. Before they had well begun it they had fallen into talk on men and books, which pleased and interested them both, and long after they had finished they lingered on over the little table at which they were seated together, all unconscious of the sunward flight of time.

CHAPTER IV.

HERCULES AND OMPHALE.

IT was full and brilliant morning when the last guests at the Christchurch ball left the lights and the garlands behind them, after the last visit to the tables, which makes so pleasant a parting for the couples who have been partnered in the closing galop.

With all her enjoyment of life, Daisy Fairfield was a girl who took her pleasures soberly enough, and, finding plenty for her hand to do wherever she went, was little given to staying out any ball whatever. At the Masonic festivity the night before, Bones and Tompkins had exerted all their fascinations in vain to win her to their wishes in that respect, and had appealed to Mrs. Pepperharrow to no purpose, Daisy laughingly representing her as the flinty-hearted chaperon who was not to be trifled with.

The soap-boiler's lady was indeed ideally qualified for her post; for, like the Duke of Wellington and others of the truly great, she could sleep how she liked and when she liked, and yet be ready for instant action if called upon, at any moment. She had attained to a perfection in the art almost equal to that of a celebrated advocate of late days, who, having only four hours of bed out of the twenty-four, always went placidly to sleep while the opposing counsel was demolishing his arguments, no matter at what length or with what natural aggravation of his ferocity, and then, waking directly the voice ceased, softly demolished *him*. Mrs. Pepperharrow, too, was ready to undertake unlimited journeys to the supper-room to pass the time, was so good-naturedly responsive in talk that she found plenty of elders willing to talk with her, and took a genuine pleasure in watching the enjoyments of the young people, particularly her favourite Daisy. She would stand to her post till five o'clock in the morning if Daisy wished; but quite as readily accepted the responsibility of taking her home early on receipt of the word of command. So she assured Bones and Tompkins that Daisy and she had ad enough of it, and that Bones and Tompkins, whose frank and cordial young ways had quite won her accessible heart, must remember that she was not as young as she had been. In vain Bones assured her that he didn't believe a word of it, and Tompkins broke down in unformed compliments about her beauty-sleep. The young inseparables had to escort the two ladies to their carriage, and then to console themselves with the champagne and plovers' eggs.

At the Christchurch ball, however, Daisy's rule was

broken through. I should be afraid to say how many dances after that supper she and Guy danced together. She was always superior to prejudice where she liked a partner, and not afraid of being told that she had exceeded the proper amount of dances with him.

As for Mrs. Pepperharrow, her confidence in Daisy was so entire, that she would as soon have questioned her dear usband Ugh's knowledge of soaps.

Daisy Fairfield wrote down Faucit's name in so many of those blanks, and for so many "extras," that something which was half a smile and half a blush came over the fair face, when she conned over her card with herself on waking in her lodgings in "the High" after her sleep that morning.

Some few hours earlier than she, for he had braced himself for his day's work while the Daisy's petals were still fast closed, Guy Faucit was making a similar study in the Balliol rooms.

"What a pretty woman," he thought to himself, "and how full of life and of interest in everything. How lovely she looked in the morning light, which seres and yellows nine-tenths of humanity after a dose of the gas-fumes. With that daring but perfect violet broidery of leaves which wreathed her rich white dress from the head to the foot, and made her look like a sylvan goddess, she might have brought old Apelles out of his grave. Gad! if he could have painted that superb throat of hers, set on her shoulders like a bit of marble of Paros!"

Something like these were the meditations of Guy Faucit at his dressing-table; and it must be remembered in his excuse that Guy Faucit was a classical scholar and a poet. He rolled about in his big bath that morning with an extra zest, and whistled to himself during the drying process as if he were grooming a horse, and had a vague and general sense of lightness of heart which was pleasant to his soul. He paused for a long time between two buttons, recalling with considerable accuracy the tones of the

last cordial good night and the pressure of the warm
hand, just marked enough to indicate the success of
the evening, which had passed as he put Daisy into
the carriage.

"By Jove, what a voice!" he said aloud, and with
convinced emphasis, finishing off the suspended button.

The even tenour of Faucit's collegiate way had been
suddenly and abruptly broken, though he was not of
the kind to admit or to know it yet. His breakfast
cleared away, he never did a better spell of work than
he did that morning.

There was a flower-show in the afternoon in the
gardens of Worcester College, once fabled to be so
remote from the centre of Oxford civilization as to
require a cab-journey to find it. Then the university
poet sang of the men who

Τηλεπύλῳ τ' οἰκουσ' ἐνὶ Γυστέρῳ, ἔνθα κέλευθοι
δύσβατοι ἀνθρώποισιν ὑπ' ἀγνοίης ἀλεγεινῆς;

and two academic collaborators in one of the funniest
parodies ever written, "Augustus Smalls of Boniface,"
discoursed of the classic Balliol—

—whose third floor men descry
The smoky roofs of Worcester
Fringing the western sky.

But the broad and fine street which runs by the Taylor
Buildings has dissipated the clouds of distance, and
the access to the Worcester festival was easy enough
when Daisy and Guy met again among the pleasant
glades of the college-garden, and listened to the
spirited music of the military band, reproducing in
an echo, perhaps, some of the dances of the night,
and making them shut their eyes and fancy themselves
waltzing again. It is a wonderfully pleasant chapter
in young lives, that first morning-meeting after the
first ball, where the interest has been mutually aroused
and the sympathy pleasantly kindled. It was with a
sort of freemasonry that our hero and heroine—pass me

the good old-fashionéd words, my reader—welcomed
each other iri the garden.

"Shall you be at the Worcester flower-show to-
morrow?" Guy had said the very last thing; and
Daisy had notified that she should, though it was not
till they had reached home that Mrs. Pepperharrow
received any intimation of the plan.

"But, my dear, I thought you said—"

"Never mind what I said, there's a darling. I had
no idea how pleasant the flower-show was likely to be
till they told me."

"They" remained comfortably in the vague; but
good Mrs. Pepperharrow asked no questions and suggested no difficulties, and was quite content to fall
in with Daisy's change of mind.

They had been sitting in the gardens for some little
time, attended by some of the faithful henchmen who
were enrolled in their service for the week, before
Guy's tall figure made its appearance among the trees.
Daisy's eyes had made more than one rapid little
reconnoitre all round her during the intervals of talk
and music, and contracted, perhaps, just a shade of
impatience and uncertainty, when her quick glance
detected it coming. She saw Guy in a moment, and
saw too, in another moment, that he on his side had
seen her, and was making his way towards her group
with that studied air of indifference and accident which
is invariably worn on such occasions, and suggests so
strongly either the primitive deceit of man's heart, or
the debasing effects of a hypocritical civilization. He
shook hands with one friend, nodded to another,
accounted for his presence at the flower-show by the
state of the weather, the attractions of scientific horti-
culture (he didn't know a rose from an oak, except by
right of his instinctive love of Nature), an "off-day"
with the crew, in fact, upon various mutually destructive
pleas. He was the most truthful of mankind, and told
as many falsehoods before he reached Daisy's side as it
cost him minutes to get there. If love laughs at the

D

perjuries of lovers to each other, he must find in their
little fibs to third persons a perfect storehouse of fun.
As for Daisy, she felt most becomingly and unreason-
ably pleased, and even then was half inclined to take
herself to task for feeling so. But the truth is that,
before Guy's appearance at the ball,—where she had,
on the strength of that one look upon the river-bank,
vaguely expected to see him until she gave it up as
too late,—she had extracted from the innocent and
willing Bones a few leading and interesting particulars
about "Faucit the other." Faucit Telamon, Gosling
called him, in distinction from P. W., who figured
in his dictionary as Faucit Oileus, or the oily one.
Gosling's acquaintance with Daisy Fairfield, however,
was to be a thing of later date than Oxford days.
Though he was a Balliol man, and proud of his cox-
ship, most of his mates and pleasures were to be found
at Christchurch, which was the foster-mother of most of
the Gosling family, and numbered his elder brother, the
Viscount Gander, among her nurselings at the time.
Jemmy was indeed sent to Balliol to keep him out of
his elder's heir-apparentish influence, and out of respect
to a family tradition, which credited him with comparative brains. His successful matriculation at Balliol
was long remembered in the records of the race, and
justly set off against the various "ploughs" which
rather roughed his subsequent career, till the heroic
efforts of Faucit, who took a fancy to the boy, "pulled
him through" the last struggle, and entitled him to all
the honours of B.A.dom.

But the Honourable Jem has landed us in a
digression. We are indebted for it to Bones, who
bore to Gosling the astonishing generic likeness which
characterizes a certain class of ingenuous youth, and
sets an apparent limit even on the creative powers of
Nature. It is as if she had to turn out a certain
number of industrial products every year, and, having
to break her best dies when once used for moulding,
keeps her common ones constantly at hand. Bones

described Faucit to Daisy just as Gosling would have done it, with the same enthusiasm and in the same vernacular, which is more descriptive than eloquence. How completely Faucit had taken his beloved college to wife, with her laurels for a dowry, and was certain to be master of Balliol some day or another; how he had once proposed to read for the bar, but had been persuaded by the other dons to stick to his Oxford work, where he was the means of colonizing half the university with fellows from Balliol, and keeping her glories fresh in the schools and on the river; how he managed the college as he liked with that strong will of his, and had done so in his undergraduate days, when he was an autocrat at the college-meetings; how vainly, when the sceptre left his hand, that ass Spooner and others had fought for it, with results approaching to intestine anarchy; how devoted he was to his old mother, who had a small income of her own, but was indebted to Guy's work for her home and most of her comforts; how impervious he was to feminine attractions, though all women liked him for his nice and pleasant manners with them; and how the universal tongue of rumour wagged at him for a bachelor foredoomed;—all these particulars and more, with a sort of "He's a jolly good fellow" refrain pervading his ditty, did Bones of Balliol confide in choice recitative to Daisy Fairfield's ear. As became his age, he was quite unsuspecting, and attributed entirely to his own eloquence the welcome apparition of Guy Faucit at the ball. Well-pleased was he that Daisy should, as he expressed it to his familiars, "cotton right off" to his favourite hero; and when, after they had gone in to supper together, he came to claim his dance and saw them deeply engaged in each other's talk, he retired with a discretion beyond his years, and apologized to Daisy for his desertion afterwards on the transparent ground that he could not find her, lest she should be disturbed in mind at his neglect. With the prologue supplied thus liberally by Bones, Daisy, at the end of the Christchurch ball, knew a great deal of Faucit's story and character, and was free to weave herself some pleasant fancies in guessing at more.

There was no disenchantment on either side in the Worcester Gardens, as there sometimes is in these episodes of ball-room romance. For in truth here was a pair ideally fitted, in all the circumstance of glorious youth, of kindred tastes and sympathies, and of outward semblance, to repeat the time-honoured process of falling in love.

"You at a flower-show, Mr. Faucit, as well as at a ball!" said Daisy, when he had installed himself at her side after the first smiling welcome. "I shall begin to disbelieve altogether the stories I have heard of your severe life."

"I don't think there is much severity about it, Miss Fairfield," he answered. "Perhaps it's because I'm so fond of pleasure that I don't look for it at places where I don't enjoy myself. That sounds more like being selfish than severe, doesn't it?"

"How lucky you are in being able to take your pleasures as you like them. A woman's are all mapped out for her, and some of the maps are very badly done. But I think we have an advantage over you. We don't always want to be 'doing,' as the stronger among you do. We can shut our eyes and enjoy such a summer day as this, with the flowers and the music, without very much asking why."

"And do you think I can't?" said Faucit. "I think if I might light a pipe under the trees here, put on my oldest shooting-coat, and look at all the pretty women without being asked to talk, I could like a flower-show as well as anybody. It is because we always *are* expected to do something in places where there's absolutely nothing to be done, that I don't profess much love for this sort of thing."

"Well, you needn't talk to me if you don't wish."

"That's another thing."

"Is it?" she said, innocently. "Why? As far as

I am concerned, if you won't be alarmed at the confession, I would even permit the pipe."

"Miss Fairfield! you don't know what you're
saying. The idea of a don smoking in a college
garden! Why, we should have half the undergraduates taking fire, and doing the same."

"And why shouldn't they?"

"I can't imagine."

They laughed pleasantly together. They felt
amazingly content with the world and with themselves, and were in the mood to laugh at very little.

"Nothing is so terrible to humanity, Mr. Faucit,
as a vague fear of consequence. If all the undergraduates smoked, what would happen?"

"Judging from the effect upon myself, there would
be much less noise. But the result of such a crime
would be something like that of being named in
the House of Commons—known only to Providence.
Mrs. Pepperharrow, what is your opinion of tobacco-
smoking?"

History must not fail to record the material fact,
that Faucit had been duly presented at the ball
to Daisy's guardian, and had impressed her very
favourably. She was no doubt apt to be favourably
impressed, but on this occasion the impression was
more marked than usual. Perhaps there may have
been some expenditure of pains on Faucit's part in
producing the result. He was not a man who often
failed to please, when he wished it and tried.

"He is a most remarkable young man, my dear,"
she had said to Daisy when they were going to bed:
"quite what one has the right to expect in these alls
of learning. It's rather awful to think of what e'll
know if he lives to be seventy. But then I suppose
he won't. I've heard these scholars always wear themselves out young."

"I hope he won't do that, dear Mrs. Pepperharrow," Daisy had answered, "I don't think he
looks much like it at present."

"No; but it's deceptive. Heart disease always makes a man look big, like my poor dear husband. Then, to be sure, Ugh does eat a good deal; so it may keep is strength up."

Mrs. Pepperharrow was well content to let Guy and Daisy talk and improve acquaintance at her side without interfering in the dialogue. Happy and many-coloured groups passed and repassed them, with the lazy interchange of looks and comments of those who come to see and be seen. Personally appealed to on the merits of tobacco, Mrs. Pepperharrow had her opinions ready for active service.

"I think it's a nasty abit myself, Mr. Faucit," she said, "and I wonder at the young men liking it as they do. The way it makes curtains smell is sometimes very bad. I ave never felt so sorry as I ought for their cutting off poor Sir Walter Raleigh's head; though indeed as he invented potatoes as well as tobacco there's a good deal to be said for him."

"Oh, Mrs. Pepperharrow, what an idea! Will you take us through the tents, Mr. Faucit? I haven't visited the show proper as yet."

"Certainly," answered the Oxonian. "It's always the thing to be done at these places. Walk in at one end of an intolerably stuffy tent, with a last lingering look at the fresh air outside; pretend to admire Prize 1 and Prize 2 in flowers and fruit, which look like unhealthy specimens of their race, with livers artificially enlarged like Strasburg geese; speculate why Prize 2 didn't get Prize 1, to argue knowledge; 'melt at a peach, and rapture at a rose;' and so out again at the other end, followed by the next batch, like the visitors in the Tower of London. I warn you that I know absolutely nothing of flowers, Miss Fairfield, and that I shall be delighted to escort you."

"If you discourse in that way, Mr. Faucit," answered Daisy, "it will be better than several lectures on botany. The proper study of mankind is man, and we can consider him in relation to flowers."

"So clever of you to talk like that," sighed Mrs. Pepperharrow, as the three entered bravely on the ordeal of the tent together.

The appearance of her friend Dr. Parley, who was a man compact of science, and his ready offer to guide her through the maze, came opportunely enough to leave the young couple to their own devices, to wander on their way upon the path of flowers. The doctor was a floral enthusiast, and expatiated to Mrs. Pepperharrow upon the forms of development before them, in good Latin words as long as Jem Gosling's historic stumbling-blocks, listened to with admiring reverence, which culminated at the end in "So clever of you to talk like that. I am sure I shall understand the Latin language better than I ever did before. I had no idea that the Latins had so many flowers in their time."

Guy and Daisy, meanwhile, looked at the flowers or passed them over in a very hap-hazard way, neither of them affecting an interest they did not feel, but finding more and more how many subjects of talk they had in common. To their fresh-air natures, the poor imprisoned plants had something of the effect that the hapless eagles in the Zoological Gardens have upon the observer's mind in certain moods, producing a longing to unbar the cell and let them out, under the influence of the look of "heimweh" in their dulled eyes, turned upon the free sky spread so temptingly over them. The show flowers in tents are always dreadful, flower-shows having long been what everything is now-a-days, mere social pretexts—pretexts for things good enough in their way, but apt to divert and to spoil a good many healthy interests.

To the genuine cricket-mind, for instance, the Eton and Harrow match of the day is but a sorry substitute for the old fights of the public-school week, which meant cricket and business, instead of fashion and champagne. In the middle of carriages six feet deep, and the small fire of remarks about anything but cricket, innocent of the difference between point and long-stop, and showing no personal interest in either side, the mind reverts regretfully to the days of the 'chaffing-gallery,' and enthusiastic sisters who knew as much about cricket as the boys. It is a pretty show, now : but one of many.

Flower-shows, however, were always privileged follies, and the exhibitions at Oxford were a degree more depressing, from the floral point of view, than their neighbours. Except by the hideous tradition of the Temple chrysanthemums, which coincides with such satiric mockery with the opening of the legal year, and the condemnation of unlucky suitors to a course of Westminster air, they have not been often matched in that way. Little enough of their influence, however, seemed to fall dispiritingly upon Daisy and Guy.

"Would you really like to see my rooms ?" he was asking her when they came out of the tent, where, notwithstanding his description of it, they had been going the rounds for an unconscionable time.

"I should indeed, and very much. The undergraduates have been very pleasant and hospitable to us; but, except Mrs. Pepperharrow's friend, Dr. Parley, we have seen nothing of the inner life of a don. You have no idea what dangerous theories I might have formed of the class if I had not met you. I shall never allow now that a don can't dance."

"I wish that I had had the chance of meeting you at the Masonic ball. But, at all events, I must try to disperse your dangerous theories as much as I can, for the credit of my race. Do you go back to town the day after to-morrow ?"

"Yes, in the morning."

"Are you engaged all to-morrow ?"

"Only to the concert in the evening, and at the theatre in the morning, you know."

"Oh, yes, the event of the Commemoration, where you will see the degrees given, and hear the undergraduates in their glory. I wonder what sort of theories you will form of that part of our community upon the occasion. Can't you come to luncheon with me afterwards? I think I can promise a don or two whom you will really like to meet."

"I'm sure I shall. But I must ask Mrs. Pepperharrow.—Mrs. Pepperharrow, Mr. Faucit has kindly asked us to have luncheon at his rooms to-morrow, after the theatre."

"Where, if you will allow me, Mrs. Pepperharrow," said Guy, "I shall be able to point you out all the celebrities, and translate some of the Latin."

"So kind of you, Mr. Faucit," answered the worthy lady, resuming her charge. "I've been earing a great deal of Latin in the tents, and perhaps I shall know some of it again. But we shall be giving you a great deal of trouble in coming to luncheon."

"None at all. Our bachelor rooms have such a treat so seldom, that it does them real good. Will you come?"

The chaperon agreed without further pressing, and the arrangement was made. They came out of the gates of Worcester together, and Guy Faucit took his leave, bent upon his duties to the Balliol crew. Daisy Fairfield had seldom looked prettier than she did at the rather formal dinner which Dr. Parley gave that night; but, from what cause deponent sayeth not, she had been seldom more silent or more abstracted.

CHAPTER V.

OXONIANA.

THE proceedings in the Oxford theatre, supposed to be the central fact of the Commemoration week, impressed Daisy Fairfield with an unfeigned and ill-pleased wonder, and supplied her with the materials for a searching cross-examination of Faucit, who had stationed himself

at her elbow, which he found very difficult of answer.
Why, on this of all days in the year, the dignified university should turn itself into a common bear-garden,
allow its own elected officers to be officially pilloried
by the universal hiss of public scorn, for nothing
particular except doing what they were appointed to
do; * specially invite famous authors, famous soldiers,
famous statesmen and diplomatists, to receive their
honours in an inexplicable dumb-show and noise,
and to hear there the names of favourite heroes and
leaders, perhaps, proposed for general execration;
expose ladies and young girls to a fire of very imper-
tinent and unseemly banter, and in more than one
instance to considerable fright;—and all this for the
behoof of a gang of juvenile rowdies, resembling a
boxing-night sixpenny gallery in everything but the
wit and the musical ear—will perhaps puzzle the
future historian of English manners as much as it
puzzled Daisy Fairfield. That young lady detected
the beaming countenance of Bones in the front row of
the rioters, evidently in a state of profound satisfaction,
with himself and the whole scene, and gravely ignored
the condescending efforts which he was making to
attract her notice. She "had it out with him"
afterwards, as he expressed himself, in a manner which
"made a man feel himself quite small, you know."

"Three cheers for the ladies in dark blue" was
the cry most in favour in that day's gallery, led by
choragus Bones, and suggested to his original mind by
the rich deep-hued dress which Daisy wore in honour
of her hostess-city, with a soft lace ruff for boundary-
line to unite it with the graceful throat. She felt
anything but comfortable under the salutation, which
she quite understood to be intended mainly for her, as
representative of the class apostrophized, and shrank
into her shell as much as she could.

* I am delighted to hope that this is a thing of the past; and
to see that the Vice-Chancellor of the day feels as if the undergraduates were "his own children."

" ."Oh, Mr. Faucit, how very rude and noisy! I shall be glad to get away."

"."It's abominable," answered Faucit, thoroughly vexed. ".I can't think why on earth this sort of thing isn't put a stop to. It goes from bad to worse every year, and will end in putting a stop to Commemoration altogether."

"If they said any single thing worth hearing, or that one could laugh at," she said, "one wouldn't so much mind. But they're dull enough to be respectable!" And a discordant, many-throated howl went up, as a figure in cap and gown came into the hall.

"Yah! yah! yah!" like the shouts of some fictitious semi-human breed in a fancy of Dean Swift's.

"Who's that unhappy man, and what has he done?"

"That's the proctor; and he is a very good fellow who has done no harm to anybody."

"Oh, P. W.?"

"No, that was last year. Who on earth told you about P. W.?".

"Mr. Bones, who is actively engaged in denouncing P. W.'s successor, and trying to catch my eye, which is not to be caught."

".The young scamp," said Guy; "he's there, is he? I'll give him a talking to afterwards."

"Oh, don't say I told you. And I suppose one oughtn't to mind; youth will have its fling," added this experienced worldling.

"It needn't have its fling at other people."

Suddenly the howls swelled and gathered into one stupendous yell.

"Yah! yah! yah! Take it off! take it off!"

"Good gracious, what is it now?"

"Vir doctissime et reverendissime."

"Who's that?"

"That's the public orator reading something in Latin."

"Yah! yah! yah!   The man in the straw hat!"

"Yah! yah! yah!   Take it off! take it off!"

"Three cheers for the ladies in dark blue!   Hip!"
But the diversion was vain, and succeeded no further
than the first hip.

"Yah! the straw hat!   Take it off! turn him out!"

The storm gathered and arose; proctors and un-
popular statesmen were forgotten; the ladies in blue
and in green were set aside; the face of the public
orator grew impatient and disgusted; a distinguished
foreign ambassador who had come to be honoured
looked about him in blank and undisguised amaze-
ment; the men of the Faucit type felt and showed
themselves thoroughly ashamed, and even the Boneses
in the gallery began to wish themselves away, while the
majority of its tenants felt themselves more and more
the heroes of the hour, and the guardians of public
decency and refinement.   Many of the ladies looked
towards the door and meditated on the chances of
retreat, while Daisy's face flushed with disgust and
anger.

"Dear me, Mr. Faucit!" said Mrs. Pepperharrow.
"What are they a-goin' to do?"

The poor lady fairly relapsed into a more primitive
stage than usual of her early English.

"Nothing, Mrs. Pepperharrow," said Guy, re-
assuringly.   "It will be over directly."

But the yahs arose.   The solitary offender in the
straw hat, a well-bred and distinguished man of letters
who lived in retirement, and innocent of Oxford's
jealousy for good manners was there by invitation, was
for a long time placidly unconscious of the cause of the
uproar.   As it began to dawn on him, he frowned and
took root, and looked thoroughly determined and resentful.   But modesty and indignation mastered him as he
became the mark of all eyes, friendly and unfriendly,
and at last he beat a sudden retreat into the street,
whence he went straight to the station, and back to his
home, to be a foe to university education ever after,

and briefly to describe the youth of Oxford as "Brutes." There he did them wrong; but they were queer cattle once a year, in my time.

A shout of triumph from the gallery followed the fugitive; and proudly conscious of having vindicated the laws of breeding, the undergraduates, with trencher caps in different degrees of dilapidation and unsightliness, graciously permitted the proceedings to advance to something like an intelligible close. The public orator's well-turned attempts to frame the most modern English sentiments in classic Latin were favourably, if rather satirically, received; and the sonorous couplets of the bard of Newdigate were hailed with an amount of encouraging applause, due perhaps as much to the re-appearance of the English tongue on the scene, as to the sentiments expressed. The general sense of relief experienced at this crisis, even by the most accomplished classic present, is apt to invest poetry of the Newdigate type with a halo not its own. An imposing figure was Pope-Scott of Christchurch in the rostrum that day, as he declaimed the peroration of his work in decasyllabics of a faultless cæsura :—

"Majestic centre of enfranchised art,
Do in the wondering world thy glorious part!
For ever and for ever, though to-day
Man's short-lived fabrics melt for aye away;—
Though not to us be given the power to mould
The godlike forms and harmonies of old;
Not ours the skill to bid the marbles don
The grace which erst the Parthenon put on,
And shape Athenæ's arches as they rise,
Broad-based on careless Genius, to the skies;
Not ours with master-hand and eye to trace
The bold proportions of the stone-girt space
Which mighty Cæsar's * giant walls embrace;
Though the deft voice of fair Pentelicus
Be in her sweeter secrets mute for us;
Though lost the painter's and the sculptor's lore,
Yet still for ever (as I said before),

---

* *sic* in MS.

> Thy name, fair city of the violet crown,
> Shall travel on the wings of Memory down,
> And live embalmed, until the death of Time,
> Linked with all virtues, and a single crime."

"Hear! hear!" and "Go it, Homer!" from the
gallery; and "Where did you get that last line
from?" from some freshman more audacious than the
rest, who was promptly snubbed and bonneted by his
neighbours. There was a well-pleased smile on the
faces of the groundlings, and as Pope-Scott bowed and
withdrew, to be escorted home with the honours by
admiring Christchurch friends, the select audience of
the somewhat mixed entertainment dispersed and
melted away.

"I certainly have heard something very like the
last line before," said Daisy.

"Pardon me," answered Guy, as he strolled with
her along Broad Street towards his rooms. "Byron
expressed an exactly opposite sentiment; and boldly
to improve by adaptation is one of the greatest arts
of poetry. Like his predecessor Goldsmith, Pope-Scott
touches nothing which he feels he does not adorn."

"Yes; but what does he mean by the single
crime?"

"I can't imagine, and you shouldn't ask. Mystery
is the soul of peroration."

"Well, it was a good young poem, well delivered.
What city did he say it was about?"

"Athens. I believe that the closing lines are
modified from one which he wrote last year on Rome,
when he ran second. You may infer it from the
reference to Cæsar's walls, obviously left by an over-
sight on the part of the poet and the examiners. What
part of the poem did you like best?"

"The touch of nature implied in the simple
expression, 'As I said before.' It went straight to the
heart."

Daisy's face was rippling with little smiles as the
two indulged in these grave comments.

"You are quite a critic," said the other as gravely,
"and have every qualification to call yourself 'we.'
Yes; you are right. Artistic Bathos is an essential
in a Newdigate poem, and is in this instance handled
with a master-touch. Pope-Scott has written many
lines which should live by his use of it. In a prize
poem of his at Cheltenham, upon a distinguished Irish
soldier (Pope-Scott is, I believe, a native of that
imaginative country), occurs this celebrated couplet,
the climax of a fervid description of the hero's
honours—

'He on the Curragh, so report prevails,
Has stood parade-ground with the Prince of Wales.'"

Daisy broke into a happy and delighted laugh,
and fairly clapped her hands. "Oh, what a delicious
poet! Why haven't I met him?"

"It might have been too much for you. To go
back into the prosaic world of London, after such a
glimpse of the Muses as a poet's society would have
given you, would have been too much of a disenchantment. I hope his pentameters will leave a pleasanter
recollection than the howls in the gallery."

"I didn't like that. Why do you dons permit it?"

"We shan't for long, I hope. But nothing in
England is so dangerous an enemy as a vested interest,
however odious to everybody. This has been a sort
of Guy Fawkes day with undergraduates from time
immemorial, to let the steam off."

"I should make them consume their own steam, by
act of convocation."

"I don't know. Boys will be boys."

"Then why do they call themselves men?"

"Your logic, Miss Fairfield," said Guy, "is becoming hard to argue with. Luckily for me, here we are
at the foot of my staircase. Will you come up?"

Daisy Fairfield and Mrs. Pepperharrow were soon
installed in the comfortable rooms on the first floor,
overlooking the green inner quadrangle of the college

of the first Balliol and Devorguilla his wife, and the enclosure of their next neighbour Trinity beyond, divided by the party-wall over which adventurous but gated spirits in the two colleges had once established a mutual right of way. The imprisoned Balliol man would make his escape, by means of climbing this wall, through the gate of Trinity; while his Trinity brother could as conveniently reverse the process, raising no suspicion in the minds of the deceived college-porters. Tompkins and Bones had pursued the unhallowed sport for some time; and it was while they were taking their walks abroad together, both under sentence of gates, under this convenient *ad eundem* arrangement, that they had fallen into the hands of P. W., who had been the author of the conviction. This discovery leading to inquiry, the illegal traffic was exposed and suppressed. Hence much of the Homeric wrath which burned in the bosoms of Tompkins and Bones, who had both suffered from a brief rustication in consequence.

Quietly enough the old quadrangle slept in the sunlight that day, as the little party went through. A few undergraduates were scattered about it, a knot of them engaged in a game of bowls upon the smooth stretch of turf—for in those days lawn-tennis had not descended, like the Colorado beetle, upon all the green spots of English earth. The college-scouts, a worthy race of men apart, who seem to have brought into their line of life a distinct academic flavour, and look as if they had a second-hand acquaintance with Plato and Aristotle, were carrying their masters' luncheons to their respective rooms, under those flat-topped covers which are as peculiar to the soil as the mortar-board caps; and the whole scene, even though the unusual presence of more than one bonny lass enlivened it to-day, had that strange out-of-the-world flavour which belongs to the enclosures of colleges, and perhaps to no other place, not monastic, since the Thames embankment edged itself in between the Temple and the river.

In old days, when the hum of work was hushed,

and the resident Templars were wandering back to
chambers from their clubs and coffee-houses, the same
feeling was yet more strongly in the air over the
green gardens, water-lapped, which stretched at the foot
of Paper Buildings and of Garden Court.

A small party of men were soon assembled in
honour of Faucit's two visitors. They were men well
chosen, whose talk gave Daisy genuine pleasure, and a
glimpse into the more ardent spirit of earnest university
life. They were old pupils of Faucit, or men of his
standing; and it was clear that among them Faucit was
an acknowledged leader, which gave the young lady secret
satisfaction. For they were all well worth listening
to, had conquered their fellowships in various colleges
of Oxford, and talked and thought in a style very different from good old Dr. Parley's friends and guests.
All were impregnated with the young reforming spirit
which was springing up everywhere—treated Oxford
politics as part of the scheme of the world outside
rather than narrowed them in any academic sense,
and on some matters, perhaps, were apt to speculate
more freely and openly than University traditions
might be supposed to sanction. But there was nothing
said to shock Daisy, though a little to open her eyes;
and indeed Faucit himself, though as broad in his
churchmanship as in other matters, never cared to
encourage some lines of thought in his company. He
was known to have commended Gosling's primitive
views on theology, rather than those of more enquiring
minds.

"I am told," that youth had said, "that Science and
the Pentateuch don't hit it off. But I don't interfere
with that myself, and leave them to settle it between
themselves."

Daisy's own love of reading delighted her with
Faucit's library; and Elia the gentle, and Landor the
massive, gave a pleasant conversational sauce to the
dainties on the table. Then an inspection of the pictures led to a welcome interchange of art-talk, in which

E

attractive field of discussion most of the men were more or less at home.   Daisy herself was deeply imbued with the genuine love of picture-lore, which is a part of the furniture of.all imaginative minds, though her travels in picture-land abroad were so far bounded by the Louvre and Dresden, where she had spent some weeks the summer before, while still in her chrysalis condition.

"No bad beginning, Miss Fairfield," said Guy; "and no bad beginning and end either, if one wants a deep draught of one spring.   I have seen my galleries pretty thoroughly, and that San Sisto picture has no rival for me anywhere."

"I cannot fancy it surpassed, Mr. Faucit," she said. "I used to go to the gallery morning after morning; and tempting as my Battonis and Correggios were, I couldn't help spending half my time upon one of the settees before it, all alone in its grandeur, and worshipping like a votary.   It was more worship than anything else."

"You were not far wrong there.   I never can forgive the Dresdeners for giving those Holbeins a similar post of honour.   They are no more to be compared to it than a batch of sign-boards, clever as they are."

"Those eternal copyists are still harder to forgive, I think; preventing you from getting a proper view of the pictures, and, in spite of yourself, attracting your eyes from the originals to those dreadful daubs of. theirs, though I dare say they are very good in their way. This San Sisto engraving of yours is a wonderfully fine one.   Is there any picture in the world, but that, with that wonder in the eyes?"

. "Only one that I know—the Foligno Madonna at the Vatican.   And there one misses the child, whose look is more startling than the mother's.   The mother looks as if she were afraid of the child, with all her tenderness towards it; but the child looks as if he were fearful of himself, and the strange child-knowledge .he must have had of what he was."

"Yes; it is a glorious picture. I should like to see the Foligno."

"Rome is a treasure-house to come; but to me that is its best treasure. I never can care, in comparison, for the more famous 'Annunciation' in the same room with it. It is noble and beautiful enough; but that incredible divinity lives, to me, in those two other Raphaels alone. By right of those two pictures, Raphael has it all his own way, to my mind, as much as Shakespeare among the playwrights."

"Yes; but still I love my Titian."

"Ah, so do I. And when you meet him at Venice you'll love him more."

The art-talk ran pleasantly on, transporting the talkers to many lands in turn, as better than any talk it can. The beggars of Murillo and the cavaliers of Velasquez introduced them to the *patios* of Seville, and the rich art-beauties of the empress of cathedrals, with the cabinet studies of nature, which may be seen in the bright-coloured streets through any of her half-opened doors. Then, by a natural transition, the stately fane of Toledo, with the surroundings of that half-dead and depopulated city of the past, and the grim solitude of the chill Escurial church, fit nurse for Philip's bigotry of blood-thirstiness, were discussed by travellers who had had eyes to see, and kindled a longing for wider-wanderings in Daisy Fairfield's receptive mind.

Guy Faucit, perhaps, thought how pleasant it would be to be her guide among all these wonders, afloat in a Venetian gondola, or afield in a Valencian tartana, through scenes where tourists vulgarize in vain. He fought his traveller's battles over again, inspired by his listener's interest; shivered over a Madrid charcoal-stove in an inclement September, warmed in his great-coat, and racked with a headache afterwards; he escaped from being boiled alive in Lucerne, to be frozen in a sudden hailstorm on the top of Pilatus, and so brought upon the scene two of his companions

who were enthusiastic mountaineers, and could initiate
Daisy into some of the deep mysteries of higher climbing, at which Faucit confessed himself no adept. Like
all true philosophers, he had for his principle live and
let live, and saw no objection to men doing these things
"if it amused them;" but how or why it did, baffled
him except from the philosophic standpoint. He
expressed the view mildly enough to Longshanks of
New, of peaks and passes celebrity; but Longshanks
was ready for him.

"Faucit sees nothing in Alp-climbing, Miss Fairfield,
because he hasn't given it a fair trial, and wasn't
bitten at starting. And here am I who can see nothing
in boating, or conceive what pleasure a man can find in
turning his back to do his work, fixing another man's
flannel shirt for his entire object of vision, and convert-
ing himself into a mechanical pendulum. So our odd
world goes round. We like our likes with all our
might, and see nothing in what other men like. Then,
unless we discipline our minds, we get angry with
them for liking what we don't, proceed to argue them
out of it by fair means, and foul afterwards, and so
cause persecutions, religious and political, all because
everybody ought to agree with us. Here's your health,
Faucit, and thanks for a very pleasant luncheon."

"With mine in return," laughed the host, "for
such a complete edition in little of Longshanks's philosophy of history. I have known greater men say
less in more words. And I am sure that Mrs.
Pepperharrow agrees with me."

"That indeed I do," said the worthy lady; "and I
ave enjoyed listening to you all very much. As for
the old masters you've been talking of, I think they're
quite perfect, and I'm always wanting my husband to
buy them. But e says the new masters are what e
understands better, and they ought to be encouraged
because they're alive."

"That's philosophy quite as good as Longshanks's,
and of great value to many worthy men," said Faucit.

The luncheon was over and the party broke lazily up, not the least successful of the parties of that Commemoration. To two of them, at all events, it was a very great success. Faucit, a capital host at all times, had never been a better one than that day. Though essentially a "man's man," he never, like many of his kind, showed to better advantage than with ladies, for he had for them much of that instinctive deference and old-world courtesy whose decay Charles Lamb so feelingly deplores. He never gave up his own style of thought and talk in order to fall in with their supposed love of other subjects than men's; but, on the other hand, he never "talked down" to them by translating himself into another language, as if he were dealing with a different race, after the fashion of some popular orators when addressing an audience of working men. I doubt if any affectation on earth, though the result of mere want of tact, is more intensely provoking to those addressed, or those in sympathy with them.

With Mrs. Pepperharrow Guy established himself that day as a favourite; and as for Daisy, he never had a more sympathetic listener or a more well-pleased guest.

Fast, fast, fast, the meshes of the net closed round those two; and when Guy parted with his guests at the gate, to go back and meditate over a sociable pipe with Longshanks, an old pupil who wanted some advice upon some question of New College municipal politics, it was with an understanding that he meant to be at the concert in the evening. He was there; and there again the pair took up their parable, over whose earlier stage of development there is no further need to dwell.

For some reason not to be defined, Daisy carried away quite a lofty impression of the knowledge of musical art possessed by the undergraduates of Oxford; and Guy himself was astonished at the effect produced upon him by Ponder's performance of "Oh, ruddier than the cherry," and Piper's declamation of "'Twas in Trafalgar's Bay." He even wrote an eulogistic article on Oxford music for the 'Saturday Review'; but it had the rare fate of being returned, with all apologies, by the editor, who thought that Mr. Faucit must have allowed himself to be carried away, and said that his musical critic was unable to approve of the sentiments expressed.

The next morning—*mirabile dictu !*—Faucit might be seen at the station, seeing the ladies off, and accepting a warm invitation to call in town, that Miss Fairfield's parents might thank him for all his kindness and attention, to which she knew that really she had no claim at all, she said.

"It was so very good of you," Daisy added, demurely, "to waste so much of your time upon us."

"So very good," echoed the chaperon.

"I didn't waste a minute of it," Guy said. "My work and my boat will both profit by the change. Good-bye."

"Good-bye."

It had been arranged that Guy was to start for the English lakes with a reading party of young pupils immediately after the Oxford and Cambridge match and the Henley Regatta, which followed the break-up of the term. The pupils were astonished to find their plan disarranged, and to be asked to postpone the expedition for another month, to the close of the London season. When season, reading-party, and long vacation were all over, still more astonished and much distressed was the Oxford world, and not his college alone, to learn that Faucit of Balliol, after six years of tutorhood, and with an established Oxford position, had made up his mind to leave the place and the life, and to study in London for the common-law bar.

CHAPTER VI.

THE IDYLL.

THE chronicler of Guy Faucit and Daisy Fairfield uses his privilege here, and skims rapidly over the next scenes of their history.

It was the end of July before Daisy flitted to Switzerland with her parents for her first visit to that fairy playground; and it was the end of July before Faucit found himself installed in a cottage at the head of Grasmere ·Lake, with some candidates for " Greats " assembled for a reading-party. A reading-bee, perhaps, it is called now-a-days, as the dictionaries of Mark Twain and Bret Harte tend more and more, alas ! to the supersession of Johnson and Webster in the old country. They were pleasant things, those reading-parties, in the days when I, Balbus, friend and contemporary of Faucit, was of them. They differed much among themselves, for sometimes there was much reading and sometimes there was none, which turned more upon the character of the coach-in-office than anything else.

There was no lack of work when Faucit was to the fore. If after a short experience, and the few days grace allowed for settling down, he made up his mind that any one of the pupils, the while on pleasure bent, was not of reading mind, he gave him a gentle warning first, and then sent him about his business. He liked his pupils to do him credit as well as themselves, and would have no shirking; so, believing that a little leaven leavens the whole lump, he disposed of black sheep summarily.

Dear old boy ! how he comes before me as I think of him. We were the firmest of allies, and had many a literary taste in common. But my inveterate mistrust of literature, when veiled in the classic guise, made a subject of chronic disagreement between us,

and any success I may since have had in life has been
in the teeth of his sombre prognostics. I shied at the
fascinations even of poetry when presented to me by
Greeks—

"Timui Danaos et dona ferentes,"

and the last French play, novel, or political treatise—
the last I fear not the most—had greater charms for
me than I could find in Plato. I wasted my time
systematically in what my father called heroic idleness
("I do believe, Tom," he said to me once, "that if
your foot slipped out of the stirrup on horseback you
would prefer riding on like that to taking the trouble
to put it in again"); and yet, alive and merry at it
matters not what year, I cannot find that I am a whit
the worse of it, in "purse or person;" but discover
that I work at congenial occupations, albeit in no
licensed profession, as hard as need be.

Well, well; it is no easier to arrive at the expedi-
encies of life than it was in Solomon's time, in which
respects that worthy old gentleman acted as a kind of
moral "taster" to the universe. Years afterwards,
thriving on unlicensed occupations in spite of experience, morality, and everything else, I ventured to say
to the elder Mr. Balbus, himself a renowned and
capable classic, that the great advantage of a classical
education was this—you never regret having been idle.
He laughed at the joke, but resented the inference.

I am not writing of myself, however, and must not
forget that if my lovers—need I say, after the beginning,
what lovers they were before their month of frequent
London meetings was over?—are to interest others in
their fortunes, that obtrusive little vowel number three
should be kept as much as possible out of sight.

Guy Faucit's ideas on the classics, and, indeed, on
most matters, were more my father's than mine; and
the magnificent energy with which he did everything
he put his hand to was part of the strong, sweet nature
of the man. Pupils of his could never fail to catch the
infection more or less, and the Grasmere days were not

soon forgotten by those who were with him there.
They were all honour-men except Jem Gosling, whom,
out of affectionate personal regard, Faucit admitted
into the company, as a sort of little dog in attendance,
giving him a special portion of his time in the evenings while the others were grappling with the higher
Aristotelic problems, or learning from Thucydides—the
discovery, perhaps, to blossom later—how excessively
ill a man can write his own language, however beautiful, and yet be famous. That eminent historian is a
perpetual encouragement to writers who can't write,
and lives again, for the placid cynic, in many a modern
misleader of youth, in the ranks of the 'Nineteenth
Century' or the 'Fortnightly Review.'

Into the Grasmere Lake the party plunged in the
morning soon after seven, for the introductory swim
which was to brace them for the day. At eight, after
the short household prayers which Faucit would never
neglect—odd, men said, in that as in most things—they
tackled one of those Oxonian breakfasts which are the
memory and the despair of older digestions, and haunt
like Tantalic phantoms the egg and bacon of later
years, where the new Sangradism allows so much.

"Nothing I know," said Bones simply, on one
occasion, "so sharpens the appetite for breakfast as a
fried sole and a good bit of steak."

When the soles and the steaks and the porridge and
the marmalade had vanished, and the tea and coffee
had been corrected by the early beer, there were four
hours of steady work to be done.

Faucit was a passed master as a guide to the
classics, and would have made me like them if any one
could But I never took kindly to any of the set
except Aristophanes, whose honest chuckle over everything and everybody was amazingly to my taste. Why
doesn't our good friend W. S. Gilbert, quaintest in his
line of modern English humourists, take a hint from the
old fellow, and take up 'Demos' again in his last new
dress? I am fond of those old Greeks now, I don't

know why; and perhaps I only wasn't then because I was expected to be. We are a contrary lot we mortals, and that's a fact.

But, "like them or lump them," it was a great sight to see Faucit, with his hands deep in his trousers pockets, and the short pipe clearing the mental atmosphere, walking up and down the little lake-room expounding, while the pupils listened or took notes, or asked and answered questions. He had the whole thing at his fingers' ends, and could dress up Plato's Republic improvisedly, in sympathetic and attractive English of his own. At another time he could tell anecdotes from Herodotus in a familiar style, quite after the old gossip's manner; and even on the perplexing mysteries of Aristotle's Ethics he could throw an original light, and moralize—as to me he often did—on the dangers of the career of the apolaustic man. If sometimes he attributed to the philosopher deep meanings and purposes of which he must have been entirely innocent, who shall blame him? Do not even the commentators of Shakespeare the same?

Half-an-hour's "yard-cricket" in the front of the house, with the centre-piece of the door for a wicket, and a tennis-ball to bowl with, and then the honest early dinner, made the young students fit for their afternoon of hill-work. Long stretches over the slopes of Fairfield, excursions into the smiling little district of Rydal, or pilgrimages to the valley of St. John, whose grim serrated rocks seemed to the more imaginative among them to wear the very shape and form which once shone castle-wise, "in morning splendour full and fair," before the eyes of the Knight of Triermain on his love-quest—scenes where Faucit's loving knowledge of his Scotts and Wordsworths made him as much at home and as pleasant a companion as on earlier but not more classic ground—filled out the long summer afternoons till supper-time, and the two hours more of work which followed before turning in. Varied sometimes by boating on the lakes, sometimes perhaps by plunges into the pleasant circle of the local society, where bright eyes were glad to welcome these cheery young squires, and to beam their best on them (Gosling had a special aptitude for making himself acceptable to the owners of those eyes, whom he generically classed as "Maries" from that hour)— those Grasmere days ran into weeks which left a sunny memory behind them. Every now and again a period of grace was allowed, when the more enquiring spirits shouldered knapsacks, and started for a tramp over passes and valleys, by rattling "forces" and smiling meres, to shelter for the night in some cozy "Angler's rest" of the old pre-company pattern, white and clean as its mistress's apron, and nestled under the shelter of the everlasting hills.

Pleasant days! pleasant times, full of enjoyment for the moment and retrospect for the future. I know not how it may be with others; but for me, as I grow older, these memories seem to grow more vivid every day; even as oddly enough the very classical gentlemen whom I neglected so heartily at the time, as I fancied, seem to exercise an increasing influence over my thoughts and work even when I don't take them up again. They come and wax unbidden, those associations of the past; and scenes and events which seemed at the time to make but slight impressions upon a mind then more set, out of work-hours, upon odd corners of itself than anything else, come all of a sudden, as I sit down to write or to remember, out of the little nooks of the brain-house into which they must have crept all unawares. And out they come full-grown, like so many awkward Minervas.

It was the summer of the comet-year, perhaps; and many a night-drive home from Keswick, or from handier Ambleside, would our party have after a longer field-day than usual, when the whole firmament seemed lit, and the stars put out, by the lústre of that old phenomenon, which has lost none of its strangeness in losing all its terror. It has been explained away,

thoroughly; but there it was, all the same. Somebody did it. And Faucit would quote to the reverential Gosling the haunting lines of the northern
poet :—

> "Oh, on thy sparkling prow to ride!
>   To cleave the depths of Heaven with thee!
>   To plough the twinkling stars aside,
>   Like foam-bells on a tranquil sea!"

And Gosling would intimate, with much conviction,
that he didn't understand it much, but it was "doosid
fine." Fair fall thy criticisms, honest Jem! They
were better than wiser that I wot of.

Guy Faucit, meanwhile? What was he thinking
of all this time? He never lost himself in his work,
for his pupils said that he never went at it harder, and
he carried more than one of them into a triumphant
first. But in the walks and on the boats he was not
quite so companionable as usual, except with one rather
silent member of his regiment, with whom he consorted
for choice to the surprise of the others, and smoked
many pipes.

When one of those parties among Gosling's friends
"the Maries" took place, Guy was apt to excuse
himself, take the opportunity of strolling off alone with
some book in his pocket, which usually stayed there,
throw himself at full length upon the turf which slopes
suddenly down into the waters of Grasmere on the
Rydal-ward side, or sit there dreamily and "corrig"
loose boulders into the lake below.

Unwitting of other presence than his own, he one
day nearly "corriged" into another world Jem Gosling
and a Mary, whom that seductive youth had persuaded
to go a-flirting with him.

They were lying on the slope below Faucit, and the
boulder shaved the Honourable James's nose. He
said afterwards that the Clipper was jealous, and must
have a love-fever on him. Guy laughed, and looked
very kindly at the lad. His heart had stood still for
the moment when he found what an escape he had had.

Ah! that love-fever! It must run its course like other tertians, though many doctors try their hands at stopping it, or at "throwing it out."

What were Guy's meditations on the lake-side those lonely afternoons? He had nothing but his fellowship, and the little that would come to him from his mother. The dear old mother! how irregularly he seemed to write to her now. He must run down to Devonshire directly the reading-party broke up, for he longed for a kiss to the silvery-hair, a welcome from the silvery voice. It would be a long time, he trusted and prayed, before that little came; and then it could not change his life.

He had resolved upon an Oxford career; for with his fellowship and his pupils, and what he made by his pen—not much, perhaps, that last, for journalism is not an El Dorado, even when exclusively followed—he had now a very good income to boast of in those rent-free rooms of his.

But—ah! those buts! How they come breaking in upon our best soliloquies, worrying our strongest purposes, breach-making in our favourite castles of the air!

Suppose he changed his plans now, and left Oxford, what should he do? He could keep his fellowship, of course, as long as— Exactly. "But" again. Why wasn't his what they call a married fellowship? but it wasn't. Besides, he was twenty-eight, and an old don. Could he make enough by his pen to make a profession of it? impossible to say. And it ·was, he knew, very hard and up-hill work. The bar? that resource of all the ardent spirits with no special professional bent of their own, that mystic profession which "leads to everything," but begins in nothing, except expense, and, alas! too often ends there. Besides, he could not bear the idea of law. That wouldn't matter to him, though; and that thought was soon put aside.

Sir Benjamin Brodie, speaking of his own original

distaste for medicine, had said that any man worth his
salt could teach himself to like any serious work he
had to live by. And the saying was quite after Guy's
own heart. Why hadn't he done like his friend
Wilmot, who took his first at the same time, and an
Oriel fellowship directly afterwards, and then went
straight to London to read for the bar?

London—there must be great advantages in living
in London, of various kinds. There was a very pleasant
smile on Faucit's face at this point of the secret
discourse. What a pity somebody wasn't there to see
it! Wilmot had been called now three years, and was
already well spoken of on the Western Circuit, where
he had made quite a hit by holding some briefs for
more advanced juniors, and had distinguished himself
on his own account at Exeter sessions, on some knotty
point of settlement law.

He, Faucit, had some friends among the Exeter
attorneys, and he could be called in three years from
November, if he began at once, and ate the first steps
of his way to the woolsack, as by custom recognised
and provided.

Three years! he would be thirty-one. Well—he
wouldn't be less if he began later. And really he
must do something. This Oxford business was growing
impossible—wouldn't do. He believed that half the
difficulties of the bar were fables, if you had brains
and stuck to work. And wouldn't he? Why at thirty-
five— Then the shadows of Guy's magic-lantern began
to shift and move, and to be lit by soft prismatic hues
radiating from the basket of Alnaschar. He saw a
prosperous and successful life before him, not prisoned
in the quadrangles of sleepy Oxford, but in the busy
turmoil of London the magnificent. He saw himself
working and rising—first remarked, then distinguished,
then great, and passing away in the fulness of years, to
leave, as his best legacy, his name behind him. He
saw many things; but in and through them all he
saw just this. Pledged first, then waiting, then

united; always kindling, helping, comforting, consoling; he pictured to himself one fair and perfect woman, ever and always at his side.

It was on one evening towards the close of that lake sojourn that Faucit made to his pupils the announcement which our readers were privileged to learn at the end of the last chapter.

What was she doing the while, that lady of the dream? Far away, perhaps, on the terrace which looks down on the curling little river which runs by the town of Berne, where the opposite heights rise suddenly and picturesquely up, and the mighty giants of the Oberland, shaded and softened by the distance, keep watch and ward on the horizon, Daisy Fairfield was sitting alone, with half-an-hour to herself before the *table d'hôte.* Her hands were folded on her lap, and her eyes were set steadily upon the beautiful mountain vision, as the shapes of Schreckhorn and Finster-aar-horn were imaging themselves firmly in that keen and open mind. And in the double process of thought which runs so oddly through our lives, even while she drank the charm of that masterpiece of landscape in, she too was dreaming out her sweet and maidenly dream. Oh, so pure, so true, so maidenly! so full of that fearless innocence of life and thought which, when a man is brought for the first time fairly face to face with its inner secrets, teaches him first to be ashamed, and then to rejoice—to rejoice with fear and reverence over what God has done and does, even over what God can pardon and undo.

As the young girl sat there, framed like an Ary Schaeffer with the distance in her eyes, one after another the passers-by turned back to look at her; involuntarily, courteously, for she was not one of those who may be looked on too rudely. But she was conscious of no look, no gaze; she seldom was. If Guy Faucit had known how rare indeed was the glance which had followed him that first day on the banks of the Isis, he would have been many inches a prouder

man. So the passers-by looked at her unrebuked, and
whispered about the "belle Anglaise," or the "schöne
Engländerinn," in their various tongues; and Daisy
sat dreaming on.

Sometimes—and in spite of myself—the tears come
to my eyes when I write and think of her. My own
dear wife, Dorothy Balbus, owns her for her best and
dearest friend : for this is no tragedy I am writing,
thank God, though the drama leads through many
paths of stone and thorns. And there is no name more
often on my wife's lips and mine than the name she
now so beautifully bears. She was thinking of Guy
Faucit even as he was thinking of her, in a sweet
fancy of love and dependence, yet of mutual help.
What it meant, her dream of marriage, she neither
knew nor asked herself, in any exactness of shape.
She knew that she loved Guy Faucit, and was very
proud and ambitious for him; and though no word
had been spoken on either part, I think she knew
that he loved her. She had talked much with
him, as she came to know him during their frequent
London meetings, — he had been at her father's
house, and often, and had neglected no place where
she might be,—of his future and his plans of life,
and had urged him much to come to London, and
boldly to try the bar. He was too good to waste
on Oxford reclusion. At first :—for afterwards, as
the better knowledge became better still, there came
a certain shyness over those urgings of hers, and she
said less. He noticed it, or thought he did; and passed
to much self-questioning as to what it might mean.

When they parted in London he had, we know,
formed no definite idea of leaving Oxford; and something of her doubts was in her fancies now. Would
he really go back to college, and not find something
to do in London ? If he did—well. She didn't know.
Of the fears and reasons that held Faucit back she
knew nothing. She was rich, or would be, in the
world's goods, and how could she use them better than

in helping a great man to a great career ? For he could be great, she was sure. And I think I can do no better justice to Faucit's sense or to Faucit's honour, than by saying that the thought of Daisy's money was not only the last that occurred to him in the matter, but struck him as a serious obstacle in his way. How could he come forward for the rich merchant's daughter, with neither position nor means, and even with brains unproven for the achieving of either ? And therein, perhaps, Guy Faucit measured the canons of society only too well. Meanwhile, however, whatever the future might have in store for them, among the fairest scenes of nature in her most various moods, and among all the surroundings of men and women who knew nothing of what was passing in their hearts, though they rubbed elbows every day, Guy Faucit and Daisy Fairfield thought from morning to evening, in very plain English, of nothing in the world but each other.

CHAPTER VII.

MOTHER AND SON.

In a quiet corner of Devonshire, by some one of the tiny Combes which lie between Teignmouth and Torquay, and make the coast-walk from one of those places to the other one of the prettiest which the pedestrian can find on a summer's day, Guy Faucit had found a home for the long-widowed mother, who had till then been his love. He always came back to the old lady with fresh and renewed affection; kept her when he was away constantly informed of all his doings and all his plans, and found in her a wise as well as an admiring adviser. With all her pride in Guy's Oxford successes, and all her sympathy with his enthusiasm

F

for his pursuits there, she had a knack of shaking her head over his monastic theories of life. Charmed with her only child's exclusive devotion, and repaying it with womanly interest—how much did she not think of him, after all, in comparison to all his thoughts of her?—she nevertheless was very firmly convinced that the boy ought to marry and would marry, and returned to the charge upon that point with unfailing pertinacity. Many and many a friendly battle-royal did the two have together in the bright parlour—I like the old-fashioned word where yet not out of place —where the roses clustered round the porch, and on the other side of the little trim garden the limes shut out the road. During his visits to Devonshire, which he made a point of paying for some substantial part of every vacation, Guy carried the old mother about under protest to many of the parties and gatherings which went on in the hospitable western county, at which mother and son were always more than welcome. They provided her with a circle of friends who were sure to look after her and find company for her when he was away, for he didn't like to think of her as dull or too much alone.

Now it happens, that to the well-balanced taste the young ladies of Devon are possessed of many and great attractions; and Mrs. Faucit was firmly persuaded that quite the majority of them were secretly in love with Guy already, and asked nothing better than to meet him half-way, if he were disposed to the mysterious step called "coming forward." When the parties and gatherings were over, thus much would she expound to him in the profoundest confidence, while he gravely smoked his pipe by the roses. There had been a little difficulty over the tobacco at first, Mrs. Faucit having been brought up in ante-nicotian days when smoking was an illicit trade, and relegated to the kitchen or the harness-room. Guy had given in with the best of graces till his mother began to find that she grudged so much of his society to his pipe, and thought it best to make advances to her rival, who now lived with her on the pleasantest of terms. She had been heard to confess that she even liked it, and the final victory was achieved by Guy's machiavellian craft. Mrs. Faucit always said that she could detect the slightest trace of tobacco in a room for days afterwards. For four or five nights consecutively Guy smoked in the dining-room, with the due precautions, after she had gone to bed, and confessed one morning when the old lady's blissful ignorance was apparent. The next night he didn't smoke; and at breakfast Mrs. Faucit, demonstratively sniffing, declared that the smell was intolerable. But she was of a candid mind; and on the weakness of the proposition being demonstrated, she gave in. So the pipe among the roses became a recognized institution; and their beauteous majesties of the garden bloomed none the worse for it.

Here, in the parlour then, many and many a time after they had come home, did these two who were all in all to each other discuss how they might become less. Guy would explain that it was impossible; that the Fates had shaped him a course at the university, where, though a wife was a forbidden luxury, a mother was not. When his position was definite enough; when a certain professorship, which was generally regarded as his reversion, had fallen in his way, and he had fairly settled down to his stride, his mother was to leave the Devonshire cottage and keep house for him at Oxford, as he should leave the rooms in Balliol, and set up a homestead of his own. He had mapped out his future upon these definite lines, and he did not mean to disturb it.

"I've married my mother," he said; "and the day shall come when she shall be a hostess well-known in Oxford circles, and all the pleasantest society in the place shall meet in her drawing-rooms."

This was his filial castle in the air; and men have built worse before now, I think. But Mrs. Faucit could not be brought to agree.

"Marriage, my dear old boy, is the law for all nice people; and you were never intended to be one of the exceptions. You ought to be independent, of course, and to be able to make up to any one you choose, and go into Parliament, where you would get a great name, and be asked into the ministry directly. It is simply too bad of James Foster, my only brother in the world, and he with neither kith nor kin of his own, not to give you a handsome allowance out of all that money of his, and acknowledge you as his heir. Whom else has he got; and whom does he want better, I should like to know?"

"Don't talk about him, mother," said Faucit, whose face always grew dark at the mention of James Foster's name.

"But I must talk about him. How can I help talking about an only brother with his tens of thousands a-year, and my poor sister Mary dead and gone? I wish you'd write to him."

"Mother! how can you even think of it? when you have so often told me yourself of his conduct to you and my father when you married, and always afterwards."

"Who knows but he may have been right, my dear? Your poor father with his half-pay—quarter-pay I called it—and I with my little bit of money; no wonder that he thought the marriage so rash and wrong."

"Rash and wrong! when he could have helped you had he cared, without even feeling it! Don't talk any more about him; I hate to hear his name. All his endless meannesses afterwards, about trusteeships, and Heaven knows what besides, didn't make things much better, did they? Daring to dictate to my grand old soldier-father, and pretend to look down on him from the heights of the stocking-trade! He had better find his needle's eye to creep through and make haste about it, the old miser!"

"Oh, Guy, what a very shocking quotation!"

"Awful. I am the profanest of men, as you know. Uncle James indeed!" and Guy laughed. "Shall I ever forget the last and about the only time I ever saw him, when I suppose I was about thirteen years old? Don't you remember, mother, when he drove past us in his gig, and said, 'Is that your boy, Kattie? Why, he's not brown—he's black!' Pleasant creature! how I should like to kick him!"

"Well, dear, it wasn't nice," said the mother with a sigh, who would have done anything for that boy of hers, and was moreover of a placable disposition. "But quarrels in families are such weary things; and I do believe that if you wrote to him—"

"I shan't, you know, mother. We're not rich, but we're comfortable; and if I go on as I am we shall be more than comfortable some day. I don't like family-quarrels either, and have no objection to making up, even with old grey-shirtings. But—*que messieurs les assassins commençent.* When Mr. Foster comes with his hat in his hand and begs our pardon, perhaps we'll ask him to tea. And now let's change the subject. Who was the last young lady you said was breaking her heart for me, at the Powderham archery meeting yesterday?"

"I didn't say breaking her heart, dear. I wish you'd be more accurate."

"But you implied it, you bad old woman; you know you did."

"Well, dear, Alice Maitland is a very nice girl indeed, and it's no use saying she isn't. And Maitland's bank is one of the oldest and best in London."

"Alice Maitland is nice, and the bank is even nicer. But I think, mother, that I like Rose Plummer better."

"Do you, really? Well, Rose Plummer is a very nice girl too, and will have a nice fortune, though she's not as rich as the other. But Sir John Plummer has a great influence in the county, and might sit for it if he liked. Still I do think you oughtn't to flirt so dreadfully with both of them. It isn't fair upon the poor girls."

"How odd you women are about each other," laughed Guy. "The moment we like a girl, and talk to her a little more, or waltz with her a little oftener than usual, it isn't 'fair'; and we are always expected to 'mean' something. I can't make out how on earth anybody ever marries anybody, as you're always pulled up before you've time to find out anything about a girl except that you rather like her. I don't believe the girls agree with you a bit, or expect anything, or wish for anything except to be left alone for a while, just as the men do!"

The old lady shook her head. "You don't know girls as I do, Guy. How are they to know what men mean?"

"Easy enough, I should think. But I tell you what it is, little mother: if they're what you make them out they're a poor lot, and I don't want to have anything to do with them."

"But, Guy—"

"But, mother. Now let's have some backgammon." And the champion of the river and the tennis-court proceeded to devote himself with a single heart, unscathed by the influences of Alice Maitland and Rose Plummer, to the mysteries of cinq-quatre and deuce-ace. Mrs. Faucit shook the box and returned to the charge.

"Nevertheless, Guy, I should like to see you with a good wife."

"Very well, then; find me one. Flirt with her yourself, propose to her yourself, and come and live with us."

"No, dear, I shan't."

"Well, then, I shan't either."

The discussion stands for many which· went on between the mother and son, before the summer when Guy Faucit met Daisy Fairfield at the Christchurch ball, and came ·down to the Devonshire cottage from

the lakes, with a new life and a new feeling stirring
in his heart.

* * * * * *

"Then you are in earnest this time, my dear
child ?"

"I am afraid I am, my mother, very much."

"God bless you, my son. I am sure that Miss
Fairfield is all that I could ever wish; and I shall be
so glad and proud to welcome her."

"There's a good deal to happen before that,
mother," answered Guy, laughing. "I've got to win
her, you know, to begin with."

"I don't think there can be very much doubt about
that," the mother answered, in a tone of very placid
conviction.

Guy laughed again.

"You dear old prophet of good, may your confidence be well grounded. Let me look at you,
mother mine."

He rested his two hands upon her shoulders, and
looked down from his height of vantage upon the soft
smooth bands of silver hair.

"Can you give up the dream of the Oxford home,
and think of me as the hard-working barrister in
smoky old London, toiling for the dear life and the
dearer love ?"

"I never believed in the Oxford home, my boy;
and I always told you so. And I shall love to think
of the work in London, which is the only place for
a man like you. I must do my best to help you."

"What, mother? It shall make no difference to
you whatever."

"Oh, but it must."

"Oh, but it mustn't. Why, I have calculated
means, and I shall do splendidly. I shall take small
living-chambers in the Temple, not to be at double
expense. I shall write a good deal more than I have
done, for I think I have the connection for that already;
and with my fellowship, which is a good one, I shall

be more than able to manage. Not a penny off the help that I have been able to give the mother."

"Oh, Guy! it is not right. It is I that should be helping you."

"You dear old lady! you look like it, don't you? Why I wouldn't lose a bit of the pride I have in helping to keep up the Devonshire cottage, not even for all the Miss Fairfields to be found!"

"That doesn't sound like being properly in love," said Mrs. Faucit.

"I think it does; and I don't think Miss Fairfield would agree with you."

"But the Bar is so expensive. Ain't there all sorts of fees at starting?"

"I've saved enough to pay them. You know what an old screw I am; quite a touch of uncle James. Yes, mother, I am going to try my fortune in London, like so many waifs from Dick Whittington downwards. It's a face to do it for, isn't it?"

There was a photograph in Guy's hands.

"Yes, dear, it's a lovely face, and a good face. My Guy would never have chosen any other. God bless you and guard you and help you, my boy, and as you will be as good a husband as you are a good son, may He grant you your heart's desire.",

Very fondly the two kissed and embraced and parted; and it was with a heart purified and a will strengthened by the mother's blessing, that Guy Faucit started bravely on the London career which has seen so many win, and so many, to all outward seeming no less gallant and no less deserving, founder and fail.

CHAPTER VIII.

TERM-EATING.

THE young Balliol fellow settled to his new work with all the will in him, and soon began to find the truth of the maxim of Sir Benjamin Brodie, with which he had comforted himself. After the historians and philosophers and poets who had grown such familiar friends with him, he found it difficult at first to realize the attractions of style and thought to be found in ' Byles on Bills,' or Fearne's ' Contingent Remainders'; and ' Smith's Leading Cases' led at times to wandering thoughts, and to a sense of almost impossible boredom.

In spite of himself he reverted to some dearly-loved point of classic controversy, and detected himself in the act of fighting old battles over again on the old ground, somewhere in the fields of thought. But I have elsewhere spoken of Guy's great power over himself, for he had realized early in life the truth of the maxim which Dickens laid down, which sooner or later every man must realize who is really to succeed in anything. He had mastered while still at school the secret of "patient ungrudging attention," to which Dickens attributed all his own success, though in the case of that high authority perhaps there was something more to start with than falls to the share of most men.

So at it Guy went again all the harder for these deviations of the compass; and it was a sight to see him, both his hands holding tight to his hair, and the elbow-seams of his coat suffering considerably from their violent contact with the table, grappling with the "construction," as the grammarians call it, of some sentence of inordinate length, without apparent verb, and with neither beginning nor end, in which the potent, grave, and reverend authors of our law-books can give many points to my old enemy Thucydides himself. I hold the authors of law-books as a race altogether apart in the wonders of their style, and their mastery of that art of meaning-no-meaning which is so heavy a tax on their readers. Except some of the propounders of the new scientific gospels, I know of none to match them in that way. I hate a page which has to be read five times before any meaning can be distilled from it, and then turns out to be either gibberish, or else some faultless platitude which might have been expressed in a line if it was to be expressed at all.

Thus not long ago, in the 'Fortnightly Review,' I think, did I find myself studying a profound treatise on the Laws of Rhyme, from which I thought to gather instruction and advantage. One half-page held me riveted for a long time, for it was beautifully fine, and I felt that when I once understood it I should realize some great truth. I was on the eve of discovery, and meditated on my author profoundly. I forget the exact words he used, but they were something like this—

"In rhyme, everything depends upon a certain assonance and a certain assured sequence in the collocation of what we call the vowels and the consonants; and if the strict conditions therein implied fail to be watchfully and systematically observed, the result is a lapse of the delicate concord of musical sound which seizes and arrests the cultivated ear, once attuned to the eternal laws of harmony and proportion," etcetera, etcetera.

That, or something like it, went on for a page; and at last I found that it meant exactly this, nor less nor more: that a "hat" rhymes to a "cat," but not to a "bag."

It was a great consolation to Faucit, after much wrestling of the spirit and internal perplexity over the abstruseness of English law, to find that nine-tenths of the abstruseness lay in the way in which it was put —or rather wasn't, the "putting" being often conspicuous by its absence—and to discover to his great satisfaction that half the pages he read might have been boiled down into as many words. Writers who undertake to write, especially upon knotty subjects, ought to go through a competitive examination first, based upon primitive syntax and words in not more than three syllables; for with rare exceptions, never yet has writer won the big prizes save by simplicity of style. Be as eloquent as Ruskin or Newman, if you can; as witty as Thackeray; as scholarly as Cockburn; as fanciful as Charles Lamb; but mark that the whole setting of the wit and the eloquence, the scholarship and the fancy, are this and only this—simplicity. And for the sake of long-suffering mankind, observe one maxim more. When you have nothing to write about, let it alone. The "laws of rhyme," for instance, are briefly contained in the summary I ventured to give of the valuable thoughts of my "assonant" friend. Rhyme has just that law, and no other. "*C'est si facile de ne pas écrire,*" was de Morny's answer to the unsuccessful dramatist who complained to him that "*ce n'est pas si facile d'écrire une comédie.*"

Having solved this original problem to his satisfaction, Faucit worked with a will. As he looked at the uninviting calf which began to invade his beloved book-cases, and felt it his duty to furnish the little chambers in Garden Court in orthodox legal fashion, he sighed sometimes over the artistic Balliol rooms. But the purpose that was in him was far too strong for vain regrets, and apart and away from that, the ambition of London life soon began to hold him. If he was not the Cæsar that he had been at Oxford, the dominant nature of the man asserted itself in his new life as it did everywhere.

In the debating societies which met in and about the cozy taverns just east of Temple Bar, to be remembered in future generations, probably, only by the hideous landmark of the city griffin, where law questions were debated with zest and interest by the

self-educating among the sucking advocates, Faucit
made his mark at once, as he had done before at
the Union, on the grave question whether Mr. Disraeli
was or was not fit to lead the Conservative Party, or
whether the Oxford youth would or would not lend
its support to the foreign policy of the day.

I fear that the majority of us, for I too tried my
'prentice hand at the bar, were content with the
education provided for us by the benchers, in the shape
of dinners in hall.

Beginning his work in November, when the fees
and the fogs begin circulating together, Faucit
deferred till after Christmas the necessary course of
reading with a pleader, as he preferred to know something of the elements of his business before he began.

The hundred guineas were rather a wrench; but, as
he told his mother, he had saved money, and all
luxuries he retrenched at once from his manner of
living. No more delicate little scout-laid dinners, or
choice bottles of wine with a friend; only the homely
mutton and the frothing beer, which my healthy-
minded young athlete liked just as well. It disturbed
him a little to think that he might run to fat, but
he forestalled the danger by a vigorous course of
fencing at Waite's rooms in Soho Square, and an
occasional migration to Lord's for a turn at the
tennis.

A very pleasant set of rooms were those of Faucit's
in Garden Court, looking down from their third floor
upon the green little gardens of the Middle Temple on
the one side,—no embankment stood between that and
the water then,—and on the other on the plashing
fountain at the head of the steps, which was such a
pleasant object both to look and to listen to, like an
oasis of rest in the deserts of law-strife. For what
reason it was improved off the face of the earth I know
not; but when its innocent babble was extinguished,
there was mourning among the dwellers in Garden
Court.

I had myself been called to the bar some three years when Faucit took up his quarters in the Temple; and very welcome was his arrival to me and others of his Oxford contemporaries. I was taking the law easily, as I had taken the classics; and failing entirely to achieve Faucit's patience over his law-books, I felt that if I was ever to arrive at greatness in the law, it would have to be thrust upon me by imperious circumstance. Imperious circumstance did indeed try it for a time, and threw many briefs and a good round practice in my way; but Nature was too strong in me even for circumstance, and my incorrigible idleness was the cause of much mourning in the Balbus family, who predicted untimely ends for me which have not yet come to pass.

Fred Wilmot was the third of the Balliol chums who now re-united in the chambers in Garden Court, and consorted in frequent companionship together.

Fast friends we were in those cheery days, though Wilmot was the very reverse of me, being all that the Wilmot family could desire, and penetrated with legal ambition and legal lore. His was a light which, in consequence, now burns and shines as it ought, for is not Wilmot the acknowledged leader of his circuit, and sure of speedy promotion to the bench? Only a morning or two ago I was reading with admiration an argument of his in a case in which a clergyman had been imprisoned for breaking the law, wherein he proved, past my contradiction, that an eminent judge who was responsible for the proceeding had broken it in half-a-dozen different places himself.

Wilmot and Faucit had many a deep discussion upon law together, as in old days upon Aristotle or Plato, at which, as in old days also, I assisted as an admiring listener—my remarks, when I made any, being with much consent treated as trivial. I was not in any way regarded as a serious person; and it was a puzzle to many, myself included, why I chose my special friends, or was chosen by them, from among the more studious spirits of my time, when I should obviously have herded with the drones.

I am no nearer to any philosophic system of life now than I was when I read Mill, and didn't believe a word of him; but I fancy that through all that idleness of mine there must have been a large amount of observation and meditation at work, which was to bear fruit for me later, when my emancipated spirit had got out of the legal shell, and had become free to circulate in a literary atmosphere of its own.

As for Faucit, none of us ever had any doubt that he would come out clear first in anything and everything he chose to put his hand to. Young as he was at the work, he soon found his connection in journalism extending and growing solid, and felt with relief that if the bar failed him he would after all have a profession to fall back upon. But he would not let the pen tempt him too far, or use it for anything but a help at starting.

A few years before, and even journalism had been under police supervision in a barrister who meant business.

"There are callings," said Lord Ellenborough, "in which to be suspected of literature is dangerous."

But more liberal ideas were beginning to prevail, and even solicitors to allow that a man cannot live upon hope while he is waiting for their briefs, but must help himself as best he may as long as he does it with a due amount of reticence. So Guy Faucit stuck resolutely to anonymous work, and suppressed his personality in literature.

As for me, in a weak moment I wrote a farce which was acted in public, and audaciously claimed the authorship. Then all was over, and my prospects were blasted. They have never recovered. Never mind.

"John, my son," said an anxious parent to a co-barrister and co-author of mine, who had like proclivities, "how can you be such a fool as to write a play? If you stick to the bar you may become a Brougham."

"I may," he said; "and if I stick to the plays I may become a Sheridan. One's just as likely as the other; and of the two I prefer Sheridan."

John held to his evil courses, and is now making a very handsome income of his own. It is very wrong; but he is. They have balances at their bankers, some of those dramatists, improper though it be.

Very strange and very wonderful are the ways of fate; and no stranger lot than Faucit's did she hold in that mysterious urn of hers. There was to be no calling to the bar, no legal name or legal success, for him from whom his friends all hoped so much. Rather they did not hope; they felt sure. Yet, in one year from the day when we dined with him by way of chamber-warming in Garden Court, upon a feast of oysters,—cheap then and plentiful, and consumed by the young votaries of Themis, not grudgingly or sparingly, or in the uncomforting shifts of Blue-Points or French immigrants, but in rich native luxuriance over the counters of Prosser,—and of beefsteaks and beer, the dream was to be over and the future gone, and our model and hero, all his moorings severed and lost, was to drift away out of sight, as lost to us as Merlin in the hollow oak, and even in the minds which held him dearest to linger but as a memory. We should have made more of him that winter, Wilmot and I, and of all the rich stores we drew from his strong sense and scholarship and shrewd imagination, had we known what and how soon was to be the end of that pleasant chapter in our lives. He was one who needed confidence and sympathy, and was expansive with his close allies, though with the many he was reticent about himself.

So it was not long before Wilmot and I knew the reason of his change of plans and life, which had puzzled us at first, well aware as we were of his attachment to Oxford, and of his tenacity of purpose.

He was one of those men who seem bound to live heart-whole, and supplied a crucial test of the absurdity of predicating such a thing of anybody. When they do go, these ironclads, they do. Faucit concealed nothing from Wilmot or from me, who kept his counsel. He felt pretty sure that he had made an impression upon Daisy Fairfield's thoughts and heart, and had a confidence in her very fine to see. He was in no hurry to speak; but if she cared about him—and he would spare no effort to make that certain—she would wait as trustfully as he. She knew well enough what his thoughts and wishes were, he said, even when they parted in the summer. Or if she doubted them, what did she think when, towards the close of November, when he had settled well down in harness, they met face to face in one of the winter exhibitions?

Very warm on both sides was the shake of the hand; and Guy's quick eye had already detected the faint sweet flush which brought the rose-tinge to the clear face, whose every line he knew so well. Many of its myriad expressions he had still to learn. So, alas! had she, poor child!

"You in London, Mr. Faucit?" she said. "Can Oxford spare you just now?"

"I have left Oxford," he quietly answered.

She looked quickly up, and spoke slowly, with a certain pleased surprise.

"You—have left—Oxford?"

"Yes; I am living in chambers in the Temple, and am reading hard for the Bar."

"I am very glad," she answered, frankly and straightforwardly. "I am sure that you will make yourself a great name in that profession before long."

"I shall try," he said gravely. "At all events, you see I have taken your advice."

"Did I advise you to do it?"

"More than once. Have you forgotten?"

"No; I remember now that I did. But I should

not like to think that I am responsible for so grave a change of purpose."

"Very many have advised me to it as well as you," Guy answered. "Indeed, most of my friends, I think. So if I turn out a failure I won't sue you for damages. But somehow I don't feel as if I should."

"No, indeed. For earnest men, Mr. Faucit, there is no such word as fail. I suppose you will live like a hermit in your Temple chambers."

"Not quite, I hope. I never believed in shutting oneself up as the best way of working. Change of mental air is the best receipt for everybody. I shall hope to come and call in Portland Place very soon indeed. Have you been back long?"

Jesuistry, Master Guy. He knew perfectly well she hadn't: for had not he and I walked past the house in Portland Place only three days before, and seen the blinds down? Guy walked very often up Portland Place. He found the air of the Regent's Park bracing, he said.

"No," said Daisy; "we stayed a little time in Paris on our way home, and only came back yesterday. I have so much to tell you of our Swiss tour, and all the delight I had in it. When will you come?"

"Shall you be at home to-morrow?"

"Yes; by five o'clock."

"Will you give me a cup of tea then?"

"Yes."

And the next day, at that pleasantest hour of social interchange, the bright silver tea-urn in Portland Place once more took up the accompaniment to the old, old song.

CHAPTER IX.

FAIRFIELD AND CO.

THERE were signs that winter that all was not well with the house of Fairfield. How is it that people know or suspect mischief in the business air? There are no outward and visible signs. The house goes on as usual; the payments are as sure and regular. In the City the same routine goes on with the steadiness of clockwork; and at the West-End Madam has her dinner-parties and receptions, and Miss her horses and her enjoyments. But there are unaccustomed clouds on the face of the master of the house; certain asperities and inequalities in his ways and speech which betray themselves to the home-observers who know him so well. And in the City chambers there are conferences between the partners, frequent and unusually protracted; and the confidential clerk, who is the marrow of the concern perhaps, is summoned to assist at them, and comes out looking rather grave, though nothing escapes him which his curious juniors can build a theory upon. But Dick confides to Harry over the mid-day chop and pint, and Harry wonders if the governor can possibly be shaky, though that anything can really be wrong with Fairfield and Co. seems an idea too absurd to be entertained seriously, etcetera, etcetera, etcetera,—*La calumnia e un venticello,*—and Harry and Dick, unconsciously enough, perhaps, set the stone of talk rolling, which, unlike the fabled rock of Sisyphus, has a knack of working its way up-hill all by itself when it is once started.

People in the City spoke doubtfully of the old ship Fairfield and Co. A younger partner had come in, bitten with the new theories of City-progress, and was bent upon enlarging the operations of the firm.

Old Threadneedle, the confidential clerk, very much disapproved of the new partner, and was for keeping the house in the old and quiet grooves in which she had run without a creak for so many years. He disliked the new order of things very much, and maintained that if the City was to become a colony of Jews and Germans, and to exist for nothing but for the forcing of hothouse fortunes, the old English traders should hold the more to the old ways, and keep a quiet corner to themselves in the middle of the scamper.

But in that, as in many things, Conservatism and Obstruction grow something mixed, and the tyrant Progress insists on having his way. It was surely by some odd freak worth the meditations of the political enquirer, that it was just when the City was growing more and more revolutionary in her own business-ways, that she suddenly ratted in her political creed, and turned Tory.

Mr. Fairfield, the head of the house, was to those who knew him casually not a nice man. His externals were against him, for his architecture was of the florid-combative order, and he was big and overbearing of manner. His voice was harsh, and creaked and grated in the sound—peculiarities aggravated by the fact that he had a sensitive throat, and was always losing the voice he had. His eyebrows were bushy, and his hair rebellious, more like a white wire-fence than anything else. He was rather a bully at home too, or poor delicate Mrs. Fairfield's frightened face belied him. She was always ailing, poor little lady, and nobody ever quite knew what with till she went quietly out of the world without any particular reason, a few years after the time I am writing of.

Some people there are who are ill in that indefinite way all their lives, and thereby cause pitying affection in some, and irritation in others.

Mrs. Fairfield irritated her husband, who was assertively strong and rude of health, and furious with the local weakness in his bronchial arrangements, which was tiresome without being in the slightest degree interesting. Moreover, he could have got rid of it in a fortnight by drinking less wine. Moreover, he knew it, and was exceedingly angry if anybody told him so.

He lectured Mrs. Fairfield on her partiality for doctors, who, indeed, did the poor lady very little good, making general remarks about want of tone which were both obvious and feeble. They were particular about the wine she drank, which varied according to the medical fashion of the season. This year it was hock. Indeed, each season has its special vintage from the physician's point of view as much as from the vine-grower's. However, I don't think the faculty did Mrs. Fairfield any harm, or that there was any harm or good to be done to her, simple, neutral-tinted soul. She clung to Daisy with a fond and close affection, which the young girl returned with interest, watching her mother with a protecting tenderness very good to see. She was a bulwark often between her and the lord-and-master's tempers; for Mr. Fairfield was in his way very fond and proud of Daisy too, and rarely showed any disposition to bully her. Indeed, with all her sweetness of nature, Daisy Fairfield was not easy to bully. Any attempt of the kind missed its mark somehow, and made itself look foolish, and perished of inanition. There was a sort of uncompromising and fearless straightness about her, clear-set in the great blue eyes, which baffled dictation as much as it subdued impertinence. The latter, somehow, was out of the question with her altogether.

Daisy Fairfield was fond of her father for his love for her; and I cannot help thinking that it takes a great deal to prevent a child from being fond of a parent. I doubt if anything but absolute and proved un-love will do it, for the fifth commandment is by nature very easy of keeping. He had great schemes for her in his head, and meant to make her an heiress worth a great man's wooing—great of course socially and by right of purse, as such folk measure greatness. He had but one other child, a son whom he regarded with much contempt and some aversion, as a very weak vessel indeed.

Dick Fairfield had shewed no propensity for making money, but a considerable one for spending it on himself. He had declined to have anything to do with the business, in which he was to have succeeded his father, as Fairfield after Fairfield always did, and as there was no second to fall back upon, "Fairfield" must in another generation be but a *nominis umbra* in the house, where the new partner would reign supreme, under such fetters of Threadneedle's forging as he would submit to. Dick had gone into the army as such men do, not to fight, but to loaf; and his father, finding the business hopeless, had allowed him to do it because of the social consideration he supposed would belong to it. But in starting him he had given him clearly to understand, that as he declined to care for the House of Fairfield, the House of Fairfield would not make an eldest son of him, but that Daisy would have her full share of the goods her father might leave behind him. Dick accepted the condition vacuously, as he did everything, being indeed slow both of heart and of intelligence, and a wonder to everybody in that he called Daisy sister. Such wonders of kinship are constant, family un-likeness being often more curious to speculate upon than family likeness.

Daisy thoroughly disapproved of Dick; and fully shared her father's feeling that he should have felt it a bounden duty, being the only son, to conquer his tastes, or rather want of them, and stand by the house and the business.

Poor Mrs. Fairfield, of course, could never be brought to see this, which nettled her husband considerably. She thought the army delightful, and the uniform most becoming; and she sympathized deeply with Dick's grievances when, as now, he was relegated to unattractive quarters in an out-of-the-way part of Ireland. He ought to have made a stipulation with the Horse-Guards, when he joined, that he never was to leave London.

Daisy Fairfield, perhaps, did not keenly regret her brother's absence, and for her that Christmas season, which followed on Guy Faucit's plunge into the troubled waters of legal life, was a happy and memorable time. It is a happy, if a restless time, for those of us to whom it is given, that during which the heart's first real fancy takes steady shape and form, and the feeling that "it may be" deepens into the conviction that "it must," the belief that "it will."

Guy Faucit, with his friends and his introductions, at once found himself welcome in the society I described as Daisy's in a former chapter. He was a man to become an acquisition and a favourite at once; for his Oxford fame had of necessity preceded him to many places in town, where many a man now in advance of him at the bar owned him for tutor and adviser, and looked up to him with unabated reverence.

Good Mrs. Pepperharrow, who was one of the first people on whom he called, killed a fatted calf for him at once, and sent him down to dinner with Daisy. Mrs. Pepperharrow was preternaturally gorgeous, and full of an important move in life which she was going to make. She was about to "take up her hassocks," as a friend of mine describes the progress of migration, and inaugurate a mighty palace in the south-west of London, which she hoped to make a fashionable centre.

"So good of you if you'll come and help me, Mr. Faucit," she said, "with some acting or a little music, or some *tableaux vivants*" (I cannot attempt to reproduce the appearance these two words would assume in the spelling). "I'm sure you're very clever in that way."

"Indeed, Mrs. Pepperharrow, I know nothing at all about them."

"Oh, Mr. Faucit, you can't expect me to believe that. A man of your intellect, who can do anything e likes to do without an effort. Daisy dear, wouldn't Mr. Faucit look well as the Earl of Leicester, with you as Amy Robarts—wasn't that her name?—and me as Queen Elizabeth? Then there would be appropriate music beind the scenes, and a good supper downstairs. Mr. Faucit, you really must promise me to do the Earl of Leicester."

"The Earl of Leicester, Mrs. Pepperharrow," said Daisy, "was slight and delicate and romantic; and you will have to starve Mr. Faucit down, which I am sure isn't at all in your way. And I'm sure I don't look a bit like that spiritless Amy Robsart."

"No, indeed," said her neighbour, in a low voice. "Flora MacIvor, or Minna in the 'Pirate,' would be more the line of part to fall to you."

"Are you to be the desperate Cleveland, then?"

"*Absit omen!*" muttered Guy in a low voice.

"Which means?" asked Daisy, half hearing.

"Which means that I was quoting Latin at dinner, which is atrocious; I should have been sconced for it at Oxford. I wonder, Miss Fairfield, if such an inveterate old don as I must be by this time will ever be civilized up to London level?"

"We shall all try what is to be done with you. Mrs. Pepperharrow, do you think we can ever make a London man of Mr. Faucit?"

"My dear, I'm surprised to hear you. I'm sure Mr. Faucit would be what he liked anywhere; though whether we ave to be different in Belgrave Square from what we are in Portland Place, I'm afraid I don't know. I've heard that you ave, and I wonder how it's done."

"What makes you change from such comfortable quarters as these?" asked Faucit.

"My usband Ugh as made a great it," said the lady, rushing at the sentence gallantly and losing every fence. (She generally saved some.) "I'm sure we were rich enough before, and very thankful we ought to be, when there's so many poor people about, and so hard to know what to do for them."

"Nobody knows better what to do in that way

than Mrs. Pepperharrow," said Daisy, looking very
kindly on her friend.

"Well, I know that I try, my dear. And, Mr.
Faucit, the poor are very hard to manage sometimes,
and do take one in so. I wonder if they're any better
in Belgrave Square."

"Are you going there on a voyage of discovery?"

"We're going there because Ugh as more than
doubled all his money this year, and is likely to go on
making more and more of it now e's once begun. And
I think we ought to do our duty in the states to which
we are called, and to see more of the aristocracy.
Not," added Mrs. Pepperharrow, hurriedly, "that we're
going to neglect old friends. Neither Ugh nor me
would do that. Oh dear me! Ugh's going to sleep;
look at him nodding at the other end of the table, and
Mrs. MacGunter not attending to him because of the
canvass-backed ducks. Ugh, dear—ahem" (with knife
and fork accompaniments on the table). "Ugh!"

The soap-boiler recovered with a start, and poured
some wine into Mrs. MacGunter's plate.

"You'll come and see us very often in the new
ouse, Mr. Faucit," continued the speaker, having
recovered the interruption; "and as for Daisy here, I'm
going to take her to all the best places and all the best
things of next year's season."

"And make a fine lady of her?" said Faucit.
"Painting the lily and gilding the gold."

He spoke rather low.

"Mr. Faucit!" said Daisy as low. "You don't
generally pay *banal* compliments."

"I don't think I ever do," he answered. "I was
quite in earnest. I cannot see Miss Fairfield in the
character of a fine lady."

"Thank you," she said, laughingly. "Perhaps I
can. Why should you think that I am free from the
ambitions and the weaknesses of my sex?"

"From what I have heard of it, the society craze
is neither an ambition nor a weakness. It is a fever,

apt to leave the whole system in an unstrung and exhausted condition."

So the talk glided on into the usual philosophies about the emptiness of fashionable life and the hollowness of society, which came of course with tremendous force from these two experienced young moralists. It is astonishing how, in London, that same hollow cavity is proclaimed and proscribed by the flutterers on the edge, who hasten to tumble into it one after another on the first appearance of an opening.

Guy and Daisy were not near enough to the mouth yet, so they were free to talk with a grave superiority which impressed Mrs. Pepperharrow but little, as far as she heard their conversation, carried on, it must be confessed, in something of an undertone.

Have I spoken of Daisy Fairfield's voice? Guy's eyes were sometimes half-shut as he listened, to dwell on the music of the notes. His hostess was on a more fashionable life intent, and undismayed by the auguries of good-natured friends as to the snubbings she might have to bear. She relied upon her Hugh's purse, and her own placid persistency of nature, which, combined with the fact that you might as well be rude to a cushion, had served her in good stead in the battle of life. They had begun at the bottom of the scale, she and her husband, and had loved and comforted each other in their honest way throughout. If such people do set their hearts upon social conquests, they do it so innocently and thoroughly that there is no blaming them, and perhaps they win because they deserve it.

The Pepperharrows' wealth made very many people happy; and in the hands of such trustees as they, it is apt to increase fast. Fortune, indeed, seemed bent at this time upon showering the favours they most desired upon them.

Early in the year, just as the big house in Belgrave Square was being prepared for the opening of the season, it fell to the lot of Alderman Hugh Pepperharrow to preside over some ceremony in the city which was graced by the presence of royalty, and carried with it some special significance deserving of special commemoration. Within a few days, to his wife's undisguised and pronounced delight, and with the effect of some shame-facedness on his part, veiling much inward satisfaction, the soap-boiler arose Sir Hugh Pepperharrow from under the gracious hand of his sovereign. And it was under such a smiling fortune as this that the ' Peep-Hole' and the 'Flunkey,' and other organs of the fashionable world, previously primed in the matter, announced beforehand some of the wonders which were to await the *élite* of the *beau monde* in the *salons* of the popular lady of an excellent knight. On such matters we always write in reverential, if sometimes doubtful, French. Even at the same time that fickle and dangerous goddess of the wheel was, alas! steering for a lea-shore, and bringing gathering rumour in her wake, the older vessel of Fairfield and Co.

CHAPTER X.

COMING EVENTS.

No rumours about the house of Fairfield or its fortunes reached the ears of the student in the Temple; nor did Daisy in Portland Place suspect any reason whatever for her father's increased irritabilities. He growled and glared more than before, and he visibly increased his allowances both of port wine and brandy-and-water, much to the girl's annoyance and distress. She had seen the effect of too much indulgence in these luxuries upon him too often not to hold them in profound horror, and she had very often been able to prevail on him to mend his ways by judicious remonstrance. Mrs. Fairfield had an unfortunate knack of inter-

fering at exactly the wrong time, and in exactly the
wrong way, and returning weakly to the charge when
wisdom lay in silence. People like this poor lady
are always doing it—unlucky social martyrs, who are
quite undeserving of the cruel process of snubbing,
very incapable of bearing. it, and yet always to a great
extent bringing it on themselves.

The effect of Mrs. Fairfield's mild but pertinacious
words was usually to increase the evil; but with his.
daughter Mr. Fairfield had the grace to be ashamed
of himself and of his bad tempers, when they outgrew
the reasonable crossness which is permitted to every
right-minded head of a household, in order to signify
that he is Sir Oracle, and wants the barking to himself.
Under the crooked influence of the bottle the crossness
sometimes broke bounds considerably, and took ferocious forms which Mr. Fairfield had forgotten all about
the next morning, till his wife began to narrate them
in a suffering tone when he woke, making him swear.

Daisy would say nothing till long afterwards, when
some quiet and perfectly good-tempered allusion,
lighted up sometimes by some of the humour which
had been rather freely bestowed upon this young lady,
made papa feel very uncomfortable and very conscious,
and grow quite good for a time. If some of the
guardian angels would only learn her method, and
refrain from triumphing over prostrate guilt at times
when forbearance is not only mercy but wisdom, con-
versions would be more numerous, and there would be
less creaking in the domestic wheel.

But of what am I discoursing? Is it possible that
well-bred young ladies can even be conscious of
aberrations of this class, much more take notice of their
existence? Faith, yes; coffee-taverns and Sir Wilfrid
were in their infancy then; and, indeed, I doubt if
good Father Noah's weakness is yet dead amongst us,
and perhaps there are a good many houses, if we
unroofed them, where the properest young maidens.
would be found very well used to the sins of fathers

or brothers in this matter, and speaking of them and rebuking them very candidly indeed.

Daisy Fairfield, certainly, had a way of going right to her mark about everything, and her mind and taste, at this period, were making rapid growth under the influence of Guy's companionship. Sadly indeed, and very gravely, did she note how this failing of her father's was growing upon him now. He was not a drunkard, nor did he often exceed the extreme limits imposed by decorum. But he drank too regularly and too much, and it was a vice that did not suit him. He was not one of those genial fellows who break up homes and hearts with the most exhilarating signs of good-temper; for when he had well drunk, Septimus Fairfield was not genial. If he had been less prone to the weakness for many years past, Daisy and his wife might have been more ready to suspect that he had something on his mind. As it was, they thought with perturbed spirits of the facile descent of Avernus, and hoped that the old gentleman would yet mend his ways.

If it had not been for this little rift within the lute, my favourite's enjoyment of this winter would have been perfect. Day after day, and time after time, the intimacy between her and Guy Faucit grew and prospered, and I think they understood each other very well, with that best of understandings which comes about between two loyal hearts like theirs, as the inevitable stream proceeds upon its course. He learned how to assure her of his meaning without definite words; to convey to her, by many a pleasant intimation which she would live upon for days, the depth of the purpose and the reality of the love that were in him; and at the same time to make her see why and how he did not care to come forward to her father empty-handed, but waited for the not far-off time, when, as he hoped, he might have something like a secure home and a definite future to offer.

When first she realized this, it may be that her

hero rose higher than before in her esteem, and that she, too, on her side, vowed in that simple maiden heart of hers that she, if so God would, was ready to wait in a quiet confidence for the moment when he might think himself justified in saying all that was in his heart. She made no concealment from herself of the answer which hers was prepared to give him.

There was no hurry. She was young, and the battered old world was young too for her; young enough to give her the full enjoyment of itself, its friendships and its pleasures, its allurements and its innocent uses, which the sceptics only sneer at when they have employed them badly.

When they met at the winter dances, the delight of the evening was in her waltzes and her talks with him; but that did not prevent her from dancing through her card with partners many and various, getting out of them all the good they had to give her, and grudging to him no little of the same kind of enjoyment. A pleasant look of understanding would pass between them at such times now and again, and the whole of their love-story was coloured by the radiance of a perfect trust.

I myself, who made her acquaintance through Guy at this time, was favoured with a good many dances and conversations with her, and thought that I could have wished no better fortune in the world for the friend for whom nothing seemed to me too good, than the companionship, through all change and chance, of such a rare creature as this.

She was so wonderfully frank and fearless, spoke of Guy with such unconcealed but modest interest, and interested herself so honestly in his friends, just because he had made them his.

She learned to laugh at me and with me for my avowed incapacity for legal learning, sympathized thoroughly with my hopeless predilections for the side of the world which men have agreed to call Bohemia— though what the word precisely means, and what are

its latitudes and longitudes, the social geography book
sayeth not in any plain terms—and comforted me
when, as sometimes happened, I felt inclined to cry
out on my own un-seriousness, by auguring for me a fair
measure of success in the irregular pursuits which it
was my bent to follow, wherein one may stray without
a licence, and work in the morning, or in the middle of
the night, or all day, or not at all, as seemeth the
unchartered libertine best in his own eyes.

Never had woman a happier knack of talking just
upon the subjects which most interest the person she
is talking to, not from any sense of duty, or with any
sign of that detestable process known as " pumping,"
but because she knew that men are best on their own
ground, and she loved to pluck from all the highways
and hedges of human nature the very flowers which
grew there the most naturally.

So it was that Wilmot came to the conclusion that
there could never be a barrister's wife like that; while
I, though quite agreeing with him in the name and
interests of Faucit, secretly felt that Daisy Fairfield was
born to share and to console the lot of a literary man,
and that after all it was to be hoped that the tyrant
Circumstance would end by dispensing that lot to Guy,
who had already shown his capacity to accept it.

Indeed, my chief despair about my own prospects
rose out of that capacity of his. Every article he
wrote for the 'Saturday,' or for the magazine with
which he was for the time connected, teemed with
an amount of knowledge and information which seemed
helplessly beyond my grasp. I wanted to be well-
informed; but it was all in vain. I was baffled by
politics, bemused by science, drugged by history, while
law drove me frenzied to the nearest oyster-shop.

I was incurably and conscientiously frivolous, and
read my fate in the pitying glances of my friends, and
the light subjects on which alone they would discourse
with me.

I used to think of my future gloomily—to see

myself a pauper, a tide-waiter, a wanderer living on my poor private means, and might never have found my destiny at all had I not one day chanced upon a French farce which amused me. I then and there wrote an original play (upon the same subject), and my groove was found.

We have all our grooves, my brethren, I verily believe, if we will but with patience wait for them. I have cited Sir Benjamin Brodie's dictum because Faucit believed in it. I didn't, and I don't. No power on earth—none—would, as I am convinced, have made me like or tolerate the law, through no fault of mine, who did not make myself. Neither could the good Fairy Bountiful herself make me hum "God save the Queen" so as to be recognized even by Her Gracious Majesty, often as she must have heard it, and on innumerable keys—even though, like Bully Bottom, I have a "reasonable good ear for music. Let's have the tongs and the bones."

I liked Daisy Fairfield heartily, just as I liked Faucit, and for the same personal reasons, which are at the bottom of all our real likings and dislikings. I abominate Jones because he doesn't appear to want my company at the club; when one day, lo, we meet in the coffee-room, he greets me warmly and we have a pleasant talk about nothing in particular, and thenceforward Jones is in my best books. Good fellow, Jones. Probably a precisely similar process has taken place in Jones's mind about me, and he has been cursing me for a stuck-up beggar, when I have been avoiding him because I thought he didn't care to speak to me. Faucit, no doubt, used to abuse me, in the round unvarnished terms of college youth, for not sticking to anything; but when the Dean of Chapel of our joint undergraduate day augured worst of me, and the master couldn't account for my proceedings except on the assumption of some mysterious deficiency in my brain—it was Dr. Phlebotham, I think, who once upon a time, trying to "reduce" me, said the cerebrum was possessed of too much white matter, and too little grey, or blue, or something—Faucit fought my battles in confidence, and vowed to them that Balbus would do very well for himself some day. The Dean hoped that I should; but my last essay upon the Theocritean philosophy had been something altogether too superficial for Balliol. I had insisted on treating that writer purely as a poet, "the poet of the Bucolics, a Syracusan by race, and the son of Simichides, as he said himself," and had more than inferred that he had no philosophy at all, and would have had as little to say for himself in that way as the needy knife-grinder.

Poor old Dean Parley! worthier and kinder soul never breathed; but he measured us all in the self-same teaspoon, and his classical curriculum was as the bed of one Procrustes, ordered to suit all lengths.

Of the brilliant minds and leaders of my college day, who were going to ignite the Thames, and witch the world with noble workmanship, only one or two have struggled to the front at all in the many-marshalled battle of Life, and those who now live and move in the eyes of men were for the most part but a poor sort of creature, ranked with the drones and pricked with the unworthy. Nimmo, the billiard-player, has made one of the finest fortunes of the day by coup after coup in Roumanian railways and Mexican contracts, wrought through energy of purpose and subtlety of brain; Scourfield, the thrice-rusticated, who would do nothing but hunt, is known through the wide world as a fighting special correspondent, whose rides and escapes astonish the generals as much as his letters delight the penmen; Mopus the solitary, who seemed to have neither foe nor friend nor occupation, and neither in books nor sports would ever do anything, is the famous poet of many editions; while Sternhold of the four first classes makes indexes in Lincoln's Inn to the statutes other men draw up; and the wondrous Impey, the distinguished Ireland, Hertford, and what not? who even in those days was too well-informed to believe in anything but himself, is incapable of making a speech, or saying Bo to a British jury; but devils unbeknown for the Solicitor-General, and saves him, as that officer confesses, a considerable amount of trouble. The wheel goes round, and the little pitchers crop up. There was not enough allowance made for mental varieties in those college days, and too much of pains taken in picking out the plums. It happens sometimes that the batter is good, and the plums are naught. Ever and again, though, the great stamp of true and original power asserts itself at the outset to all eyes; and neither tutors nor rowing men—neither friends nor examiners—were even then mistaken in their gauge of Faucit's capacity. Hard and sad enough was the discipline the Dispenser had in store for him; but as I write and remember, may discipline and Dispenser be thanked, it is bearing its late fruit now.

I was much with Faucit at that time, and made number four with his sweetheart and himself in more private boxes than one, contenting myself with the task of absorbing Mrs. Pepperharrow, whose conversation and character rewarded me thoroughly for my devotion, being to me a source of never-ending delight. Whether she attached any meaning or seriousness to the romance unfolding itself before her eyes, I am not sure. But such was her confidence in Daisy, that whatever that young lady did was sure to be right for her good-natured guardian, who made Daisy a prominent figure in all the mind-pictures she drew of the ouse in Belgrave Square.

"Quite a mansion, I assure you; and so elegant. I am sure if we might ope for anything from your pen for our first performance in the theatre, it would be sure to be a feature, Mr. Balbus. A man of your intellect, you know. But I'm afraid you wouldn't have the time."

I had just followed up the fatal farce with a melodrama, also of French origin, on the strength of which, not without some inward spasms, I called myself an

H

author. It is the only line of life I wot of in which a translator takes to himself that privilege. Yet do the sins of the adapter recoil upon his own head, for there is a general impression abroad, both in the public mind and the managerial, that an English playwright cannot invent his own plots. Why I don't know, as it is the easiest part of the business, which may be fairly inferred from the number of novels which every year provides. The impression has crystallized into a maxim, however; and it is proved by the simple process of attributing a French origin to all the plots one does invent. So it falleth out that in consequence of the sins of his fathers, and mayhap of his own youth, the British dramatist has a hard time of it. He is always told that he cannot invent his own plots; and when he does, he is told that they are not his own.

Not long ago I assured a friend of the absolute originality of a story of mine which had just had some success upon the stage; and he asserted it on my authority at a dinner of some gentlemen "in society" a night or two afterwards. The assertion, he told me, was met with roars of laughter, and the assurance from one of the guests that he knew the dialogue by heart and could repeat it in the original French!

Pleasant, truthful creature! "In less than a week there were some people who could name the father, and the farm-house where the babies were put to nurse" What can be the secret pleasure, I wonder, of railing by precept and detracting by rule?

But what am I, that I should keep Mrs. Pepperharrow waiting upon my wrongs? Her honest mind was troubled with no misgivings about degrees of authorship; and she recognized in me one of those mystic beings at whose shrine she bowed under the generic name of genius. Large and catholic was her interpretation of that word. Muggins, the eminent amateur actor, whose powers of facial expression (grimacial expression Jem Gosling once christened it) distanced J. S. Clarke in his most india-rubber mood;

Josephine Parrott, the eminent *tragédienne*, who learnt all her parts after the fashion of Pendennis's friend, Miss Fotheringay, and concealed a world of emotion in those beautiful eyes so effectually that it never got out of them; Binks, the successful manager, who did such wonderful things for art that the great upholstering firm of Shoddy and Co. made quite an income out of him (his plays he bought in Paris, but encouraged native art by insisting that all the characters should be called by English names, and that new English repartees should be written for them, thereby proving his respect for the French author's work, and how little that author knew what was good for him)—the drawing-room comic singer of the hour, whose name is immaterial, for he is always the same; Balbus the dramatist; Faucit the scholar and Saturday Reviewer; Mr. Millais, the Bishop of Winchester, and Mr. Gladstone, were all welcome to the routs of Lady Pepperharrow that was to be as representatives of Genius.

She was an honest, kindly, and admiring soul; and small idea enough had she of the consequences which were to follow, when she took Daisy Fairfield under her affectionate wing. She had no daughters of her own; only two or three sons, who had taken to country-pursuits, and were but little at home, eschewing the society which their mother so loved. So Daisy filled a void in her life, and willingly gave the time she could spare from the duties of her own home to the service of her friend. Faucit's polite attention during the winter charmed the old lady, who made him exceedingly welcome, and gave opportunities many and various for meetings whose significance would scarcely have escaped the keen eye of Fairfield papa, and would very little have pleased him. But for the preoccupations which were growing upon him at this time, he might have scented danger even as things were. But he was revolving schemes of his own for Daisy in his own mind, with as small thought of her as the slave-dealer has of the feelings of his plumpest Circassian.

H 2

Kind Mrs. Fairfield had inklings of her own on the matter, for Faucit rallied to the five o'clock urn not unfrequently, and one day she hinted something of her thoughts to her daughter, who met them with a very becoming blush, a little laugh, and a kiss. Daisy was very happy in her simple paradise. Fearless of the man she loved, and undoubting of herself, as she would be fearless and undoubting if ever the day should come when she might seal at the altar the compact already firm and fast in her inmost heart, she went on her way rejoicing, and adding day by day more splendours and more adornments to her castle in the air.

> "O, but she would love him truly;
> He should have a cheerful home;
> She would order all things duly,
> When beneath his roof they come."

Daisy Fairfield was modestly conscious of a heart and mind beyond the average of every-day women; and she knew the rich gifts of love and help that she could bring in her hand to the man she could accept as worthy of them. Young as she was, she had attracted admiration enough to turn a light head lightly; but she had formed her ideal from the first, and her ideal protected her till it came in living form, and a very attractive living form too. She recognized in Faucit's nature the complement and magnet of her own. She had the artist's eye to admire his physical manliness and the woman's perception to read his steady truthfulness of character, and the perfect simplicity with which, conscious on his side of his own superiority to most of the men surrounding him, he referred it without doubt or question to the source whence he believed it came, and read the lesson of humility so—as it was meant to be read—as so few will deign to read it.

That it was his business to do his best with the talents intrusted him, be their number five or ten, or, as he expressed it himself, to "stick his nails into the work that came to him to do," was a conviction with which all Daisy's nature sympathized. And it was the opinion of the chronicler of these events, as he watched and protected his two favourites as best he might, flirted with Mrs. Pepperharrow in a manner to endanger the soap-boiler's rest, and regarded Fairfield papa with a suspicious and unaccommodating eye, that Nature never formed a pair more nobly fitted to fill a royal space in a rather commonplace world together.

CHAPTER XI.

MY LORD AND MY LADY.

IT was the Baroness Luscombe of Lusmere who kindly undertook to issue the invitations for the opening festivity at the new house in Belgrave Square, about which the 'Peep-Hole' and the 'Flunkey' had been busied with starry paragraphs for weeks before.

The blushing honours of the soap-boiler's knighthood were brand-new upon him; for it was in the February of the winter of which I have been writing that his sovereign singled him out of the mistered herd, and gave him antlers in the shape of the *manche à son nom*, which was so impressive to Sir Barnes Newcome, the banker.

In the ensuing month of March, when the sun even in London was pitilessly clear, just out of perversity, and because the east wind was so pitilessly cold, Lady Pepperharrow welcomed all the world and his wife to Glycerine House, Belgrave Square, to the first of the festivities with which the name of that hospitable mansion was to become eternally connected. It was unfortunate that it was Lent, certainly; for the hostess would gladly have respectea every prejudice and every feeling under the sun; but it could not be helped; and this comparatively quiet season had its advantages, for a beginner in the field of fashion, over the later months, when dates are all filled up, and the fixed stars of the social firmament reign supreme.

Lady Pepperharrow was at present but a comet with a good deal of tail, so she took the advice of Lady Luscombe, and of that distinguished authority Lord Pentonville, to whom Lady Luscombe introduced her, and compromised with worldliness with a sigh. Nor did the good lady surrender her ancient prejudices without the knowledge and sanction of the Rev. Mr. Birmingham Pope, the favourite minister of her new district. She had frankly consulted him, on her coming, upon the poor of his neighbourhood, and what help she best could give him in his work, and fairly astonished him by the roundness of the cheque with which she presented him. He quite stammered his acknowledgments, and owned that from the wealthiest neighbourhood in London he did not get quite so much help in that way as he could wish; for indeed, whatever his social proclivities and concessions to mammon, Mr. Pope was a man who did a great deal of good from the incomings of his church, and would gladly have done more.

"The subscriptions, I must own, Lady Pepperharrow, are not what I could wish. But above all things we should be charitable; and I know that the members of my congregation have calls and duties in the country which conflict with their opportunities here. An open hand like your ladyship's will be a blessing not to be over-estimated."

Mr. Pope delighted Lady Pepperharrow, and was installed as her confessor in ordinary without loss of time. He was consulted about the great house-warming —if a word so ordinary may be applied to an event of such magnitude,—and while respecting the lady's hesitations he fully endorsed the opinions of her secular advisers in the matter. Lady Luscombe herself, he assured her, was a very particular person, and would only advise a great entertainment like this in Lent under exceptional circumstances. Lady Luscombe was no doubt quite justified in considering the circumstances exceptional, and there was now-a-days a decided advance in the liberality of public opinion upon these matters, which he himself could not but regard as a healthy tendency, if not carried too far. Those who still cherished scruples on the point would consult their own feeling in staying away; but he was far from thinking that, with proper safeguards, pleasant and general social intercourse was not in itself both lawful and commendable at all periods of the year.

If Lady Pepperharrow had further doubts, they were banished by Daisy Fairfield's straightforward intimation, that she could see no conceivable harm in her friend giving a party in Lent if her friend liked, and it was more convenient than any other time. As Daisy's ways and opinions of thinking were always very simply in earnest, her verdict in the matter, as on most matters about which Lady Pepperharrow consulted her, was accepted as final.

Lady Luscombe was the first high step in her humbler sister's social ladder. The Lord Viscount Luscombe, gouty and aristocratic almost beyond the permitted limits of aristocracy and gout, passed his days in the fond delusion that he was a Liberal of the modern advanced school. He was a country gentleman of olden family and good though moderate fortune, who, determining to devote his abilities to the service of his country, was as a series of matters of course elected member for the county division, early introduced to the lesser loaves and fishes of official life, and by steady gradations developed into a Secretary of State.

When the Liberal Ministry of 18— was formed, it was in all quarters felt that Mr. Fulke Vavasour was entitled to a post in the cabinet, from the eternal order of the proprieties. No better reason could be advanced or was suggested. In that position he was found by some of his colleagues, upon trial, to be so eminently and entirely respectable, that upon a reconstruction of the ministry he was translated to the House of Lords, without office, it being thought and indeed stated that his independent support in that position would be of the highest value to the government.

Wilkins, the advanced member for Radborough, accepted the vacant portfolio. It was early in the session which followed upon these events that a measure was inadvertently suffered to pass the House of Commons, which was rightly regarded in well-informed quarters as a serious menace to the existing social system; and the House of Lords, with the pronounced interest in political matters, and the unselfish patriotism which distinguishes them as a body, rose to the occasion. They were assembled in London in numbers quite unusual for the season of the year.

Lord Luscombe, whose independent support was the implied condition of his peerage, could not be expected to give it against his conscience, and both spoke and voted the other way. He afterwards wrote to the 'Times' in vindication of his principles and action, and the letter was very much admired. A yet more extraordinary result of the political crisis, and a more convincing proof of the keen political insight and anxiety for the public weal which is the true basis of the sturdy English character, was the fact that a whole army of Peers, many of them unknown by name to the more ignorant sections of the public, left their hunting-boxes and their country-houses, and their winter watering-places in the Capuan South, to rally round the throne and the constitution. They did not listen to the arguments on the other side, for they knew the value of time; but voted with the unanimity of the players in the 'Critic,' and saved the country. Some of them, it was even whispered, were so much in earnest that they had never been inside the House before, and couldn't find their way.

The 'Peep-Hole' recorded the arrival of the Earl of Deadhead at Claridge's, from his villa on the Mediterranean; while the 'Flunkey,' in this respect beforehand with all rivals, announced that Lord Pentonville, who had been staying with some distinguished friends in the neighbourhood of Newmarket, had taken up his quarters at his bachelor residence in Mount Street, Grosvenor Square. Even those inseparable friends, the Duke of Surbiton and the Marquis of Norbiton, were visible in London. The great heart of the country, no doubt about it, was thoroughly stirred.

So much the better for our friend Lady Pepperharrow. These throbs of the country's heart sensibly quickened the circulation in her drawing-rooms, in the exceptional pre-Paschal season which resulted from the political crisis. Lord Luscombe, who was very much respected in the city, and had many mysterious things to do with odd and sundry Boards, had, in the course of his financial operations, made acquaintance with Mr. Pepperharrow, and thereout, it must be admitted, sucked no small advantage. He had been put up to a good thing in connection with the *coup*, which established the soap-boiler's fortune on such a solid basis; and it was whispered that he was the first cause of the claims of that gentleman to social recognition being brought to the notice of H. M.'s advisers in such matters. And learning from Sir Hugh Pepperharrow the nature of the " buffets and rewards "—for I am told that in such things the two go hand in hand—on which his better half had set her heart, his lordship showed himself not ungrateful. He called upon the lady and dined with her, in his wife's absence from town, at Luscombe Abbey; and gave her matter of conversation with her friends and intimates for a long time after, until lords and ladies grew as plentiful with her as peas in June.

During many of those parties of four of which I have spoken, I heard of nothing but Lord Luscombe's merits, while the other two, pleasantly and entirely unmindful of such subjects of talk, were straying together in fields and byways of their own. And Lady Pepperharrow having confided to his lordship her wishes and ambitions about the opening of the house in Belgrave Square, Lord Luscombe in a gallant moment undertook that his wife should be her sponsor.

Lady Luscombe was not especially pleased when she heard of the task assigned her. Certainly a greater difference of style and externals between two women could not well be imagined than between her and the lady given her as a *protégée.* Marian Fulke Vavasour was barely twenty when she made her appearance in London life under that name, as the young wife of the rising statesman, thirty years older than herself. For at fifty Mr. Fulke Vavasour was still rising; and he might never perhaps have attained to his highest altitudes but for the rare gift which pertained to his wife. As the French say so neatly of a characteristic which once, at all events, belonged signally to Frenchwomen, *elle savait tenir son salon.* The cold and somewhat fishy, but observant eye of the countymember had detected this gift in her, when he met her at her father's table in his voyage round his constituency. He found in her exactly what he wanted: good family and undeniable connexion; no fortune, which would make her dependent; much ambition, which would make her helpful; and an appearance and manner which must make his house and table infinitely attractive to the class of people he wished to attract. For his, too, was a genuine parliamentary ambition, of the kind which has furnished so many officials of a uniform and serviceable type. He had a steady plodding brain, with no heart to distract it; no domestic affections, and no taste for pleasure whatever, though he shot his covers solemnly every year in a pair of characteristic gaiters, and never enjoyed the sport so much as when the game was shy, and he could talk blue-book over his gun to some congenial spirit, invited to Luscombe Abbey for that especial purpose. He worked as hard as any clerk in his office; some sceptics indeed, conversant with the ways of those gentlemen, said a good deal harder.

Therefore Mr. Fulke Vavasour was a man who deserved to rise.

In the civil contract entered into between him, bachelor, of the one part, and Marian Teesdale, spinster, of the other part, and attested with certain mutual but unbinding affirmations in the accredited clerical formulas, there was no disguise or pretence upon either side. The lady was weary of the refined and pretentious poverty in which she had been brought up from her cradle, and the never-ending bickerings which made her home a picture of small discomfort; and was quite ready to marry Mr. Fulke Vavasour for his lands and his position, provided he fully understood that it was for them she did it. For she was straightforward enough in her way. She knew, and she let him know, that in her opinion she fetched her price, with her good looks and youth and breeding, and the wits and accomplishments which she had quietly and sedulously cultivated, to fit herself for the place she had always intended to fill. Mr. Vavasour was just what she wanted. He might have been ten years younger; anything younger than that she did not wish for, for she liked what was *posé*. But as it was it was well enough. So too his fortune might have been larger, in comparison with the growing extent of fortunes now-a-days. But it was good and solid, and would serve; and with a name and position such as his, there were ways and opportunities of increasing it by wariness and venture properly combined.

To Marian Teesdale, to do her justice, money was a means as much as an end, for she wanted to lead, and she could not do that through money alone. Before she attracted Mr. Vavasour she had steadily, and two or three times, refused a prosperous manufacturer of half his years and treble his fortune, who was a very presentable man, and very honestly in love with her. She saw at once that she could do nothing with him except possibly conquer for him the position of a *nouveau riche*, which to her meant no position at all. She had drunk in the bluest traditions of race with her mother's milk (or rather with her foster-mother's, who was a farmer's daughter,—It is odd, but so . .), and was honestly and scornfully surprised to see how " her mother did fret and her father did fume," at her determined rejection of Mr. Thomas Hodges' proposals.

Poor people ! their narrow means, and, of course, large family, had half harried them to death, though all that interest could do had been done for all the little male Teesdales. Unluckily that is not much now-a-days, in cases where idleness chooses to graft confirmed incapacity upon original want of brain. Competitive examinations were almost as great a bugbear to poor Mrs. Teesdale, and as much the object of her denunciations, as " them dratted schoolboards " are at this present time to the casual farmer's wife we meet in the railway-carriage. And indeed there had been more plucking of little Teesdales in these merciless ordeals than the Mother Goose could comfortably bear. The parents may perhaps be pardoned even by the sternest moralist, then, if it was with pronounced regret, and after considerable argument, that they let the manufacturer's fortune go. Marian had a bad time of it when he returned again and again to the charge ; but she held her own very calmly. The parents implored in the name of her brethren, who were as many as Joseph's ; and she frankly answered that, though she would do what she could for them if she could do it some day in her own way, she held their interests altogether secondary to her own, and as they didn't seem to be able to do anything for themselves, she couldn't honestly feel that she cared two straws what became of them. She retorted very justly, and therefore all the more provokingly, upon her father all the continual variations of *noblesse oblige,* with which he had played upon her from childhood ; and the hapless man felt that it was difficult to make Theory square with Practice, when the latter took such very substantial form. I think, on the whole, that it was hard upon him. However, so it was ; and matters took their own way, which, after all, thanks to the young lady's tenacity of purpose, turned out eventually much to his satisfaction. Mr. and Mrs. Teesdale, to do them justice also according to their lights, much preferred Mrs. Fulke Vavasour that was, to Mrs. Thomas Hodges that should have been, and magnanimously forgave her at the altar to which she conducted them.

The common moralizing about the bargain and sale of children in this country of ours has always struck the present chronicler, at all events, as a good deal exaggerated. The sweet young victims, in nine of these convenient marriages out of ten, sacrifice themselves with a good grace and much of their own accord. Negatively, no doubt, parents may have brought them up to the theory of the thing, and may so far be gravely responsible for the evils which follow in its train. But often and often, I believe, if the reverse of the medal could be read, which carries the pithy motto instead of the stamp, we might learn that some of these wicked parents, with their lives half lived and all laid out, with many a stray example and moral in their minds,—sometimes, perhaps, their own among the number,—are not even willing participators in some of the ceremonies of St. George's; have even warned and besought a headstrong child in vain. She knows better; life is before her, and with the watchfulness that she will exercise, and the experience by which she will profit, will yield for her fruits they were not able to gather. It is all very well for papa and mamma to deny that happiness can reside in carriages and horses, and dresses and jewels unlimited. She and her friend Clara have talked it all over and thought it all out, and for them they know that it does. So the fair Iphigenia cuts her own throat at the altar smilingly, and Father Agamemnon, so far from lending a hand to the sacrifice, turns his head away and covers his eyes, even if he does sanction the affair with his presence. Are not these things sometimes so?

Marian Gresham Teesdale on her side, and John

Audley Fulke Vavasour on his, knew very well what they were about. She assured him very honestly that in this case there was no penniless but cherished suitor in the background; but that she liked her chosen husband as well as anybody, and sympathized in his pursuits and his ambition. In a very short time the marriage bore its purposed fruit. A self-possessed and admirable hostess, whose conversation was sensible and brilliant both, and tact and courtesy unfailing, Mrs. Fulke Vavasour soon made her rooms and receptions a fact in London life; not in its social phase only, but in its political. All the leaders and supporters of their own party found Lusmere House a centre; though, by a careful exercise of that same admirable quality of tact, the hostess succeeded in the most difficult of all tasks, preventing it from becoming too exclusively a party-centre. A pleasant leaven of opposition gave lustre and interest to the whole; while to art and literature, in the persons of their more famous and favoured sons, Mrs. Fulke Vavasour held out open arms. Nor, while contriving that all this should be, did she neglect the other task she had set herself—that of improving and enlarging her husband's fortune. She made quiet and keen inquiries into the mysteries of city life; to her it was in the first place owing that her husband became, as we have described here, interested in City matters; the state of trade and of railways, under careful and secret guidance, became to her a thing of familiar knowledge; she was careful that nothing unbecoming to, or inconsistent with, Mr. Fulke Vavasour's political position should at any time or in any way be connected with his name; and the Luscombe estates grew and waxed and prospered quietly— so quietly that men hardly marked how the parties at Lusmere House, and the circle at Luscombe Abbey, increased gradually in brilliancy, and in the outward and visible signs of wealth and solidity.

Alas! to what good? Once or twice during the first few years of their union the Fulke Vavasours hoped for a child. But the hopes were disappointed, and after a time they were not renewed. Barren as it had been loveless, the marriage was denied that blessing which sometimes sows an after-seed of love; and as they grew nearer in interests, Mr. and Mrs. Vavasour grew further apart in heart. They were little together except at the hours and times of ceremony, and a separate circle of private friends grew up round each of them. Long and close were Mr. Vavasour's private interviews with his wife; but if a reporter had been present he would have found them very like a man's visits to his solicitor. Marian was her husband's first man of business, and a good one, and he knew it. In some cases, that is no bad bond of a better union, where wider sympathies agree. But here the lady was bright and intellectual, the gentleman dull and plodding; while to him she was as cold as he. Then out of the dulness and the ploddingness came a great blow to them both, which has been already told. There are times in politics which want strong men, and are apt to put averages to the right-about. Mr. Vavasour's greatest social honour was really his final failure, and they both knew it. They both knew very well why at the age of sixty-two, when many politicians have the world still in their hands, the House of Commons minister blossomed into the pensioned-off lord. His wife wanted him to refuse; but the intimation that he must not, while very courteous and considerate, was too clear to be mistaken. Mr. Fulke Vavasour was a failure on the post after all, in spite of all his wife had done and all the diplomacies she had used, and the shadows gathered darker round the loveless home.

CHAPTER XII.

LADY PEPPERHARROW'S HOUSE-WARMING.

WHEN Lady Luscombe came to London, at her husband's wish, to preside over Lady Pepperharrow's house-warming, and to play the social godmother to that excellent but inappropriate lady, it was in pursuance of the compact between herself and her husband which both thoroughly understood. Fastidious in taste and choice, the centre and the favourite of her society, and famous as the first of hostesses from one end of polite London to another, Lady Luscombe was not fond of throwing her ægis over unqualified aspirants, or sending out invitations for other people. I am not sure, indeed, that she had ever done such a thing before. But she was sore, and smarting from the recent blow. The Lady Luscombe would never, she felt, be what Mrs. Fulke Vavasour had been; and she saw the prizes she had toiled and contrived for slipping from her grasp, and the objects for which she lived failing her. She was a woman of ready resource, and was ready for a change of part at once. She knew that her political reign was over. As hostess even in the political world she might yet hold her own in a sense, no doubt; probably the chief regret felt by the heads of the ministry was, that in losing Fulke Vavasour they lost his wife. But it was her husband's position which had given her its weight, and it was gone. When she surveyed her Fulke's sleeping face, to all outward seeming unperturbed by any sense of failure or rebuff, and the open mouth, which had just swallowed a coronet, snoring contentedly on, it is certain that her ladyship felt a weariness, an indignation, and a resentment coming over her which were much at odds with her wifely duties.

Had she nursed him all those years for this? that his abominable stupidity—yes, stupidity—should, after all, have brought their joint career to wreck? It is absolutely on record, that after the catastrophe, on the night when she so gazed upon him, the high-bred Marian then and there, in the silence of the night and the recesses of the bed-curtains, sate bolt upright, and shook her sleeping lord violently. He never knew till his dying day what was the shock that woke him. It is a fact that these lofty beings have their vulgar passions like other people.

But the first purpose of the lady's life being frustrated, the second remained. Love could scarcely do more for many husbands than ambition did for Fulke Vavasour. I can never bring myself to write of the Right Honourable gentleman as Vavasour without the Fulke. For her husband the keen-witted Marian continned to scheme, almost from habit of thought, perhaps; for, with no son of his or hers succeeding, what had she really to scheme for? But she had resolved on this course at starting, and it was too late to change.

Lord Luscombe could no longer hope to be an influential minister, but he might be made a very rich man, through those City boards and City mysteries I have told of; and the City, instead of Downing Street, now became the metropolis of Lady Luscombe's land of action.

It is not necessary to tell in detail how it was that, as I have already mentioned, the fortunes of Lord Luscombe became connected with those of Sir Hugh Pepperharrow, who had just munificently presented the City with a strange and fearsome monument (which was carefully set up in the middle of a crowded thoroughfare where there was no room for two cabs to pass before), and was knighted accordingly.

Lord Luscombe and his wife quite understood each other on all matters of business; but when he learned from Pepperharrow, after much hemming and ha-ing on the part of the soap-boiler, what it was that his Martha had set her heart on, and how she desired to accomplish it, his lordship, who had dined with our old friend, was secretly doubtful how his Marian would take it. But the Pepperharrow connection was vital to him at the moment, and he propounded the sug-gestion, which, to his surprise, was received without cavil.

A few months before, and Marian would have cer-tainly declined to open her house to the Pepper-harrows, much more to adopt the lady as a social *protégée.* Lord Luscombe hinted thus much to her, and was puzzled by the tone of covert scorn with which it was answered, that their position in life was changed, and their views and objects must change too. Wealth at any cost, Lady Luscombe explained without definite words, was thenceforward the Luscombe pro-gramme. So Lady Pepperharrow's guests were bidden to the opening festivity of Glycerine House by the Baroness Luscombe of Lusmere.

Very splendid the west-end mansion looked that night. The mysterious *coup*—I write about a thing which I do not in the least understand, and never shall—had put the Pepperharrows among the financial giants, and everything was worthy of the occasion, when Lady Pepperharrow first put her foot down to trouble the Belgravian waters, and to occupy her large space in the eye of the social journals.

The staircases were bright and sweet with rich exotics which lined all the walls and filled all the recesses like silent and many-coloured chaperons, there to look after the young people with a friendly interest. The lights were softened by judicious shades, and set off the whole scene *a giorno,* as *giorno* should be, clear but not obtrusive. The rooms were furnished with genuine taste, with no pretence of show, but a full sense of richness; there were people who did say that one Daisy Fairfield, the hostess's particular favourite, had been carefully consulted and actively concerned at every stage of the furnishing, and had relentlessly vetoed several appalling combinations of greens and yellows, and a Pactolic superfluity of gilding, which had at the outset much commended themselves to Lady Pepperharrow's Oriental fancy—and the sofas and settees were an invitation to confidences and treasons.

It was strongly asserted that young Cooington, of the Home Office, never left Milly Swansdown's side the whole evening, in that tiny room which "gives" on the first staircase. There really was no more than space for one couple in it, and it was much in demand. But Cooington and that bold girl held their own in a way which—well, which was very disappointing to other young people with whom they were beforehand. And Milly's eyes always looked so round and simple and surprised, when anybody looked at her as if she had been holding the fort long enough.

The large long room, which was the principal attraction of the house, was filled and busy with the buzz of guests. At one end of it, a perfect bijou stage had been erected as a permanent fixture, under the careful superintendence of Muggins, who had superintended more amateur stages than any man alive; who talked theatre all day, and dreamed it all night, and was wont to salute his friends, at all times and places, with appropriate quotations from John Maddison Morton—a humourist, by the bye, whose whims and oddities, being confined to the little yellow books which have no connection with literature, have never been half recognized for their spirit of exuberant fun.

The Theatre Royal, Glycerine House, was constructed to serve for every sort of entertainment, from opera to recitation, from *tableau vivant* to scientific lecture, and was opened that night with a miscellaneous concert, in which the stars of the hour, as many of them as had risen in London at that early season, figured and quavered to the equally miscellaneous audience.

Lady Luscombe had done her work well, for everybody was there. Men busy with the affairs of state, whom the poor lady looked upon with a sad eye askance, as they offered their congratulations on her husband's honours with as little of an air of condolence as possible, talked aside in corners of the crisis of the · hour; and Society shook its head in the wrong place, and instinctively took the wrong side, as the spirit of the club and the drawing-room in such cases prompteth it. Noble lords mutually congratulated each other on the public spirit which had brought them to town at such a time, and wondered where Lady Luscombe had picked up her new client, and who she was, as indeed did everybody in the room except the small knot of personal friends whom Lady Pepperharrow would not forget in her invitation, even though they had all to be submitted to the approval of the higher authority.

The world of pure frivolity, the world of dancing and of flirting, were to the fore in force, looking very young and very happy, or else very aging and very bored. Every sort and all sorts, whom Society gathers under her motley wing, came out of curiosity, out of idleness, out of habit, out of love, out of the main chance, out of business, out of any of the thousand-and-one motives which carry people about, night after night, to meet each other over and over again without giving themselves the time to get anything new to say, in the inexplicable whirl which solved perpetual motion long ago, when Mrs. Noah sent out her first invitations for the ark. So good Lady Pepperharrow's rooms, large as they were, were crowded to their full capacity, and she stood gallantly perspiring at her post at the head of the great staircase all the night, till a pitying Duke—it was his Grace of Surbiton—asked her to come and have some of her own supper.

The Marquis of Norbiton had bet him that he would not do it, for the Duke was very young indeed, and had been with difficulty persuaded to leave his hunting-box and come out in the character of a legislator, even by the gravity of the situation, which he confessed he did not fully grasp. But his ancestor had come over · with William the Conqueror, and planted the first tree on Messenger's Eyot: so he rose to his duty, and gave his vote in the House of Peers, shoulder to shoulder with Norbiton.

The two young men, who said but little even between themselves upon the subject, agreed thereafter that politics were doosid slow, and abandoned a public career. Indeed, they were scandalously attacked by some low fellows in their local papers, for voting at all, which after their trouble in leaving Leicestershire was doosid ungrateful, and they felt it.

Surbiton and Norbiton were delighted with the Pepperharrow festival, and especially with the magnificent appearance of the hostess, which even Daisy's influence had not been able to keep entirely in check. Some of the patterns, denied to the curtains and chintzes, had surely blossomed out in her attire.

The two young noblemen watched her with a sort of fascination all the evening. "She'll bob herself into two, Sur, I know she will!"—until the Duke felt impelled to make the recorded bet, and conduct his hostess to supper, an attention for which the poor wearied soul, at the summit of its honest ambition, was unfeignedly grateful.

"I couldn't have done it," Norbiton said to himself gravely, shaking his head as Lady Pepperharrow's feathers fluttered through the door of the supper-room below; "but Sur always has the doose's own way with him."

Thus did these budding rulers of ours beguile the time which they were sacrificing to the labours of the Senate.

It was as one of the hostess's small knot of personal friends that I was included in the gathering I am enabled to describe; and I watched much that was going on with the supercilious envy and contempt of youth, embittered by a deep sense of social wrong and the inequalities of rank.

"Why should we, my dear Faucit,"—I began. But I am bound to say that Faucit, by this time hard at work in a pleader's chambers, and getting more law into his head in a day than most men can digest in a week, gave no encouragement whatever to my radical sentiments, passed the rights of man lightly over, told me that I should be very glad to be a lord if I could, and sought metal more attractive by a certain young lady's side.

Deserted and snubbed, I turned upon little Binks the manager, who had gotten himself an invitation through his dear friend Muggins, whom he had assisted in contriving the Glycerine stage. He was in a very bad temper, Binks, at the failure of all his plays that season, and profoundly disgusted with the British public.

"Never know where to have 'em, Balbus, never! They won't go to anything but trash, blessed if they will, unless it's Shakespeare, or something else that they go to because their fathers went. And I can't do Shakespeare, confound it! I hate blank verse, because I can't speak it, and you mustn't cut it. If you do it don't scan. As if that mattered! Don't know what to make of the public, blessed if I do!"

"Binks, my boy," I answered, "you are wandering. The abused public are Tom, Dick, and Harry; and as a rule, with but few exceptions, they go to the good things in whatever line, and they won't go to the bad ones. Being human nature in the lump, they cannot well go wrong. Therefore, Binks, when I find an actor, or an author, or a manager, abusing the British public, I say unto myself, say I, 'Here is a man that knoweth not his own business.' Be modest, Binks, and instead of abusing the British public, try and give them something worth seeing."

"Ha, ha! upon my soul! mean something of your own, Balbus, I suppose. Got something by you you think would suit me?"

"Indeed no," I said. "I don't keep things by me, or make suits of clothes on spec, on the chance of their being made to suit the wearer afterwards. You see authors have to live as well as you, without the advantage of drawing a weekly salary. No, Binks, I have nothing by me; but there are plenty of plays in your drawers which would do very well, I'll be bound!"

"Bosh, sir, bosh! all bosh from beginning to end. Englishmen can't write plays, and those who can won't unless we order 'em. Vanity of authors quite awful— quite disgusting—'pon my soul."

"Vanity, my dear Binks," I answered, "has been described as meaning a conviction that you can do things which you can't do, and are not your business. Now, when I bring a play of mine to rehearsal, the first thing you actors do is to come round me in a body, or one by one, tell me that this ought to be cut out and that altered, and at last so daze me, that if I don't stand out the play is soon no longer my own. In other words, you insist on teaching me my business instead of doing yours, which is either acting my play or letting it alone. I only ask to be allowed to know my business. I don't teach you to act, though the Lord knows some of you want it. On which side is the vanity, Binks?"

"All nonsense!" said the manager. "Of course we must know all about plays, and you can't. I've tried everything this season—all the pieces which have been the greatest goes abroad. Had one from the German, one from the French, one from the Italian, and one from the Dutch, and none of them brought a penny—not a penny, by Jove. Now I don't know what to try."

"Burn your dictionaries and try English, something which hasn't been a go abroad. Good night, Binks."

Having launched my darts and avenged myself, and being in a better humour with the nobility and gentry in consequence, I strolled about among the bright rooms, after listening for a while to the gymnastics of a popular soprano, who ran up to the chandeliers and down again in a way to defy catching. But when I caught sight of Guy Faucit and Daisy Fairfield in close talk together under the shelter of a favouring plant, which might have been transported from the tropics as it stood, after one quick glance I quietly drew away, unnoticed by them. In that one look at the man's face and at the girl's, I knew that my dear old friend had made his confession, and I knew too how it had been answered.

I never saw Daisy Fairfield look so well as she looked that night, the happiest she had ever known, as it was to be her happiest, poor girl, for many a long year. I do not even remember what dress she wore, but I know that the basis and the ground of it were white, seemingly and gracefully adorned. I remember the one purple flower which was set behind the ear, so small and so close to the head; and the wonderful gloss of which nature that evening had been more liberal even than usual to the sunny hair. In that one glimpse I caught of her face, the shy smile which played about the lips matched so perfectly with the deep seriousness in the eyes, that the two expressions made up one. And as she listened to what Faucit was telling her half under his breath, but in that firm full voice of his, or as she let a few words fall from her in answer, she opened and shut her fan mechanically with her right hand, as the elbow rested upon the arm of the couch on which they were seated side by side. I can recall the quaint watteau patterns upon that fan, a present of Lady Pepperharrow's, and the laces which fringed it, now. Asmodeus the chronicler claims his privilege. What was it that the two said?

" Yes, Miss Fairfield, I love you very earnestly. I have done so since the first day I saw you by the river, I think. Haven't you guessed it?"

" I hardly know, Mr. Faucit, indeed."

" But you knew that I didn't intend to speak. I wanted to have something to offer you better than a law-student's belief in himself before I told you what I have told you now. It isn't much, is it?"

" With you I think that it is," she said, very simply and frankly; and Guy's overfull heart gave a great bound as she said it. " It isn't as if you had not shown what you can do, at Oxford."

There was a pretty pride both in the girl's look and tone.

"Supposing that to be so, the race is not always to the strong."

"To the strong and patient," she answered, "I for one believe that it is."

"But I haven't been patient after all. If you knew how resolved I was not to speak, till I had at least been called to the bar!"

"And what was I to do all that time?" asked Daisy, with a smile which made poor Guy's heart beat faster and faster. Her frankness was so perfect and so winning, so free from any taint of forwardness, so full of utter trust. It never seemed to enter Daisy's head, from the moment when Faucit opened all his heart to her, that she was to play at hiding any of hers from him.

"I suppose you were to wait," he said, with a happy and half-embarrassed little laugh; "and understand all about it all the time. That was to be your part in the comedy."

"Perhaps I should have grown a little tired of it," she said. "But I would have waited!" she added suddenly, then blushed fairly at herself.

"And will wait now?" he asked.

"Yes," she said simply; "if you wish it."

"I must wish it. For I have nothing in the world till I can make it."

"But I have."

"I know; and that's just what I'm afraid of. People would say I asked you for that."

"Do you care much for what people say?" she answered him. "I shouldn't."

"No; but your father might say so. You wouldn't."

"I!" And there was a touch almost of reproach in her tone.

"I was stupid even to say it."

"Well, you were—rather." This with a smile. "But papa is not nearly so hard as you think him. He'll do anything for me; and he will know that you mean to work and to get on. What better use can a girl find for money, than to help a man who means to do that, at starting ?"

"You are not a girl," said Guy; "you are a very noble woman."

"Am I?" she answered. "I feel very like a girl to-night. You have made me forget my trouble at home."

"That was what made me speak, you know. I thought you seemed annoyed and anxious about this stranger—this Mr. Brent, you spoke of; and I couldn't help telling you that there was some one who—some one that—"

The athlete broke down in the sentence; but it served.

"And, Mr. Faucit, you were right; and you will be a real help to me. When papa brought this Mr. Brent to dinner and introduced him to me last night, I thought there was something odd in his manner which I couldn't understand. And the man himself was familiar—rudely so even. I haven't been able to shake off an uncomfortable feeling all day, and came here as if something was going to happen."

"Something has—hasn't it?" asked Guy.

"Yes. But not quite like that."

"What is this Mr. Brent?"

"I don't know. 'Something in the city,' which sounds like anything in the world, from a diamond-merchant to a crossing-sweeper. I don't want to think of Mr. Brent again."

"And I don't want you to think of him. You have told me that I may go and speak to your father to-morrow, and tell him everything?"

"Yes, Mr. Faucit."

"One thing more."

"What's that?"

"You haven't answered my question yet."

"What was it?"

"Whether you love me or not?"

"Haven't I?"

"Not in words. Won't you? Do you?"

"Yes; indeed I do."

"Ah! And when will you begin to call me Guy?"

A big pause. Then she said, "Now, Guy."

*　　　*　　　*　　　*　　　*

"What a lovely-looking girl!" said to Lady Luscombe, a little later, as Daisy was walking through the rooms, a dark and singular-looking man with a pale oval face, and jet black hair parted in the middle, who seemed some six-and-thirty years old, if any clear guess at his age could be made. He had nothing distinctive in his dress, which was very simple; but everybody who looked at him looked at him again, and it was to be noted that all who spoke to him spoke to him with marked deference. Lady Luscombe was leaning on his arm, and he was twisting a hoop-ring round the fourth finger of his right hand.

Lady Luscombe looked carelessly up, as she had been absorbed in some close conversation with this man which the remark interrupted. Her eye was caught too, at once, not more by the beauty of the girl, than by the air of refinement which was especially Daisy's own.

"She is indeed," she said. "I wonder who she is. As I don't know her myself, and never saw her before, I must ask Lady Pepperharrow."

"The young lady doesn't look much like a friend of our gentle hostess," said the other, with a sneer in the words which his tone hardly marked. "But whoever she is we must know more of her. She must be an ornament in your rooms this season; it is always an advantage to introduce a sensation. A fine-looking fellow with her, too; a Briton of the true broad-shouldered Viking type. She is too good for him, and he can be dispensed with."

"He is very much absorbed by his pretty companion," Lady Luscombe said.

"Clearly. Calf-love to be killed young. There's

Pentonville. He'll find out all about the girl's parentage, prospects, and general health in five minutes.
Pentonville ! "

A tightly-booted and short-sighted little gentleman
hopped across the room.   " W—w—w—"
    " Well ? "
    " No—what !   W—what is it, Lestrange ? "

CHAPTER XIII.

MR. JOHN BRENT.

MR. FAIRFIELD was in his study, closeted with a
friend. The friend was not a person who excited feelings of sympathy at the outset. He was little and
dried-up, like a medlar; and looked as if the drying
process had taken place as much inside as out. His
face wore the livery of the burnished sun in the
especial form it assumes in complexions which have
been tanned and dried in India, from an improper
understanding of the conditions of Indian life. Mr.
John Brent looked as if he should sit for a picture of
liver. He had a little iron-grey head of hair, which he
brushed back as far as he could, so that with the help
of the baldness at the parting the revealed expanse
might pass for a high forehead. The real forehead,
which is bounded in anatomy by the frontal bone, was
so low that there was nothing of it, the bone of
boundary being nearly in his eyes, which were pink and
ferrety, and winked like sickly stars. Little iron-grey
whiskers, ending half way down his face, and looking as
if they were gummed on, they stuck so close, completed
the physiognomy of the man very consistently. His
voice was shrill and weak, and worked on one note or
in an exasperating manner. Neither his tones nor Mr.
Fairfield's grating voice were agreeable to listen to;

more especially as on the occasion which, had now brought them together, there was considerable excitement on both sides.

Mr. Brent had been the Calcutta correspondent of the firm of Fairfield and Co.; and it was with Calcutta that the younger partner in the house had been coquetting, with the disastrous results which our story has already foreshadowed.

When Mr. Brent, himself a man of realized fortune, came home from Calcutta to settle down in nabobhood, he brought with him the sentence of death of the firm of Fairfield and Co. if he chose to pass it. The whispers on 'Change which heralded his coming were as correct as they were ominous, and Mr. Brent was not a man to let any foolish feeling of sympathy stand in his way, or prevent his claiming his pound of flesh to the full.

It is not necessary to tell, nor could I exactly do it, the process of events by which Mr. Brent had become the arbiter of the fate of the house of Fairfield; but financial operations on a large scale are apt to lead into no-thoroughfares of the kind, and I am grateful to the Providence which has ordered my lot in other pastures, and saves me from great fears, if from lofty hopes, for the fate of the salt-cellar on my modest table.

Mr. Brent had had his wings somewhat singed by the operations of his correspondents in London, though those financial pinions of his, on which he sailed home, were very broad indeed. He resented the injury, and armed with divers acceptances and other documents of a pernicious nature, he came to London breathing flames and fury against Fairfield and Co.

The early history of John Brent had absolutely nothing in it to interest anybody. He was one of those gentlemen who make themselves; and in his case nobody could grudge him the exclusive credit of the manufacture. It may safely be predicated of him that he landed in India with the traditional half-crown in his pocket, as Benjamin Franklin came to Philadelphia.

"After all, when you come to think of it there's
nothing in it. Anybody could have done it," says Mark
Twain, in the funniest essay he ever wrote. These sort
of people, not that I would compare Benjamin Franklin
with John Brent, always do begin life with half-a-crown.
Where do they get it from? and why is it always half-
a-crown? The unvarying character of the sum makes
one suspicious of these self-making gentlemen.

Alexander Dumas, — *the* Dumas, — the dear old
Dumas of 'Monte Cristo,' and 'D'Artagnan,' and the
'Tour de Nesle,'—not he of the morbid Aspasiac school,
whom the soul of Binks loveth and worshippeth as a
great creator, which indeed he is so far, in that, while
another made the world, he made the half-world,—
Dumas the first confessed to an original capital of two
louis. "My son," he said, nearly at the end of his days,
when he was being reproached with his still incurable
prodigalities, the big-natured, generous old giant, " My
son, there is no charge I deserve less. Sixty years ago
I came to Paris with two louis in my pocket, and
look," he added, turning it out, "I've got one left
still!"

John Brent was not a prodigal, being indeed one of
the meanest persons to be found on a summer's day,
and his half-crown had made a very large number more
when he came to England to enjoy the fruits of his
toils and scrapings. "This was a way to thrive, and he
was blessed," after the measure of his desires. What
sort of enjoyment he would manage to extract from his
riches might have been a problem to any one who
examined him in Mr. Fairfield's study.

Now it came to pass that Mr. Brent had no wife;
and that one of the first things he proposed to do in
England was to buy one. He was sixty, no doubt, well
rung; but he had been what the world agrees to call a
man of no vices, and he flattered himself that his health
and constitution must therefore be those of a young
man, of necessity. He was as angry with his liver as
Mr. Fairfield was with his throat, and would not admit

that it could be out of order, or that excessive desk-work and inordinate cheese-paring, coupled with a masterly neglect of all the humanities and liberalities of life, could produce anything of the ill effects which properly follow upon vicious careers. Virtue and self-denial, he felt or asserted, had been his rules of conduct. He had neither chick nor child, and if he had any relations in England, he did not intend to find them out or to acknowledge them. His memories of them were of the vaguest, dating back to the half-crown days, when, as likely as not, some tipsy or improvident father had turned him out of the house to shift for himself. It may well be that it was not so; that the *res angusta domi* had been no fault of any one's, and that the parting had been one of bitter tears, and much heart-breaking on some poor struggling mother's part. Perhaps on the boy's too, for if there be some people who seem to be born bad, and some who have badness thrust upon them, assuredly there are very many men who achieve badness for themselves, by a course of deliberate egotism, beginning perhaps in no source that can fairly be called evil. Such men are, indeed, self-made. If there was any such love and tenderness in the far background, there was no trace or shadow of it upon John Brent's spirit now, and he started on his proposed St. Martin's summer with a clear tablet. Whether he had married before, in his youth, I do not know. If he had, history has no record of the first Mrs. Brent, who certainly left no child, and probably died of a broken heart, or of the want of sufficiently generous living. It didn't matter to Mr. Brent, and it doesn't matter to our story.

When Mr. Brent had been but a few days in London, and had brought the head of the house of Fairfield to the verge of distraction, he called one day in Portland Place, and he caught sight of Daisy. The little Indian was overcome by the gracious vision, and saw his opportunity at once. It was in his power, by no great pecuniary sacrifice on his part, to tide over the difficulties which beset the London house, to save the credit of Fairfield's, and to start the firm fairly on its way again. For this Mr. Fairfield had recourse to entreaty, and brought all the influence he could to bear, without being driven to expose the true condition of affairs to the world, in order to work upon the feelings of the arbiter of his destiny. But the arbiter had no feelings to work upon, and frankly said that it was a mere matter of business. He bore no ill-will to Fairfield's whatever, but there was no reason in this case for suspending the ordinary course of events, and he did not see that any consideration was or could be offered which would or could make it worth his while to be merciful. On what compulsion must he ? tell him that. Everything to this sun-dried anatomy was mere bargain and sale, for he was so effectually tanned as to keep out feeling or sympathy as long as the tanner of Hamlet's grave-digger could keep out the water.

Mr. Fairfield saw nothing before him but ruin. He had not even provided the refuge from the storm secured by a large settlement on his wife, which in such cases has often enabled the bankrupt merchant, while hundreds of people who unfortunately trusted him are left penniless and destitute, to retire into obscure misery on five or ten thousand a year. Perhaps Mr. Fairfield's reliance on his house's credit had been too high ; perhaps he had a conscience of his own in spite of all his failings. In any case so it was. Keeping his counsel as best he could at home, but causing real and increasing uneasiness to his wife and daughter, he saw something very like want stare him and his family in the face, when Mr. John Brent cast eyes of favour upon Daisy. *Vera incessu patuit Dea*, to him as to mortals of higher and finer grain, this stately and attractive young lady. Mr. Brent did not deceive himself in relation to the purchase which he desired to make, and quite understood that even with his money he might find a deficiency in the market of the precise article he wanted. Therefore he regarded the appearance of

Daisy upon the scene as absolutely providential. I
have not alluded to a fashion of Mr. Brent's, which gave
especial offence to many of those who had dealings with
him, of constantly referring to Providence the issue of
his keenest bargains. In fact, I don't like to talk or
think about it, for to me I know of nothing more
terrible than this particular form of hypocrisy. It gives
me a feeling of nervous dread for those who indulge in
it. Mr. Brent's moral lectures to Mr. Fairfield, on the
ordained and divine consequences of commercial remiss-
ness, had exasperated that combative old man more
than anything else. But indeed it was curious to see
how subdued his arrogance was in Brent's presence, and
how supplicatory his tone became.

The returned Indian saw at once that in Daisy
Fairfield, if only she should prove a dutiful and amen-
able daughter, he had found exactly what would suit
him best, and fulfil his domestic ambition. Here was
a woman to make his table attractive, to amuse his
declining years when they should begin to decline,
which, in his opinion, must be a long way off yet, and
till then to shed fresh blossoms upon what he secretly
believed to be still the fervour of his youth. He saw
at a glance, in which he was not peculiar, though his
own penetration pleased him very much, that in externals his victim's daughter was all that heart could wish.
Mr. Vavasour did not know better what he was about
or decide more methodically, when he paid Marian
Teesdale the compliment of selection. Internals did
not matter; for Daisy was evidently young enough to
be moulded by a husband of his tact and experience.
John Brent had, he thought, a very successful way with
women.

And so, on the morning of the day of Lady
Pepperharrow's gathering, the day immediately preceding that which finds him in the study in Portland
place, the Indian millionnaire without much prelude
propounded his scheme to the English defaulter, as he
took very good care to let Fairfield know, in plain

K

terms, that he was. He had not been informed of the domestic history of his correspondent, and till he accidentally saw her, he knew nothing of the "one fair daughter, and no more," whom, like Jephthah, judge of Israel, and the excellent Polonius, the poor father from his heart, and in his way, really loved passing well.

Matters were at a crisis, and Fairfield was resigning himself to his fate. The junior partner, who was young and go-ahead, and had feathered his private nest on the chance of cold weather, about which he said nothing, shrugged his shoulders and preached some philosophy to his elder in a curiously provoking way. He was really shocked to find how culpably careless Fairfield had been in not providing for his wife and family, as every good citizen was bound to do in such uncertain times, in the precarious state of business. Poor Fairfield, driven to bay, indignantly declared that there never had been anything precarious in his business at all, never need have been, and never would have been, but for the rashness and experiments of the junior partner, who expressed pity.

"My dear sir! As if it is possible for any intelligent man not to move with the times! What you call rashness and experiments are courage and prudence at once, in the altered conditions of city-life. Why, my dear sir, America would annihilate us, literally annihilate us, if we did not keep pace with her as far as we can in the race of commercial enterprise. She has great advantages against which we must in any case find it hard to hold our own; but you would handicap us so completely that all English trade would go to the wall. Your theories, my dear sir, are impossible, exploded, out of date. It is true that we have been unfortunate; but though I would not say anything to add to your distress of mind at such a time,—my own is deep, my dear Mr. Fairfield, very deep,—I must in justice to myself, say, that our misfortunes are chiefly to be attributed to your most ill-timed conservatism, and the manner in which you have thwarted—yes, my dear sir, I must say thwarted—all my schemes for the welfare of the house."

Mr. Brent, who had never in his life risked a rash experiment of any kind, entirely endorsed the junior partner's views, and between them they almost persuaded the unhappy man to regard himself as the prime mover of his own disestablishment. To do him justice, he thought more of his wife and daughter than he did of himself in the ruin which was coming upon them all. The junior partner put on his shining hat, and gloves of faultless kid, and with a clear conscience betook himself to his club for a basin of soup, and some particular Amontillado, whereon to meditate on the fresh start that he should be able to make when unencumbered with the old-fashioned concern which, after all, he was well quit of, as soon as the nine days' wonder should be over.

Honest Threadneedle, the clerk, went to his chophouse hopeless and crest-fallen, with something very like tears in his eyes, and denied himself his usual beer. Mr. Brent was left alone with Fairfield, and came straight to the point.

"You have been constantly asking me, Fairfield, if there was no consideration on which I would consent not to press my claims against your house."

"Yes, I have. There is nothing in the world I wouldn't do, if you will but give me the time to tide over the difficulty," answered the other.

"Tiding over difficulties like yours is all nonsense and sheer self-delusion," said Brent, sharply. "You've got into a bad way, and you'll only flounder into worse."

"Still you might show me some consideration, after all our dealings together."

"In the name of common sense, why?"

"We have done a great deal to build up your business and your fortune, Brent, and that you know," growled Fairfield, though the growl was in a key sufficiently subdued.

"And what of that?" snapped Brent. "It was all in the way of business, wasn't it? You didn't build up

K 2

my fortune, as you call it, out of charity and consideration for me, did you ?"

" No," acquiesced the other, shortly.

"No; of course not. You did it for business, pure
business; and if you had taken the advice of your
highly intelligent and most honourable junior partner,
you wouldn't have· been in your present position, nor
have placed me in mine. However, I shan't waste any
more words on recrimination or on sentiment. Sentiment in trade is silly. Let us come to the point. I
h ve found the consideration you have been looking.
for."

"What do you mean ?" asked Fairfield, eagerly.

"I mean that I have found the consideration on
which I will not only defer, but forego, all my claims
against you ; and not only that, but do all I can to put
your house safely on its legs again."

"Brent !" gasped Fairfield, getting up from his chair.

A good many men would have hesitated and stammered considerably before making the suggestion the
other had to make. Not so Mr. Brent, whose comfortable confidence in himself was equal to all emergencies.
He neither stammered nor hesitated at all.

"I think I have told you, Fairfield, or perhaps I
haven't, that now that I want to settle in England I
want to find a wife."

"A wife !" said the other, in a tone which would
have conveyed to anybody else the conviction, that to
Mr. Fairfield the idea was entirely' new.

"Yes, a wife, and a young wife. I can make her a
fine settlement, and she will be very happy. I want to
marry your daughter."

Never till that moment had Mr. Fairfield been in
such immediate danger of apoplexy. He grew blue
through his natural red, stammered and wondered
enough for both, and like Aulus the dictator, scarce
gathered voice to speak, or indeed to think.

"My daughter—Daisy—marry—you ? You haven't
even seen her."

"Yes, I have. I saw her yesterday. I can put half my fortune into your business, and set it on a sounder basis than ever."

The conversation which followed would not, perhaps, be very nice to record. But one or two things which Fairfield said made the other man's eyes glisten in an unpleasant, snake-like fashion, and he showed his teeth in a way to prove to Fairfield that not till that moment had he fully realized how much he was in John Brent's power. John Brent dined that night in Portland Place, with the result on Daisy's mind in the last chapter recorded.

It was on the next day, on the morning after Lady Pepperharrow's *début* in the world of fashion, that the two men were again together in Mr. Fairfield's room. They had a long talk together, and Mr. Brent took up his hat and went away with a comfortable sense of satisfaction. Mr. Fairfield sate in his arm-chair by himself, and had some brandy-and-water. Then a servant knocked and disturbed his meditations, and told him that a gentleman was upstairs in the drawing-room 'with Mrs. Fairfield, and had asked to see him. The name on his card was Mr. Guy Faucit.

"A friend of my wife and daughter, the young fellow who has dined here three or four times," muttered Fairfield to himself. "What does he want to see me for?"

He was not sorry to change the current of his thoughts, and when he had finished his brandy-and-water he went upstairs.

CHAPTER XIV.

THE COUP DE GRÂCE.

MRS. FAIRFIELD was sitting on a low chair before the fire, looking very small and frightened. Guy Faucit was standing on the hearthrug near her, frank and much in earnest; and it was clear that the conversation which had been passing between them must have interested them both in a high degree. Mrs. Fairfield fidgetted in her chair when her husband came in, and looked at him appealingly, rather like a dog who is doubtful whether he has or has not been guilty of some breach of the law, and tries to discover from his master's eyes whether he is going to be beaten or not. Faucit met him in a comfortable, straightforward way, with no consciousness in his manner that there was anything unusual to be said, and the two men shook hands.

"I asked to see you, Mr. Fairfield," said Guy, "because I have something especial to say which I wish to say to you myself."

"What is it, Mr. Faucit?" asked the other, who knew his visitor as a man who had dined at his house and made himself pleasant, but had paid him no special attention. There was not much in common between them to make it otherwise. It is possible that Mr. Fairfield was not fully aware of all the five o'clock teas and other meetings which had taken place, though there had been no conscious concealment in the matter. "Can I be of any service to you?" The merchant's manner was nervous and pre-occupied, and he did not sit down, but walked about the room.

His wife watched him uneasily, and then made an appeal to Guy.

"I think, Mr. Faucit, you had better go now. We can talk about this afterwards."

"No, Mrs. Fairfield," he answered, "I have nothing

to hide. I came to ask you, sir, if I may marry your daughter ? "

The declaration was point-blank enough, certainly; and I think that, under the circumstances, Mr. Fairfield was a good deal to be pitied. He had been thinking about his daughter, of course, since Brent had propounded his scheme, and about nothing else. Even in that short 'time he had begun to reconcile himself to the notion of the marriage as far as he was concerned. John Brent had given him a full account of himself, and he was richer even than Fairfield had imagined. A more distinguished son-in-law would have been, more agreeable to his taste, no doubt; but the fortune and the security were the chief thing, after all. And the anxiety of the last months had so shaken and worn the merchant under that hard outside of his, that there was hardly any price he was not ready to pay to feel secure again. Fairfield and Co. safe and sound once more, and starting afresh under better auspices than ever; the reign of reason resumed, for Fairfield knew his man, and the odious junior partner suppressed and outvoted :—all this made up a prospect which effectually dazzled Daisy's father, and blinded him, in the attractions of its horizon, to the unsightly character of the foreground. It must be remembered, besides, that Fairfield was not recognized as an agreeable person himself, and did not resent the odious characteristics of Mr. Brent as a man of a higher nature would have done. He hated the man certainly, because he was in his power. But if he got out of it he didn't see why they shouldn't pull well enough together.

Yes; but Daisy? Mr. Fairfield was an autocrat at home, and his daughter had never failed for a moment in duty and obedience. But all the softness in his nature had been for her, and he would have spoiled her, probably, if she had been to be spoiled. He was an affectionate father to her, and in spite of domestic rubs, and his constant impatience with his wife, there had been always something between them which was even like sympathy, different as their ways and natures were. With her keen sense of fun, Daisy could not help feeling how intensely irritating her poor mother's placid submission, or tactless little provocations, must be to the old gentleman at times; and her care in smoothing difficulties and averting collisions was exercised as much for the sake of one as of the other. At the bottom of Daisy's character, however, lay a firmness which the father strongly suspected, though so far it had shown itself only in everyday directions. He had more than once been on the verge of confiding his whole trouble to her, and deserved genuine credit for denying himself the confession, from real unwillingness to cloud her opening life. What shape might that firmness take in the face of such a proposal as John Brent's? Daisy would not disobey her father by taking any step he disapproved, that he knew; but whether she would obey him to the extent of doing what she rebelled against herself, was another question. Therefore he was meditating the time and way in which he was to make the full state of the case known, of which Brent consented to let him be the judge, and he had nearly concluded that the sooner it was done the better. Brent suggested frequent visits to the house, and many opportunities of wooing; but Fairfield shrewdly suspected that the opportunities might not turn as much to the wooer's advantage as that gentleman flattered himself. It would be a plunge when it came, and it might be better to take it before the waters had been sounded too closely for reefs.

Meanwhile, it had been with much satisfaction to both that Fairfield had been able to assure Brent of the important fact that there was nobody else in the way. To that effect had been almost the last words which had passed downstairs; and then, suddenly, and with the inconvenient promptness of a stage-apparition, started up before the merchant's eyes in his own drawing-room, one of the finest-looking young men he ever saw in his life, who, with no prospects or position that he had heard of, yet as coolly as if he were a prince of the blood royal asking for a glass of wine, demanded his daughter without prelude or warning, and obviously, as the father felt in a moment, with the daughter's own leave. The daughter was suddenly assuming an importance in the world quite out of proportion to the due order of things. Wasn't he to be considered in the matter at all? he began to think, in the general confusion of faculties which was taking possession of him. And the effect of Guy Faucit's bomb-shell, suddenly discharged into this disorganized camp, was to throw Septimus Fairfield of Portland Place and Mincing Lane, merchant, after his first struggle with perplexity, into a most tremendous rage.

Guy Faucit has been kept, by this disquisition, a long time waiting for his answer, which, when it came, was strangled at its birth in a neckcloth, and was simply this—"Good heavens!" Mr. Fairfield's veins swelled before Faucit's eyes, and his complexion became Homeric in its purple.

"You have taken me by surprise, sir! you have taken me by surprise! I really don't know how to answer such an extraordinary thing. I really—God bless my life and soul!"

Mrs. Fairfield detected the signs of gathering wrath, and interposed in a nervous tremor, "Septimus dear, Mr Faucit doesn't mean any harm."

"Good gracious, Jane, don't talk in that way. Mean any harm! God bless me! God bless me! Do you know what you are asking, sir?" in a tone of positive bewilderment.

"Yes, Mr. Fairfield. I am asking for your daughter to become my wife some day. I am asking with her own permission."

"You are? And you have absolutely, sir, absolutely accepted my hospitality to abuse it in this manner, and taken advantage of a girl's passing fancy to attempt

to secure her affections without her parents' knowledge ?
I never heard of such a thing."

Faucit's face was flushing slowly, and his manner
very grave. He was on the point of appealing to Mrs.
Fairfield whether she had not been well aware of what
had been passing under her eyes, when he read in her
face such an unspoken appeal on her side, that with
instinctive generosity he let that defence go. He had
been enough in the house to guess that Mrs. Fairfield's
lines were not cast in the smoothest of places, besides
gathering much from Daisy. But he answered Fairfield
steadily.

"I have never done anything underhand in my life,"
he said, "and should not have begun with your daughter.
I have never disguised my wishes from the moment I
formed them, and I have not lost an hour in speaking
to you since having Miss Fairfield's answer."

"You should have spoken to me first, sir!" said the
other, growing more and more angry with Faucit's calm
superiority of tone. He felt already that he was not
coming out of it well.

"I cannot agree with you, Mr. Fairfield. A man
has no right to presume so far on a woman's consent
as to speak before he gets it. He can hardly pay her
a worse compliment than that."

"I shall not be lectured about the claims of a parent,
sir!" stormed Mr. Fairfield, who, in the perplexity of his
position, was forgetting himself very fast indeed.

"Septimus, dear Septimus!" murmured his weaker
half.

"Upon my soul, ma'am, I believe that you must
have known of this business and never told me! this
most discreditable business! To trade on the passing
fancy of a young girl——"

"Mr. Fairfield, I cannot let you speak like that,
even though you are her father. I don't believe Miss
Fairfield's feeling for me to be a passing fancy; but
that you can find out from herself. I have the right to
know the strength of my own feeling, and to ask

you if you will one day allow your daughter to be my wife."

Guy's manner was so studiously respectful that it was difficult to quarrel with it; but the weakness of Mr. Fairfield's cause made him quarrelsome. He disliked the vision of Brent in the background very much indeed, and felt that the Indian's chances would be materially lessened by the appearance of so singularly personable a rival. He still kept up his favourite tone of bluster, though he perceived even in his wrath that bullying was thrown away on his troublesome visitor.

"What prospects have you, sir, may I ask?" he said. "I have heard that you are only reading for the bar."

"That is the case, Mr. Fairfield," answered Guy. "I can pretend to no position and no immediate prospects; but—"

"I knew it, sir, I knew it, and could have sworn as much!" The merchant was inwardly delighted with his chance, for if Faucit had had definite prospects to offer, his position would have been more awkward. "Yet you presume to come forward and ask me to give you my daughter, who has been accustomed all her life to a position which I do not intend her to lose; on the strength, I suppose, of all that you mean to do when you are called to the bar! No, sir; I assure you that I do not intend her to lose it, or to share a crust with anybody! I shall wish you good afternoon, and beg that I may never hear of this again."

"Mr. Fairfield," said Guy quietly, but in a way which enforced a hearing even from the man he was speaking to, "I hope that you will regret this some day. Nothing will tempt me to show any disrespect to Daisy's father, or to use hard words with him. You give me very hard ones, and, as I think, without reason. I have a very honest love to offer, and I gave up a good and secure position at Oxford that I might be able to offer it. I don't think you should have spoken to me as you have. My Oxford work gives me the right to look for a fair measure of success at the bar, and I have already a good connection in the writing-way."

Mr. Fairfield grunted at the display of this last card of poor Guy's, which he might as well not have played. "The writing-way," in the eyes of Mr. Fairfield, was a rather disreputable road to starvation.

"I never supposed," Faucit went on to say, "that you would sanction any immediate marriage with your daughter."

"Immediate indeed!" said the other. "What on? On my money, do you suppose?"

"I suppose there would be nothing unreasonable in thinking you would help your daughter," answered Guy. "She thought so. But I should myself prefer to wait till I had made a good start for myself."

"And keep a young girl dancing attendance upon hopes for the best years of her life, I suppose. Fairness to her, if you meant that, should have prevented you speaking."

"I don't think so myself," said the other. "It is far fairer to speak than to leave any one in doubt of a serious feeling. But I see that I have made a mistake in speaking to you, and for the present I shall not say any more. Good-bye."

"Stop one moment," said Fairfield. "Am I to understand that you give up this foolish nonsense altogether?"

"I shall never give it up," answered Faucit.

"And you tell me that to my face?" shouted the other, whose temper, in spite of himself, had been quieted by Faucit's tone, but now boiled over again. "I tell you, sir, that I forbid you now or at any time to think of my daughter. And mind, let me hear nothing of any more meetings of any kind! Before you go, give me your word that you will not attempt to see the young lady again."

"I don't think that you have the right to ask me for any promise of the kind," said Guy. "Neither Miss

Fairfield nor I, you may be sure, are likely to do anything to be ashamed of."

"Oh, Mr. Faucit, I'm sure you won't, either of you," interrupted the unlucky third at this disagreeable scene. "Please go now, and don't come again at present. I am sure Mr. Fairfield doesn't mean anything unkind, do you?" But her lord and master was only fuming.

"Good-bye, Mrs. Fairfield, and thank you for all your kindness," said Guy, pressing the good-natured hand. "I can't say good-bye to Daisy before I go, can I?" he added to her hurriedly.

"She is out for the day, indeed she is," answered the mother. "But you are sure to hear from her or me."

"Of course," said Guy. And with another grave salutation to the excited man of business, he was gone. Even while he was still on the stairs, he heard the storm bursting upon the head of the devoted Jane.

Guy Faucit went quietly home to his chambers, revolving. This was a check at starting which he had not been prepared for, though he told himself rather angrily that he ought to have been. He had taken Mr. Fairfield too much on trust from Daisy, instead of believing in his own conclusions about her father's purse-pride and want of refinement of mind. There was a little injustice in this, as we know; and if the merchant had not been fairly driven to the wall by the situation, of which Guy and Daisy were equally ignorant, it is probable that his daughter would have had no very great difficulty in bringing him round. She had made Guy feel so convinced that this was the case, that he was fairly astounded at the ferocity of his reception, though he had not of course supposed that Mr. Fairfield would jump at his offer. He felt rather annoyed with Daisy, therefore, as well as with himself, for he could not disguise from himself that the merchant's objections were of a nature altogether too strong to be conciliated as they had hoped. Well, it could not be helped: the course of true love was going to run roughly, as usual, and the flinty hearts of fathers to inflict the usual bruises on the supplicating hands knocking at the door of them.

Another man than Faucit would have been more down-hearted than he. He could not, in spite of his annoyance, as yet regard the situation very seriously. He felt as sure of Daisy as of himself, and smiled as he thought of the father scheming for ambitious marriages, or trying to argue her out of her love. Probably he should not see her for a few days, and their meetings might even be suspended for a longer time than that. But the separation was one which they could both accept, and was too unreasonable to last.

Guy knew that he should hear from Daisy the next day, and her letter would tell him the line he must take, which it rested with her to decide. He thought that he knew what the letter would be, and could indulge his fancy in watching her think it out and write it, with its calm assurance of the future and counsel of short patience, and regret that for the moment she had misled him.

With these thoughts in his mind he smoked his pipe placidly enough in his fireside corner, rather amusing himself mentally at the remembrance of Mr. Fairfield's angry airs of Bashawship, but withal a little puzzled by their vehemence, suggestive of something in the air which he couldn't quite understand. Then he migrated to his writing-table, and added a postscript to the letter which he had written to the old mother down in Devonshire, in the first flush of his happiness and pride, making her, as he had done throughout, the confidant of all his proceedings, all his hot and cold fits, wherein the cold had played but a brief and bracing part, and anticipating the day when "the two sweetest women in the world" should come to know each other.

Daisy had sent through him, in that first part of the letter, a sweet and tremulous message of her own.

"Dearest Mother," added the postscript, "I shall let this letter go, as it will tell all the story. But we have counted without our host, if I may describe by that name a gentleman who has incontinently kicked me out of his house, abused me for presumption and fortune-hunting and other pleasant things, and generally behaved like the Emperor of China with a fit of the gout. Indeed, I think Fairfield Papa rather resents the indignity of *not* being Emperor of China. My Daisy made rather a mistake in sending me to him; but it will all come right, and I am not much disturbed. When I can write of her as 'my Daisy'—doesn't it look nice on paper? but if you could only hear how it sounds!—nothing matters very particularly. We shall bring Timour round between us, Daisy doing the best part of it. I am sure to hear from her to-morrow, and I think I know what the letter will be. God bless you, little mother. This bonnie conquest of my bow and spear will draw you and me together closer than ever.

"Your own son,
"G. F."

Guy worked well on to his usual hour that night, and slept the sleep of the just without dreaming of Daisy, though he wanted and expected to dream of her. He told me long afterwards that he kept on dreaming of me all the night in a perverse sort of way, and resented it in his sleep as a personal injury, wanting some one else, and not knowing why.

When the laundress had done the fire and cooked the chop, and Faucit came out of his bedroom to his bachelor-breakfast, the post brought the expected letter, and his heart jumped at the sight of the well-known hand. It was a good hand, free and firm, but womanly, and he treasured many scraps of it in small notes of invitation or thanks. It must be admitted that, in the presence of his unseen Asmodeus, Guy kissed the new-comer two or three times before he opened it. But when he did open it, what he read was this:

"I am too deeply sad and sore to know well how to write to you. But you must forget last night, Mr.

Faucit, or that I was ever able to call you anything else. I will not say that we shall never meet again, because I hope that one day we shall; but it cannot be for a long time, and never in the way you wish. I cannot help hoping that this will not prevent your persevering at the bar, for you were born for a great success. But whether you do this, or whether you return to Oxford, my best wishes, and my prayers too, will. always be with you. My father owes you an apology for the manner in which he received you yesterday, and so do I for having exposed you to it. Will you let me make them both, for him and me? I am afraid you will be very grieved and very angry, but if you knew everything you would not blame us so much. I could not let the post go without writing, as I knew you must expect it; but perhaps if I had had more time, I might have written in some other and better way. But when good-bye must be said, perhaps it doesn't much matter how we say it. Good-bye.

"Always your friend,

"DAISY FAIRFIELD."

Guy Faucit read the letter through and through, and again through, without being able to grasp and comprehend it. A dismissal!—like that—and from her! whom he had believed in as in Truth. When he could bring himself to grapple with it fairly, he read in the letter a clear and final decision. If he had laughed at Mr. Fairfield's pronouncement of his sentence, he knew now that the Court of Appeal had positively confirmed it, and without reason given.

Daisy Fairfield was right when she wrote, that Guy would be grieved and angry. But she did not quite know how sternly so. He was simply stunned. With his strong instinctive sense of right and honour, Guy felt, as soon as he could feel, that if there were reasons in the case, as the letter hinted, apart from that of his position and hers, which the father had so rudely given, those reasons should have been told. I do not think that he made enough allowance there, in his fulness of manhood, for the gentler and more shrinking fibre of which the noblest womanhood is made. But the result of his view was, that he disbelieved in any such reason at once, and, in the first flush of indignation, at all events, accepted the whole thing as over. It was enough for Guy to make up his mind that if Daisy Fairfield had been what he had believed her, she would not have written that letter. She was only a flirt then, after all! How cruelly letters often miss their mark, and what harm they do.

Daisy Fairfield, I think, confidently expected some answer. Either Guy would write, or come, and there would be an explanation between them. The reader will divine, of course, that she had learned the state of his affairs from her father on her return home that day. But Guy neither came nor wrote, but met the blow with characteristic silence. For two or three days he worked on as hard as ever, but said nothing to any one of what had passed. Then he grew sleepless and nervous, and felt that he did not work well. Then he announced that he should take leave of absence from his pleader's chambers for a time, and went straight down to his mother's in Devonshire.

CHAPTER XV.

OVER.

YES; they are deceptive things, those letters, and have caused in this world an infinity of misunderstandings, some of which are destined never to be cleared up. My conscience is good and my digestion sound; yet I shrink from the post instinctively, and rejoice when

L

fate casts my lines in a place where there is no afternoon delivery. I am unable to understand the frame of
mind so common to women, which makes the post hour
a delight and a curiosity; and always feel a sense of
grateful relief if a day comes which brings no letters
with it. It seems to me like so many possible disagree-
ables the less. Quarrels without end, misconceptions
without number, rudenesses, intended or no, which
would be impossible at a personal interview, are sown
broadcast all over the country every night and morning
by those agents of mischief, bearing the Queen's head
on them. Very sad are the offences which rise through
them, never to be explained till explanation comes too
late; and all, very often, because the receiver cannot
read between the lines, or tell anything of the workings
and strivings which possessed the writer's heart, but
could find no voice upon his pen.

Very different would Guy Faucit's frame of mind
have been, and very different his course of conduct, if
he had seen the expression upon Daisy's face when
she wrote him that farewell letter. Had he been
there to see, he would have seen the tranquil and
trustful face moved to a very tumult of passion which
he had never suspected in her. One of the fears
which he sometimes expressed to his mother was, that
there was even too much about her of the φρόνημα
νηνέμου γαλάνας—the spirit of an unruffled calm. Its
charm was great, but it sometimes perplexed him;
and it was that perhaps partly which led to his rapid
acquiescence in the outward seeming of her letter now,
and his belief that in that stately way of hers she had
only been playing with him all the time, and was really
like the rest of womankind, worldly in her heart. He
had thought her something so very different, had held
her so priceless in his esteem, apart even from his love,
that for her sake he was beginning to believe that even
the rest of womankind were better than the romancers—
those of their own sex especially—are so fond of painting
them; and he could not bear to have his idol broken.

If he had only seen! If she had only had no second thoughts, but had sent him straight off, without after-thought or reflection, the passionate adieu which first she trusted to the paper, dashed off through a very mist of tears. It was an adieu, no doubt, as was the other; but it would have brought him within the next hour to her father's house, had he been ten times as roughly expelled from it the day before. An instinct led her to shrink from reading that letter when it was finished, for she knew that it was right and true, and the envelope was in her hand to close when that evil spirit called Expediency whispered to her to pause and to think, and she took the letter out and read it through. Then the hot tears fell faster yet, and the brave heart beat still more loudly, and the blushes gathered round the tears, and she leant her head upon her hands and thought. Could she, Daisy Fairfield, have written to one to whom she had given herself but the evening before, in the language of a passion so undisguised as that? What if he, that manly and perfect lover, should think such lack of reserve un-maidenly? Oh, no, no; and she wrote with a sore heart and toiling head the other letter, whose meaning she thought he would surely read behind the words. Could she have such a love in her heart, and he not see it? Could she disguise from him, however carefully she wrote, the passion of pride in him, and happiness for both which had lived in her all that day, from the moment she knew from his own lips that what she hoped was true, and that she had conquered her hero for her very own? No; he would answer her, he would demand to see her; and neither she nor her father, nor any one in the wide world, would have the right to refuse him. So she sent the second letter, and she put the first away—away in a desk among her girl's treasures, where she read and re-read it many a weary time in the year to come. Long, long after, with a blush she showed it him.

She had come home from Lady Pepperharrow's

very bright and full of hope. When she gave her mother the good news, the mother rejoiced in it for her daughter's sake, and promised her to love Guy, and think him the most perfect and fascinating of human beings. Indeed, she liked him very thoroughly already, for he had always shown her all the deference and consideration, which so wins old ladies' hearts from the young and strong.

Mrs. Fairfield, however, shook her head over her Septimus, and very much doubted if he would look at the matter in the rosy light with which the imaginations of mother and daughter invested it. To them, it was clear that Guy Faucit would be Attorney-General and Lord Chief Justice in no time, if he did not feel tempted to take to politics and become Prime Minister; but it was on the cards that Septimus Fairfield might regard this brilliant future as not proven, and require solid guarantees from any candidate for his daughter's hand. Mrs. Fairfield knew that her husband regarded himself as a very considerable personage indeed; and moreover, she augured ill of the present condition of his temper, with which he had visited her of late so much.

"It's that dreadful brandy and water!" she murmured.

"Not so much the water, I'm afraid, mamma," said Daisy.

"And I'm sure I tell him about it often enough. Every morning, regularly nearly now, I have to have a long talk with him."

Daisy smiled a little.

"Perhaps there's something wrong in the City, mamma. The City seems to be always going wrong and always coming right. I can't feel out of spirits now, dear, and I'm sure everything is going to turn out for the best. You will see Guy—Mr. Faucit—before he speaks to papa?"

"Yes, my dear," said Mrs. Fairfield. "I shall be very fond of him for his own sake, as well as yours;

and he'll be a great comfort to us all—as great as poor Dick."

"I hope so," answered Daisy, something almost like a sneer curling the pretty lip becomingly enough for the first time since we made her acquaintance. "From something papa said, I believe some of Master Dick's bills have to do with those tempers of his just now, and if so, I'm sure I can't blame him. If there's nothing to do in Ireland, without the pretty language Dick bestows on the place, why is there anything to spend? Money spent on nothing travels a bad road."

The young moralist was very angry; and though the poor mother believed firmly though resignedly in her Dick, she was but a weak cudgel-wielder in a weak cause, and soon reduced to her final argument, a sigh; which always led to Daisy's, a kiss.

Daisy was not in a mood to dwell on unpleasant subjects, whereas nothing so much as a piece of good news, or a glimpse of happiness, moved Mrs. Fairfield to the verge of tears. She always cried over her congratulations to a friend upon anything, and drew little morals which had nothing at all to do with the question, like an undeveloped Cassandra. She shook her head now over the prospect of how Septimus would take it; but could not discourage her daughter, who at the moment was armed with a full confidence in her own powers of pleasing, and with general auguries of a successful issue for everything.

"He's a very good old father, that of mine, and never likes saying 'No' to me. He won't begin to like it now, when it would be 'no' to the whole happiness and ambition of my life. Besides, what would be the use? I shan't change my mind now, and I'm sure Guy won't."

And the young lady sang herself off on her way to her room, rejoicing. She went out at the time when Guy's momentous visit was expected, from some instinct of modesty and shyness, and betook herself to her friend Lady Pepperharrow, jubilant over the success of her festivity the night before.

"Oh, Daisy dear, wasn't it delightful? All the supper was eaten before the people went away, and everybody said such kind things. There was a friend of Lady Luscombe's who told Ugh he was like Luke Somebody, which Ugh didn't quite understand. E was a Roman nobleman who gave suppers, and was in the best society of his day. Do you know what is other name was?" enquired her ladyship of Daisy, to whom she was in the habit of referring all her doubtful points in the field of knowledge; and she had many.

"Lucullus?" asked Daisy, laughing.

"That was the name," said the other, quite satisfied. "But this friend of Lady Luscombe's is quite the most remarkable man I have ever met, and so very interesting. Directly you see him you know that he must have been a corsair, or a refugee, or a Fenian, or Don Juan, or something like that. Then he as such a beautiful name—the Count Lestrange. E wants to be introduced to you."

"Does he?" answered Daisy, happy with an infinite content which made Lady Pepperharrow wonder.

She had never seen her favourite look so well, and wished that she could introduce her last admiration, the Count, at once. As it was, she made Daisy promise to dine with her on some early day, to meet Lestrange and the Luscombes, and Daisy was well pleased to promise anything just then. Her heart was full to the brim; and she had all a girl's longing to confide in her friend, and listen to all the delightful sympathy which was sure to be hers. But she had made up her mind that her delicious secret was to be kept until all had been happily arranged at home. So she wandered with Lady Pepperharrow from room to room—watered the drooping flowers, and arranged the demoralized furniture, and was so handy and happy, so laughing and helpful, teasing her friend and caressing her, and so entirely childlike and radiant, that Lady Pepperharrow would fain have adopted her then and there, and have installed her in the new mansion as sole lieutenant and director.

It was a pity that she could not; but there be many such pities in the world. Daisy wouldn't even stay all day, neither to dinner nor to tea; but growing a little impatient as the afternoon wore on, and she threw frequent looks at the clock, insisted on departing prematurely, on the plea that she was wanted at home, and left her hostess with a kiss and a hug which were not to be forgotten for hours. I like to linger over poor Daisy's short-lived happiness, which was to be dissipated at once and cruelly when she reached home.

Her mother met her in the hall with a frightened face, and in a few sentences told her what had happened. "Your father was very angry, dear, and I'm afraid he was very rude. He forbade Mr. Faucit the house, and said that he had not behaved like a gentleman."

Daisy's face flushed to the hair.

"Papa told Mr. Faucit that! On what excuse? how could he dare—?" She checked herself, but she looked very tall and very straight as she stood there.

"I don't know what it means," said the mother. "I'm sure that there's something wrong that we know nothing about, or he never could have spoken like that."

"Where is he?"

"In the study; and he asked to see you directly you came in."

"He shall see me directly," answered the girl, crossing the hall.

"Oh be careful, be careful, there's a dear child! Don't make him worse."

"You need not be afraid, mamma; I feel very quiet indeed. But I must know why he has done this at once." And with a short firm knock at her father's door, she went in, with a sense of strong indignation and of rebellion in her heart. If there was to be anger in this matter, let it be with her, and let her know the reason. She resented a slight to Guy Faucit in a way that would not be denied.

Her thoughts changed when she saw her father.

He was huddled in his chair before the fire, and looked
ten years older. The high colour seemed to have left
his face, and there was a dull pain in his eyes.

"Is it you, Daisy?" he said, in a voice very unlike
his own, when she came in. And that was all.

"Yes, papa. What is this that has passed?" She
took a chair by his, and rested her hand upon his
arm.

"It is a very painful thing; and of course you
know."

"I know that Mr. Faucit has been here, and why.
But I do not know why it should be painful, unless it
is that you spoke to him in a way which nobody can
deserve less."

"I can't agree with you there," said Fairfield
quickly. "He was bound to let me know before proposing to my daughter."

"I do not quite see why, papa," she answered,
getting up and resting one arm on the mantel-piece,
while the other hand played with her glove. "It is I
whom he wants to marry. He was bound to let you
know directly he had proposed, and he did."

"He led me to believe that you care for him,
Daisy," said the other; "but I can scarcely believe it."

"Why not?" she said. "It isn't very difficult to
believe." She smiled a little, hoping that the worst
was over. "If you knew him, papa, as you will, you
would not very much wonder."

"Good God, Daisy! You don't really care for the
man much!"

There was real anguish, real regret, in the old man's
tone; and Daisy knew then that the worst had to be
heard. She turned very pale, and was very still for a
moment.

"Papa! what is the matter?"

"You can never be his wife, Daisy."

"Never is a long word," she said, "especially for
two people who know their hearts as we do. If we are
to wait, we can. But why are we to wait?"

"You do not know him, child."

"Yes, I do. I have been learning since last summer to know him. I have known myself still longer, and know this: that if I ever should meet with anybody who could win me like that, I should not change to him. You are very fond of me, father dear," she added, and knelt at his feet looking up into his face, "and cannot wish me to change."

"He has neither a penny nor a prospect," argued the father, fighting against the confession which he saw must come; for he knew what her answer must be.

"He has all the prospects which brains and energy can give to a man who means to make his way, and to make it for my sake," she said very proudly. "And you have the money to help us at the start easily, if you like, as you always said you should if I married to please you. There is nothing in this that should displease you, papa."

He struggled with himself for a time with an unfeigned misery in his heart, looking round and round for rescue in his thoughts in vain. Then he got up from his chair and walked to the window, turning his face away from her, and without prelude spoke.

"Daisy, I am ruined."

"Papa!"

She did not take it in at once; but he came to her and told her. Very gently and very lovingly, for him; for she was, after all, the pride of his heart and eyes, and she had told him enough to make him feel the heartbreak he was preparing for her. He said nothing of the man Brent as yet; he could not, and it was not now the time if he ever could. But clearly and briefly enough he put before her the situation as he had too well realized it. Ruin and poverty, real and hard; and something like—too like—dishonour even in that. Nothing need absolutely be known for a time, and the difficulty might be tided over, perhaps. But for the penniless lover there was neither place nor hope, and Daisy must forget her dream.

"It has been very short, dear," he said appealingly.

"Yes, very short, papa. Not longer than my life."

She went quietly to her room, when she had learned all that she was then to learn. She looked at the thing as such a woman would look. Money or poverty with her would make no difference to Guy; but money or poverty, for him, must to her make all the difference. He was going to be a great man; and proud as she would be to help his career, she would never mar it. Was she right? I do not know, though I think not. A love like that of those two is too great and rare a blessing to be lost or to be denied upon any terms at all. But the young, when like them, have always the spirit of sacrifice, and do not learn the absolute supremacy of the great claim, till perchance they are too old to profit by the learning. Besides, there was more in the background, and Daisy felt it. When she left her father's room, it was with the knowledge that all was really over, and that Guy and she had better meet no more. Nor was she privileged to tell him all the truth. So she wrote the letter which she knew must be sent, in a spirit of impossible pain. Then — womanlike — desiring the parting and dreading to meet, she hoped and waited for days for an answer — for him. Neither came; and the world went on its usual round again. Daisy dined at Lady Pepperharrow's, and made new acquaintances in a world new to her, with the band of an iron sorrow round her heart. But her charm was as ever, and as she saw and heard no more of Guy, it gathered fresh armour from her pride. Except the four, none knew what had passed.

It seemed the very perversity of fate, that I who knew and loved these two so well, should, on the very morning after Lady Pepperharrow's party, have left England with a friend for a tour in America, long out of the way of letters and of news. I left with a happy heart for them; and after a shake of the hand with both, that last evening, which was meant to convey my unspoken congratulations on the unconfessed truth.

Of the sadness which followed I knew nothing till months afterwards, when it was all too late. Guy never wrote a line to me for years, and for years I never saw him again. When next I met Daisy, she was a Daisy whom I had not known. To his other chief friend, Wilmot, Faucit spoke no word either; but left him to guess. He guessed, as men do guess where their dearest friends are concerned, all on one side. When next he met Daisy a short time afterwards, he bowed to her and wanted to pass by. In arms as was her pride, she mustered courage to speak to him, and she spoke with a cold constraint she would willingly have avoided.

"I have not seen Mr. Faucit lately," she said. "Isn't he well?"

"He has left London, Miss Fairfield."

"Altogether?"

"Altogether, I believe."

And the golden dream was over.

CHAPTER XVI.

ALONE IN THE WORLD.

GUY FAUCIT went down to his mother's to find her very ill. Unselfish in her loving devotion as she always had been, she would not interfere with her boy's work in London by complaints about herself, and her letters to him neither admitted nor showed any change in her. He was shocked when he saw it, almost into forgetfulness of what had brought him down. For her, she had rejoiced greatly in her son's coming; for a fear was upon her that her life was drawing near its quiet end. She had never been strong, and the cold of the winter had tried her severely. And she longed to have her boy with her for a time, if that was to be, as in the old days. If before she left him she could only know that she left him in safe hands, that he would not want a woman's love to care for and to tend him, without which, in one endearing form or another, she held a man's life to be very much alone, she would be well content to fold her hands, and go to the place of those who had gone before. She wanted to know, she longed to hear, that all was arranged between her boy and Daisy; and then she hoped to make the new daughter's acquaintance thoroughly before the end, and to have some sweet confidences with her over Guy's manifold excellences, to tell her how impervious he had been to all the reigning beauties of Devonshire, and how she had been beginning to despair of his ever finding any one to suit him, in spite of all his mother's entreaties and advice; when suddenly she heard from him how Daisy had descended from the blue, and at the first description made up her mind to welcome the new Mrs. Faucit to the place and heart of the old. She would be able to tell her many things of Guy's tastes and ways, besides all that she would learn for herself, and smooth the path of perfect confidence which those two should tread together after she was gone. Would she have the opportunity of fulfilling this desire of her heart? The warning was upon her, and she knew that her time was short. Therefore she rejoiced with a great gladness over the first part of that letter of Guy's to her that we have seen, and was painfully affected by the last. She hoped with her boy that all would come right; but felt that Mr. Fairfield's opposition, against which her brave maternal pride rose all in arms,—indeed, she had strongly urged Guy to speak out; for whom could man desire for a son-in-law better than he?—might too surely put an end to her dream of knowing Daisy.

And on her side, the girl of her son's heart was cherishing a kindred hope; for much, very much, of Guy's talk with her was of his mother, in those times when they were coming to understand each other well; and for that, as for other things, she loved him more and more. She was full of a wish to love Guy's mother too, for her own sake; and on the night when she promised to be his they found room for their schemes for the mother in Devonshire, even in the happy after-talk of self which followed upon their common confession.

"Oh, Guy, do you think your mother will care about me ? Won't she hate me for taking you away from her ?"

"Ask her that yourself, dear," he had answered.

And the sweet tremulous message I have told of, sent in Guy's letter, made the disappointment which followed all the harder to the old lady. That message was all she was ever to know of Daisy, who never forgot her regrets for the loss, in the after time. Thank God for the faith of some of us, which tells us inwardly, with a full assurance, that elsewhere, if not here, those lost knowledges shall be. I would not hold a blanker creed than that, for the price of the world's ransom.

Mrs. Faucit scented danger in the air when she had Guy's news, and though pained and shocked to the heart, was not surprised, when she heard very briefly from him a few days afterwards, that Mr. Fairfield's dismissal had been ratified by Daisy in a way which he could only regard as final, and that he must have been mistaken all along. All the mother's heart went out to her boy in his disappointment, and she wrote at once and begged him to come to her. She was not well, she told him, by way of further inducement, and would be very glad of his society for her own sake, as he would value hers now for his.

"I do not understand quite what has happened, my boy," she wrote ; "for you speak of it very shortly. I hope all is not so ill as you think ; but if you will come here, I can advise you and talk to you as I used in all your boy's troubles. Do you remember? We stupid old women are wiser in some things than wise and clever men like you."

He kissed the faltering handwriting, and reproached himself for not seeing sooner how much it did falter; and he came back to the true mother's heart for comfort and for love.

He found it there in full; but he found too surely, at the same time, that he was come only to lose the sacred consolation when he pined for it the most, and would miss it sorely indeed. His mother was fading very fast and unmistakably; and seeing her as he did, without warning and without preparation, he realized it at once. She was unwilling even to speak of herself, could care for nothing but her longing to pour balm into the wound which had gone so deep. At first she tried to persuade Guy that there had been some mistake in the matter, some misunderstanding which would certainly and easily come right. She wanted to write to Daisy herself—had not the girl written first to her?—and ask her, as she had the right to do, for some fuller explanation of what had passed. But Guy Faucit had the pride of Lucifer, as such men have, and he would not hear of any compromise here. If she had anything to explain, let her. Though at the time his trust in Daisy had let him pass it by, he felt deeply afterwards the sting of Fairfield's insolence, which his daughter's action seemed to sanction. She had been persuaded that he wanted her money perhaps, after all.

"Would you let such a suspicion rest on your son, mother?" he asked.

And the poor mother was not strong, as she had been, and could not make head against a determination which was too great for her, as it had often been in lesser things. She admired that powerful will of her son's, which was with him so strong a characteristic; but she always feared it for him, and many a time had prayed earnestly that it might not some day take the invidious shape of self-will, and wreck him. She learned to agree with him as to the meaning of his disappointment, too. A fuller account of the inter-

.view with Mr. Fairfield showed her that he must be one of those men, of whom she had seen so much in her own life, with whom the world and the purse were the be-all and the end-all. Such a man as that was the fit father for a worldly child, and the Daisy of her son's fancy must have been a dream of delusion. So grieving from her soul for her son's disappointment she saw that it was idle to talk with him about it, and she accepted it as an accomplished fact, as he did.

He put the subject aside after the first few days; and with his strong power over himself, he hid from his mother resolutely and successfully his fierce struggles with his own pain. His duty here, at all events, was clear and straight before him, and he took the duty up in the strength of his great love for the mother who had been everything to him, till this enchantress deluded him for a time for her own amusement.

The doctor of the place confirmed him in his first fears, and told him that his mother was surely dying. It might be a question of a few weeks or of a few months, but the sentence had been passed and written down. In those weeks or months Guy would not leave her, but devote his heart and soul to making the passage easy to that world of rest and un-striving, whence he himself felt pitilessly far. So he crushed down all his own selfish regrets, and comforted his mother by the assurance that there was no harm done, that the episode in his life had been too short, and he had never allowed himself to build upon its issue, and that no doubt some day the proper wife would be found for him, for whom the mother's soul longed. After all, a London flirt would never have done. So before she died she came to think it was for the best, and that her worshipped son had but passed through the waters so many pass, with nothing worse than a wetting. He had never, perhaps, been to her what he was during those closing days.

When the bright spring came, he could wheel her

out in her chair into the garden, and sit by her side chatting and reading.

There was no pain, happily, attending her peaceful end, and he brought all the resources of his mind to bear upon his dear love. That love was dearer to him than ever, now that he had realized its full truth by contrast, just on the verge of losing it. She tried ever and again to persuade him to go back to London, and resume the work he had so zealously begun. But he put that aside altogether. There was plenty of time for that, he said.

The end waited three months, and came noiselessly and without warning, as gently as the visit of a friend to the quiet sick-room. They had been talking seriously and soberly all the long summer-afternoon, with the insects droning their peaceful monotone outside, and the long June shadows creeping lazily over the lawn, on one of those days of still heat when Nature seems crouching for another spring, chiefly of the things above and the things beyond, and the mysteries of that life which had been the mother's chief reality through all her varied days of trouble and of calm. Chief of all her happinesses and prides in her son was her knowledge that he shared that faith as she would have him share it, in the unquestioning obedience and unmurmuring love of a child—the faith that is in one sense higher than charity, in that if it be real it cannot fail to include it. He took up at his mother's request the book they both loved so well, and had read together so often, during those last months especially. And in the deep voice filled with reverence he read to her the opening words of the wonderful chapter in Hebrews— "Faith is the substance of things hoped for, the evidence of things not seen." Her head fell back in her chair, and she gave a faint cry. He was at her feet in a moment.

"Where are you, my boy?" she whispered. And he took the weak arms and clasped them round his neck and pressed his lips to hers; and in that

mother's kiss she died,—died as she had always wished
to die,—in the full confidence of love, alone with him
whom most she had lived for, with the loftiest words of
Divine prophecy leaving, in his voice, the last earthly
echo on her ear. She knew the euthanasia she desired,.
and it was given her.

He did not call for a moment, for he knew that she
was dead. Then he kissed her again, and there broke
from him one low cry. For her the evidence of things
not seen was now turned to the things themselves; the
things hoped for belonged to hope no longer, and the
glass she had seen through darkly was broken down,
to let the fulness of light in for evermore. But for
him the fall of that irrevocable fate was as a sentence of civil death in the grey and purposeless world,
which had for him now no meaning left; and he rose
up in that dear dead presence, feeling himself hopelessly alone.

*   *   *   *   *

He went quietly through the days before the funeral,
and through the business which had to be done, like a
man in a dream; to all outward seeming unalterably
calm. Then he saw his mother laid in the quiet
country grave, and noted with conscious pleasure the
signs of affectionate interest and respect which were
shown on every side. She had the gift, that lady, of
being truly loved and sincerely mourned, after the
fashion of the things that pass away, and leave their
trace of sorrow, though it be not a deep one, upon the
general hurry of surrounding life.

Guy had every sign of sympathy and kindness
shown him,.but his nature took refuge in itself, and for
a day or two still he lived quietly on at home, with no
companions but books and thoughts. His mother's
death left him the master, with his fellowship, of some
few hundreds a year; and he had all his plans of life to
make again.

He must do something, he thought; and his mind
began to revert to the old rooms at Oxford, for the bar

seemed to have no attraction now. But the rooms at
Oxford now recalled Daisy Fairfield, from whose image
the strong will could not shake itself free, though he
did not know yet how deeply it was graven, distracted
as he had been from his first pain by his care for his
mother. In spite of himself Hope began to lift its
head again, and he began to wonder if there could have
been, after all, some strange misunderstanding, and if
he had not been over-hasty in yielding at once to pride.
Was it possible—that last night—that Daisy did not
love him?

A letter from Wilmot, with whom he had exchanged
one or two, came to him at this time. It discoursed of
many things, and it told him, casually and quietly, that
his friend Miss Fairfield had been a great success that
season in London, and that she was going to be married.
The stroke went home to the desolate heart; but this
time Guy was resolved to know something more, and
by an impulse he did not care to master, he wrote one
brief line to Daisy.

"I hear that you are to be married. Is it
true? If it is not, I think that you owe it to me
to tell me so. If it is, silence will be enough. I shall
wait a week for your answer, though I hope not to
wait so long."

He waited for a week, and no answer came. No
line, no sign, no message. Within one week more, Guy
Faucit was on the high seas, alone upon his road to
South America, with no definite purpose in his mind
but to find out places he had never seen, and to be as
if he had never been to all who had known him. He
left behind him directions that the cottage should be
sold, and from time to time communicated with his
lawyer. And he picked up strange friends and strange
acquaintances, and gathered much wide knowledge of
life and lands, serious, self-contained, and silent always.
And he was a wanderer on the face of earth for seven
years.

CHAPTER XVII.

THE COUNT LESTRANGE.

I WAS moralising, some chapters ago, probably little
to the satisfaction of my readers, upon the trials of the
post. There is another side to those trials on which
I often reflect, when I see a brief paragraph in the
papers stating that John Noakes, letter-carrier, has been
arrested, and that so many hundred letters have been
found in his possession. So many losses perhaps, so
many sorrows, so many misunderstandings, not to be
repaired. The form of theft is an amusement which
certainly seems on the increase.

It was my lot not long ago to be living in a country-
town about half-an-hour from London, for a space of
some eighteen months. In that time I had seven
correspondences with the General Post-Office—which
has so little to do in its own line of work that it has
just taken the telephones under its fostering care, on
the ground that the Crown bought them before they
were invented—upon the subject of letters of mine which
never reached their destinations. I had many more
such losses, about which I was too fairly disheartened to
write. Once I received a peremptory summons from
Her Majesty's Collector of Taxes, about a form which
he said I had neglected to fill up and return. I had
done it weeks before, and was able to tell him the day.
His answer was that he was very sorry he had troubled
me, for six or seven others in the district had given him
the same explanation. I appealed to everybody at the
General Post-Office, from the temporary Chief to the
permanent clerk; I represented that the staff at the
local office should be overhauled or changed; I consulted the tradesmen in my town, who told me that the
state of their post-office was notorious, but as for the
General Office, "Lord, sir; you might as well complain to the king of the Zulus." Still I tried, and to

M 2

all my appeals I got but one answer—that "it should be looked into." The answers were nearly always signed by the same gentleman, whose name I grew to hate; afterwards, to my cynical delight, knighted for his "eminent service to the State." How I chuckled when I read of the appointment! Once I wrote to him with gentle satire, hoping that next time he would vary his formula, and tell me that it had been looked into. He answered me quite placidly by return of post, as before, that it should be. It never was. No change whatever was made at the local office; and the imperturbable official in charge always asked me at what exact minute of the day and in what exact box I had posted the lost letter, necessarily long before. At last I kept record and was able to answer him. He said, 'Ah'; but proved to me that I had not ascertained my facts with sufficient exactness. I could not swear whether my last letter went by the 4·10 post or the 4·20, three weeks before. It was idle to expect redress if I was so careless as this. I was quite beaten; gave up complaining; and if I had letters especially important, at last used to take them to town with me, to post at my club. And I reflected, seeing a correspondence in the paper about a monument to Sir Rowland Hill, that the monument he would best have liked would be that his successors should do some of the work the country pays them for. I wonder if he used to write and say it should be looked into.

John Noakes happened to be employed at the office in Devonshire when Guy Faucit sent his last appeal to Daisy Fairfield; and whether it was that he was then trying his prentice hand, and experimenting on the touch of stamps, or was a hardened offender, who stole letters out of pure "cussedness," as others upset railway-trains, he was the link in the chain of events which form this history, which prevented Daisy's hearing from Guy. Such a part in life do commonplaces play. I cannot tell what would have happened if she had received the letter, or that it would have made any difference in the catastrophe. But I do not want Daisy Fairfield to lie under the suspicion of having kept silence upon such an appeal. Wilmot's news, however, was unhappily too true; and when Mrs. Faucit was dying in the Devonshire cottage, she became the affianced wife of Mr. John Brent. Upon this part of Daisy's story I cannot bear to dwell. "*Fais ce que dois, advienne que pourra,*" was so entirely her motto, that I think at no cost should she have been led into so perverted an idea of duty, as to sacrifice herself to become the wife of a man she did not love, with her heart full of the image of another. I can never believe that anything ever really justifies that, though the largest of allowances is often to be made, and never larger than in Daisy's case. The nets which circumstance wove for her were very closely meshed indeed.

Guy Faucit had gone down to Devonshire; Daisy Fairfield had dined at Lady Pepperharrow's, and made the acquaintance of Lady Luscombe, and was by her being initiated into the social mysteries of a more fashionable world than the old circle in which she at first began her going-out life, crushing down the deep pain in her heart, and wearing the customary mask which the world demands of its votaries; aimless and objectless and sad, but winning general admiration wherever she went. She would have stayed at home and looked after her mother only too willingly, and thrown all this aside. But she did not want her story known; still less did she wish that any talk should get abroad of the condition of affairs at Fairfield's, which her social success would help to dissipate as much as anything.

The sword of Damocles still hung suspended over her father's head; and Mr. John Brent, patient and catlike, bided his time.

Now, it happens that Mr. John Brent had a singular auxiliary at hand when he began to lay his formal siege and advance his parallels. Some years before he had made the acquaintance, out in India, of a man who had been introduced to him in connection with some

intricate city business at home, who seemed to come
from nowhere, and have no very definite occupation,
yet to occupy positions of influence and trust at all
sorts of times in all sorts of places, and to possess,
for the purpose of confidential missions, a special and
striking gift for swaying the wills and winning the
ears of men. When he made his first appearance in
Calcutta circles, young, though not in his first youth,
he impressed men at once with the idea of almost
universal knowledge, of a satirical power of observation,
which strengthened his position indefinitely by making
everybody half afraid of him, and a charm of conversation which very few could resist.

The sinister but handsome face, the low musical
voice, of which no word was often lost, and the acute
intelligence which grasped all the sides of a situation
at once, made an exceptional and impressive personage
of the Count Lestrange. Why he was a Count, and
where the Countship came from; whether he had in-
herited it from some ancient race, or gotten it for
himself from some grateful sovereign of a court large
or petty, in recognition of secret services to a starving
exchequer; whether Lisbon, or the Holy Roman Empire,
or the capital of the Cannibal Islands, all which places
seemed equally familiar to him, was originally responsible for the decoration, was never exactly known.

Men muttered and questioned at first, and talked
about "adventurer" and "impostor," and used harder
words than that. But from the beginning they did not
care to use these expressions very loudly, or provoke a
certain cold and dangerous glitter which had a knack
of coming stealthily into the Count's eyes, and taking
by surprise the offenders who had not marked its
beginning. Moreover, there were things whispered
of his having "killed his man" more than once in
countries where it was not yet impolite to do so, and it
was said that, even where it was not polite, he had
been known to make it so.

So gossip and ill-report died away in the wake of a

man so desirous of pleasing where he was allowed, and
of making himself generally useful; and the quarterings
of the Prince of Ark and Ararat were not more unques-
tioned by society in the course of time than those of
the Count Lestrange. He stood well with the Roths-
childs, had been trusted by the Torlonias, and had
recovered bad debts for Overend and Gurney's among
the most morally dilapidated of South American re-
publics; and when first he made acquaintance with
John Brent, in the interests of a firm which was working the Great Magnibonium Railway at an increasing
dividend to the subscribers of thirteen-and-a-half per
cent., but had not for the moment as much ready cash
in hand as could be wished, he had just been engaged
in examining some Parsee schools in the south of India
on a commission from the British Government. This
was the man who became, upon his homeward visit to
Calcutta, the adviser and intimate, and "fidus Achates,"
of Mr. John Brent.

I am no master of the involutions of finance, especially in the hands of such a keen diplomatist as the
Count Lestrange; nor do I know how it was that he
first discovered in Brent the man to serve him in the
matter of the Magnibonium Railway.

So he did, however; and from his fortunate connection with that concern, which announced a dividend
of fifteen per cent. shortly afterwards, and then collapsed
with a stupendous crash which half-ruined hundreds of
confiding shareholders,—who had not reflected that such
a rate of interest for themselves probably represented
proportionate injury to at least as many others unknown
—dated Mr. Brent's first great rise in the world. He
was quite as careful about it as he was about everything; and when the crash came, it hurt him no
halfpenny in purse or credit.

The confiding shareholders filled the newspapers
with lament and woe; pitiful stories of half-pay officers
and maiden ladies, who had justly expected not less than
a safe fifteen per cent. for their little all, resulted in

tears and sympathy from many of the benevolent, and subscriptions from some; leading articles, pitched upon the highest key of morality, held up the directors to the reprobation of honest men; and some of the directors were finally brought to trial and acquitted, as having been on the whole confiding, whereupon the leading articles recanted, and expressed their sympathy.

Mr. Brent, meanwhile, had nothing to do with the thing except to realize (if I make any mistake upon this difficult ground, I must ask the reader to believe that the incorrectness lies in the narrator, but not in the events narrated); and Count Lestrange, who, without a profession or a penny of capital, used to set down his brains as worth so much a year, and made it about as regularly as a government official receives his salary, was paid too in his own modest way, and pocketed his fee for his services. But he made out of the transaction, in the pulling of the secret strings, something else which the dangerous adventurer valued more than money. When John Brent came back to England, he, on his part, who had netted the house of Fairfield, was somehow in Lestrange's power.

It was this same Magnibonium Railway business into which Fairfield and Co. had been drawn through the activities of the junior partner; and Mr. Fairfield had, by a course of events of which he was really the victim and the dupe, and not the promoter, fallen into the danger of being one of the scapegoats of the concern, and having one day to stand in the dock to answer for the Magnibonium Railway. The junior partner, much to his annoyance and surprise, for he had fancied himself warm and safe on the windy side, and had certainly taken every possible precaution to make himself so, was one of those who did eventually stand there, and escaped as related, to begin business under new colours afterwards, and to do very well for himself in the world indeed.

It was in the autumn of the year of which I have been writing that the Magnibonium catastrophe came, and during the weary months which preceded it, Mr. John Brent was pursuing his object calmly and relentlessly. Daisy was being slowly and hopelessly drawn into the toils, and her hapless father was breaking in health and constitution fast and surely, under the pressure of his lingering suspense. He clutched at straws, and clutched in vain, and made appeals to Brent which might as well have been addressed to the monument.

> Come sul capo al naufrago
> L'onda s' avvolve e tesa,
> L'onda su cui del misero |
> Alta pur dianzi e tesa,
> Scorrea la vista a scernere
> Prode remote invan—

So his troubles crushed Septimus Fairfield as he looked for a plank, and looked in vain. He might have found help elsewhere if it would have availed him. Lady Pepperharrow, if she had known of the situation, would have made her Hugh sell Glycerine House to help Daisy; but the Magnibonium toils were too close for that, and could be loosed by Brent only. And Brent himself, in all the complications of this labyrinthine business, which utterly baffled the general reader who tried to understand them from the newspaper reports of the trial of the directors, was in some way in the hands of Lestrange, who used him. So consistently tortuous had been the proceedings of the Magnibonians, that everybody was in somebody else's power, like the personages in the famous dead-lock in the 'Critic.' Everybody,—except Lestrange, who pulled all the strings and worked all the machinery, and was paid his fee for his services in some indefinite but truly respectable way; who was able to do many a friend a good turn during the winding-up of the gigantic skein; materially advanced the fortunes of the house of Luscombe, among others, by means of it, and gave some evidence in court which much damaged some and much distinguished others,—shedding quite a lustre, for instance, on the character of John Brent,—being finally complimented by the judge upon his disinterested labours and his brilliant services to the shareholders in the hour of their need. The few of those who could after-wards afford it felt themselves bound to subscribe for a handsome piece of plate, which was presented to the Count after an elegant oration from Cicero Wrigley, Esq., in the names of those of the misguided share-holders who owed him their preservation from entire shipwreck.

It has been already told how, at Lady Pepper-harrow's festival, the Count Lestrange first saw Daisy Fairfield in the very flush and radiance of her new-born happiness. The Count was a connoisseur in beauty, and had seen so much of it in all parts of the world, that he was slow to move to anything like admiration, though every pretty woman gave him pleasure. Of late, his devotion had been quietly exclusive in one quarter. Familiar with all phases of the world, he had some seasons before first come to London from abroad, in which vague region, though he was supposed to be of an English family, he had been born and bred, or said so. He came on a diplomatic mission from some German court, well accredited and with good intro-ductions, and made his way in society at once. He was accepted on his own merits, as such men sometimes are, without much inquiry into antecedents. The German court had got him from another German court, on some mission or another, which other German court had got him from somewhere else. He was a kind of reputable Autolycus, picking up the unconsidered trifles which gradually make a career, and knew capitals and men so well, that life seemed to have given him the best education in her power. She taught him by the process of passing him on, till he anchored, as much as he could anchor, in the great port of London. He found his sphere there at once ; for he suited London, and London suited him. The fascination of the sunless city for foreigners who come there with good introductions, and

do not fly from the first appalling aroma of soot into
the bluest wilderness they can find, has always been
very great. I believe it to be a fact, that if the *attachés*
of the world were polled, they would vote for London in
an overwhelming majority. They find the Circean
arms of society open for them all, a sort of republic
under a monarchy which is the harmonious result of
England's incongruous growth, the idlers at their idlest
and the workers at their best; brilliant talkers still
surviving, and surviving with less of egotism than was
wont to be a talker's bane; women with less of restric-
tion than ties their hands in some countries, and not
too much of freedom to wound the taste as in some
others; and, stoutly as an Englishman I will maintain,
on the whole the prettiest in the world. Lestrange,
out of his wide experience, maintained it always, and
vindicated his position by pointing to the theatres.

"There is the test," he said. "I see so many
actresses, that in society proper I am no fair judge.
Sweet are the society beauties who grace the albums
and shop-windows; and why on earth shouldn't they?

> "'Small is the worth
> Of beauty from the light retired;
> Bid her come forth,
> Suffer herself to be admired,
> And not blush so to be desired.'

"The beauties are quite right, and should not 'to
parties give up what was meant for mankind.' For one
young acolyte who burns his incense to the original in
a London drawing-room, a thousand chawbacons may
smoke their pipes in Yorkshire under the sweet nose of
the copy, and never offend its delicacy. But for one of
society's sweethearts, I can show you a dozen pretty
actresses in a day whose trains she ought to carry.
Where is the theatre abroad where one can feel sure
of such a feast to the eye? I don't care about brain-
sauce, which spoils it. I like to feel like a Turk in his
harem, when I disport myself in my stall at the Fantasy,
and pay my half-guinea for my whole seraglio. The

theatres of England prove the prettiness of her women, and I care not who says me nay. ' *Vive la Bohême !* '" It was when he had expressed these lawless sentiments one day that Lestrange sate down at Lady Luscombe's piano, and confirmed them in a ballad in which he had embodied them :

Joyeux pays des gens joyeux,
Les beaux esprits de ce bas monde,
Pour te donner à nos aïeux,
Vénus sortit jadis de l'onde.
La belle reine de bonté
Protégera tout cœur qui aime,
Et vit toujours, dans sa beauté,
Pour les enfans de la Bohême.

Le musiçien va fredonnant
Les doux airs de son répertoire ;
Le peintre vient en exploitant
Les belles couleurs pour sa victoire ;
Le poête rêve le beau,
Chantant en dépit de soi-même :
Le luth, la plume, le pinçeau,
Ouvrent pour nous nôtre Bohême.

La route parsémée de fleurs,
Voilà bien d'autres qui s'avançent ;
En foule viennent ces chers pêcheurs,
Les gens qui jouent, les gens qui dansent !
Il est heureux, le Bohémien,
Car pour bien égayer sa serre,
Il sait trouver, sur son chemin,
Les belles filles de la terre.

Versons le bon vin pétillant !
À l'avenir ne songeons guère :
Si le sort pour nous est méchant,
À l'avenir buvons la bière !
Nous donnons gaîment d'une main,
Quand nous avons la bourse pleine,
Et de l'autre prenons demain,
Des bons amis qui ont la veine.

Que l'avocat ne frappe pas !
Il trouvera la porte close ;
Et n'entre pas que dans le cas,
Où il serait causeur, sans cause :

Le médecin n'en est pas vraiment,
Qu'il tue à part sa clientéle !
Il faut, pour y aller gaîment,
Assez de cœur, et de cervelle !

Le dévôt maudit son voisin,
Tous les Dimanches à la messe,
Mais prêchera pour nous en vain
Son évangile de tristesse :
Qu'il se fasse sa propre loi,
Faisons y guerre, et à outrance !
Nôtre devise, c'est la Foi,
La Charité, et l'Espérance.

Tout las de travail,—où de vin,
Bien doucement quand on sommeille,
Là-haut, un petit chérubin
Sur nous exprès sans cesse veille ;
Ainsi, quand au dernier moment
La Mort à nôtre porte sonne,
Saluons-la en souriant :
"Viens ! je n'ai fait mal à personne ! "

Nous croyons à la vérité,
La droite ligne de la vie,
De l'amour et de l'amitié
La vraie franc-maçonnerie ;
Le sage ne croit à rien,
Excepté toujours à soi-même ;
Mais le bon Dieu, qui fait tout bien,
Chérit ses enfans de Bohême.

The Count trolled the verses out, or some of them, for eight stanzas of a song are more than propriety admits of, in days when the poet is naught and the composer everybody, and words are but as pegs to hang tra-la-la's upon. Having been a writer of song-words, among other things, I speak feelingly. It is not long since I beheld, if I may for a moment borrow one of the oddities of type affected by that manliest and most human of living story-tellers, Charles Reade, a song advertised in a music-seller's window thus, or thusly :—in which last phrase I am borrowing again, with the true effrontery of a scribbler, from Artemus Ward—

MARY JANE,

THE WORDS BY ALFRED TENNYSON,

THE MUSIC BY BUNKUM BARRE,

DEDICATED TO AND SUNG BY

BOANERGES BULL.

Once Bunkum Barre did me the honour to set some words of mine, in which he failed, with the most faultless completeness, to catch a single idea out of those with which my geniuskin of song had inspired me. "Most extraordinary thing," he said to me, conscious of his success. "I find that our popular composer, Herr Tutl Te (a mere impostor, my dear boy, I assure you), has set these same words of yours, as I think, in an inferior manner. But you will admit, my dear Tom, that the *rhythm is the same.*"

I looked at him feebly and humbly, and admitted that it was. As the "rhythm" depended on the words, I failed to see how it could be otherwise. Seeing that the wretched word-writer finds three things out of four, the ideas, words, and rhythm, and leaves the fourth, the tootling, to the composer, I never could see why he should be printed small and the composer big, and the two paid on a like scale of proportion. But such is the author's life, from time immemorial. He is the one man presumed to have no weekly bills. I have written songs, and the composer has composed everybody to sleep with them, and taken the cash and the big letters. I have written a play, and the actors have "made" me; and written another to be made again by some more of them; whereas where they have failed, which has not been unfrequent, to catch a single idea, or indeed, with exceptions, to speak a single word of mine, they have been much commiserated for having to do with an author who handicapped their talents with such ideas and words. I have served for six months at hack-work, as hard as Jacob, for Skimpington the religious book-

seller—might I not rather say, the seller of religious
books?—and at the end been refused one penny in
payment, on the ground that I had no "contract," not
indeed being apt to make them in such relations. I
have been driven to law for my money,' and after a
year and a half's delay got it from a judge and a jury, to
be robbed of more than three-fourths of it immediately
afterwards by that exquisite and rational product of
British law, the taxing-master, who sits in a room of his
own and placidly reverses, to all intent and purpose, the
"judgment" and the "order" of Her Majesty's High
Court of Justice, in the absence of the hapless, though
successful litigant, who has spared every penny of
avoidable expense, and is fined for succeeding. The
taxing-master hath a villa in the wholesome suburb of
Scurviton-on-Thames, and draws his unmolested income
quarterly. And the religious bookseller lives in
splendid opulence, and cares no straw whether he pays
me what he owes me or not, provided I am duly
mulcted for venturing to annoy him, and wanting to
be paid like other men. Oh, that he would sell fewer
prayer-books, and read more! I like irreligious
publishers much better, and find them indifferent
honest.

This is digressive, and remote from Lestrange's song.
The Count's wonderful voice, a rich tenor baritone, and
refined musical skill were among his chief passports, as
such gifts and acquirements are, and deserve to be, to
social success. That success of his was great and
immediate. He could talk with the best talkers, do
innumerable services unobtrusively, and have the name
of a "thorough gentleman" for the asking. So great
was his musical gift, that at a concert where the best
signors and mesdames of the day discoursed their most
highly-paid songs, he would win from a frigid audience
the one loud *encore* of the evening, by some simple,
thrilling, perfect ballad, which set half who heard it
dreaming, sung with an art beyond the reach of skill.
At last the professionals came to him with a sort of

deputation, asking him to ask payment for singing among them, because it wasn't fair.

He thought of it for a time, but would not, having plans and notions of his own. And in the first blush of his London success, he became an unfailing feature at the Vavasour receptions we have heard of; the right hand of Mr. Vavasour in the City, and, still more, of Mrs. Vavasour at home. She was his devotion.

When the cruel title came, he understood better than any one else how to soothe and soften Marian's bitter and bravely-hidden mortification. And when she and he came to Lady Pepperharrow's house-warming, it was from Luscombe Abbey that they came.

CHAPTER XVIII.

THE PITY OF IT.

The Count Lestrange's keen eye for beauty was held and fascinated by the first apparition of Daisy Fairfield. She was looking her loveliest on that evening at Lady Pepperharrow's, and we know the reason why. So did the Count at once, with an intuition which would hardly have failed a less keen observer than he was, when he saw her at Guy Faucit's side. She was very sweet and very fair, and he knew that he was in the presence of the most perfect specimen of her kind whom to his taste he had seen.

He set Pentonville to work at once, and through that well-qualified agent of social inquiries, he soon learned all he wanted to know.

The name came upon him with a surprise. "Miss Fairfield, the daughter of the merchant!" he said. "Really!"

This, then, was the girl about whom John Brent

had spoken to him only that morning, as the young lady upon whom he had cast a favourable eye. Lestrange fairly laughed to himself, with an old silent laugh, as he thought the combination over.

Lady Luscombe's quick eye followed him with suspicion, and she asked him what was amusing him.

"I will tell you some day," he said; "or rather, it will tell itself before long. I see a plot in my mind's eye; and you know that I am fond of them."

He was introduced to Miss Fairfield that night, and he met her at dinner a few evenings afterwards, when that sad change had come over the spirit of her dream. He was courteous, sympathetic, watchful, and laid himself out to please. He did not altogether succeed at first, as well as usual; for there was something in the girl's royal instincts which took alarm. But he met her at a good time for his purposes, whatever those might be.

She was deeply wounded at Guy Faucit's departure without further sign, and inwardly resolved that he could not have cared very much for her, after all, or he would never have taken her so instantly at her unwilling word. She missed his companionship though, painfully, not only as the lover's, but as the friend's; for all her talks with him had been an education to her, and had widened and enlarged her mind.

This gap Lestrange was more able to supply than any one else, for he was a man of wide culture, as well as of deep observation. He, too, was able to talk of art and books out of the overflowings of a fuller knowledge than Guy's; though the cynical flavour of his comments and criticisms, delicately veiled as it was, was very different from that of the discourse which came of Faucit's frank and open-air nature.

During the months of that London season,—during which poor Daisy, taken up by Lady Luscombe and others at once by right of her rare beauty, blossomed out into the great world with a canker-worm at the

N

stem,—Lestrange had constant opportunities of "form-ing." the girl whom he adopted as his pupil.

Everything fought for him. The entire change of life and associates, in which she found the best distraction possible for her sad thoughts, made her glad of the attention of one who knew her new world so well.

Terribly sad those thoughts became within a few days of her father's scene with Guy. First, he told her that things in the City might recover; then, that it was only a question of time when the crisis should come; then, that she could save his fortune, his credit, and his character, and she alone; then, that she could save them but in one way; and, at last, that that way was John Brent.

Every step was taken with Machiavellian precision; for John Brent directed Mr. Fairfield, and Count Lestrange directed John Brent. Scarcely had he made Daisy's acquaintance, and understood Brent's purpose, than he determined to forward it with all his power.

I do not wish to examine too closely into the motives by which he was actuated, for they were mixed and many. Moreover, Lestrange was one of those terrible characters with whom one meets, thank God, very rarely, though one does meet with them some-times, who love evil for evil's sake, and have made it their good. It is in itself motive enough for them. Such people are an awful scourge, perhaps a wholesome warning. Let no man speak of "dispositions." To them, as to all, the choice between good and evil is open at the first; and when they have entered upon the downward course, constant and constant are the opportunities offered of return. Then constant less and less; and at last, none at all. Their perception of right and wrong has grown fairly confused; and their ears are no longer open that they should hear the passing of the sad, remorseful, sighing sentence, "Ephraim is joined to the idols. Let him alone:" or know of the irrevocable moment when it is passed, if indeed such a sentence can ever be irrevocable, which mercifully we cannot know, though it is well for us to fear it.

So the nets closed round Daisy Fairfield, for whom Count Lestrange had conceived a deep and dangerous admiration from the time when first he began to talk to her. The frank and fearless spirit, the entire absence of self-seeking, and comparative indifference even to admiration,—though she would have been less than woman if she had not enjoyed, even in her trouble of heart, the conquests of her beauty,—delighted Lestrange, who had grown weary of the monotony of worldliness which he found upon the surface wherever he went. Here was a task worthy of his power and skill, and in accordance with all the principles of the nature which he (and none else) had made his, to subject this high-minded woman to a process of mental degradation. In the future he may have had other views.

The months which Guy spent by his mother's side in Devonshire, Lestrange devoted to this unworthy game. The world, at that time, affixed him much to Lady Luscombe, and for good reasons of his own he had to conciliate her. The adventurer's main purpose in life was very definite to himself, though unknown to all beside. From the first, he had made himself indispensable to Marian Vavasour, whom he magnetized at last into an entire and dangerous confidence. In her social empire he had been an admirable vizier; in her schemes for wealth he had brought all his craft and mastery of city politics to bear in helping her. Marian Vavasour had told him a fact which was concealed from every one else in the world but the family physician. Her husband had serious heart-disease, and his life was of short purchase. The Count Lestrange knew well what she and he might do together with the gathering rent-roll of the Luscombe lands, and he meant to marry the widow of Lord Luscombe.

It may give a better idea than anything can of the admiration he conceived for the beauty and the nature

of Daisy, to say, that for the moment she shook him in
that intention. Daisy Fairfield would have a good
fortune, which he could save, with her father's credit,
through John Brent, as well as the Anglo-Indian himself. And as his wife she would do the Count credit
indeed. But a little reflection cured him of that idea.
The position which Marian Luscombe would give him,
and the peculiar fitness which he recognized in her and
in himself, to make them an important place in the
English world, was a matter which he was not going to
throw lightly away. So for his further objects he
decided to second John Brent's purposes, and not to
thwart him. In this he congratulated himself upon a
good disinterested action. For what else could it be, to
save such a girl as Daisy from ruin and obscurity,
and the shame which would result from her father's
exposure, and probably his public trial, by the only
means left by which to save her? So he went upon
his way. Drop by drop he instilled into her ear at the
many parties, dinners, gatherings at which they met,
the theories of life which for the moment it suited him
to entertain. He said no word to her of his knowledge
of her father's position, and the designs of Mr. Brent.

"Yes, Miss Fairfield," he said to her once, "like
others I have formed my conception of duty. As far as
in this world we can understand it, I think that it is
to family and to name. Self-sacrifice for that is the
highest point to which we can rise."

"Do you really think that?" she said.

"I do," he answered. "I am myself my own architect, such as the building is; and I think myself bound
to honour the building."

"And if self-sacrifice, in such a cause, meant misery
and wrong?"

"I should hold it to be all the higher self-sacrifice."

And Daisy thought, and thought again.

Lestrange was far too clever a player to intimate to
the girl anything of personal admiration, which could
be construed into anything more than personal defer-

ence. Too clever far to use the ordinary common-
places about the value of wealth and station to such a
pupil as this, he played upon the chords of the higher
common-places of sacrifice and unselfishness. He used
the general ways of worldlings in his subtle and suggestive fashion, not for example, but for mockery. And
so by degrees, studied and sure, he undermined the
foundation of a higher and a nobler faith.

Daisy Fairfield, meanwhile, became the favourite of
the hour, and the recognized Cynthia of the fashionable
minute. She clung to good Lady Pepperharrow with a
despairing fondness, as she felt the ground slipping more
and more from under her feet. She used her own new-
born fashion to help her friend to the desire of her
heart; figured as Diana Vernon at her *tableaux;* as
Mrs. Mildmay, or Madame de Fontanges, at her private
theatricals—nobody ever acted anything but 'Still
Waters Run Deep,' or 'Plot and Passion,' just then—
willingly and carelessly enough. It was her first
step into the public life from which she had rather
shrunk before, and surprised her hostess as much as
it gratified her. The rouge and the applause had
been little enough to her taste; but she did not reject
it now.

"You acted like an angel, dear," said Lady Pepperharrow, after one of these performances.

"Very likely," she answered. "I never saw an
angel act. But not nearly as well as any half-trained
professional actress from the theatres would do it, on a
salary of fifteen shillings a week."

"Oh, but, my dear, ladies have such an advantage."

"As professional ladies, of course. But not as
professional actresses."

And Lady Pepperharrow, without at all understanding it, recognized in her favourite's talk and
her favourite's ways a tone entirely new to her. She
asked once or twice what had become of that nice and
distinguished Mr. Faucit, who had seemed such a friend
of Daisy's. But she had but off-hand answers, and

knew nothing. So Daisy laughed and talked and dined, and the wheel went round and round.

One day,—it was late in the season, and some two days before Guy Faucit's mother died at his side in Devonshire,—Faucit's name was accidentally brought up in conversation at some small and familiar dinner-party, by some one who knew of him. Daisy bit her lip a little, and turned a little white; and Lestrange, who was sitting next her, filled her glass with wine, or beckoned to the servants to do so.

"Faucit!" he said. "Oh yes, I remember him. A fine, manly fellow, who was to carry everything before him. Did you ever meet him, Miss Fairfield?"

"Once or twice," she said.

"A fine career spoiled," he added, "like so many others. I met him at supper once or twice three or four months ago, at the house of the pretty singer, Dora Lane. He was her favourite and slave for the time, and I fancy the Temple Chambers didn't see very much of him. Most men would have been proud of it; but whatever his reasons were, he didn't like it talked about. The thing was kept rather dark, though it was well enough known in some circles."

He looked away from Daisy, and talked to his other neighbour.

Daisy was brilliant, almost noisy that night; and she went home late. Her father was still in his room, and the inevitable crisis was near. There had been scenes at home of late; the idler, Dick Fairfield, had come back, and with father and mother, was pressing Daisy hard; for even the poor mother knew the truth, and was fading under it, as Fairfield himself was breaking.

"Papa," said Daisy, "tell Mr. Brent I will marry him." And so she went to bed.

The next day she had her interview with the unlovely lover, and made, on her side, no disguise. His face was unlovelier than ever when the interview was over, and the terms of the bargain on both sides arranged. Daisy's was a frank and unconventional spirit, and she held her own. Whatever her terms were, Brent yielded, and the cruel thing was done. I have told my thoughts before, and do not love to linger.

There was a wedding at St. George's in the following autumn, when Guy Faucit was upon the high seas. I had myself just come home, and heard the startling news; and I watched the ceremony, uninvited, from the gallery of the church. The face of the bride was like a statue of Diana, as pale as the marble—as classical—as cold. Throughout the mockery, no quiver of a nerve might be seen. Only, when she was asked if she would love, and honour, and obey, there was a pause before she answered. Then she said in a low voice, "I will," and suddenly lifted her eyes, with a strange appeal in them, for a moment straight above her. And I, who was watching her and naught beside, saw her, with one rapid gesture, make the sign of the cross.

It was rumoured that the fashionable priest, one of the two or three who was close to her, heard her whisper under her breath—"Thy will be done."

For myself, I went home dreaming, and sate out that evening at some theatre in a dream. I have never been able to remember either theatre or play.

CHAPTER XIX.

DAISY BRENT WASHES HER HANDS.

THE marriage was over, and the deed was done; and when the Magnibonium catastrophe came, the good fame of Mr. Fairfield escaped all connection with it: so Daisy reaped her reward. But in less than one year from that day, she was without father or mother, the first of whom followed the second to the grave within a few weeks. The long anxiety had killed them both; and the cold duty which in Daisy's manner to them now took the place of the old signs of love, perhaps hastened the inevitable end. She could not help that change. Mrs. Fairfield grew smaller and smaller, and faded out: and her husband, much changed on his side, less dictatorial and gentler far, was found after dinner one evening dead in his arm-chair. He had died quietly and painlessly in his sleep.

Daisy had been dining with him that night, and was the first to find him so, when the usual time had passed for his coming up-stairs for his cup of tea.

"Papa!" she said. "Papa!"

Then as the silence awed her she drew nearer, and looked at him, and knew that he was dead. She stood by the chair quietly for some time, neither moving nor speaking, but looking into his face, with the sadness of an unfathomable feeling in her eyes. Then she bent over him and kissed the dead lips, which wore, thank God, a smile; and then she knelt and prayed. She felt for any sign of life, but there was none; and quietly called the servants. The doctor came and certified that he must have been some half-an-hour dead when his daughter found him, and discoursed to his wife constantly for months of the impression made upon his mind by the stately sweetness and self-possession which the daughter showed. She looked at her father, he said, with an expression in her eyes which haunted him, and was always tempting him to try to define it.

So Septimus Fairfield's life was over; and he had escaped the dishonour and ruin which had seemed to him so terrible, at the heavy cost of this young and vigorous life, full of the bud and sap of its richest spring. He had lived out his days in their narrow-minded span, as such men do live them; and nobody had much to say of him for good or for evil. His interpretation of the fifth commandment had been like that of most elder people—all on one side.

It is a cheap conception of duty which gratifies the

vanity of the old, and saves them trouble, and casts all the burdens on the young. When they moralize on the point, it is impossible but to believe that they think of themselves as having married not to please themselves at all, but in order to place a possible progeny under heavy obligations in no wise mutual. The progeny are apt to think otherwise during their early years. Then they grow old in their turn, and go and do likewise. And so the undying tradition of self is handed on again—to yet a generation more.

With reference to this same commandment, it may perhaps be suggested that most of us do not live under the dispensation of Moses; and that it is not that commandment upon which, according to Him under whose dispensation we are, hang all the law and the prophets.

Septimus Fairfield, like most people, had interpreted the commandment in the sense most gratifying to himself, and did not seem to think, so far as his children were concerned, that it even included his poor timid wife much. "Honour thy father" was enough for him without the context; and he certainly took no trouble to teach respect for Mrs. Fairfield by any example of his own. What his lessons lacked, Daisy's heart supplied. And to save himself in the eyes of the world, which had done little for him and paid scant attention to him or his doings, Papa Juggernaut drove his parental car right over his gallant child's happiness and life; and before he had time to profit by his drive, went to his rest apparently with a Nelson's confidence that he had done his duty. Who knows? Puzzled and perplexed by all these myriad problems of the entangled scheme of Self, we are tempted to write over half these monumental graves Ophelia's single epitaph—

> "He is gone, he is gone,
> And we cast away moan;
> God ha' mercy on his soul."

"And of all Christian souls, I pray God." Many of these leaden caskets may carry yet, locked within them, some rough gem of Christian soulhood, all unguessed, still proper for the refiner's hand, as Bassanio's casket hid Portia's image. What good had poor old Polonius, in the comedy of his philosophic selfishness which wrought to such an end, ever in his life done to anybody?

Daisy Brent went home to her husband's house, to take up her cross alone. She went to him a portionless bride in reality, though it was supposed that she had brought him a handsome contribution from the Fairfield salvage, when the house was comfortably wound up to be a record of the mercantile past, though something, as has been already told, to the temporary discomfort of the junior partner. As a matter of fact, nothing was really saved, except a modest bachelor's income, which, by arrangement between the contracting parties, went to keep the wolf from the door of subaltern Dick's quarter, and to enable him to live—when after a time the military profession proved too severe a trial for his capacities—the blameless life of self-sufficing clubhood.

Such men be the lotos-eaters of our day, in whose land it is always afternoon because they never get up in the morning, though to eat with them is to nip, and their lotos is called sherry-and-bitters.

John Brent had really got all the Fairfield money into his own hands, and in his short-sighted selfishness, he wrung from Daisy's father every doit of his bond. It was concealed from Daisy, who believed that she really brought money in her hand to her husband; for it was not difficult to hide the truth from so innocent a financier as she was. John Brent imagined that by taking her portionless he would have her more completely in his power, and he looked forward with satisfaction, the brute, even at the very hour of his marriage, to telling his wife some day that he had taken her as a pauper. Most short-sighted was this selfishness of his, which left out of sight altogether the whims of the goddess Fortune, never so whimsical as with wealth.

of such precarious making. The Fairfield business
might have pointed that moral for him; but he had
no eyes to read. It had been his purpose to retire
altogether from business; but business had been his
life, and he soon began to realize that it was as impossible for him to do without it, as it is for nearly all men, lawyers, doctors, anybody, to give up a
profession and to die out of harness. The few who
can do it are exceptionally fortunate men, who have
managed, however absorbing the nature of their especial
work, to keep in view the infinite varieties, and interests,
and fascinations of life, and to retain a hold, for their
declining years, upon the rich resources of leisure, which
is likely, through the law of revulsion, to become before
long the highest good of these worrisome days. I
who write these things avow my simple belief, that
there is nothing in life so delightful as intelligent idleness, even as there is nothing so terrible as "loafing"
where idleness is, but intelligence is not.

Now John Brent, it must be confessed, knew nothing of the possibilities, and was in sooth the veriest
and narrowest little huckster who ever scratched himself up a fortune. His married home was wretched,
for wherever he went he made his own wretchedness,
and that of all he had to do with. It was in spite
of all that the brave Daisy could do;—doing all her duty
fearlessly, and striving her best to keep, subject to the
conditions of her sale, to the terms of the memorable
and specially attested vow. I, for one, hold not that
she ever broke it. For, without any Jesuitic reserva-
tion, we may supply before the words of any such an
oath as that, even as before those of that same fifth
commandment, the introductory clause " to try our best."
And when the other side makes more impossible, so
much the worse—for the other side. Try—and when
you have failed through no fault of yours, know it; and
try again at the first opportunity possible, till the
case has become " no thoroughfare," and you can wash
your hands. It was in this wise that, after four

years of loyal battle, Daisy Brent washed her hands at last.

Sad and cruel and violent had been many of the domestic scenes which characterized those four years of domestic history. Mr. Brent became engaged again in the labyrinth of business, and his wife, patronized by Lady Luscombe and tutored by the Count Lestrange, blossomed into the dangerous honour of a fashionable married beauty. It is the old story which wants small re-telling, though I hate to think of Daisy as its heroine. Society adopted her as a queen,—petted, and *fêted*, and pictured her,—and scandal busied herself with her name, though as little, perhaps, as scandal ever did with any of its victims. She knew it, and she shrugged her shoulders, and she went her way. What other way was open to her? I do not know. Her warm friendship for Lady Pepperharrow continued unabated, and Lady Pepperharrow's house became a recognized centre of the whole frivolous world of London, dashed with much of the attractive and un-frivolous, for the hostess still retained her admiration for "genius" in its fullest power, and genius at Glycerine House, or at the country house in Hertfordshire which was afterwards added to it, was as plentiful as caller herrin' after a good haul, some with soft roe, and some with hard. Gradually, slowly, surely Daisy's character deteriorated and hardened in its outward and visible signs, though after events were to prove the tenacity of the inward and spiritual grace.

Mr. Brent occupied the position which husbands in such cases are content to hold; and, like such husbands, liked it, while he snarled at it. The liking was of course reserved for others; the snarling for his wife. Nobody, be it said, ever ventured to say much to Daisy in disparagement of Daisy's husband; for, with a touch of the old masterhood, she put such venture down. She had many struggles with herself. She might have turned *dévote;* but it was not in her, and she could not feign, especially in matters such as that. So she

kept her own counsel in her utter solitude of heart;
and tried once or twice to kindle in her brother some
spark of loving sympathy, but failed. There are few
people so apt, unhappily, to fail utterly under real stress
of heart as those of one's own kindred. There are
few, I am afraid, so prompt to desertion, so quick at
commonplace, so (unwittingly, perhaps) irresponsive to
the chords and cries of feeling. Water is thicker than
blood, in nine cases out of ten. Daisy's brother was
the last thing left to her, and he was a reed that broke
at the first handling. Thanks to his keen intelligence
and subtle power of purpose, she found her best resource
in the talk and the companionship of Count Lestrange;
and gradually, softly, surely, he undermined the faiths
and loyalties of her life.

At home, Mr. John Brent proved himself a past
master of the infamous art of "nagging," which has
wrecked so many homes. Like the dropping water
which wears out the stone, it is the most merciless of
processes, as it is the most difficult to detect. It is an
art, sedulously cultivated. Its special delight is to find
out the weak points in the sufferer's armour, to insult
his or her special prejudices, to calumniate his or her
special friends, to exaggerate and to dwell upon, to
others as well as to the victim, his or her especial
weaknesses, or to invent them when they exist not.
When some explosion has taken place under its influence, the victim is powerless to point out the particular
wound; and on "the facts" is condemned by the
Wehmgericht of kinsmanship as having been guilty
of temper, or quarrel, or anything easy to say, and
economic of trouble to themselves. And he or she—for
masculine or feminine may be the victim—is driven to
ask self the question if self is wrong, and its own senses
and eyes are to be believed. After reiterated proof it
knows and acquits itself, and goes on its way in isolated
scorn. So by degrees it came to be with Daisy.

John Brent was under a restraint with his wife under
which he fretted, fumed, and stormed, to as much

purpose as a small pool jumping at a hundred feet of rock. Thanks to her, he was in a position which he had not anticipated for himself. Mr. Brent's dinners became famous, and he officiated as the figure-head, a position which he had meant her to occupy.

Instead of Mr. Brent's wife, the world only spoke of Mrs. Brent's husband. Still, the world came; and the house in Curzon Street was renowned for the aristocratic contents of the hansoms which waited at its door.

Once, a distant cousin of Daisy's, who had an affection for her, came up from the country at some pains to see her; but only reached the house to find an empty hansom at the door, and to hear that etiquette forbade her to be received, because some great personage was paying a visit. The country-girl went home disappointed, and puzzled about etiquette; and Daisy lost the chance of a friend who might have forgotten the ties of kindred, and been a friend indeed, when a friend was most wanted. She might have risen higher than the family conception of Christianity—"Don't bother me." But the opportunity was lost.

Four years after that ill-omened marriage, the crisis came. As he had done by others, others had done by him. Mr. Brent was outwitted and out-generalled in the tactics of speculation, into which he had been completely drawn; and he found one morning that he had to begin the world again.

While his alarms about this had lasted, he had been to his wife unremittingly and basely cruel; and, bravely as she fought on, had almost fretted her into a nervous illness. She started at night, dreamed miserably, grew thin, anxious, worn, heart-broken almost, under his constant persecution. And alas, and alas! her chief comforter and sole confidant was Lestrange, whose serpentine consolations were a very mint of evil.

Husband and wife were alone together one day, when he told her, brutally, that he was ruined. She remembered how her father, too, had once had the same story to tell; and she looked at him in wonder.

"How long have you known that this was coming?" she asked. "Ruin doesn't come in a moment, as I have learned before."

"I have expected it for some weeks," he snarled.

"Why didn't you tell me before?"

"Why should I?"

"It was your simple duty," she said. "I have not failed in mine to you."

"Not failed!" he answered, with a brutal laugh. "What sort of wife have you been to me? You have deceived me from the first to the last."

"I never deceived any one," she said calmly.

Then he burst into a bitter storm of taunt and anger,—insulted her with the gossip of society, vowed she had dragged his name into the dirt, while she bore it with an unflinching and unmeasured scorn. Then, when he thought, in his perception of character, that by this manly course he had worked upon her to his purposes, he told her that she could save him.

"I again!" she said. "Am I to be always saving men who ruin themselves by gambling, and those who belong to them too? You cannot be ruined either, for you have my money."

"Yours, you pauper!" he said.

Then he told her of the truth she had not known till then, and threw it as another insult in her face. The man was half beside himself with evil rage, and furious with his wife's sovereign calm, unshaken still, though every jot of colour had left her face, save for the light which sparkled in her eyes.

Then he confessed his scheme, some trick he had contrived for a post-nuptial settlement, which only wanted her consent to place them in comfortable security. Of course she would give it, he said; but she very simply declined.

"I can give you no help to defraud your creditors," she said. "If you had not been so anxious to rob me when I married you, you would not have been in this difficulty now. But even had you not, I

would rather give up every penny I had, than help
you in such a scheme as this. I can go out and
work now."

"Work—you? Where?" And he laughed more
savagely than before.

"I don't know. On the stage perhaps; they say
that I can act:—or anywhere."

"Can't you get some of your lovers to help you?"
he sneered. "You must have made a pretty private
purse by this time."

At last the true blood rose, and the true face flushed,
crimson.

I cannot dwell on what followed; but within five
minutes after that infamous word was said, John Brent
had done something which I cannot name; and
Daisy, a red mark burning on her shoulder under her
gown, had dressed herself to go down to Lady Pepperharrow's, and passed out of that shameful husband's life
for evermore.

CHAPTER XX.

JOHN BRENT DEPARTS.

DAISY BRENT threw herself into Lady Pepperharrow's arms in a tempest of shame, passion, and tears,
the stronger for its long repression, and told her
everything. She was past silence with such a sterling
friend and kindly woman now.

"What was she to do?" she said. Did Lady
Pepperharrow think that she was qualified to teach,
that her skill in music or drawing was sufficient for
such a purpose?

All Lady Pepperharrow's kindness and sympathy, all
her personal affection for Daisy, and her resentment at
such evil as this, came to the front at once. She failed

to see that it mattered the least what became of Mr. John Brent, to his wife or to anybody. "Oh, my dear! if you had only married that nice Mr. Faucit, as I once thought you would! But people never do marry the right people now-a-days."

Poor Daisy's heart felt as if a hand had gripped it, and choked her with a sob. Daisy's schemes of teachership her friend scattered to the winds. She was to come and make her home with her at once, and be to her the daughter she had so longed for all her life. What better use could she find for some of all the money which she so honestly devoted to the engagements and amusements of others, than to make her darling Daisy its steward? She had guessed a great deal of her unhappiness with her husband, though it had been loyally concealed to the best of Daisy's power. Daisy, after some discussion of the point, could not find it in her heart to refuse such a welcome refuge after all these storms, so frankly and lovingly offered. Everything kind that her heart could prompt her to say, of the old days, of the old chaperoning, of the old home in Portland Place, and of the girl's father and mother, Lady Pepperharrow poured out in a torrent, kissing and comforting Daisy all the time, and crying over and soothing her. If there was anybody nearly as fond of Daisy as herself, it was her Sir Hugh; and he was as unfeignedly delighted as his wife when the new daughter took her permanent place at the table, at which she had always been so welcome. She would see him suddenly nodding and smiling at her from the peaceful recesses of his chair, and coaxing her to a glass of champagne, which he thought was a panacea in trouble. And as time went on, Daisy Fairfield, after some months of quiet and seclusion, became again the star of the world in which she moved, under the shelter of the Pepperharrows' home.

Two or three days after their separation, John Brent wrote to his wife a miserable, whining, appealing letter, in the hope of inducing her to reconsider her

determination not to accede to his wishes about the
settlement, for which there was still time. He apologized for his conduct to her in an abject way, which
made things worse, as such people have a habit of
apologizing. He had been so driven, so harried, so
wretched, etc., etc. Then he went on to find the scape-
goat for his offences, as in such cases usual also ; and to
Daisy's astonishment and indignation, he laid everything
on the Count Lestrange. Lestrange, he said, had been
his confidant and agent throughout in the matter of his
marriage ; Lestrange it was who had prevented him
from rescuing her father ; and Lestrange who had since
drawn him into fresh and dangerous speculations, and
constantly insinuated into his ear, in a manner which
he could scarcely trace, ill-reports about Daisy.

Lestrange was at Lady Pepperharrow's, as it
happened, on the afternoon of the day when this letter
was received. Daisy, in her straightforward fashion,
called him aside and read him the passage out of it
which concerned him. Lestrange asked if he might
look at the letter, merely raising his eyebrows. Daisy
showed him the last pages. Lestrange read them to
himself, smiling a little, and raising his eyebrows rather
higher. Then he gave the letter back, looked thoughtfully down, then said very courteously, and in a tone of
interest and hesitation,

"Mrs. Brent—excuse me ; but—is your husband
quite right in his mind ? "

"Count Lestrange ! " she said.

"Surely it is rather charitable to think he is not.
Why in the world should I have prevented him from
saving your father ? why in the world should I have
wanted him to marry a woman like yourself ? why in
the world should I have insinuated to him ill-reports
about you ? There is always a grain of truth in this
sort of thing ; and no doubt I have had, in the City and
before that in India, some business relations with Mr.
Brent, as I have with most people. But really I have
too much to do to occupy myself with drawing him

into fresh and dangerous speculations. Why in the name of the monument should I do that, when obviously it profiteth me nothing? 'Whys' are the strongest of arguments. Excuse me, Mrs. Brent, but I am rather surprised, knowing me as you do, that you even spoke to me of such a letter."

She looked at him thoughtfully, and took it back from him, and was moving it to and fro in her right hand as she answered him, in a low voice—

"Because, Count, knowing you as I do, I have never been able to trust you."

"Why not?" he asked, as quietly.

"I don't know," she answered.

"Do you consider that quite fair?"

"I don't know. Perhaps not."

"I suppose I might be offended with other people if they said so," he said in a thoughtful tone; "but somehow, not with you. It strikes me that if I had acted in any interest of my own, I should have been more likely to cross Mr. Brent's desires than to forward them, if I had known anything in the world about them."

"'Whys' are the strongest of arguments. Why?"

"Surely you must know how very deeply I admire you," he said. He said it after a moment's hesitation, with a respect in his manner so absolute that no woman could possibly have quarrelled with it, when he offered it as a defence which she herself had invited. "Your marriage with Mr. Brent was a hard trial to me," he added at once in the same tone, and then instantly changed the subject to some everyday topic with a tact which was above praise, and in spite of herself, made Daisy like him better than she ever had before.

No man, she felt, could have behaved better, or freed himself more completely from a charge at which he might justly have taken offence. She dismissed John Brent's letter from her mind with an infinite contempt, her knowledge of him, unhappily, allowing her to attribute it not to any alienation of mind, but to what she had detected him in a hundred times, the contemptible vice of habitually lying, especially where harm is to be done by it to anybody else. When one has fairly found them out, sinners in this kind must be let alone. It is idle to contradict them, for if you do they sprout up again in a new place like the Hydra's heads. Let them alone; and the heads knock each other's brains out, like the cats of Kilkenny.

Lestrange knew this weakness of Brent's well enough; and like the boy who cried wolf, the wretched Anglo-Indian was justly served by being utterly disbelieved, when by accident he said what was true. Justly served, too, thought Daisy, and with that wondrous equality of justice of which even in the world's punishments we have so many examples, in losing his fortune as he had robbed her father's, punished where he had sinned.

Lestrange only made one more allusion to the letter. "If I had committed a villainy as complicated as Iago's, with even less reason, Mrs. Brent," he said, "there would be something somewhere to convict me of it." Of course there was not.

What did happen, however, was an interview between the Count and Brent, which had the witness of a clerk, and half palsied the little wretch with fear. He had never guessed before what anger meant, in that impassive man, or how dangerous could seem such impassive anger.

"I do not easily forgive people who insult me, Mr. Brent," Lestrange said. "How dared you tell that tissue of falsehoods about me to your wife?"

"What?" screamed the wretched Brent.

"That tissue of falsehoods, sir," answered the other. "Is it not enough that you should have made yourself notorious for your cowardly and brutal treatment of that lady, just when you were on the verge of ruin from these City tricks of yours, that you should venture to slander a man of my character and position?"

"Slander! slander!" writhed Brent. "But it was all true."

"What?" said Lestrange. And he called the clerk in, who was listening already, and nearly tumbled into the room as the glass door was opened in the office which Brent had set up in the City. "I shall require an apology from you for that, written under your own hand, unless you produce instant proof of your calumnious statements about me."

The wretched Brent was like the bird under the snake's charm, and was mastered very soon. Lestrange mixed comfort with his menace, and showed Brent that he had an admirable opening in his old house at Calcutta to begin life over again, even at his age, if he would take his, Lestrange's, advice, and the assistance which, with his influence, he could give him over there, to begin the rebuilding of his fortunes. He could, as it happened, find a place for him at Calcutta worth six hundred a-year, for which his practice and experience would especially qualify him. It would give him, too, plenty of opportunities to scrape a competence together again, if no more.

Brent, who had contemplated ruin, began to whine on the new key of gratitude to his benefactor, and acceded to the two conditions demanded.

The first was, that he should sign his positive denial of the statements he had made to Daisy. So contemptuous was Lestrange upon this matter, that Brent himself began to mistrust his own senses and memory, and signed in the presence of the clerk, who signed too. The second was, that he should by deed transfer to Daisy half of his annual six hundred to place her above dependence.

Here was cause for new rebellion; but Lestrange pointed out how soon the Indian income would increase in his hands, and again spoke with lofty scorn of Brent's treatment of his wife; to him, he said, the noblest woman he had seen. And Brent acceded to everything, and sailed for India unregretted by a dog;

and the clerk described the scene, and Lestrange's magnificent conduct, to his mates and peculiars; and in course of time Daisy knew that, in return for her unjustifiable suspicion of him, Lestrange had spoken for her in a way not usual with him, had found a competence for her husband, and for herself enough to prevent her from feeling a mere dependent even in her dear friend's house, against which the high spirit would have soon rebelled; and had read with her own eyes her wretched husband's witnessed retractation of all that he had said of Lestrange. And so it was that the strange Count became. more and more the guardian, guide, philosopher, and friend of this hard-tried woman.

CHAPTER XXI.

CHECK TO THE COUNT.

Not very long after the events told of in the last chapter, happened one which caused much talk and excitement in the world in which these characters of my story moved. I have spoken of the peculiar ties which connected Marian Vavasour, in the days of her social supremacy, with Count Lestrange. Before the time of her luckless ennoblement nobody ever dreamed of speaking of the intimacy more than as a strong case of mutual friendship and liking, and Lestrange was merely regarded as a familiar intimate at the statesman's house, versed in its ways, and useful to both host and hostess. The growth of the intimacy was so gradual, so unmarked the steps by which the attitude of Lestrange towards Mrs. Vavasour grew into one of almost exclusive social devotion, that the world was very long before it could hint anything ill-natured of an alliance which had been so slow and open of formation.

As long as Mr. Fulke Vavasour's political position

remained to him, and his wife's drawing-rooms continued to be the acknowledged centre for the political
world, scandal was a powerless factor in the matter.
If Lestrange wove in his head the scheme about the
Vavasours of which I have spoken in another chapter;
if in making himself more and more essential to them
both, he never left his purpose out of sight,—he was
above all things determined not in any way to compromise the lady, or allow his name to be prematurely
coupled with hers, in any shape or form. Nothing
could have been less favourable to the fulfilment of
that ambition of his than any untimely catastrophe, or
even rumour, which could in any way prejudice the
social position which was the lady's,—which he meant
to be his own.

That crafty purpose of his once slowly formed,
he could make no false move in playing his game,
as indeed he had begun it for a smaller stake, before
he knew how much might depend upon the issue.
From the moment when he first made the acquaintance
of the Vavasours, he saw that in their house were the
chances to be found of making for himself the influential
position which it was his ambition to hold in England,
apart and away from the smaller diplomacies and
intrigues which had made up his interesting but less distinguished career. He was in no hurry, for he believed
in the preservation of his own youth; and if, like a
distinguished man of our time, he had said that he
"wanted to be prime minister," he might have betrayed
something of his inner thought. But he never said
what he wanted, and nobody ever knew. Gradually, in
Mr. Vavasour's house, he succeeded, through a careful
use of his own social gifts and subtleties, in paving the
way to his destined goal. He became intimate with
the springs of official life, to which the circumstances
of his first introduction to London had given him his
first access; he became favoured of ministers and
trusted of officials, less in the City and more in Downing
Street, and worked upon his way.

He might have found a seat in Parliament more
than once, but with it he would have lost many of
the secret opportunities for influence, which were the
object on which his heart was set for the purpose of
the hour. When he did enter Parliament, as it was
his intention to do, he wanted to be safe, and to
enter it as a man with his way smoothed and made;
he wanted to enter it on the winning side, after one
of those crises of popular feeling when the people,
having enough of one lot, give the other a turn, and
the "national palaver" starts on a new tack in different hands, and reverses the policy of its pre-
decessors, or says it does, before the eyes of an
admiring crowd.

The Horatians, say, have had a seven or fourteen
years' lease of office ; and the Curiatians are justly tired
of it.   The lawyers on the Curiatian benches, especially, are growing clamorous for the loaves and fishes
on which the Horatian advocates are waxing fat and
kicking, while themselves are fed on the bread and
water of opposition.   It is at last discovered, therefore,
that the honour of the country is in danger in Horatian
hands.   Her fair fame is being tarnished by oppression
abroad, where struggling and subject nationalities look
in vain to the land which was once their pole-star
for guidance, for sympathy, and for aid.   The old land-
marks of right and wrong, which should be the one
guidance of peoples for evermore, are becoming obliter-
ated ; and, unless the Curiatians come at once to the
helm, England is practically lost.   The Horatians, in and
out of season assured that they are wicked men, to
whose darkened minds truth is a fable, and honour an
unknown quality, become at last badgered and irritated
into standing it no longer, and appeal to the country
to tell them whether they are wicked men or not.
The Curiatian leaders rush from hustings to hustings,
appeal to Scripture and to Hampden and the rights
of men, and to the glorious records of the Curiatian
past ; for every Horatian measure, which has done any

good to the people, has been, as all the world knows, passed under Curiatian pressure.

Their burning words inflame the people, and wake them to a spirit of crusade against wickedness in general. Even quiet and thoughtful men of letters or of science catch the infection in their studies, forget the eternal law of the cobbler and his last, and rush on to platforms and into committees, much to the detriment of their wives' and children's pockets, to contribute their driblets to the ocean of talk, fairly taken in by the Curiatian moralities, and anticipating an instant dawning of the golden age. The mighty resurrection of all the goodnesses prevails. The people of England come to the hustings in flocks, and emphatically declare virtue is lord, and that the Horatians are wicked men.

All is over. There is much grinning like a dog, and running to and fro in the cities. The Horatians depart from the up platform of Windsor by one train while the Curiatians enter the down by another. The Horatians, who had arrived each with a portfolio under his arm (which to the popular notion suggests something in the nature of a photographic album), depart with the evening newspaper in its place; and in the mysterious recesses of Windsor the albums are handed over to the Curiatians, who on their return to the station display them to the populace with pride.

It is done, and virtue reigns. Then the triumphal Curiatians change their note as fast as they possibly can. They withdraw their accusations of immorality with anxious zeal, disclaiming for their most ferocious utterances anything but a Pickwickian meaning. If there is one thing, they feel with pride, for which all English statesmen are distinguished, it is the high-minded and disinterested earnestness with which each and all of them labour for the good of the people of England, according to their honest views of right. No men have ever been more remarkable for this than the late Horatian government, however mistaken their policy may have been. If in the heat of conflict hard words may have been used, it is now time to forget them. The country has discovered, to their credit be it spoken, that the abilities of honourable gentlemen opposite were not commensurate with their lofty principles, and if the Curiatian brains be of a superior cast, after all that is not the fault of the Horatians.

The Horatians, meanwhile, are not much conciliated, being a good deal angry at having been called so many bad names, and sent to the wall thereby. So they fail at first to see that it is time to forget everything on the spot in a friendly way; and as soon as the Curiatians set to work, or rather before they have had time to do anything, they begin to call names too. The Curiatians find themselves *tu-quoqued*, and taxed with vicious and unpatriotic conduct, before they have been guilty of any conduct at all. They beg the country to wait, and the country, serenely confident of its millennium, does. The "national palaver" braces itself for legislation; and in the very first speeches of the Curiatian chiefs the country detects a new and very different ring. We must conciliate, we must diplomatize, we must be Pickwickian, we must nurse the prejudices of majorities and minorities. Then out of the blue cometh a bolt; and the country, who had really begun to believe in a new era for the oppressed, and in a bolder vindication of the higher moralities as the stronghold of political battle, find that the reign of the strong has begun again indeed; that if the Horatians scourged the weak nationalities with whips the Curiatians will do it with scorpions; that, by whatever rule Russia and Austria are to be judged towards Poland and Hungary, England, Lord bless us, is quite another thing; that to throw away English money abroad is in Curiatian eyes the be-all and end-all of Horatian crime; and that for these same much-professing Curiatians, despotism, like charity, begins at home.

In the palaver, however, the world is in a tale, and

poor deluded old Demos, so much flattered and appealed to a few months before, is told to mind his own business, for discipline is good for him. The misguided man of letters or of science, deserted, angry, powerless, gets him back to his study and exchanges indignant letters with his friends, and wonders what and how soon the end of this world-doomed imperialism is to be, at present all the worse, seemingly, in the stronger hands. For verily the imperialism of the Horatians to that of their conquering rivals, is as a procession at Astley's to a charge of cavalry. The people of England, patient and quiet always, hold their tongues in mortified silence, and leave meetings and agitations, for the most part, to the mere froth of the thing. But they think as much and talk as little, as the noisier section think little and talk much. And they wait for the next battle at the polls, when they are deaf to Curiatian thunder, and stay at home. And amid a blare of town-bands and triumphal articles, history proclaims to the world a new "Horatian reaction." Even so, until the time be ripe—

> " Fu vera historia ? ai posteri
> L'ardua sentenza."

Count Lestrange was waiting for some such crisis as this, as best calculated to bring out his powers, and acquiring meanwhile a full and cautious mastery of the geography of the political chess-board. But no man knows everything ; and he was astray in his calculations when he placed his chief dependence upon his position with the Vavasours.

Mr. Vavasour's bald head, irreproachable dignity, and exceeding reticence, did not impose upon Lestrange himself, but they imposed upon him indirectly. He believed in their effect upon Mr. Vavasour's colleagues as well as upon the world, which regarded him as a type of the hard-working and self-effacing statesman, who acts while others talk. His close attention to details, and interminable though lofty fussiness, carried out the illusion in the official world; and it was regarded as certain that on the next right-about of parties Mr. Vavasour, then in opposition, would hold an especial post for which the public voice designated him.

There was a hustle and a crisis; a vote of confidence in Ministers carried by a narrow majority, and an appeal to the country, which responded by saying that it had even less confidence than the Commons, and incontinently turned them out.

Lestrange did not feel sure, at the time of this election, which way the popular wind really blew, and he waited to be sure.

But when the new Ministry was formed, the catastrophe occurred which has before been told of, and Mr. Vavasour was told off, album-less, to the Lords.

The blow to Lestrange was as great as it was to Marian. He was to have been Mr. Vavasour's right-hand man in his new political office; indeed, it is no secret from the all-knowing chronicler, that the expressions about struggling nationalities, and oppression abroad, and other similar manifestoes, embodied in the election addresses of John Audley Vavasour to his constituents, were the well-balanced periods of Lestrange's pen, which was accustomed to sift everything to its smallest, and in its briefest and most pointed form to set it forth.

He had kept well with both sides in the official world; but his great stake had been set upon Vavasour, with whose party he saw shrewdly enough that the coming mastery in the game lay. That party in office, it was quite understood that the new minister would do his best to further the parliamentary ambitions of his shrewd ally, and to find the money which, even in these degenerate days, can still, though less openly than of old, purchase in some instances senatorial honours. He certainly owed the Count, in consideration of City services rendered to his income, the fullest price of a very safe seat indeed.

Lestrange had seen through the innate dulness of

his patron as well as Marian Vavasour herself; and sedulously had the two laboured together, in alliance unconfessed even to themselves, to conceal it from the world. If Marian was provoked beyond all patience to find that the dulness had been too much for both of them, Lestrange shared her feeling to the full, and proved at once Lady Luscombe's best comforter, as he had been Mrs. Vavasour's greatest stay.

Poor Marian's disappointment and excitement—for had she not made this husband's rise the purpose of her life?—made her more womanly, more gentle, more open with her counsellor, than she had ever been; and he, his next move yet unplanned in the collapse of his game, ventured on an openness of sympathy, and an expression of personal regard and admiration, which he had never approached before. For Marian was essentially the great lady; and Lestrange's instincts were wonderfully true, however he perverted them in use. They were to him now as a second nature, born of assiduous cultivation, not of the heart, but of its best social substitute, tact.

In the long, long talk they had together, the new Lady Luscombe fairly opened her heart to her friend, and gave him a full understanding, much as he had already guessed, of that chilled and isolated heart. She had never before been so open with any one; and perhaps for the first time in her life did she allow any one to see her in tears.

It was in the course of that talk that she let him know the secret so carefully concealed, that her husband's heart was seriously affected. Steady official work, the doctor had said, would be its best palliation, though it could not be a cure. Frets and excitements would be its worst irritants.

Then and there, at once, the Count Lestrange decided on his new game.

From that day he became more and more with Lady Luscombe; more and more to her. "La calumnia è un venticello," and that wicked little wind began to blow

about in the new circles which gradually formed round
Lady Luscombe. She was born to be a leader in
society, and she remained so; but the society gradually
changed. Her political influence was gone, and indeed
she was too indignant and too mortified to care to keep
it. The life she led became of the more strictly
fashionable, the more socially exclusive, the more
entirely frivolous.

Soon she lived for society alone, in its mere confined
sense, and society rejoiced in her leadership. Fashionable beauties and indolent youth formed the crew of
the new craft, where a looser tone of manners and of
morality prevailed than on board the older vessel.

If Lady Luscombe heard of the rumours which
gathered round her and Lestrange, she paid them no
attention, and went on her own way. One thing she
did at last; when he was abroad upon some mission or
another, she wrote to him, and she wrote more than once.
She would have been startled enough if she had seen the
expression upon his face when he read the letters.

"You will be the Countess Lestrange now," he said
to himself, "I think, my handsome Marian; whether
you still call yourself Lady Luscombe or no."

And all this time Lestrange was able in his own
way to devote himself to the education of Daisy Brent,
who had become the reigning beauty of the Luscombe
set. He amused himself, sometimes, by playing her
off against the wakeful jealousies of Lady Luscombe,
who brooked no rival near the throne. But he was
always able to soothe and smooth such jealousies away;
and the rumours grew. Lord Luscombe knew nothing
about them, and pottered on contentedly enough to his
wife's annoyance, devoting himself to county politics
and Luscombe Abbey, and becoming great at quarter-
sessions, and an authority on scientific farming.

But it happened that about the time when John
Brent left England, Lord Luscombe received a letter
when he was alone at the Abbey, which made him start,
and mutter, and bite his lips. And the next evening,

unexpectedly, he made his appearance at Lusmere House during a great reception which his wife was holding, and showed himself cantankerous, ill-tempered, peculiar. Especially unpleasing and repellent was his manner to Lestrange, who smoked a cigar or two more than usual that evening in his chambers before he went to bed. But the next morning Lord Luscombe was quiet and civil to his wife and to everybody, as he remained. But he took to asking various people questions, and to mysterious colloquies which he kept to himself. With Lestrange he was as confidential as ever, and involved himself again in some City matters, to which he had been paying no attention of late. The Luscombe rent-roll was very large indeed now. He got excited over these and other things, and the doctor was grave with him, very grave; and one day he sent for his lawyer, who was with him for a few minutes only. Lady Luscombe knew that he had been; and Lestrange soon knew it; and a vague uneasiness took possession of both of them. The uneasiness did not continue long, for Lord Luscombe was seized with a bad attack, and after a few days' illness, during which he could not speak, he died. And the talk and excitement, which the opening of this chapter recorded, followed when it became generally known that the dead peer had a few days before appended to his will, which left everything unentailed to his wife, a codicil which revoked it unconditionally if she should marry again.

CHAPTER XXII.

THE PARTHIAN DART.

It was a matter of some days after the contents of Lord Luscombe's will had become known before Lestrange and the new-made widow could bring themselves to meet. To both it was a crushing blow; for if she did not acknowledge it to herself, Marian had allowed the hope of a genuine love, and of the reality of married happiness at some future day, to spring up in her solitary heart. Without allowing any difference in his manner to be perceptible, after he had learned how frail was Lord Luscombe's tenure of his leasehold, Count Lestrange had none the less allowed that manner to grow very different; and in the four years which had passed between the formation of his grand plan and its sudden and final frustration, he had displayed to Marian Luscombe a constant and watchful tenderness, an unfailing respect and devotion, which had won her heart and will completely for his own. He at all events set as much store by his conquest of the second, as by gaining the first. He was able to guard himself from any suspicion of ulterior motive by letting her trace his increased interest in her to her burst of confidence in him, not in the especial nature of the confidence. He dwelt upon the manner in which her frank confession of isolation and disappointment had touched him, and found a thousand ways of showing her how deep was his sympathy, and how thoroughly he, at least, understood the misunderstood life of whose pages she had given him a glimpse.

At first, that indomitable pride of hers had taken the alarm when she thought over all she had said to him—she who so prided herself. upon her self-sufficing nature. She was sensitively on her guard for any sign of disrespect from Lestrange to her husband, who was still her husband. Why had she allowed herself, even in her first passion of disappointed ambition, to speak of him to any-one as she had to Lestrange? For in that interview she had dropped her wearisome mask altogether, and poured out all her difficulties with her husband's dulness and obstinacy, all the efforts she had made to nurse his position and credit, and her ceaseless trials under his cold and irresponsive nature at home, in language of unconcealed scorn. Lestrange was far too good a judge of character to mistake her;

far too keen a player to make any false move in his game. While he threw into his manner to the wife at once that increase of sympathy and watchfulness, to the husband he showed himself, in the same way, more attentive than before. He was more courteous and deferential to him than he had been, not less; and advised him, taking care that the advice and the quarter it came from should at once reach Marian's ears, to withdraw as much as possible from the excitement of London and of City politics, and to devote himself to the quieter pursuits of a county magnate. Very soon had Lestrange assured himself of the gravity of the doctor's verdict, and become convinced that the end was at best a question of a very short time. He would retard it if he could, not accelerate it; and again he could be conscious of a good action. As a matter of fact, it was advisable that he should be thoroughly secure of his reversion before the end came. Marian was touched by the interest he showed, and grateful for this thoughtfulness for her husband, which was so palpably free from any unworthy or interested motive. More than once, never off his guard, Lestrange allowed her eyes to detect him in the act of watching Lord Luscombe with an expression of anxious sympathy and interest, drawing him away from some conversation in which he seemed likely to show unusual excitement, and with his quiet, restful tones and sleepless tact, soothing the peer into the placid blessedness of his natural self-satisfaction. From the moment when he made up his mind to do it, Lestrange knew well how to win the world-trained and world-worn heart which had never spoken for living man before, and by slow and sure degrees he conquered her for his very bond-slave through her pride.

Infinitely dexterous was the use he made, in the pursuit of his all-absorbing purpose, of his intimacy with Daisy Brent. He played his game with the great advantage, which under such circumstances it is, of perfect coolness on his side. If he had been capable of loving Marian, he would have transgressed etiquette, and would have alarmed her pride. So he was able to observe the advice of the old saw— " Pique her and soothe her turn by turn "—with the experimental curiosity of the practised duellist, playing with the foil of a raw adversary. He experimented, and amused himself with sundry passes for show and for self-gratification, in his duel to the death in which he meant to win.

While Daisy remained unsuspicious of any ulterior aim, and flirted and danced upon the frivolous way on which she had now resolutely set her foot, to find in the flowers which strewed it, if she could, a Lethe for the wasted intellect and wearied heart, he worked upon Marian Luscombe more and more through her; and more and more Marian Luscombe and he became coupled and united, while Lord Luscombe grew yet more lost to London sight, till the catastrophe recorded at the end of the last chapter came upon the two.

Lestrange's baffled wit and broken scheme betrayed him into a first anger terrible to see, had any one but his valet and factotum, Chaffers, been in his chambers to see it. Even there, his very rage was dangerous in its suppression; in the dead-white face, which every jot of colour had left to the lips, closed tight over the teeth; in the clenched hands and caged walk up and down, and the fierce curses muttered deep under his breath. " Where had he made his mistake ? " he thought ;· " he who had watched every point in his game like a lynx, and stopped the earth as he went everywhere. But a few weeks before he had been as indispensable to Lord Luscombe as to his wife, and trusted and consulted by him upon every petty point, at every turn. Where had been his mistake, where ? "

He sat down and growled ; and out of a casket which he unlocked he took out a small bundle of letters and counted them.

" No, they are all there ; none of them can by the merest chance have come under Luscombe's eyes."

Then he read the letters over and over again to
himself, and laughed bitterly enough.

"Frank and open enough, certainly, and not meant
for publication. What a fool Marian was to write them.
With such a weapon in my hands, I was armed against
any refusal on her part if she had been inclined to
make it; not that she would have been. I never saw
a woman more in love in my life. And all for nothing
—nothing—nothing. Good Heavens! I shouldn't be
surprised if she expected me to come forward and
marry her for love. When clever women once become
fools, they are capable of any folly, and of suspecting
men of the same capacity too. I had better burn the
letters. She might get hold of them, and appeal to
them as a weapon against me."

He took up the poker in his left hand and held the
letters over the fire. Then he reflected, and put the
poker down.

"No, I won't," he said; "I never throw away a
weapon. I've got to find a new line of battle, and no
one knows what may serve. Great Heaven! it is too
maddening, just when I thought my life's battle won
at last. More than half my life over, and I have to
begin again! Am I to go on living on nothing, never
secure of the next six months, to the end of my days?
Curse that dull-witted old lord—curse him—curse him!
To have a career in a million blighted, and by such as
he! I'll keep these idiotic letters, if only to spite his
widow. Now let me go into the park and think."

He locked the letters carefully away in the casket
with the little key which never left his chain, and he
went out.

"Shall you dine at home, Count Lestrange?" asked
Chaffers submissively as he went.

"I don't know. Don't bother me."

He went out into the wilderness of Hyde Park,
where within a few yards of the world's busiest corner
the world leaves a solitude, and he wandered about
among the paths and on the grass, switching with his

cane at the long grasses and wild-flowers which grew
about, smoking a cigar with less deliberation than usual
with him, and in spite of himself and all his trained
self-mastery, uttering an occasional audible interjection
which made a casual actor lift his head from the bench
on which he was studying his part, set him down as
"one of the profession," and go on again.

Once he turned round in his walk, and found himself face-to-face with a rosy nurse-maid, wheeling about
a little Box and Cox in a comfortless perambulator, with
their two little heads hanging out over the two sides
of the vehicle on the verge of unconscious dislocation.
The rosy nurse-maid, whom he had passed the moment
before, had opened both her eyes to a wider width, and
her mouth to match them, and oblivious of her duties,
was staring at Lestrange.

The lesson brought him to his senses at once; he said
something good-natured to the girl with an easy laugh,
and went away, leaving her to resume her ordinary
walk of life, and shake the heads of her two charges
violently into their proper angle on their necks again.

He wandered away the afternoon; he hailed a
hansom and drove the round of Regent's Park once or
twice; he dined in the quietest corner of the club he
had most recently joined, where he was least known;
and he went home to his chambers later at night than
usual, after more than the usual allowance of cigars,
planless still to any special purpose. What in the
world was he to do? Well—he must bide his time.
Something would happen to give him a new lead.
Wait sometimes on events, he thought, and events will
wait on you.

Events, however, failed the Count this time, and
gave him no special lead which might point to a secure
future. If he had been able to see in this crisis of his
life one of those calls to better things which come to all
of us, his brains and his connection would have found
him, soon enough, plenty of solid and worthy work to
do. But he had no ears for any such call as that.

When he met Marian Luscombe next, it was a
hard trial for both of them; but it became harder still
for her, when she read in the face so studiously impassive none of the sympathy the poor lady had been
yearning for, but a something new and undefinable,
which flashed to her startled nerves the electric message
of a formless fear. He looked as hard and as cruel as
death; for as the natural consequence of the feelings in
which he had been indulging since the shock of Lord
Luscombe's will came upon him, he who had never
loved her had passed into a deep phase of hate. If she
did not quite know that—out of her woman's nature,
hardened as it had been, could not know it—she knew
that there was some bitter change. She had nothing
to reproach herself with; what was it?

The feeling which had grown up in her heart for
Lestrange, unlicensed and half-confessed though it may
have been, had in its way softened her, though but for
a sad end; and the reflections which that feeling had
caused, working in a direction exactly opposite to that
in which they had acted on Lestrange, had really
brought her to think that out of such apparent evil
might come good.

She was free to accept Lestrange's hand after a
proper lapse of time; and she said to herself that she
was ready to do so, and to give up her fortune for
his sake, who had all the brains and means to work for
her, if he had the will, as surely he must have. Was
he not bound to offer so to do? Would not the world
talk cruelly of both of them, and whisper its bitter
sarcasms behind their backs about the true meaning of
her husband's will? That was the hardest part of all
her trial; as to him, who hated the very thought of
ridicule, it was the hardest too. She saw the way to
meet and brave it; he did not. So that their first
meeting was very terrible to her.

Whatever his first feeling and her suspicion of it,
however, he was able after the first to suppress all signs
of it, and to speak to her with all due sympathy, while

careful to commit himself in no wise. By various questions he tried to arrive at the reasons of Lord Luscombe's conduct, and he saw she knew, though she fenced with the subject naturally enough, and shrank from every allusion.

One day, however, when in his own subtle way, at which she could not take offence, he had pressed her hard, she put without a word a letter in his hands.

"I found this letter among my husband's papers," she said. "It is anonymous; and from the date he has marked upon it,—'Received the —— day of ——, 18—,'—he had it on the day when he last came up to town. Nobody has seen it but he and I, to my knowledge. Perhaps you should see it too. Read it, and see if you know the writer."

She gave him the letter, and got up from her seat and left the room. He took it, and he looked at it, and started as if he had been stung. It was a puling, unmanly, miserable thing, as such things are; much affecting manliness and sincerity, and putting Lord Luscombe on his guard against a danger of which, according to the writer, all the world was talking. Did not Lord Luscombe know why he was persuaded to be always in the country? did not Lord Luscombe know what was going on in town? was it not fitting that the eyes of one of his lofty position and high character should be opened to the reflections that were being cast on both, and on his name, by his wife and a man he knew too well—whose name he would not mention, though from the hints he gave, Lord Luscombe would easily discover it. He, the writer, would not sign his name, for reasons which Lord Luscombe would guess and appreciate; but the facts Lord Luscombe, if he mistrusted him, could easily verify for himself. All he asked in return for the warning,—which, as a warm admirer of Lord Luscombe's career, he could not in his conscience help giving, now that he was on the point of leaving England for several years,—was that Lord Luscombe would never say a word of his letter to any one.

And Lestrange read the poisonous letter through and through, artfully contrived as it was-to sting Lord Luscombe in every detail; and through the clumsy disguise which confused the handwriting, he knew in a moment that the writer was John Brent.

CHAPTER XXIII.

DESCENSUS AVERNI.*

JOHN BRENT had taken a characteristic revenge, and a deadly one. Sitting in a chair with the letter before him, the schemer recognized his own impotence to sway events precisely to his liking, with a sense of failure new to him. He had never failed before in anything he meant to do, and now he had broken down over the most important stake for which he had ever played, through the thick-wittedness of one of his puppets and the small spite of another. That this blow should come from such a quarter as Brent especially irritated him. He had held the man in such unutterable scorn, had amused himself so much over his infinite littleness, and had so completely controlled him, that he could not have believed in his venturing to revolt.

"So clumsily, too!" he thought to himself, as he examined Brent's awkward essays in falsifying his handwriting. "But it is always so. The roughest hands spoil the finest webs. D— the man! what a reptile it is; I wouldn't have given him credit for brains enough even for such a dirty move as this. Just after I had got him that place, too! Ungrateful little brute." The Count Lestrange honestly conceived himself a deeply-injured man; and his reflections took the turn of high moral indignation. King Lear himself could not have resented

* All downhill.

ingratitude more. But then and there a new purpose
came into his mind, which, as he thought matters over,
gave his face an expression which would have warned
any one who saw it off him like a signal of danger.
"You shall repent this to a purpose, Mr. John Brent,"
he said to himself, when his reflections were at an end.
"I give you some six years to mend your fortunes in;
and when you come home you shall find a bed of nettles
to lie on. The shallow idiot! suppose I robbed him of
the place I found for him, by a stroke of the pen?
Most men in my case would; but I shan't do that yet,
though I may some day. A bad day's work all round,
that letter of yours." Count Lestrange merely shrugged
his shoulders when he spoke of the letter to Marian,
and told her that he had no idea who the writer could
be. He asked to keep it, on the chance of being able
to find out; and she left it in his hands.

Four years more went by upon their course, and
brought no striking change in the position or the lives
of the characters of this our story. But it was a time
for three of them, of slow and sure deterioration in
different degrees of kind. When it became clear to
her that Lestrange had no intention whatever of claiming her hand without its hereditaments, the heart of
Marian Luscombe hardened into stone. While her
husband lived, she would not own to herself any feeling
which could amount to disloyalty to his name, though
under the name and guise of friendship, upon which
Lestrange had carefully traded and played, she had
admitted the Count to such a dangerous place in her
familiar thoughts and life. She remembered the letters
she had written to him but vaguely, and could not
answer to herself how nearly friendship, in the expression of them, might have trodden upon the heels
of another partnership. One day—it was many months
afterwards—he reminded her of them.

"My letters to you, Count?" she said. "Why, you
burned them."

"No, I didn't," he answered.

"Count Lestrange! you said you had."

"Did I? It was a mistake, and I must have been thinking of something else. I seldom burn letters, for one never knows what may happen."

"But—but," cried Lady Luscombe, "you promised me, on your word as a gentleman."

"Surely not," he said. "Do you think a gentleman has no feelings, Marian?" He spoke in a tender and respectful voice, with a mocking devil in the eye.

"Feelings—you—feelings!"

A great sob rose in Lady Luscombe's throat, and she walked away from him to the window. After her husband's death, and after the reading of that cruel will, she had realized what her feeling for this adventurer had become. Till the will robbed her of the future, she never definitely thought of what that future might have become. But then she did—deeply and hopefully, till the first sight of Lestrange dispelled her dream. Then, things went on as before. The man was in her heart, and she could not root him out; could not help hoping that some day, before it was quite too late, he would be touched by the love which he had so sedulously won, and make for himself some position by the right of which he might claim her. Nor did he relax his hold over her a jot. If he could not have her hand, he had still some use of her fortune, and Luscombe Abbey and Lusmere House were head-quarters not to be abandoned. So still he kept up, with cynical skill, the tradition of tenderness and devotion; still he stayed with her, played with her, consorted with her. And the world, which, as they both feared, had commented with much of sympathetic malice on the nine days' wonder of Lord Luscombe's will, began to shrug its respectable shoulders more and more. Marian had faced the first looks and the first whispers with impassive face and indomitable pride; and Lestrange had let no sign escape him, either of disappointment or form of personal interest in the matter. He openly spoke of the will, when he did speak of it, as a cruel thing to the widow, and as an unpleasing finale to Lord Luscombe's life and character. And as time went on, the world, though it did shrug its shoulders, accepted the alliance between the wealthy Lady Luscombe and the fashionable Count as one of its licensed eccentricities, and dined and danced at her house as of old.

It was after Lady Luscombe had shown some sign, as she sometimes did, of a wish to break with Lestrange altogether, and to shake off an influence which was too much of a mastery, that the episode of the letters occurred. Lestrange used them as a power, and recurred to them again and again, with every circumstance of art and malice, to strengthen his hold over Marian. He succeeded in misleading her memory and mind altogether as to the terms in which they had been written, which he exaggerated, bit by bit, till he made them an unsleeping cause of fear to her; for he more than hinted that he might one day find means to make them public, if she showed any hesitation about lending herself and her fortune to any of his schemes of self-interest. Fearing him, shrinking from him, angry with herself or his influence, but jealous when he showed signs of devotion to any one else, Marian Luscombe became Lestrange's bond-slave, deaf to other voices when it but pleased him to charm her. His motive in all this seemed insufficient enough, but for the light which in an earlier chapter I attempted to throw on such a character as his. The shock of Lord Luscombe's will, and the discovery of Brent's letter, had aggravated all the evil of the man into a finished fine art, and rooted out every scruple of which yearning and appealing good had left so much as a grain behind. "*Totus, teres, atque rotundus,*" the adventurer came out of that ordeal just as this—

"The most replenished villain in the world."

He hated Marian as he hated Brent, and as before long he hated Daisy.

Daisy Brent went downwards on the Avernian

path in her own way, meanwhile. That way had never much harm in it really, I think; for the loyal nature was siege-proof in the citadel, against the whole army of temptation. But some out-works were carried, perhaps. The misery of her life with her husband, with its strain of petty and unremitting mental torture, had gone far to spoil the sweetest woman on the earth. But with the better nature strong in her, and scornful of herself far more than of others, she let the current of her new life bear her on.

She heard nothing of her husband, would not hear; and the thoughts of Guy Faucit, never-ending, never-dying, she crushed like serpents out of her heart, and crushed out half her sweetness with them. She cultivated her beauty; she prided herself in her beauty; and as she matured and ripened in her womanhood, it put forth new shoots of honour every day. She laughed and she joked; she sang and she acted; she was the pride of the papers and the photographers; she teased good old Lady Pepperharrow, who worshipped the very ground she trod on; and when good placid Sir Hugh, full of his years and his wife's honours, was gathered to his honest fathers, she devoted her time and her energies to the task of unselfish consolation. She had not been so much her old self since she left her husband's house with that mark under her dress. She reigned supreme in the court of folly and frivolity which buzzed and trifled round her; she flirted with reckless impartiality with every courtier there, and let no one of them flatter himself that he had gained a foothold in her heart. Woe to him who passed the boundary; for he never came near to it again.

Now it fell out that, one day, the Count Lestrange transgressed. I am not careful to record the why or the how, or to tell how gradually, while keeping Lady Luscombe in his power, he allowed his admiration for Daisy to draw him on. It was in an outburst of jealousy of her that Marian brought upon herself the first scene about the letters. Careful and watchful always, bent upon his revenge on John Brent, and confident as ever in his own magnetic power, the Count Lestrange fancied at last that he had won Daisy's heart, and one day he let her know it.

The adventurer had blundered again, and shrank into himself under her flash of indignant honour. For she stood at her full height; she spoke of Lady Luscombe with personal regard; her bright colour and her angry eyes framed and lit up a lofty picture of unmeasured scorn; and he met his match, did the Count Lestrange. But he knew the falseness of his move in a moment, and he repaired it as far as it could be repaired before more harm was done. He persuaded Daisy that he had been led away; he did all in his power to soothe and to disarm her, and finally persuaded her to say no word of what had passed. After all, alas! these things were too much the way of the half-conscienced world in which they lived. She had encouraged him, perhaps, as with an air of honourable and repentant mortification he intimated that she had. So she spared him and held her tongue, and let things be as they were again, as far as she could, though studiously on her guard from that moment with Count Lestrange. As for him, he was more upon his guard than she; and, accepting the position he had made for himself, never again let look or word escape him which could suggest offence.

And so, gradually, the influence of the man's mind and will re-established its old sway over Daisy's intellect. But a new purpose began to shape itself in his active brain.

"Wrong again, was I?" he thought to himself at home. "That is a very inaccessible character. 'Tu me lo pagherai,' John Brent, though, for all that. I wonder what on earth has become of the man called Faucit?"

The man called Faucit travelled all those years away, bearing the mark upon his heart invisible and

uneffaced, like the preacher's counterpart of Hester
Prynne's scarlet letter. His love for Daisy had gathered
round all the roots of his life, and no new growth was
possible for them, till the tree should decay and die for
lack of sap. He lived the wildest of wanderer's lives :
in the bush and in the desert, on sea or on prairie,
anywhere but in towns. Most of all he loved the
strange haunts and strange ways of the men of the
sierras, whom Bret Harte has sung. He had enough to
live on, with his simple healthy ways of life; and he
made himself something of a name too, though he
carefully concealed his personal identity, by some
stirring sketches of that stirring life, in prose and
verse, which he published in America. Some echoes
of them came to England, and Daisy Brent, casting
her eyes over a set of magazine-verses one day, started
and dreamed. So ran the lines—

IN TWO WORLDS.

UNDER the forest, of its snows unladen,
   And kissing back the nervous kiss of spring,
I sit and dream of courtly knight and maiden,
   And old-world pomp encompassing a king.

Out of her wintry sleep the earth is waking,
   And birds and flowers carol her *réveillé;*
O'er West and East the common promise breaking,
   Breathes the first whisper of their holiday.

Without, the mighty forms of things primeval
   Stand all untenanted of Custom's robes ;
Within, my mind shapes pictures mediæval
   With pencil fashioned forth in other globes.

The rugged miners share my board and pillow,
   And by the camp-fire sing their lawless song;
But at a bound my thought o'errides the billow,
   And breasts the strong surf with a flight as strong.

What do I here, among the waving grasses,
   Which never learned to trim their graces wild ?
While by my side Nature's rude army passes,
   Another world still claims me for her child.

In vain I ply the axe in pass or clearing;
  In vain I fill me with the unfettered air;
Still to my eyes are other scenes appearing,
  Still my heart hearkens the low voice of care.

Among our ranks no woman comes to harm us,
  And sow us discord for our hands to reap;
No wiles and jars allure us or alarm us,
  Or wanton with the mighty arm of sleep.

Yet here, for me, though heart and will are master,
  As strong as iron and as calm as death,
The will will waver and the heart beat faster,
  Touched by the memory of a woman's breath.

Why are ye here, rude fellows of my labour,
  Thus outlawed from the bounds of woman's reign?
Read I, beneath the swart hues of my neighbour,
  Another story of another pain?

She said she loved me—and one day she left me
  Without a warning and without a word;
Of past and future at a blow bereft me,
  The cause unspoken, and the plea unheard.

Behind me honour, and high hopes before me,
  A life of earnest and a name of worth:
Her glamour shed the bright delusion o'er me,
  Her presence kept the promise of my birth.

Then fell the blow, and past and future shivered
  Just at a fairy finger's heartless touch;
And from the bondage of a lie delivered,
  I laughed that I had trusted overmuch.

Laughed! and the echo of that hollow laughter
  Rings in my heart with one eternal knell;
And the slow years which rolled their burden after,
  With all the burden cannot crush the spell.

Pines of the Sierras, spread your mantles round me
  And hide me from the past, untrodden West!
Oh that the free lands and free souls that bound me,
  Could break the fetters of my prisoned breast!

In vain, in vain! not the dividing ocean
  With all its storms one memory can drown;
While the vexed phantom of a lost devotion
  Still in the tortured bosom dies not down.

' Up and to work! the western spring invites me,
And Freedom calls me forth among the free;
But no—nor work nor freedom here delights me;
The eastern bondage falls again on me.

Eight years after the day when first he met Daisy, the wearied spirit brought Guy Faucit home to England again.

CHAPTER XXIV.

THE COUNT LESTRANGE'S WAGER.

IT was the fag-end of the London season, when the world is melting away to its pleasures and its holidays abroad and at home, when the active rush to mountain-climbing or to moor-shooting, and the indolent or over-eaten go off to German spas, and swell the coffers of Dr. Kurgemess, who is saved the trouble of prescribing anything for anybody except water, and would justly be suspected if he did. Others who are less troubled about their digestion, or less able to pander to it, follow the call of Custom, and desert their homes and their comforts for the unequalled wretchedness of sea-side lodgings, happily to the unfeigned delight of the infantry, who are made the excuse for the proceeding in most cases. Much as the Londoner vaunts his London, he spends most of his time there in considering where he is "going to" next; while the country-cousin, whose tastes or profession let him keep out of the maelstrom, may sit under the shadow of his vines in peace, and wander afield only when the fancy prompts him.

"O fortunati nimium, sua si bona nôrint,
Agricolæ."

In nine cases out of ten, the agricole sees it not, and thinks that he is wasting his days and bushelling his light out of London.

The fag-end of the season always found the Count Lestrange in town, unless he happened to be absent on one of his mysterious errands of private diplomacy abroad. For the fag-end of the season meant that he was more in request with the fag-enders than any man, with his exhaustless store of information and anecdote, and his pleasant capacity of being all things to all men.

It was only when the last roses of summer had ceased to bloom on the London dinner-tables, that Lestrange was off to carry on the social war in a round of country-houses, beginning with a campaign of deer-stalking or grouse-shooting in the North, and subsiding into the milder excitements of partridges and pheasants in due course of calendar.

Very soon in his English life had Lestrange realized that for an outsider who wants to become a social power, the royal road to the heart of the male British Philistine lies through the gun-barrel. So, being one of those happily constituted persons who do everything well to which either taste or circumstance leads them to turn their hands, he made himself a crack shot, without caring for sport the least in the world. Indeed, his utter absence of all excitement in the matter was probably one of his chief secrets of success.

I am myself a man of peace, who only carried a gun four times, and grew rather "mixed" over it. The first time, I discharged it at an untimely landrail when it was exactly a yard from my feet, and blew the creature into so many pieces that nothing but an odd feather or two was ever found. The second, I fired at my first and only snipe, a parlous bird to hit at the best of times, and nigh out of gun-shot; and with an inward wonder carefully concealed, I found that I had slain him. The third time, now confident of my powers, I took long and deliberate aim at a sitting rabbit within easy distance, who did not seem to mind me the least; and he was perfectly justified, for I missed him. The fourth, made to carry a friend's gun under protest over a field or two (there are friends who will do it still), I became lost in my own literary meditations, and forgot entirely where I was till an indignant keeper told me that I had just neglected a whole covey of partridges which had offered me a choice of shot, and were disappearing. I blankly gazed at their retreating forms; and, ungratefully, but with entire unconsciousness of a guilty motive, discharged my friend's gun straight at him. I missed him, too; but he made such a Vokes-like bound into the air, that for the moment I thought I hadn't. He never asked me to carry his gun again. And I think that he must have whispered the tale abroad; for nobody else has, either. Whereof I rejoice.

No such sins as these had Lestrange to atone for; and many a hardened cover-haunter was jealous of the cool prowess of his steady gun. In the evenings, his talk and his song were as welcome to the women as his sportsmanship had been to the men; and he brought with him to the table of Crabtree Hall all the latest intelligence gathered in the rooms of Lady Backbite, where he had been staying last.

The Count Lestrange could live at free quarters pretty well all the year, if it pleased him. And for a substantial part of the year it did. But his chief resource was, and remained, Luscombe Abbey.

It was on a July afternoon, then, as the last London month was drawing to a damp close,—the Derby had been run that year in a snow-storm, and some casual thunder-storms were all the heat that had vouchsafed itself,—that a bright fire was burning in Lestrange's chambers, somewhere off Piccadilly, among the curious little impasses of the Mayfair maze.

They were good and comfortable rooms, oddly furnished out of all parts and corners of the world, till they might have passed for a museum in little. Strange skins of strange beasts; gaunt curiosities of China or Japan; stuffed birds of tropical parti-colour; assegais and cross-bows, and muskets of antique formation; rare gems of painting and of bric-à-brac; carved chairs and couches of rich mellow wood; fantastic curtains

Q

artistically looped and draped; these things, and things like them, made up the Count Lestrange's interior. And he had so planned and so arranged its general tone and background, with a view to harmony of colour, that the whole effect was as of "a study in reds and blacks."

"A hot fire for July, even a cold one," thought the man Chaffers to himself, as he occupied himself in the arrangement of the rooms where he was the ministering acolyte. "But the Count likes it. He's an odd man, my master."

The stealthy man who acted as the Count's servant was gliding about the sitting-room of Lestrange's suite, which contented itself with being a suite of two, after the fashion of the older lodging-houses. His bed-room and dressing-room combined was separated from the other by the central folding-doors which make the despair of English dramatists, accustomed to the side-doors of their French brethren, and finding them not—when they want to hide Lady Barbara, or to withdraw the lover unobserved by a private way, with the assist-ance of the chambermaid on the left, just as the indig-nant parent enters by the right, and discovers the ingenuous daughter seated at her work, centre. What is the wretched playwright to do with one sitting-room opening blank into another, with no relief but another door opening out just at the side of it, upon the same staircase? "Doors at back in flat" are as part of his stock in trade, and the British architect rarely pro-vides them.

Was it in deference to some dramatic instinct that Lestrange's two rooms did possess a sort of appendix, in the shape of a narrow strip of a chamber opening into the drawing-room only, and like it facing the street through a slip-window?

People were facetious about that little room, and called it the Blue Beard chamber, the laboratory, the confessional, any name which occurred to them. By rights it should have been devoted to the uses of

Chaffers, who was indeed allowed to make a sitting-room of it at times. But his master did not love too much proximity, even in his useful case, and relegated him to a bed-room in the upper regions.

The ear of Chaffers caught a sound at the door, and the parlour-maid of the establishment came in. He had heard a ring at the door-bell first, and had looked out and smiled.

"Is the Count at home, Mr. Chaffers?" said the girl, a spruce and trim handmaiden, with no suspicion of the "slavey." The Count's landlady understood his ways too well for that; and her reverence for her lodger was the first article of her social faith.

"Yes, Miss Hannah."

Hannah's pretty cap withdrew itself, and silks and satins rustled in its place. The lady who wore them threw up her veil from her face, and she looked quickly and impatiently round the room.

"Where is the Count, Chaffers?" she asked, with the way of one familiar with the rooms. "I want to see him at once."

"Yes, my lady," answered the man, as with a scarcely perceptible knock at the folding-doors he disappeared into the bed-room.

Lady Luscombe, for it was she who was the visitor, looked round and round with a strained and eager look, and threw herself into an oaken arm-chair, which stood like a senator's seat of office by the round table in the middle of the room. Impatiently she tapped her foot, and impatiently she moved her head, as with her hands she pushed back from her face the bands of the whitened hair.

"I must make one more effort before I leave town, hopeless as it seems," she thought; and again the Asmodeus of romance caught the unspoken soliloquy. "My letters! If he would give me back my letters! Fool that I was, to be so led on. But that man would lead on anybody to do what he wishes, with his strange eyes, his strange talk, his fatal fascination. With

Q 2

any one else I shouldn't feel afraid, I think, for what could he do? What would he have the heart to do, if he could? Heart!" and a sad and bitter smile crossed her face. "He has none—none. He has never forgiven me my husband's cruel will, and the terrible clause which went so deeply home. I am afraid of him! afraid! afraid! and I don't know even now' whether I love him or hate him. Sometimes it is one, I think, sometimes the other. But I'am always afraid of him. What were those letters? what did they say?" the next thought said, and Lady Luscombe was on he feet again looking about the room. "I never can remember how far I trusted him. My conscience longs to feel clear; but I am always trying to recall the words I wrote to him, and I can't. Would they spell ruin, as he says? And why should I care for ruin or for anything else, in the blank life which mine has turned to? But I do care, and the thought of those letters keeps me in a fever. Where does he keep them —where?" And she began angrily to turn over the cards and letters which lay on the table in a queer old plate of Dresden red, after the impetuous fashion of the young wife in the 'Pattes de Mouche.' "And why does he keep me waiting?" she muttered at last. "If he doesn't come soon, Daisy will be here to fetch me."

She began her idle search again, even throwing open some drawer in the writing-table between the windows, and thrusting her hand among the scattered papers. At her back the folding-door was quietly opened, and the Count Lestrange was in the doorway, watching her with an amused smile. He wore the short velvet coat which was his home alternative to the frock-coat and swallow-tail of decorum, and there was no trace of white in his hair, and no perceptible change in the lines of his face, to match the ravages of Time upon her. If he had emotions, the Count Lestrange kept them in order.

"Can I help you?" at last he asked, placidly.

Lady Luscombe started and turned round; and, resting her hand upon the papers in the drawer, looked straight at Lestrange.

"You can, indeed," she said; and her eyes were full of a steady and reproachful appeal. "Oh, Count! Count! give me back those letters."

Lestrange's eyes wandered, as they so generally did, and met hers no more fairly than his answer met her invocation. His smile imperceptibly deepened a shade, and his eyes seemed looking after his smile. Like the Quaker of tradition, he only answered by a question.

"Why did you write them, if you want them again?" he asked. "The property in a letter, you know, belongs to the receiver."

"Not if he has promised to destroy them."

"You misunderstood me," he said, "as I have told you before. And I say again, if you want them back, why did you write them?"

The speaker had moved to the well-lined bookcase which filled the wall between the room and the slip-room, except the space where the door was. It was a curious bookcase, decorated with gilt sphinx's heads between the upper shelves, with corresponding feet which peeped out of the partitions of black wood at the lower ones, and rested on the black marble slab which covered cupboards below. He was leaning an elbow upon the slab, and examining his books, a favourite process with him. Lady Luscombe looked at him, went up to the table, and spoke shortly and hardly.

"Because I cared for you, and you know I did."

"And I keep them," he said,—as quietly as ever, but with that mocking devil lurking in the tone, which she never seemed to miss now, whenever, since her husband's will was read, he spoke to her of things like these,—"I keep them because I care for you, and you know I do."

"It is not true!" she said, passionately, though

very low. "You must have forgotten, I think," she added bitterly, and with all her pride under arms, "that, under my own eyes, you ventured to make love to Daisy Brent."

"Did she ever tell you so?"

"No. But I know it. You could not blind me if you tried."

"Why should I try then, if it is of no use?" he answered. "But if I did do so, depend upon it, I have not forgotten; I never forget."

"She was wiser than I," Lady Luscombe said, "for she saw through you."

"Not entirely. I don't think it's easy. But she judges me more fairly than you do."

"How?"

"She knows," said Lestrange, in his gentlest voice into which he suddenly threw a tone of pleading, "that my passing attentions to her were the result of a little pardonable jealousy—of some one else."

"Jealousy!" exclaimed the other, "and why? Daisy Brent was fortunate," she added, with an infinite sadness, and again sitting in the oak-chair by the table, "to escape those 'passing attentions' better than I did."

"Perhaps," he said, taking his seat opposite to Lady Luscombe.

Neither moved till the brief talk was done, which was to prove pregnant with result for this story.

"But such women live on passing attentions," he went on, with a contemptuous expression of slight regard for the object, which had a wound in it; "though they like them better when they don't pass."

Lady Luscombe knew these aphorisms of his, and shrank from them.

"Daisy Brent is a good woman," she said abruptly.

"I don't think so."

"Do you think any woman good?"

"Not many. But surely *you* should forgive me," he said, with the sudden pleading again in his voice from which this time he had banished the tone of mockery, " if I am not easy to please."

The change of tone went home; and Lady Luscombe answered it as pleadingly.

"Lestrange! give me back my letters!"

"Marian! let me keep them!"

"What for? why?" she asked.

"For sentiment, which rules me," he answered. The mockery came back; and a half-repressed exclamation of disappointment, weariness, anger, pain, came from Lady Luscombe. "It is all I have left," Lestrange went on, "now that I may not marry you."

"Now that you may not marry my fortune, you mean," she said bitterly, throwing all disguise aside. "You could have had me had you wished."

"Without money on either side?" said he. "We are not young or selfish, like Mrs. Brent."

"How you hate her!" was Lady Luscombe's answer after a brief pause, in which she looked at him strangely. "You say these things so often. Oh, don't deny it! I believe you want revenge upon her."

"If I do, I shall soon have it."

"How?"

"She will throw over her husband."

Lady Luscombe started, as he spoke with that deliberate slowness which he sometimes adopted. Then she laughed and shook her head.

"It would serve Mr. Brent right, bad man that he is!" she said. "But she won't, however long he stays in India. She is a good woman."

"You doubt it," Lestrange said, pointedly. "You say these things so often." Then his manner grew careless and off-hand. "Excuse me if I write a note for a moment, an answer which I forgot to send," he said.

Lady Luscombe excused him with a sign, and he took up pen and paper. Then as he was writing he laughed, as if some humorous notion had crossed his mind.

"What will you bet me," he said, "by way of a joke, of course," and he held his pen between his fingers with a smile, while looking at his note before him,—"you have grown fond of betting, you know,—that Daisy Brent doesn't run away before the end of the year?"

Lady Luscombe laughed shortly. "With you?" she said.

"Oh dear, no," and he laughed a good deal while he went on with his note. "I wouldn't have her."

"With whom, then?" Lady Luscombe rather scornfully asked.

"What does that matter? You see you daren't back your opinion."

Lady Luscombe looked at him sadly enough, and answered with another scorn in her voice, which had a ring of regret in it.

"What have you to bet, Count Lestrange?"

"Your letters," he said very coolly, still writing.

"Ah!" She started as if at a blow.

"What price do you put on them?"

She hesitated for a few seconds.

"Any price," she said.

"It's a mere fancy wager," said Lestrange, and taking up his note to read over to himself. "Shall we say—ten thousand pounds?"

"Nonsense," she answered. "That *is* a fancy wager."

"Like Shylock's, isn't it?" laughed Lestrange. "And as much in earnest, Mrs. Brent," was the aside which his thought supplied.

"Shall we book it?" he added, folding up his note.

"Seriously?" asked Lady Luscombe, puzzled thoroughly, and not understanding the drift of the scene, or seeing that it had any.

"What a question!" answered the other.

"You are a strange man," she said suddenly. "What are you?"

"I don't know. I never did. Shall we book it?"

"Ten—thousand—pounds," emphasized she.

"Nothing to you," said he. "Your letters are everything, in the view which you persist in taking of them and me."

"The view you made me take, you mean."

"Well, if you prefer it. Never mind the view; it is the value which matters."

"Is it your way of giving them to me?" she asked, very seriously. "It looks like it, you know."

"Doesn't it?" was the careless answer, which she might read as she pleased. "Why not? Shall we book it?"

"Shall I?" she said.

"I have a few trifling conditions to make," proceeded the Count. "You are just leaving London. You must collect a party at Luscombe Abbey at once, of the people whom I shall choose—all in your own set, don't be afraid. And you must give Daisy Brent no warning."

He spoke with all the careless indifference of Shylock of his single bond and merry sport; but it came over Lady Luscombe with a sense of fear.

"But this is wickedness," she said.

"Oh, no," he laughed, "amusement;" and his manner was more off-hand than ever. "And if I should require it, you must even help me a little. Bah! the joke won't go too far."

"It *is* like Shylock," she said, with the hesitation of Bassanio. "No; I don't think I'll do it."

"Think of your letters," he went on, not looking at her, "and of the use I *might* make of them."

"You would never——" she began.

"I don't know. It's such an odd world."

"I *cannot* understand you," said Lady Luscombe, completely baffled by his changes of manner, and more than ever doubtful whether this strange scene were jest or earnest, or a mixture of the two.

"Nobody ever could. Come, think how great the odds are in your favour. As you say, it's making you

a present; and without letting you feel the obligation
too much."

There was another pause, and Lady Luscombe was
ill at ease.

"Is this—bad joke—the only way?" then she
asked.

Lady Luscombe looked at Lestrange again, and
thought that she could read in his face, which she had
tried to read so often, that he really meant to make
her a present of her letters, after putting her to some
test by this impossible wager. So thoroughly had he
worked upon her fears about those letters, so vaguely
but deeply alarmed her with allusions, insinuations, and
covert threats about them, that they had at last
assumed diseased proportions in her eyes, and wore
the shape of a perpetual fear. She felt that "the
only way" was final, and she persuaded herself that
the wager was a jest; and then and last, the thought
of Daisy Brent's singular character, firm as a rock
under all her frivolity, which Lady Luscombe's womanly
perception had keenly read, came across her like a
charm.

"I know Daisy Brent," she said suddenly, lifting
her head with a kind of defiance in it. "And I agree."

"Done," said Lestrange, no muscle moving. He
took a small note-book from his pocket, and formally
he noted the strange wager down.

CHAPTER XXV.

THE SPIDER'S WEB.

"You really have the letters?" said Lady Luscombe
suspiciously, after another pause, as her hand fell upon
a pile of papers.

"Yes. You needn't look for them; they are in

that casket there." He pointed to a coffer of mediæval bronze, which stood by itself upon a small table in a recess, carved and wrought in the rich German designs of the time. "A most curious collection of manuscripts and letters that box contains," he said. "It will be quite a legacy to the memoir-hunters some day. Nobody ever has the key but myself, not even Chaffers."

He touched a small key which was attached to his watch-chain, whose pattern matched the casket. Then he began to sketch his scheme for the party to meet at Luscombe Abbey, and talked the names over with the Abbey's mistress.

"You will have Daisy's brother of the party, you know," she said.

"The soldier? No, I shan't."

"Do you mean you won't let me ask him?"

"You may ask him. He won't come."

"Why?"

"Ask him, and see. There are ways of doing these things."

He rose from the table and went to the window.

"There is the very man," he said, "calling with his sister; I wonder what brings them."

"Ah!" answered Lady Luscombe. "They are come to fetch me."

"In the nick of time," said the other. "This is the first visit Mrs. Brent has done my rooms the honour of paying them, though she has often talked of coming. Come into my sanctuary for a moment; I have something that I wish to show you."

"You don't want me to meet them. Why?"

"I want to arrange matters with you first, that's all. I shan't keep you five minutes, and Mrs. Brent can make acquaintance with my room before I do the honours. They are coming up-stairs. Come."

He spoke with a quiet tone of command to which Lady Luscombe seemed accustomed, and with him she withdrew into the inner room, as Daisy Brent and her brother entered by the other door.

Dick Fairfield was a well-looking soldier of a traditional type, with nothing much to distinguish him from other soldiers of his kind. They have the comfortable conviction fostered in their minds by admiring maidens, and still more by each other, that they are the salt of the earth ; and one grain of salt is not called upon to be more unlike another than is the case with the proverbial two peas. Civilians, I think, cherish a certain resentment against the class, for which its assertive flabbiness gives them much excuse. If no companion is pleasanter than a well-graced and active-minded soldier, the members of the thousand-and-first haw-haws are on the other side of the scale. It is so impossible to know what to talk to them about. Dick Fairfield always bored me to extinction more than any man I knew, and I could only tolerate him for his sister's sake.

We met often during those eight years, Daisy Brent and I ; for Lady Pepperharrow patronized and made much of me, and I was much with Daisy Brent at her ladyship's country-house meetings. For her I never bated one jot of my regard ; and I read the truth behind the frivolous externals of her life with much sad thought of my own. During all that time, we never spoke of Guy Faucit but once ; but there was a difference in her manner to me from that which she wore to all the world beside, which I could never fail to remark and to honour. It was for Guy's sake, I knew ; and I loved her for it. The exception to her rule of silence was when—once and at once—she cleared herself in my eyes (though, faith, I had never really been able to doubt her) by telling me the whole truth about her luckless marriage.

"I wanted you to know it, Mr. Balbus," she said, " because I want you to tell it one day to *him.* Further than that it need never go. Now let us never talk about it again."

He would have learned it soon enough, I think, if it had depended upon me. But blows like that which struck Guy Faucit tell differently upon different men; and during the whole of his long and solitary exile he gave his friends no sign, and no one but his lawyer (under the seal of absolute confidence) ever knew where to write to him. When he came back to England and settled as he did in Yorkshire, none of his friends learned it. Only one man did; and he was not a friend.

I saw little enough of the brother, and wished that little less. His remarks, when he thought it was time to make one, always managed to be particularly irritating, though without the smallest intention on his part. Some men are wonderful in that way.

Once at dinner, for instance, just after I had brought out a new drama of an ambitious kind with some success, he was sitting opposite me, and it dawned upon him, during a lull in the conversation round us, that he had bestowed none of his upon me. He did not wish to be neglectful, so suddenly addressed me with the deep deliberation which marked his manner whenever he did speak, causing the co-birds of his feather to say that "there must be a good deal in that fellow Dick Fairfield, you know, if you could only get at it."

If it was in him, however, there it stopped. It was thus he addressed me—

"I say, Balbus. Isn't it about time for you to give us another fa-arce?"

I could have hit him. Even as he bored me of old, he bores me now, and it bores me to describe him; and I shall let his talk with his sister, when they came into Lestrange's rooms, tell itself. He really liked his sister, and was at his best with her. Poor girl, I have no need to describe her, for I must have done so but too much for the patience of my readers already. If they do not know by this time what my heroine looked like, they never will; and I must have made a mess of it. I am sorry, for the women's sake, that I can find no technical description of the entrancing brown dress she wore, with the sideways sweep of gilt buttons, medalwise, the size of a shilling for the bodice, and a florin for

the skirt, which gave her the sort of Diana look which
sate upon her best of all, though she was all the goddesses and all the graces in turn.   She had that reckless
—and alas! that it must be said—fast manner which
had grown upon her of late, though in her, somehow, it
never repelled.   It never seemed real, I think, to anybody, and the fastest of her companions liked Queen
Daisy best without it.

DAISY (*taking the room in a moment, with approval*).
So the mysterious Count really lives somewhere, after
all!   This is the Castle of Udolfo.   Do you smell any
sulphur about, Dick?

DICK (*taking in nothing at all*).   No; but it's
deuced hot.

DAISY (*looking at everything*).   A blazing fire in
July!   And what an uncanny taste in colours.   The
place looks comfortable, though.

DICK (*looking at nothing*).   Don't provoke that
man, Daisy.   He's dangerous.

DAISY.   Why?   What harm can he do me? and
why should he want to do me any?   We are the best
of friends.   He fell in love with me, you know, like all
the rest, and I snubbed him for it.

DICK.   Did he though?   Damn his impudence.

DAISY.   Don't swear.   I oughtn't to have told you,
for I said I wouldn't tell anybody.   But a brother's
nobody, and it didn't matter.   It did the Count good to
be snubbed.

DICK.   He isn't likely to forgive it.   You talk
lightly enough.

DAISY (*with sudden seriousness*).   Perhaps I don't
feel so lightly, though.   (*Changing again.*)   It's a way
the men have, which means nothing.   And the wicked
Count took his whipping very well.

DICK.   I wish you'd drop him.   No good ever
came to anybody from being a friend of Satan
Lestrange.

DAISY.   That's a very shocking name, Dick.   He's
creepy, but he's very amusing.

DICK (*surlily*).   I don't see it.

DAISY.   Sense of humour deficient, dear.   Everybody thinks him so.

DICK.   Who's everybody?

DAISY.   Why, everybody.   Everybody who's anybody, you know; all the right sort.

DICK.   Slang again!

DAISY.   Dick among the prophets!   You stupid old soldier, when did you first take to preaching? (*with a dash of affection*).

DICK (*with the same, uncomfortably*).   I don't like leaving you to-morrow and joining my regiment.   Your head's in the wrong place, altogether.

DAISY (*ecstatically*).   But the heart, my Richard! the heart is in the right!   Its every pulse beats fondly for an absent lord, who is wringing from the Indian native the uttermost rupee, to lay it at the feet of his pining wife.   *Ay de mi!* I hope he'll never come back again.

DICK.   John Brent is not a good lot, no doubt——

DAISY.   Not strictly speaking.   But that's not my fault, is it?

DICK.   Still, you are his wife, and you ought to be more careful.

DAISY.   What of?

DICK.   The family name.

DAISY (*drawing herself up*).   Dick!

DICK.   Oh, I mean it, you know.   I know that you've had hard lines in life, and I like you to enjoy yourself.   But you may go too far.

DAISY.   Take care, or *you* may.   Who ruled those hard lines for me?—and Heaven only knows how hard they are!

DICK (*growing uncomfortable*).   Heaven, I suppose.

DAISY.   Not a bit of it; it was man's work all over.   I should have served Heaven better in spite of all of you, and steadily refused that man.

DICK (*sulkily*).   For that penniless lover of yours, Guy Faucit!

DAISY (*firing up in a moment*). Don't mention his name! I won't have it! I'll cherish one good memory through this unworthy life of mine, to keep my head straight. It will do it better than you can!

DICK I shouldn't like you to meet him again.

DAISY (*full of scorn*). Don't be afraid. He wouldn't speak to me if I did; and quite right too. (*Breaking into a wail.*) Oh, why—why—why did you all marry me to John Brent?

DICK. Our people were on the brink of ruin, you know. It was to save the family credit.

DAISY. A bad way. Good never came of such money as Mr. Brent's.

DICK (*with just disgust*). No. He lost it all soon enough.

DAISY. Thank Heaven! or he wouldn't have gone back to India. I am free from everything but his name.

DICK (*sententious again*). You are much too free, Daisy.

DAISY (*in arms again*). I will not have you say that again. I was persuaded to marry money, and to play my heart false, for my father's sake. But some men, Dick, would have found some better way of saving the family credit than by selling a sister's life and happiness. When you join your regiment, brother mine, take care of the family name. It's safe enough with me.

"I hope so," muttered to himself, at the end of this dialogue, a listener at the door. Then turning to Lady Luscombe, he added, unheard through their conversation by the others, "You are quite right; I am making you a present."

"Join his regiment, did she say?" thought Lady Luscombe, who with Lestrange had heard the last sentence from the open door of the inner room. Lestrange, it may be, who had cultivated a very keen sense of hearing, and could listen and talk at the same

time, might have heard more. Daisy and the Captain
did not see them till Lestrange stepped forward.

"Mrs. Brent!" he said: "You have found me out
at last. I am delighted to receive you."

"Ah, good morning!" she answered, carelessly
giving him her hand. "The reception is a warm one,"
she added, with a laughing look at the fire, "Count
Mephistopheles!"

"Madame Marguerite!" he said in a low voice, and
with an inclination of the head. And he smiled to
himself as he said so.

"Is that a sneer?" asked Daisy.

"Oh, no; a compliment. How sweet she is," he
thought as he looked at her; "it is almost a pity— You
are a dangerously pretty woman," he said to her in a
low voice, turning over some books on the table, while
the other two were talking together.

"Still?" she said, with low and firm emphasis.

"Still, if you would only let me say so."

"I shan't, you know. Count Lestrange, remember,
and take care!"

"We should make such allies, Daisy."

"Sir!"

"I beg your pardon," said the Count Lestrange.

"Only my friends call me by my Christian
name."

"You are lucky," he quietly and pointedly answered,
"to have so many friends. She will have war, then?"
he thought. "Very well."

Lady Luscombe looked at them uneasily as they
talked together in a voice she could not catch.

"Nonsense!" she thought to herself, "the girl's as
good as gold." But she was uneasy and conscience-
smitten, and wished the wager undone.

"Captain Fairfield," she said, rousing herself, "the
charm of London being over for the year, you will bring
Daisy down to the Abbey at the end of the week? We
shall be a pleasant party."

"Very sorry, Lady Luscombe," answered the soldier

R

with a genuine regret, for he thought the Abbey much pleasanter work than his duties; "but I must leave her in your friendly care. I join my regiment at Gibraltar to-morrow."

Lady Luscombe gave a slight exclamation.

"I told you so," whispered Lestrange.

"Couldn't you put it off for a month?" she asked.

"Uneasy already!" whispered the Count again.

"*I* would put it off, willingly," said Fairfield; "but my Colonel won't. I've overstayed time already, and he is peremptory."

"The regiment, dear Lady Luscombe," laughed Daisy, "is lost without Dick. The men are reported on the verge of mutiny."

"Always chaffing," muttered her brother, with his normal sulkiness.

"Chaff is the salt of life. Isn't it, Count?" she appealed.

"You sprinkle it very freely at times," he said.

"All's fair in war!" she answered, laughing again; "and—-shall we say in 'love,' Count?"

He bit his lip a little. "Do you know the meaning of that word?"

"Perhaps," she said; and there was no laughter in the voice then.

The Count watched her under his eyebrows, and he said to himself, "I think you do, Madame. We shall soon see."

"What will Lady Pepperharrow do without you, Captain Fairfield?" said Lady Luscombe, finding her invitation in vain. "She says you are the best secretary and collector in the world. What is to become of her great subscription for the conversion of the Jews?"

"Oh bother!" interjected Daisy, irreverently. "When she asked me to subscribe I said I couldn't afford it, but if she liked to send me a Jew, the dear old lady, I would do my best to convert him for her."

"And surely," added Lestrange, "the Jews are rich enough to pay for their own conversion."

Their laugh over Lady Pepperharrow's proselytizing schemes put the party in good humour with each other; and Lady Luscombe announced that it was time for her to carry Daisy off for the end of the last flower-show of the season at the Horticultural, where some friends were waiting for them.

"The last roses of summer!" said Daisy.

"Which wouldn't bloom without you," was Lestrange's comment.

"Pretty," was what she said; and what she thought while she said it was, "He makes me creep all over."

"Then you will not give me those letters back, as you ought?" pleaded Lady Luscombe once more in a low voice with Lestrange.

The Count smiled the plea aside, and made some laughing comment on the wager which was so soon to put them in her hands again.

So she sighed and accepted her fate, and offered him a seat in the carriage, if he was minded to come.

"Thank you, no," he said. "I shan't help the roses, and I have a good deal to do. We shall meet to-night at Glycerine House. *Au revoir!*"

He saw his visitors to the door with his accustomed courtesy, and went thoughtfully back to his rooms. He sate down in his chair, wheeled it before the fire, and lit up the eternal accompaniment to thought which so many as well as he have found to be its best sedative and stimulant in one. He took out the little book in which he had entered his strange wager, and he referred to other of its pages. Then he referred with care to a book of accounts, carefully kept; and his face grew rather dark as he went into it.

"Only just in time," he muttered to himself; "I'm glad I kept those letters. Yes, I have a good deal to do," ran his musings before the fire, when he had put up the books again. "I must put money in my purse, as counsels honest Iago. What says my friend? 'Pleasure and action make the hours seem short!' A fine fellow Iago, and so little understood. I must write a treatise to whitewash him some day, after the fashion of modern history, and leave that thick-headed Moor . blacker than he was first painted. Ten thousand pounds to be won before the year's end; and only just in time, for ·I'm in unpleasantly low water; and this is the chance which, as Iago says, makes me or foredoes me quite. How much did mine Ancient die worth, now? He must have been a warm man at times, and without a dollar to curse himself with at others. It's a grand thing to live by one's wits, given the wits to do it. Now then—to work out my plot. *Dramatis Personæ :*—Heroine, Daisy Brent: safe from love, she thinks. Why? Because she is one of the few who can love, and can remember. I wouldn't have risked my wager upon any chance but one. Hero, Guy Faucit: old lover, recluse and misanthrope, living near Luscombe Abbey in retreat, without an idea how near the moth has crept to the flame. And the flame knows it as little. Burn up till you blaze, my child. Ha, ha! of all the coincidences in the world, if there were such things, the oddest would be my meeting the man Faucit coming out of his lawyer's room, just when I had managed to learn of his return to England. I knew him at once, though he didn't look at me. I never forget a face. And the lawyer, with no idea that he was breaking confidence, talked to me about the strange client who wanted to find a desert for himself to live in. And I was able to suggest the very place, close to the scene of operations. Could Iago have done better, now? The worst of it is that Faucit has no money, and all women like diamonds. Now if only his old hunks and miser of an uncle, my good friend Foster (promoted to the place for the purpose), would die in time, and not leave his money away from him, it would help me wonderfully, though I might do without it. Foster was breaking up, by my last intelligence; but he's Scotch, and very tough. He has not made a will yet, I know. How shall I introduce myself to this Faucit? I want a good effect to begin with. The man's a student and poet, and dabbles in German metaphysics. Why not play upon that string? Mephistopheles they call me, confound them. I am not one of them, though I live with and by them; and they know it, and so do I, and I hate them for it, brainless puppets that they all are! And that unlucky widow and her money and estates were in my hands, but for that unprincipled will. The selfishness of these aristocrats, even in dying, is perfectly shocking. As for you, Mr. John Brent, and you, Mistress Daisy— How strange that so many motives should all work together. Ten thousand pounds! A great comfort, a small annuity. What a fool that woman is about those letters! What on earth does she suppose I could really do with them? Still, with a little skilful manipulation— Mephistopheles, eh! It would be a striking introduction."

He was smiling over his thoughts to himself, as Chaffers came into the room after his furtive knock.

"A telegram, Count Lestrange," he said.

"Ah! from Scotland!" said Lestrange to himself as he took the paper. "From my trusty agent, Foster's lawyer." And he read the telegram. "F. is worse— has had a stroke—can only live a week or two. No will . . ." "Good Heavens! how timely!" he thought. "'Pleasure and action make the hours seem short.' Can I afford to wait for a week or two, on the chance of bringing to Faucit, by way of credentials, the first news of his heirship? At all events, I will risk it for a while. Yes; I can afford it. Chaffers—"

"Yes, Count Lestrange."

"We go to Luscombe Abbey at the end of the week."

"Yes, Count Lestrange."

PART II.

The Drama.

CHAPTER I.

THE HERMIT OF THE OWL'S NEST.

SOMEWHERE in the great smoke districts of York-shire, and near to one of its main capitals of industry, there is a strange old ruin on the moorland slope. It is a wonder how it got there; for smoke and soot have laid the strong hand of annexation on the whole country-side, and antiquity seems like an obstructive to be effaced. It dies hard, however, the storied past; for men built hard and strong when they built slow and true, and by the side of the old abbeys which have crumbled down to us, the modern factory or railway-shrine has an odd appearance of insecurity as well as tawdriness.

I am not prepared to give the exact birth and parentage of the old Yorkshire castle where my story now reopens, which had lost both use and name in the lapse of years, and is known in the neighbourhood only as the Owl's Nest. Though scarcely six miles distant from the big trade-city, the hum of whose wheels seem almost to reach the ear, as at times the wind brings palpable news of it in a thick pall of fog fighting to be free, it might be in the heart of a desert but for such evidence as that. Green slopes spread upwards to the hilltop behind ; and the wild moor heatherland faces it in front from the other side of a sudden valley, with a stream running townwards at the bottom, clear and sparkling, and innocent of the pollution waiting for it so little further down.

The ruin itself forms a complete though broken quadrangle, uneven and overgrown. A big old tower occupies the north-east angle, and another the south-west, while a straggling parapet unites the two in either direction. In the north-west corner stands the antiquarian gem of the whole — an archway nearly perfect in preservation, as it is quite perfect in form, a pure specimen of the lancet arch which will not, somehow, be imitated with any exactness by anything we moderns can contrive. Those secrets are as lost, seemingly, as the lost books of Livy, and must be as much the despair of architects as the galop in " Gustave " of dance-composers, or as that " *vilaine bête vivante,*" the stone-horse which Romans know, was to the French professor of drawing, who exposed the sins of its anatomy by example. " *Pourtant, messieurs, la mienne est morte,*" he said. It was through this arch-way that the quadrangle might be entered, when I was there. Perhaps it is gone now, though I am writing but of a very few years ago. Mine is a story of our own time ; but it is a time which goes fast upon its way, though weighted perhaps now and again, in spite of trains and telegraphs, with the drag called Boredom. There was the arch, however, and there was the old tower opposite to it, which also gave access to the enclosure through a passage choked, till you knew where to find it, by a thick growth of laurels. The walls of the old tower, of which two sides were standing, formed the angle then, and stood boldly out as a shelter against sun or wind for any one who cared so to use them. Stray picnic-parties from the city came there now and then, bringing their sheaves with them ; for there was no inn near to help them to their picnic-needs. There was no house at all but one small cottage, just on the other side of the road, which ran under the northern parapet from tower to arch. Beyond the road the ground rose boldly and suddenly into the picturesque slope leading up to the top of the hill, turfed and green, and good riding-ground for some miles.

In the cottage, when this part of my story opens, was living a solitary man. The few waifs and strays who belonged to the neighbourhood were of the kind who have no visible habitation or known means of subsistence, but are as offences in the eyes of the Law, which expects everybody to be moderately well-off. They seem to have lairs in the grasses, like the warriors of Roderick Dhu. These few, however, had a kindness for Mr. Fraser, the stranger who had suddenly taken up his quarters among them a few months before, and had an eccentric way of his own of doing them good. He talked very little, and smoked very much; did unobtrusive kindnesses, and hated to be thanked. Nobody knew anything about him, or cared to ask. He had not written a letter, nor had he had any, since he came. He was a man who seemed well on in middle age; dressed very roughly, but always like a gentleman; big and muscular, with a growing suspicion of portliness. The face was fair and clear, with the pink English complexion which turns so soon to bronze, and the eyes of the true Saxon blue, too prominent, but good. The features were strong rather than handsome; the forehead, both broad and high, giving its chief character to the face. The mouth did not present itself for criticism, having retired into the recesses of a thick beard and moustache, which curled all round and over it, and were so grey as to give the man an appearance of age which the features, closely looked at, and the hair many shades browner, were inclined to contradict. The brown was of a silky softness, and irrepressible in its tendency to curl, which it owed partly, perhaps, to the owner's disbelief in oil-colours for the head, and faith in cold water. The nose was like most noses,

without form and void, but did the face no harm as
it attracted no attention, and did not invite it, being
in fact, as the same owner said of it, "good enough to
blow." Six good feet of height, and a stonage coming
nearer to fourteen than to thirteen on the average,
served to carry this very healthy specimen of English
humanity, and formed a whole curiously at odds with
the utter solitude of his life. There was nothing about
him of the broken man, but everything of the elastic
one, shown in everything he did—in the firm step breast-
ing the heather, in the steady hand throwing the line,
and the keen eye to back it; or in the strong forehead
which bent over his beloved books, and seemed to shut
out without an effort every thought and every image
disconnected from the page before him. He looked
the man of action, every stout inch of him, and not the
dreamer. But it was the dreamer's life, apparently,
that he had elected to live. And the face bore
one clear and lasting mark—the mark of a great
sorrow.

He fished the trout-streams, and he shot the moors,
and he shot and fished well. At other times he left
both rod and gun at home, and shouldered a thick stick
for company and not support, and strode for miles
and miles in the bright northern air, he, and the stick,
and the dog Frisco. Frisco was a noble brute of mastiff
breed, who had come from the golden gates with his
master, six thousand miles away. The mutual affection
of the two was a pleasant thing to see, as they strolled,
or sate, or talked together, as men and dogs do talk
sometimes, when they understand each other thoroughly.
Frisco slept at the foot of his master's bed, and took
especial interest in watching the morning tub which
braced the giant for the day; and he seemed to know,
before the master knew it himself, what was to be the
occupation of the morning. The large, true, intelligent
eyes, with a strange and surely a beautiful world of love
and thought behind them—shall we penetrate the
secrets of that world, perhaps, some day?—seemed to

be always on the alert to discover his friend's plans and wishes.

One curious habit of Mr. Fraser's there was, worth recording. He was fond on Sundays of walking to a little barn-like church some miles away upon the hills, which gathered under its wing the few and far-between worshippers to be found thereabouts, and watching them go in, and listening to the cracked old bell. The people of the village of Mould-on-the-Moss, for so was the little hamlet called which owned this parish church, watched him with much curiosity. For he did not go in himself. He looked, and smoked, and thought, and went away. Once or twice, upon week-days, he found his way to the village and asked the sexton for the key. A character, in those parts, was Delves the sexton. Then he stayed alone in the church for five minutes, and came out more grave than ever, after a spell of what he called thought, which was really prayer. The man was no unbeliever, but was one perplexed, as yet, by the eternal—no, not eternal—problems of suffering and wrong. The buzzings of the Agnostics had something puddled his clear spirit, and the smoke of the pit troubled him.

A large portion of his time, rain or fine, the stranger passed in the old Owl's Nest. He had chosen for himself the corner I have spoken of, where the two walls made an angle. Here he had rigged up a water-proof tent where he could smoke and read in all weathers. Here he was smoking and reading on the day when my story re-opens, without the tent this time, for it was a glorious September afternoon. It had been a long wet summer, and had given up, as early as May, all idea of being anything else. So September came with one of those Indian bursts with which it often does come after seasons of that kind, to apologize for shortcomings in the handsomest manner. And the man called Fraser sate with a rich meerschaum between his lips, with a colour on it like the top of the clouted cream, fresh made in its own country, cloud-compelling.

and deep in his book. He was sitting in a rough wooden arm-chair, and had as rough a table before him, with a brandy-and-soda on it in a long glass, from which he sipped occasionally and with no especial zest, being one on whose face temperance and self-control were written in every line. The book he was reading was German, and it was the second part of "Faust."

"Not a bad translation, I think," he thought, taking up a note-book in which he had a habit of scribbling odd scraps of verse or casual quotations in pencil. "Listen, Frisco, old boy, and give me your ideas."

Frisco lifted his head, and wagged his tail once, as one who was all attention, while his master read.

"What do you think of it?"

Frisco wagged his tail twice, with approval, and lay down again.

"What is the use of it all?" muttered his master to himself, impatiently. "Why, in the name of common-sense, do I live this useless life, as if I were a debtor hiding from his creditors, or a man who had done something to be ashamed of. We have nothing to be ashamed of, Frisco, you and I, and we don't look it. Your tail is as the tail of an honest dog, and you would have nothing to say to me if I wasn't worthy of you and it. But I can't help it. I—I— Oh my darling, my darling, with your voice as sweet as Heaven, and your face as true as Truth, is it possible that you could have told that long lie to me? Yes, you did. Well, be it so."

He took up the book, and the strong will mastered the wandering fancy at once. The masterful look came full upon the brow and face. Frisco, who had been watching the sudden outburst with infinite solicitude, looked satisfied and shut his eyes. And neither man nor dog, absorbed in their own reflections, noticed the entrance of another figure on the scene.

CHAPTER II.

BEAUTY GOSLING.

IT was a very pleasant figure in its way—that of a fresh and pink-faced youngster of the class who look eighteen all their lives, till the balls, and the clubs, and the late hours, and all the dissipations, take a sudden revenge and age them all in a moment.

The Honourable James Gosling had as little beard as Orlando, but cherished the soft down upon his delicate upper-lip with infinite solicitude. His face was singularly handsome, and recalled the pictures of Byron; but the eyes wore a perpetual look of innocence and surprise, being withal very round and very open, which marred the resemblance. Like the ambered fly, he seemed incessantly wondering why he was anywhere, and why on earth he should be expected to do anything. Nobody, perhaps in consequence of this, expected him to do much; but the clinging affectionate nature made him welcome everywhere; and he was allowed to purr away for hours in the snuggeries of fine ladies, hard to be found at home by more pretentious visitors; just as at every gathering of men, in all lines of life, he was sure of a welcome. Painters and actors loved him well; and he believed himself closely connected, in some important way, with artistic life. The bright summer-picnics on the river, organized by some pretty actress whose 'head wore the manager's crown without seeming to lie uneasy for it, were never complete without the butterfly patronage of Beauty Gosling. He entered the quadrangle quietly through the lancet-arch, and it became evident at once that Frisco would permit the intrusion. For the dog was the first to look curiously up; and he made no remark at all beyond a wag of recognition. Gosling nodded to the dog familiarly, and drew nearer to the man he had come to see, whose thoughts and faculties were pathfinding in the poet's land.

"There he is," muttered the visitor to himself, "at it as usual. Pipes and Poetry! Why a fellow who is such good company for any fellow should keep out of every fellow's way, I can't make out."

Then he came forward.

"Faucit!"

The strange solitary started, and came back to earth slowly and half-composedly, as a man wakes from sleep to his troubles or to his happiness. He looked his visitor a little in the face before he answered him, not without something of the friendly smile on his, which this youth of the ruddy countenance was well accustomed to see.

"Fraser, young 'un," he then said, quietly. "I've often told you to forget the other name, as I have. How are you?"

"Thanks—I'm fit. Old Luscombe was a judge of champagne, and his worthy widow don't spare it. Consequently, with the morning's dawn, I'm fit."

"That's very satisfactory," said the other, paternally.

"Doosid. I can't say as much for you, though. You look awfully bad about the eyes, old man. Damme, a fellow might take you for a hundred."

The man called Fraser, no other than our old friend Guy Faucit, winced a little. But he only answered, slowly, and with something like a sigh—

"The fellow wouldn't be far out."

"Humbug!" was the cheery comment. "Got any B. and S. handy? Thanks!" as the other pointed to the rough table; "that's lucky. I tooled the little mare over from Luscombe Abbey—the six miles in the half-hour, and I'm doosid dry."

"Help yourself," said the other, nodding, and passing a corkscrew.

Then the eyes began perceptibly to travel dream-wards again, and he took up the book he had laid down.

"What's up with him?" thought Gosling; and met the situation by patting Frisco's handsome head, and bestowing on him a few well-appreciated words of caress. "What are you reading?" then he said, abruptly.

"The second part of 'Faust.' Do you know it?"

"No. I didn't know there was a second part. I know the first,—Gounod's, you know,—but I never read that. Let's have a look."

He leant his arm familiarly on the older man's shoulder, and looked over it.

"All right," said Faucit. "I'll begin your poetical education, Jemmy. Read this."

He pointed to the book with a smile.

"Ah! German; I know that from the printing. Haven't got any English about you, have you? I'm better at that, though not too good. My godfathers and godmothers in my baptism neglected my languages dreadfully."

"There's some English for you, then."

"Whose is it? the German fellow's?"

"His German, and my English. I've just been making the translation."

"The doose you have. At the old game still. I should have thought you'd dried up down here. Tell it us?"

The other recited his lines slowly, as he had recited them to the dog, as if to test them again to his own ear. Again he began to seem unconscious of company, and to be passing into a world of his own.

The solution of the question, "What are your thoughts like?" would have interested any observer who watched the strong set face.

Gosling was not much of an observer, perhaps. He listened to the lines with eye growing rounder and rounder, like a pool into which a stone is sinking; and the pathetic, half-animal expression, of dumb speculation as to what he was meant for, came into his graceful face.

"Ah!" he said, as if deliberating more than was

usual with him ; "doosid fine that. I don't know what
the blazes it's about, but it's doosid fine. I'm stoopid
about poetry, except burlesques. The little Whyte
Chappel puts me through them sometimes. Old man,
you're dreaming," he suddenly added, with a genuine
ring almost of yearning in his tone. "Wake up!"

The quick ear of the other caught the intonation
just as his sensitive nerve felt on his shoulder the shy,
sympathetic touch of the boy's hand. (Gosling was not
a boy ; but he was always called so.)

"You're right, Jem, I was dreaming." He shut up
the book, turned round with his chair towards Gosling,
and looked at him with a real and evident interest.
The other had a pull at his brandy-and-soda, with as
evident relief.

"Tell us about yourself, come," said Guy. "I'm
fond of your cherub face, my boy; it does me good.
And you're a good fellow to leave your fun and your
smart friends as constantly as you do, and come over
for a chat with the hermit, as they call me. It must
bore you tremendously."

"Bore me ? humbug ! Do you think I'm likely to
be bored by my old coach, who was so awfully kind to
me up at Oxford ? "

"I didn't do much for you."

"You pulled me through my divinity, which I
swear no one else could, and looked after me like a
trump. And that was eight years ago : and then you
bolted from Oxford, and shied up your fellowship, and
the fellows said you went abroad, though nobody knew
why or where; and everybody forgot you, and I never
heard of you again till I spotted you down here the
other day, beard and all, calling yourself Fraser, and
cutting everybody. Then—didn't you keep my brother
Gander square with the dons all through? Dear old
Gander ! he's gone no end of a howler on the turf
since; but he never forgets you—nor do I, nor the
governor, nor any of us. Damme ! there ! "

The speaker delivered himself of his tirade without

reflection of any kind, walking up and down, to Frisco's obvious astonishment, finishing the brandy-and-soda in distracted gulps, and filling up the glass now and again with an absolute unconsciousness as to which of the two liquids he was pouring out.

"Drop that, my child," was the quiet answer.

"Hanged if I do! What man of my time at Oxford would forget Clipper Faucit? Look here— you've no call to run to seed in this way. It's not right. Brains are rare; and you mustn't do what you like when you've got 'em. I wish I'd got 'em; for I'd try. I've kept my word since I spotted you here, by accident, though I don't know that I ought, and said nothing about you; but now they're all coming here to spot you, and I've come to let you know. Don't bolt."

The other had jumped to his feet, followed by Frisco's eyes.

"How do you mean, coming here?"

"I mean what I say, though I know that ain't worth ·much. I tooled over this morning because I promised to keep dark about you, and Lady Luscombe's lot mean to picnic here to-day, and I thought I ought to let you know, though I've said nothing. I say I wish you'd join us. Beastly things, picnics, but awfully nice people. Do come."

"Thanks for the warning," answered the other quietly. "I'll keep out of the way. Don't talk nonsense."

Gosling's face fell visibly, but he incontinently proceeded to talk again; while the recluse subsided into his chair, and gradually, into absence of mind.

"Like the rest of the fellows. Whatever I say is always nonsense. They call it 'bosh,' but it's the same idea. Hang it, I say, do come! The Luscombe isn't a bad lot, though she gives herself airs and all that; and her niece Carrie Beaufort is awfully jolly—spoons me rather, but her aunt don't see that. The aunt wanted Gander; but *he* didn't see that. Then there's Lady

Pepperharrow—wonderful old woman—always wanting to convert everybody—though nobody knows what to. Everybody laughs at Lady Pepperharrow, but everybody likes her. Then there are some good men. There's Lord Pentonville, otherwise old Pen., otherwise ' Hard Labour '—supposed to have turned nine hundred —rum 'un he is, but a doosid good fellow! Then there's Norbiton and Surbiton, you know—one's a Dook, and the other's a Marquis. Always together, and no good without one another, like the men in Leech who took two to show the pattern. And Count Lestrange —Gad, you must know *him!* Talk about rum uns! Comes from Greece, or Poland, or Japan, or somewhere that way, with a sort of title which he picked up somehow. Queer beggar; been everywhere, and knows everything; belongs nowhere, and lives on nothing. Licks us all round at shooting, billiards, and the lot. Sings like a bird, and spoons like a turtle. Nobody likes him, and everybody asks him; everybody's afraid of him too, except the Brent, who's afraid of nobody. She's at the Abbey too, under the capacious wing of the Pepperharrow. By Jove! the Brent!—there's form!— the best out; and all the men mad about her. Don't she carry on a few? Got a husband out in India; liver, and all that. I should stop there if I was him. She's splendid—Daisy Brent."

The Christian name struck suddenly on his friend's ear, though it was some time before it seemed to reach his sense. During Gosling's chatter he had rambled far away; and it wanted time for him to catch the threads again.

"Who's that?" he said. "What were you talking about?"

"Why, the people at the Abbey."

"Oh, I beg your pardon. I was dreaming again, and I didn't quite hear."

"Oh, damme!" said Gosling, pathetically. "Doosid hard lines, that I can never get the fellows to listen to anything I say; and I talk a lot, too."

"You do, Jemmy," the other answered, with reflective gravity.

"Don't chaff. If you don't listen, of course you
won't come."

"Come to what? oh, the picnic. No, not to-day."

"No, nor to-morrow, nor any other time. I must
go and look after the picnic lot, I suppose. You must
own that it was very good of me to let you know about
them, when I might have let you in in spite of yourself.
Bother the picnic. I'd rather be out in the turnip-
fields, bar the Brent."

"I wonder, Jemmy, if you will ever grow any older,
and take to talking English?"

"Why, what do I talk now?"

"Goodness knows! a tongue without a name. Your
Greek was bad at college; but your present style is
incredible. How soon will your friends be here?"

"Precious soon now. Very soon I mean; and I
must be off. But I shall come again, mind. I'll
never let you off till I unearth you for the public
benefit."

"Don't take the trouble. I'm past praying for."

"Ah, I shouldn't be much good to you in that line.
Well, it's a sell; but by-bye."

He clapped his friend on the shoulder, patted Frisco
on the head, and was off through the arch. The dog's
eyes followed him with what might have been an
expression of disappointment at his master's obstinacy.
The master's eyes were on the book again, before his
visitor was gone.

"If you'd have a turn at prose," said Gosling, for a
last word, shrugging his shoulders, "it would do you a
lot of good. Adoo!"

"How that boy used to make me laugh at Oxford,"
thought Guy Faucit, letting his book fall upon his knee.
"And he's not a bit changed. Why can't I laugh now?"
ran the thoughts translated into words. "Eight years
ago was it? Yes, just eight. Eight years ago I was
still in the old rooms at Balliol, coaching, with my old

friends about me, and my dear dead mother to spend vacation with. An authority in the schools and on the river; popular, happy, very happy; with a past I could be proud of, a present I could enjoy, a future I could trust in. I was twenty-eight, and felt eighteen. Now I'm thirty-six, and feel—what was it he said? A hundred? Yes, about that. I wish I felt it in body, but I don't."

He rose from his seat and stretched his arms, instinctively feeling with his left the muscle of the right. "I believe I could pull the dark blue through yet, between Putney and Mortlake. How long must I go on living" (and restlessness and impatience began to take possession of his manner), "at a moderate calculation? But this isn't living. Mind, heart, and will —that's life; and they died eight years ago. She did it well, that girl. What's become of her? What's the name of the man she married? I don't even know."

He bit his lip and bent his forehead, and threw himself into the chair again. Once more he took up the book, but this time the will played him false, and he could attend no more.

"I wasn't born vindictive, I think," he said to himself aloud; "but sometimes I feel that if I were to meet the woman who changed me like this, it might be bad for her."

The laurels in the angle behind him, which have been before described, were gently parted as he began to speak, and a man's pale face looked through. It was a very pale and sinister, but attractive face, and full of breeding. He heard the words, and smiled, and stepped forward quietly behind the speaker's chair. Frisco saw him, and growled low but angrily. But the new-comer took no notice of him, and for the moment the dog did no more.

"I shall go mad with these fancies!" cried Faucit, who did not hear the growl, his head resting on his arm on the table before him. "Faust, eh?" he said, with a bitter laugh. "Faust, who conjured up the devil! I should think so. Who wouldn't conjure him up, if he came with the old gifts in his hand? Faust got his money's worth, anyhow, and was a cur to turn round on his best friend. Come to me, devil, come to me, and take me at your own price, if you will give me back one hour of the old spring: the youth to begin the world, the money to command it, the friends to make it easy, and the love—to make it real! Yes, and more than that—the revenge that makes it even! Money—youth —friends—love—revenge!"

The strange soliloquy ended, and was suddenly answered as thoughts sometimes are, though scarcely perhaps as these were. The man who had entered through the laurels came forward, and touched Faucit on the shoulder. He was in a riding-dress, booted and spurred, and leant familiarly over him.

"Excellent things, all of them," said the intruder. "What are you reading?"

CHAPTER III.

A STRANGE VISITOR.

"THE devil!" cried Faucit, jumping to his feet at the sudden address.

"Are you?" was the dry answer. "Not an easy subject to read."

The student looked at his new visitor with an almost startled curiosity. He was a singular contrast to the one who had just left him. The pale face was oval in shape, and the well-set head was covered with jet-black hair, parted in the middle, and lying close to it, without curl or wave. The nose was straight and cleanly cut, as all the features were, with a constant expression playing about the nostril. The thin, rather colourless lips were shaded by a narrow black moustache; and a short pointed beard met the mouth below. The eyes were small, black too, and very piercing, with a habit, however, of looking away from the person spoken to, if he on his side was given to looking others straight in the face. The forehead was low, but had a character of its own; and the whole face, which had in it a kind of strange magnetism, impressed men at once with a subtle sense of intellect and influence. In age the man might be about forty-five or fifty. He was of about the middle height, as the average of height goes in men of his class, and singularly thin of build and constitution— a characteristic made the more marked by the black dress he wore, high black hat, frock-coat closely buttoned, black trowsers strapped over his well-shaped riding-boots, and broad black necktie tied in a loose bow under his turn-down collar. In the centre of the white shirt was one small stud of bright diamond; and on the fourth finger of the right hand he wore one ring— a curious production, apparently, of German or Italian mediævalism. It was a hoop, of three rows of gems, the centre being made of a dozen small pearls, while the two outer bore nine stones in the same order—an amethyst, sapphire, aquamarine, ruby, opal, emerald, aquamarine, sapphire, amethyst. He was fond of showing this ring in the different lights that fell upon it, and of looking into it himself, and into the spare and small, but strong expressive hand which carried it, whose two forefingers, laid together, started and curved apart from each other at the middle joint—an odd sign, some say, of a power of impressing the individuality upon others. The feet were small and shapely enough for a pretty woman to be proud of; and even in his riding-boots he was shod coquettishly. Gloves he did not wear, being too fond of his ring. The whole man, with the strange surroundings of the scene and the wild thoughts that were tossing in Faucit's mind, created on the latter an immediate and very powerful effect.

Seemed as from some enchanter's cave,
Or some deep vault beneath the wave,
   To an unholy prayer,
Some spirit not of middle earth,
Yet human-seeming, form and birth,
In mocking tone of covert mirth,
   Made answer then and there.*

Most effective of all was the voice in which the stranger spoke — a voice curiously soft, sweet, and deliberate. He spoke very low, yet with such quiet distinct emphasis that no word was ever lost to the listener's ear.

"Who are you?" asked Faucit, abruptly, after a brief pause.

"Never mind who I am. You are Guy Faucit." The speaker was not looking at the other for the moment, but turning over the leaves of the book which had been dropped on the table, behind which he stood, tapping his boot carelessly with his riding-whip.

"My name is Fraser," said the other roughly.

"I think not." And the visitor laid the book down, and seated himself easily in the chair just vacated, with no appearance of familiarity, but as little of diffidence. The face of the man with the two names grew rather dark and angry, and Frisco, who had been *couchant regardant*, contributed another low growl to the dialogue. "Good dog," said the stranger, in an offhand way.

"What brings you here, whoever you are?" asked Faucit, who had taken his place towards the centre of the old quadrangle, and with his two hands in his pockets was taking the measure of the intruder, with an expression both of mistrust and uneasiness.

"You do," answered the other carelessly, and with perfect good-humour. "You called me, didn't you?"

"Called you?" said the student, puzzled.

"Am I different to what you expected? I was always a gentleman, you know; and can only dress as one."

* "Old Play."

"Oh, I'm in no humour for mummery, sir," the other answered, shrugging his shoulders impatiently, and turning away. "This old place is as open, of course, to you as to me; but as far as I am concerned, you are not privileged."

"Pardon me; I'm a privileged person. And we are wasting time, which is precious to me, though perhaps not to you. What price do you offer," and the speaker rested his right arm upon the rough table, leaned forward with a new seriousness in his tone, and looked at the younger man, "for the commodities you were asking for?"

"What commodities?"

"Money and youth, friends and love, and—revenge."

"Did you hear my thoughts?"

"Well, I ought to apologize; but you think so very loud. A pretty place this, but in baddish repair, and draughty in the winter, I should think. But to return: what price do you offer for those four things?"

"To you?"

"To me."

Guy Faucit burst into a laugh, which moved the other in no wise from his seriousness.

"Ha, ha! this becomes amusing. Like my prototype in the book there, to any one who will give them to me, my soul, if you like it!" Recklessly and bitterly enough were the words said.

"What? in the nineteenth century? You don't keep pace with modern thought, I see."

"Ah, you don't believe in a soul?"

"If *I* didn't, my occupation would be gone. I'll be liberal, and on the chance that, in spite of modern theories, you have a soul, I'll take it."

"Done!" said the other, laughing more naturally and with more good temper, as if he were grasping the humour of the notion. "But you must tell me your name, you know."

"How material you are. I have had so many.

But, in the present century, I am called the Count Lestrange."

"Well," said Faucit; "and you live—— ?"

"Don't ask too much," answered he, with a rippling kind of laugh, which was a kind of smile in sound, placidly expelling and savouring the while a cloudlet of well-graced tobacco-smoke from a scented cigar. "Don't ask too much. I am staying, not living, at the Abbey near here, Lady Luscombe's place, on business. Her party are excellent people, from my point of view."

He sent a puff of smoke through his nostrils, blew an upward breath after it, and trimmed his nails reflectively with a small ivory pocket-knife. By this time he had seated himself, with his legs comfortably crossed, on the small chair which faced the other's from the side of the table where the laurels were. Faucit was not sitting, but standing, and watched him restlessly.

"Ah!" he said, "at Luscombe Abbey. You know Jem Gosling then?" he added after a pause.

"Your pupil?" answered the man who called himself Lestrange. "Yes. I expect to be very intimate with him some day. He is a finished specimen of that fashionable remove of the new school, whose language is slang, whose topics scandal, whose diet brandy-and-soda. You indulge, I see?" he said carelessly, looking at the remains of Gosling's visit.

"Very seldom," said Faucit.

"I'm sorry for that. It's such a useful agent of mine, and so active now-a-days. This age will be known in future history as the brandy-and-sodaic period, or as the age of B. and S. — brandy and slang."

Faucit laughed shortly, and it was a cheery laugh to hear, with the ring of a very sound pair of lungs in it.

"You're a strange fellow," he said, already under the influence of the indefinable charm of this new acquaintance.

He took the chair opposite the Count's, and produced a short meerschaum which had safely passed all
the dangers of colouring. He looked at it with fondness as he took it from its case, knocked out a small
remnant of ashes, tested the passage with a preliminary
draught or two, then filled it from a battered old pouch
with mechanical precision, and was proceeding to light
up when the other interrupted him.

"You smoke too, I see," he said familiarly, but
without any suggestion of impertinence, "a short pipe,
and Cavendish tobacco. Quite right. Another of my
agents. Let me offer you a mild cigar, against my
own interests," he added, bringing out on his side a
dainty cigar-case mounted with a cipher, and stocked
with cigars on one side and cigarettes on the other.
"I always lay in a stock when I call in at the
Havannah."

"Thanks," answered Faucit, declining the offered
case. "I prefer a pipe. It's such a companion," he
said, with half a sigh.

The Count Lestrange looked at him as he lighted
up, and did the same himself for a fresh cigar.

"Like a wife," he said, abruptly. "Have you got
one?"

"A wife! No. Why do you ask?"

"Because I prefer cigars," answered the Count,
carelessly.

"I don't follow you," said the other.

"Don't you? A pipe is the type of a wife. Let
me look at yours. Yes," he went on, taking the pipe
which Faucit handed him with evident curiosity, and
interest in his strange visitor. "Yes, very nice for those
that like it; sweet, well-coloured, and ripe. But how
much time and pains did it cost you to bring it to that
perfection? How much watching, coaxing, humouring,
and occasional nausea? Neglect it for a while, and
the colour will die out. The game may be worth the
candle, perhaps, when you have succeeded in producing
a pipe like this. But how many pipes are there that

won't colour, and will burn? That's why a man so often marries a widow, a worldly-wise woman, or a practised flirt. He buys his pipe ready coloured, forgetting, poor devil, that it was coloured to suit other tastes."

There was a slight smile at one corner of the mouth and an indefinable something in the voice as he said the last words, which could not be seized, but left an uneasy impression on the ear.

"What a singular parallel," said Faucit, uneasily, the pipe suspended in his hand, his legs crossed, and watching.

Frisco growled.

"Shall I carry it further?" asked Lestrange. "I prefer cigars. Look!" and he let a thin stream of smoke curl round his moustache. "You can buy them coarse and cheap, if you please. At the worst, you can throw them away half-smoked, and for a minute they leave a rank taste behind them. But choose them well, as I do. Savour the first whiff, the sweetest of all! let it burn slowly, evenly, tenderly; you know at the beginning that it can't outlast an hour. It turns to ashes as you smoke it—yes. Black if it's a bad one, and gone in a moment. But see how my ash clings still, white, firm, and round, till the last taste is gone and the last kiss savoured, and then melts at a breath, as this will, to the four winds of memory!" And he flipped the white ash away.

"Go on," said Faucit; "I like it."

"It would carry me too far. I find a doubtful specimen even among my best sometimes, which comes to a knot in the middle, and goes out. I can knock off the ash and relight it, if I will; but it will never smoke the same again, and I prefer to throw it away. There are plenty more where it came from." And the soft voice took the same tone again.

"True enough," observed Faucit, half-attracted and half-repelled. "But I smoke a pipe because it's cheaper," he said with a laugh.

"Ah! and a wife is not. All parallels break down somewhere," said the Count, laughing too, pleasantly, at himself, "and that's where mine does. But why consult economy?" he went on. "You're rich enough to please yourself."

"Rich! I!" answered the recluse. "After all, you don't know much about me."

He spoke rather abruptly now.

"Don't I?" said the other, careless of the change of tone, and speaking even more quietly than before, and with deliberate emphasis. "After your mother's death, when you had left Oxford, for reasons of your own you took another name, and travelled abroad for some years; then you settled here a few months ago, buying the little cottage close by, and spending your time here. It's an odd idea," he added, looking round the time-worn old place; "but I never quarrel with anybody's taste in the matter of residence. Mine has been thought peculiar, you know," said the Count, with an odd smile, and half-shutting his eyes, which were on Faucit's face.

The hermit was growing visibly restive under this curious visitation, and his annoyance showed itself in his voice and manner, as he got up from his seat, shut his pipe up in its case with a snap, plunged his two hands again, British fashion, into his trousers pockets, and began to walk restlessly about the enclosure, Frisco prowling after him protectively. The Count watched them, but didn't move.

"There are many ways," said Faucit impatiently, "in which you might get as much information as this, sir, if you care to take the trouble to pry into other men's affairs. As you know so much, you may be aware exactly what my fortune is."

"I am."

"You are welcome to the knowledge," said the other with a short and irritated laugh, "and to the fortune, if you like. Of all miseries, a competence is the worst."

"Avoid vulgar errors," said Lestrange, shaking his

head with an air of admonition. "It's an excellent thing, only men don't use it properly. Yours is not a bad competence, though."

"Splendid. A few hundreds a year."

"Forty thousand," was the cool reply.

"What?" The sharp question rang through the ruins, as the man turned full round on his visitor.

"That was about the figure of your Uncle Foster's fortune, I think?" said the Count, with a new but undemonstrative seriousness in his tone, while those magnetic eyes of his shifted a little, now that the other was looking straight at him.

"My Uncle Foster! Where did you learn so much about us? He behaved infamously to my mother, and we have never met for years. His fortune is no concern of mine, for he will never leave me a penny of it."

"I know that." And Lestrange made a study of his ring. "But, like men of his character, who dislike leaving pennies, he wouldn't leave it to anybody else either. He died in a fit of apoplexy, without a will. You are his heir."

The quiet phrases, dropped softly and impressively one after the other, fell upon Faucit's ear without reaching his sense, and he felt like a man talking in a dream.

"Died!" he said, putting his left hand to his forehead, and trying to think. "Where and when?"

"In Scotland—last night. I had the first intelligence, naturally." And the speaker smiled the same odd smile again.

"Who are you?" suddenly asked Faucit, very shortly and sharply; as if half in the mood for a quarrel.

"I have told you," answered the other, with the simplest frankness—"the Count Lestrange. You needn't have sent for me if you didn't want me."

"Sent for you! nonsense. Why did you come here? What do you mean? Did you say that my uncle was dead? did you say that I am his heir?"

" I said so, certainly."

Faucit came straight up to him, sate again on the chair he had left, rested his left elbow on the table, and looked over it.

" You don't look as if you were joking; and I warn you it might be a bad joke."

" I never joke," answered the Count, quite unruffled. " Why should I ? it's such an inferior amusement. You are the happy owner of forty thousand a year."

" Will you swear that this is true ? " asked Faucit, his teeth setting as he spoke, and his face looking very strong.

" I will. I swear that it's true."

There was a pause of some moments—one of those pauses which seem all silence, all round and everywhere. The strange Count might have cast a glamour over the whole place. A sudden cloud-rack had for a time darkened the September brightness, and the old ruin seemed napping in the shade. A few sheep-bells outside set the silence off. Frisco had grown quite quiet, and might have been fascinated. And the throbbing of Faucit's heart seemed to him as loud as the sheep-bells.

" I can't realize it," he said, when the silence became pain.

" You will," said Lestrange, looking at him. " Think it over."

He got up, laid his right hand lightly and with a sort of patronage on Faucit's shoulder, passed him by as he buried his head in both his hands, then crossed to the old lancet-arch, and leaned against the buttress, watching the other with a smile.

CHAPTER IV.

IN GOOD SOCIETY.

"Well!" There had been another and a longer pause before the Count spoke again. "I have given you the first thing you wanted, and the most important."

"Yes," said Faucit bitterly; and a whole history seemed to have passed over his face. "Money buys everything."

"Vulgar error again; it doesn't. But it buys that which does buy everything—opportunity. Opportunity makes friends, love, everything, and the best that can be made, for those that care for them; and all opportunities are open to the rich man, who has the brains and the wish to use them."

The strange philosopher was speaking very freely and pleasantly now, with a careless kind of cheerfulness which had its effect upon his listener, who smiled.

"I suppose that's true," he said.

"Of course it is. The talk about bargain and sale in hearts is overdone, like every other talk now-a-days; and I say nothing of sham love, which of course can be bought, but it isn't worth it. But a woman has a thousand opportunities of loving a rich man where she has one of loving a poor one; and the lovable rich man wins love—real love, such as it is—where the lovable poor man fails. Opportunity. Am I boring you?"

"No, indeed. I'm glad to listen."

"The same with friends. A fool, rich or poor, doesn't make real friends. But if a good fellow be rich, he can give dinners, lend horses, and display his qualities. That makes friends:—real friends. Opportunity."

"But opportunity cannot buy youth," said the other, shaking his head.

"Pardon me," said the Count, in the same cheery tone. "Given a good constitution, it secures the means of managing it. And that is health; and health is, youth. Q. E. D."

The speaker was still leaning against the arch, and beheading with his riding-whip some of the taller of the wild grasses which grew in rank luxuriance about it. Faucit, as he turned round in his chair, and nursing his knee with his two hands, looked at his visitor, remembered his Roman history, and thought of Tarquin. The oddest associations, the most incongruous memories and ideas, were jostling each other in his puzzled brain. The whole scene and its surroundings were so strange: he had been living of late so unreal and unhuman a life, —he to whom in the old days the company of good friends and good cheer had been half himself,— and, above all, the feeling that in spite of himself he did not resent the intrusion of this singular stranger with the Satanic credentials, was strong upon him. As for the news of the fortune, he could make nothing of it yet, beyond the feeling that from this moment his life was in some way changed. He could not go on playing at hermit on forty thousand a-year.

"Whoever you are," he said to Lestrange enquiringly, in comment upon his last theorem, "you seem to have thought of these things."

"Of course I have," was the answer, as the riding-whip brought down an unusually tall specimen, which looked like a chief of his tribe. "Money's no use to me; but I have as much youth as I want, as many friends as I want, and more love than I want. It's troublesome sometimes," he added in a lower voice, more to himself than his companion, whistling thoughtfully between his teeth.

A woman's voice came from outside at the moment —a rather hard and worn voice, but a gentlewoman's.

"This way," were the words addressed to some one with the speaker; "through the arch here."

"How odd!" said Lestrange, with a soft laugh, and

stroking his moustache. He turned round to Faucit
and came back to him. "That's Lady Luscombe,"
he said to him with quiet emphasis; "an excellent
.woman and a good friend. Here is your opportunity;
use it—and buy her!"

Lady Luscombe's face, as she came in through the
arch, was like the voice which had heralded it—rather
hard and worn. Yet it was a sad and handsome and
not unkindly face—the face of a woman of forty, with
the well-preserved figure of ten or twelve years less,
and with features good and regular. The nose was
aquiline in shape, and the complexion, especially round
the cheek-bones, rather high. The eyes were of a light
gray, wandering and distressful, but honest enough, and
expressing the general sadness of the face like an omen.
Her smile was pretty when it came, which was rarely;
and she was softly dressed, in grays and laces. The
hair was smooth and abundant; but white—quite white.
She looked like a woman who had fought the battle of
life, and lost it.

The two companions who were with her made a
strange contrast. One was a rotund and rubicund
matron some ten or fifteen years older than she, with
an expression of the most absolute good-nature, ex-
haustive and exhausting. She had no features, so
they need not be described. Audrey's question—"Lord
warrant us! what features?" might sum up a good
many people besides Lady Pepperharrow.

The chief impression left by her on the mind was
a gorgeous daring of costume, in which the most pronounced combinations of red, green, and yellow resulted
in a vague whole suggestive of a Bird of Paradise.
As "The Bird," indeed, she was consequently known
to Beauty Gosling and his set. Beauty had a knack
for nicknames, and bestowed them freely. He had
also been known to christen Lady Pepperharrow as
"the h-less one," with reference to a weakness of hers
which she rather impressed upon her friends.

The late Sir Ugh Pepperarrow, who had been very

properly knighted for boiling soap in unusual quantities, was a great trial to his relict at the start of his name, and again half way through. Nobody quite knew why Lady Pepperharrow was fashionable, but she was. That she was a guest of Lady Luscombe in itself showed that: so did it that she and her hostess were now escorted by Lord Viscount Pentonville, who could make any social coin current which he chose to favour, whatever its metal.

Pentonville had ruined the domestic happiness, Gosling used to say, of more husbands than any man since the days of Don Juan, through a new Don Juanism of his own, of a kind unimpeachably moral. He took up young married women and posed them as beauties, supplying a new one where his unfailing instinct detected satiety beforehand. It was whispered indeed that he was secretly connected with two or three of the leading photographers' houses, by a financial arrangement convenient to both sides. And it was more than whispered that he was the author, subject to editorial correction as regarded the English, of the social paragraphs, dealing with these ladies' dresses and private lives, which were the principal attraction of those two flourishing weekly newspapers avowedly established for the purification of society,—" Peep Hole," and " The Flunkey."

Lord Pentonville, however, was not a recognized author, and in the excess of his modesty never signed his name to anything he wrote; the privileges of the English press, of which Englishmen are so tenacious and so justly proud, entitling him therefore to deny his own works when advisable. Indeed, as his editor, technically speaking, wrote his articles for him, he considered that he kept on the windy side of the divine law in exercising his privilege.

The fabulous number of years attributed to his Lordship by Gosling was justified by the appearance of his face, which was wrinkled and puckered and needle-scored to an extent which made him look as if he had been engaged in a long prize-fight with Time. He wore a pronounced and defiant little wig, which he flattered himself baffled observation. From a subtle study of the processes of Nature, he had it made white, added an incipient baldness at the temples, then dyed it to a rich brown, then greased it well with the fashionable unguent of the day, and felt himself a power. The effect was to the last degree weird and wiglike.

Lord Pentonville was very short-sighted, but despised eye-glasses; and peered into people's faces, after a method quite his own, with a little pair of oysterous eyes of no particular colour. He had to stand on tiptoe to do it, in most cases, for he was most diminutive, and his walk resembled a sort of little trot, the oddness of which was increased by the tight trousers which he always wore strapped over his shiny and corn-producing boots.

Gosling maintained that old Pen was obliged to trot and to strap, because he must fall to pieces if he didn't, like the cab-horse in Leech's picture, which tumbled down directly it was taken out of harness. Such as he was, however, a very great man and arbiter of society was little Lord Pentonville, the glass of fashion with its own mould of form.

"This will be the very place for the picnic, I think, Lord Pentonville," said Lady Luscombe, as the three entered the quadrangle, in a rather tired and uninterested tone.

The two men who had watched them enter had drawn back a little into the angle of the ruin, and were not at first seen by the new-comers.

"Ca—ca—capital," answered his Lordship, who was balbic of speech, and kept an old sort of tune to his trot in his talk. He had a way of stumbling over his first word, and bringing out the rest with a rush, like a man who has broken a fence down. "I'll tell them to bring the hampers at once. P—plenty of animals, and no p—ossible place to sit down."

"How ot it is," sighed Lady Pepperharrow, fatly.

"It's an odd place too. But, Lady Luscombe, do look at the colouring. It quite reminds me of the old masters. Such wonderful people as those old masters were, you know. Not but that I think dear Mr. Long Locke's beautiful paintings quite as appy in their way. His renderings of the light and shade are so bold. You quite wonder where he gets them from."

"From science, dear Lady Pepperharrow," said Lestrange, coming forward. "Science is the modern alkali, by which we learn to correct the too pronounced acids of Nature and Religion."

"Dear me, yes, Count Lestrange," answered the lady. "You always say such clever things. But then everybody hasn't your gifts. And I wish you wouldn't say anything uncomfortable about religion. I'm sure I don't know what I should do without it, and without the comfort of dear Mr. Birmingham Pope's prayers. He always dresses so beautifully, that I am sure they are always answered."

"Always?" said Lestrange. "Surely he prays every day, and as fervently as for everything else, that *all* the nobility may be endued with grace, wisdom, and understanding. That prayer has not been answered yet—at least to the full extent," he added, glancing at Pentonville, who was contentedly absorbed in various little trots of discovery about the quadrangle.

"There's somebody here," said he, peering. None of his senses were exceptionally quick.

"It's Count Lestrange," said Lady Luscombe in a low voice. Her expression had suddenly flashed into life when she saw the Count. There was a strange interest in it, and a stranger fear. "Have the riders arrived then?" she said to Lestrange.

"Not yet," he answered, with a shade of familiarity in his tone. It was but a shade; for by shades only did his voice or his face vary. "I came on before the rest to have some talk with a friend of mine. This," he said, pointing to Faucit without further prelude, "is the Hermit of the Owl's Nest, of whom you have all heard. We were speaking of him at dinner last night." Faucit came a little forward and bowed gravely. But he turned his face away as much as he could from Lady Pepperharrow. He had given a slight start when first he saw her, and had watched her unobserved with an expression upon his face which gave evidence of strange associations. It was something which had in it an echo of tenderness. As for the lady, she had paid him no attention. She and Lady Luscombe now acknowledged the bow with some surprise, and Pentonville peered.

"That old f—f—f—" he began to ask, turning to the Count.

Faucit winced.

"Fellow?" suggested Lestrange quietly.

"No, person!" snapped Pentonville, like the shot of a saloon-pistol.

He resented assistance.

"Let me introduce him more formally," said the Count.

"No—not now," said Faucit to him in a low voice and hurriedly.

"Nonsense!" the other answered, in the same tone. "What did I tell you about opportunity? Lady Luscombe—Lady Pepperharrow—Lord Pentonville, let me introduce—"

"Any friend of yours, of course," said Lady Luscombe, constrainedly.

"He is sure to be so distinguished," murmured the other lady, with a patronizing sigh, which brought a strange smile into Faucit's face.

"Let me introduce my friend—"

"Fraser," said Faucit in the same manner again.

Lestrange smiled.

"Mr. Fraser," he said, with the gesture devoted by Fashion to an introduction. "Better so at present," he added to himself, looking at his ring. "It suits my own views precisely."

"D—d—d—delighted, I'm sure, quite delighted!"

said the peer, rushing at the colossal Fraser, standing very much on tiptoe indeed, and inspecting his new acquaintance's middle shirt-button. After which examination he shook hands inquisitively, button-holed the Hermit at the same level, and became confidential.

"Ask him to join the picnic," said Lestrange to Lady Luscombe, still engaged with his ring.

"Your whims are endless," she answered.

"Humour them. Ask him." And the request was like Queen Elizabeth's to Sussex.

"That Mr. Fraser!" she said, hesitatingly, and puzzled, as she looked at the rough unpicnic-like figure before her.

"That Mr. Fraser," he repeated emphatically. "Wasn't it with that object we came here? You remember your promise?" he added, and the brows knit a little.

"To ask him—first to the picnic, and afterwards to stay at the Abbey. Yes; but—I hadn't understood. He is so strange-looking a.man."

"At present. We will remedy that."

She looked at Lestrange.

"Tell me your object," she said abruptly, and after a pause.

"When it is gained. I beg of you—"

"Really, Lestrange,—"

"I beg of you." And he emphasized the second word very courteously, but more markedly than he often did. And as he did so he took her hand and kissed it. Nobody else heard the dialogue.

"When you ask like that—" she said, slowly.

"You can't refuse me. I know your kindness. Thank you." He kissed the thin, well-shaped hand again, and turned away.

Lady Luscombe stood still for an instant, then went up to Faucit, an imperceptible shudder coming over her.

"You are the gentleman who has come to live in those ruins, Mr. Fraser?" she said.

"I don't exactly live in them, Lady Luscombe," was the answer, given in a very honest and straightforward fashion. Nobody could mistake the thorough gentleman, and Lady Luscombe did not.

"Don't you?" she said. "I thought you did."

"Such a sweet place for a romantic mind," interjected the soap-boiler's memorial, whose eye Faucit avoided throughout.

"Eg—g—g—gad! I should think he'd be more likely to die in 'em! Most extrorny taste at your age; I shouldn't like it even at mine! Don't you find it devilish dra—dra—dra—"

"Draughty?" said Faucit, shortly.

"No, windy!" And his Lordship trotted off to Lestrange. "D—devilish odd taste, isn't it?" he confided.

"Devilish tastes are for hot temperatures, you know," said Lestrange.

"Ah—y—yes—of course."

Hard Labour retired uncomfortable, and tumbled over Frisco, taking his hat off and apologizing immediately: "I b—b—beg your pardon," he said, and peered again. "D—damn it, it's a dog!"

Frisco, who had retired into a corner and given up the whole thing as beyond his comprehension, accepted the apology with much self-restraint, and a wag of his tail.

"We have made up a picnic here to-day," said Lady Luscombe, continuing the conversation she had been holding with the supposed Fraser, "and it will give us much pleasure if you will join it. My party will be here directly."

"Picnics are not much in my way," he answered. "I don't look like it."

"Still, if you would. But if you don't feel disposed—"

"I will dispose him," Lestrange interrupted.

Lady Luscombe drew back.

"Then I leave him to you," she said, disguising an

uneasy look. "Lord Pentonville, will you explain to the servants what place we have chosen."

"C—c—certainly!" answered Pentonville, with an air of extreme agility, as he trotted out through the arch. "You are too exacting, Lestrange," she whispered under her breath.

"They say—that love is always exacting."

"Love!" She threw volumes into the word. "Lady Pepperharrow, will you come and look for the others?"

The two men were alone again together.

CHAPTER V.

THE COMPACT AND THE VISION.

"WELL, you will join the picnic?" said Lestrange. "No, not I."

"I think you will, for all that."

"I dislike that style of people more than I ever did," said Faucit impatiently. "There's a sort of ridiculous assumption about them, as if one were a clay of an inferior kind, made by a different manufacturer. It irritates me, and I don't like it."

"Perhaps the manufacturer is different," observed Lestrange. "It is difficult to think that a man like yourself, and a Pentonville, are turned out by the same hand. I should be inclined to attribute him to the classic Demiurgus; unless," he added, reflectively, "I had something to do with him myself."

"It's just the inferiority of the creature that makes assumption so enraging. I wanted to kick him."

"That is a very improper frame of mind for a hermit," said Lestrange. "It's a poor little snob, no doubt. But snub downwards is snub upwards, and he gets as much moral kicking from one side as he gives on the other. It's all very even. An odd country this England of yours, where everybody seems to be saying, 'Please find me somebody's boots to lick, and bring somebody else to lick mine.' I happened to be the other day in a picture-gallery, near a princess of the blood-royal, some degrees removed. She had with her her little girl, aged five, necessarily another degree removed. To them enter, as the stage-directions say, two fashionably-dressed young ladies. A mixture of awe and gratification filled their lovely eyes, and each bobbed twice—I cannot call it bowing, for it was an odd jerky motion effected by the crooking of one knee —to the great lady. Then they left-about-faced, and bobbed again, positively, to the little girl—the crook being a shade less hooky. It was a very touching sight; and I was as much amused by the quiet look of fun in the princess's face, a very bonny, good-natured looking woman by the way, as by anything else in the little scene."

"Who were the bobbers?" said Faucit. "Ladies'-maids?"

"Oh, dear, no. They were the beautiful ladies Diana and Castalia Coldharbour, daughters of the Duke of Freezeland, whose ancestors came over with the Conqueror. It's the old story of the bigger and lesser fleas. If you spoke to those girls, they would chill you with a look. The blueness of their blood suggests an underdone joint. It was never even warmed through."

Faucit laughed a good deal. "Yes, it's all very funny," he said; "and I confess I'm out of it. Why on earth did your friend Lady Luscombe ask me to join her picnic?"

"Because you are not justified in being 'out of it' any longer. Because you've got forty thousand a year."

"Does she know that too?" asked Faucit, astonished.

"Yes," said the Count. "I told her."

"What on earth, and why on earth—"

"What business is it of mine, and why should I interfere? You needn't be angry with me; I haven't used an unpleasant means of introduction, have I? and I don't even charge a commission."

The man's good breeding was so perfect, and his easy familiarity so free from any suspicion of discourtesy, that a less well-tempered man than Faucit was couldn't have taken offence if he had tried. Faucit was not inclined to try. Apart altogether from this proffered fortune, which was like a vision of fable-land, he was thoroughly interested and held by the conversation and manners of his new acquaintance.

"Then your Lady Luscombe wouldn't have asked me, if it hadn't been for this fortune-in-the-air?"

"In the air, eh? you'll find most of it in a very solid form. No, she wouldn't; why should she? She has a niece to marry," said the Count, looking down and trimming his nails.

"Oh, is that all? Only another edition of the eternal old story. A girl to sell—wanted a purchaser. I'm sick of all that, and have heard far too much of it; and I don't buy damaged goods, or any other goods either. Her ladyship is early in the slave-market, no doubt, but she's too late for all that. I don't want to have anything to do with her niece, her picnic, or her. Moreover, I don't wish to meet that older lady, for reason of my own." And the speaker's face grew very sad.

Faucit hadn't said so many words in a speech for a long time; and Frisco, whom he was accustomed to talk with in the fondest but fewest monosyllables, looked up from his ruminative attitude in the corner with undisguised wonder at the new ring of the familiar voice. Then his eyes fixed themselves again on Lestrange's unmoved face, with every evidence of much inward exercise. If one may attempt to explore into the course of a dog's thoughts, he had begun to conquer his first violent prepossession against the Count, on discovering how his master gradually thawed in his company; but was now, in spite of himself, coming back to his original feeling. It is much the same with us.

We take an instinctive dislike, feel that we must be wrong, argue ourselves out of it, and are quite on good terms for a time; then suddenly and helplessly relapse, to dislike for evermore, and to give up struggling against it. Very often, too, it is some sudden exhibition of moral shadiness on the other side which explains and justifies the relapse. The other side, perhaps, says the same of us. Therein instinct proves itself a truer thing than reason, and begins new matter of speculation as to the real positions of the different animals, man included, in the scale of intelligence. Faucit himself, among the various literary torsos which at one time he had accumulated in his drawers, had written a good part of an empiric essay—'On the Causes of Johnson's Dislike for Dr. Fell.'

For the present, however, a quiet rebuke from the Count was the only result of the other's outbreak.

"In the new career which is opening for you, my dear fellow," he said, "I strongly recommend you to avoid misanthropy. It's a common assumption, and neither real nor wise. Amuse yourselves with your fellow-creatures, make friends with them, make use of them, make all you can of them, but don't always impute bad motives to them. Our motives are like ourselves, a mixture."

"It strikes me that you imputed the bad motive," said Faucit, laughing. "The lecture comes badly."

"I beg your pardon," answered Lestrange. "I stated a fact, and you instantly drew a misanthropic inference. Nor did I suggest that the motive, if it be one, was bad. It strikes me as exemplary. Miss Caroline Beaufort is a very nice little girl, and you look as if you ought to make a model husband. What can an aunt do better? Come to the picnic."

"Indeed, I'll do nothing of the kind."

"Well, stay here with me a little longer, and it will come to you. Don't move; you mean to join it."

"Eh?" said the other.

"I read acceptance in your face, and I can tell you

the reason. Your little tirade just now was a disguised
farewell to the stylitic life, and to roots and water.
You are tired of misanthropy as a profession."

"Do you really want to persuade me," said the
recluse, "that you are so fond of your fellow-
creatures?"

"I said nothing of the kind," answered the other.
"The operations of your mind are electric. Between
affection and aversion there are many shades of feeling.
Now you are going back into the world, cultivate indifference. Will you take me for your mentor?"

"I suspect," said Faucit, "that you would soon
have enough of me. We are men of a very different
sort."

"All the more likely to agree. If I propose to take
the mentorship, it is to serve us both. My knowledge
of the physical, and still more of what I may call the
moral geography of what is known as the world, is,
though I say it, oddly varied and complete. I keep a
sort of chart of all the reefs and shoals, and I know a
lighthouse when I see it, also if it is given to revolving.
I know when the appearance of solidity is deceitful;
how thin and how many the strata underneath. I can
distinguish the soil which only wants surface-draining
from that which is barren at heart for evermore. I
have also—having set myself early to acquire it—a
singular power and influence over the wills of men. I
can be of great use to you, Faucit, in launching you
in the world (and there is thus much gained already,
that I hear no more objections); and I am interested
in you for reasons which I can explain later."

"Tell me one," said the other, on whom the fascination was growing.

Lestrange hesitated a little, and looked a little
away.

"For one thing—I knew your father," he said.

"Who died when I was a child?"

"Yes. And was very kind to me when I was one."

"The introduction is quite enough," said Faucit,

rising from the grass, on which he had thrown himself down to listen. And he said it with relief in his voice, as if it were a pleasure to feel that he had an excuse for encouraging this self-presented acquaintance. "Why didn't you say it at first? Let us be friends."

He held out his hand to Lestrange, and the two men shook hands. The small nervous fingers disappeared in the other's large grasp, and Frisco, with a slight wag of the tail, and an inaudible growl, witnessed the compact then and there made between the Count Lestrange of the one part, and Guy Faucit, sometime called Fraser, of the other, signed, sealed, and delivered in the dog's presence that blank day of September, in the ruins of the Owl's Nest.

*　　*　　*　　*　　*　　*　　*

"I don't see yet, however," said Guy Faucit, "of what service I can be to you."

"You will be to me," answered Lestrange smilingly, "what the Lord Viscount Pentonville's beauties are to the Lord Viscount Pentonville. He produces them, and he shines by the reflection of their graces, and in the coruscation of their photographs. Why shouldn't I speculate in a man, as he does in a woman? Men are a much better investment, and more interesting altogether. Besides, are your powers of imputation disappearing already? You are a rich man and I am a poor one; and you can serve me in thousands of ways."

"That's true, of course," answered Faucit; "and I'm sure I shall be very glad. You're worth it. But the sweetbread comes just in time to mumble, for I've few enough teeth left. I'm old to invest in."

"Nonsense," said the Count, cheerily. "Youth was one of the commodities you were asking for just now; and with money and friends I have brought it you. What can you want, to begin with, younger than a picnic, and Lord Pentonville?"

"Who is good enough to take me to be older than himself," said Guy, rather angrily.

"Yes," said Lestrange, observant and amused; "I

don't think you look so," he added drily, measuring the
man's broad proportions with his eye, which had a
touch of envy in it. "What an athlete you must have
been." The eye twinkled, and the smoke curled up,
for Lestrange had lighted another cigar, being seldom
without one.

"Must have been ! I am."

Guy Faucit followed the instinct of strong health
and a strong frame, took a long draught of the bright
moorland air into his lungs, expanded them, hit out
with both his arms, and then played "double attack"
with them on his big chest, which answered to the
summons like a mellow cathedral bell, some such
celebrity as Tom of Lincoln. Lestrange fairly laughed
out, on a note distinctly louder than he had yet
allowed his voice to take, bating no jot of its music.

"Vanity, eh ?" he said, still laughing. "You're
young enough."

"Not for picnics and fashionables, hanged if I
am," answered Guy, suddenly forgetting his personality.
"After all, Count Lestrange, I don't know who you
are, or why you take so great an interest in me. But
though our introduction has been a strange one by
ordinary rules, I shall be glad to have any amount of
talk with you, if you care about it. Who wouldn't ?
There isn't much in my talk ; but I can't stand
your Pentonvilles, and that sort of people. I'll see
you whenever you like, but d— your friends."

"Of course—that's my object," said Lestrange.

Faucit laughed in spite of himself.

"You won't join us, then ?" the Count went on.
"Money and youth don't tempt you. What about
revenge, and love ?"

"I don't really want revenge," the other said,
gravely ; "that was a momentary thought. 'I will chide
no dweller in the world but myself, against whom I
know most faults.' No, I don't want revenge ; I'm not
so bad as that."

"As to want revenge ? it's a very natural need,

and a very healthy passion; much healthier than love."

"Love!" Guy said, with utter bitterness in his voice. "The sort of love that fine ladies, with nieces to marry, come dinners-in-hand to offer you! I put my own meaning on that insulted word, Count Lestrange; and I've done with it once for all."

"So much the better for you," was the answer. "You must be a very exceptionally lucky man to be able to put a limit on the illimitable. But I don't believe it, I'm sorry to say; for I can't imagine that I have met the impossible for the first time, after all my experience. Why were you asking for love just now, Faucit, if you don't want it?"

"All men wish to be loved—sometimes," said the other, very slowly and dreamily, with his eyes turned into some unforgotten past.

"Do they? It's not bad,—if they can't make themselves feared;" slowly on his side, and very low and clear.

"Feared!" echoed Faucit. "I've no desire for that."

"It's much more useful," said Lestrange, communing with his cigar. "People will do some things for those they love, everything for those they fear."

Once more the same uncanny note might have been heard in the voice; and once more Guy Faucit's straightforward nature took the alarm.

"You might be a dangerous mentor for a younger man than myself, Count Lestrange," he said; "but such as I am my creeds are formed. One might almost think you had studied philosophy with the master you assumed just now. Yes, my creed is formed; and as one of its first articles, I believe in love,—God help me, —though I have done with it long ago."

There was a pause on both sides, and on both sides the "interval of sound" was filled by tobacco-smoke.

"Yes?" then Lestrange said, quietly. "Tell me the story."

He spoke with an evidence of interest; for he saw

in the face of the other the longing to speak which possesses us all at times, most of all after long-enforced repression. And Guy Faucit had kept his counsel for many solitary years; nor had any one till now had the power to make him break it. He had been tempted often, on ship-board and in bush-land, in strange cities and stranger settlements, amongst the various companions, rough and gentle, with whom he had from time to time consorted, to break the spell of silence which became now and again almost intolerable. But the hour and the man had never come till now. Nor now had he much to say.

"Shall I?" he said, drawing at his pipe and looking straight before him. He spoke more to himself than to the other, and dropped his sentences one by one, as if they were wrung from him with a sort of pain. "The story's a very old one. I cared once for a girl, who—as I thought—cared for me. It began ten years ago, and it ended eight. My mother warned me that she might be frivolous and heartless, and of course I didn't believe her. Of course my mother was right. It was just at the time of my mother's death,—when I had gone down from London and seen her die,—when I most wanted love and help—"

The pause lengthened, and Lestrange remarked quietly—

"Just the time when they fail. Yes?"

"It was then that I heard that the girl had thrown me over for some rich man or another. Nothing very new, is it? That's all."

He got up from his seat with a sigh half of relief, knocked the ashes from his pipe, and walked slowly to the opposite corner of the quadrangle; there he stood looking on the ground, and tapping the grass absently with his foot. More and more and more, the afternoon shadows crept slowly over the scene.

"And you have never seen her or heard of her since?" Lestrange said, watching the set face closely.

"Never."

Guy spoke the word between his teeth, and the shadow that fell on him for the moment was not quite good to see.

"Should you like to do so?" asked the Count, after another pause.

Faucit started, as if a new train of thought had followed on the last. He took counsel in his heart before he answered, and seemed to be arguing out something with himself behind his knitted brows. Then he said curtly—"Yes."

Lestrange took a small photograph from his pocket, and held it out to Guy. "Is that anything like her?"

Guy Faucit looked at the other for a space as if he did not understand, then took the portrait from him. All the blood rushed straight from the face to the heart, leaving the giant for a moment as colourless as a dying man; then rushed back again with a strong reinforcement, and overflowed cheek, and throat, and forehead. His eyes seemed literally to fasten upon the picture before him, and the tempest that shook the man all through seemed for a moment as if it would throw him from his feet.

"How did you get this?" he said, and in a whisper.

The Count paid no apparent attention to the emotion of his companion, but treated the whole matter with the same pleasant air of commonplace. "I like," he said, placidly, "to keep the portraits of people who interest me."

"But what is it?" insisted the other, still in a voice not his own. "It is herself. Where is she?"

It was not from Lestrange that the immediate answer came. Suddenly, from the road behind, a woman's laugh rang out upon the ear, like a silver peal of bells of infinite beauty, in which one of the bells, perhaps, has gone a little bit wrong, and caught a note not quite the others' in the strain. It came without warning, and went crisply through the air. A quick smile flitted over Lestrange's face as he slightly raised his eyebrows and twisted his ring, and half muttered to himself, "Curious. I'm always in the right time."

Upon Guy Faucit the effect of the sound was startling. He literally staggered on his feet, turned again as ashy pale as a snow-drift looks in a dull twilight, and fell back against a projecting part of the wall, behind Lestrange, breathing hard and quick, and like a hunted man. His eyes were fixed upon the road, over Lestrange's shoulder, with half a hope and half a terror in them. Full upon the little knoll behind the road, bathed in a capricious sunbeam which flashed out to frame the picture, sprang and stood the figure of a very beautiful young woman, one of the daughters of the gods, divinely tall and divinely fair as Helen of Troy herself. And a Helen of Troy she might be, worthy a ten years' siege. The full but lithe figure was fitted to a marvel by the shapely blue riding-habit she wore, and the little man's hat, coquettishly worn aside, took the station of Mercury on the mass of soft fair hair, seasoned with countless threads of sunny gold. The complexion was of the pure marble white which is surely the most perfect of all complexions—the veined white of the statue-world, which suggests delicacy of constitution till the flash of interest or of exercise belies the charge. The firm and well-cut hands, not too large for beauty, but not too small for use, were carefully gloved in becoming gauntlets, and one of them had gathered up the habit's folds, while the other tapped her boot with the whip it held.

"All who love me, follow me!" she said out in a laughing voice, apparently to some one behind her. And she stood as upright as a dart, and looked down like Galatea from her pedestal upon the two men in the foreground. Or rather upon one of them. For Lestrange, as the vision appeared, answered the other's last question quietly.

"There she is," he said; and with an imperceptible movement placed himself more completely between

U

them. If his object was to keep Guy out of sight he might have saved himself the pains. For after one long deep look, which seemed to take the picture into the very framework of his heart, to stay there for ever, Guy Faucit fell back, like a man utterly dazed and overcome, into the angle of the ruin which screened him from every part of the road, with one set, yearning, stifled cry—"Good God!"

CHAPTER VI.

DAISY BRENT.

THE visitor shaded her eyes with her raised hand, and looked into the quiet quadrangle, from the centre of which the Count Lestrange was directly facing her. Of the other figure she saw nothing, and nothing of the strange drama which was passing there. Before anything was said, Frisco struck a sort of preliminary note by shaking his head, and crossing quietly to the angle where his master was, to take his place beside him.

"Ah, Mrs. Brent!" said Lestrange, raising his voice without any perceptible modification of the tone, and speaking with familiar acknowledgment.

"The wandering Jew!" laughed she, nodding to the speaker with a manner not indicating any special respect.

> " 'Und aber nach fünf hundert Jahren
> Will ich desselbigen Weges fahren.'

"Shall I translate it for you?" she added.

> "And when five hundred years are o'er,
> I'll travel the self-same road once more."

"I never want to be translated to."

"I know you don't, and apologize. I believe you are the inventor of language; but you always look in your element in out-of-the-way places, most romantic and Byronic of men. What plot are you constructing down there, Manfred ? "

"You know as well as I do, as, like the rest of the world, I only act under your ladyship's orders. I'm constructing a picnic."

"Have you found a good place ? " she asked; "one where my satellites will show to advantage ? "

"Capital, I think," he answered. "Look about you from your point of vantage, and admit that I have done my spiriting well."

Count Lestrange went towards the parapet, and with a rapid motion of the hand signed to Faucit to keep his post. There was no fear of his leaving it, for his eyes having done their part over Lestrange's shoulder, his ears were now drinking in the sound of the rider's voice. Did he remember it as he heard it now ? or did his quick sense detect in it, even in the few syllables of courteous badinage which were passing between her and the Count, something curiously differ- ent from a voice which had once been the music to which his life was set, and had left its melody behind with him wherever he had gone ? There must have been something of this last discovery, and something in it which even in its sadness was not all pain. Were there others in the world who could have suffered as he, and why ?

Meanwhile the Count was leaning carelessly over the parapet upon his elbow, looking up at her whom he had called Mrs. Brent, and she was taking in the scene with evident enjoyment of its rich and quiet beauty.

"Did I not see some one with you ? " she asked.

"With me ? why ? "

"Another of your bad habits, Count. Like the Quakers, you are always answering one question by another. I fancied I caught sight of a figure in the background, which vanished at my coming like a ghost with a bad conscience. Perhaps it was a phantom

U 2

herdsman who haunts the ruins, as he is no more to
be seen. I oughtn't to drive even a ghost away,
ought I ? "

"You ought to bring him back to flesh and blood,"
said Lestrange. " If I were a ghost I should revive at
the sight of you, I'm sure," he added, with a shade of
admiration in his tone which failed to reach Faucit, but
did not escape the quick ear of the woman, better versed
in the fashions of Lestrange.

"I'm not sure that you are not a ghost," she said
hastily, "of some uncomfortable vampiric order. Only
if you rose you would never do it like other ghosts, but
come up sideways like the creature in the 'Corsican
Brothers.' However, I'm not going to stop here all
day, set up on a mound like a Chinese idol. If you
have found the right place for the picnic, well and
good ; and it looks most interesting and mysterious,
made to set you off to advantage, and in every respect
what it ought to be. O dear ! I wonder if there is anything there that will interest me ? "

"I think so," said Lestrange, very quietly.

"Then I shall be with you like a flash of lightning,"
answered she, laughing, " followed by my thunder, at a
long distance."

"Who's your thunder ?" asked the Count, laughing
too.

"My swells! slow, but sure to be after me." And
she burst into a brighter and merrier laugh than before,
which had in it an infinite grace of girlishness and
innocence too, and seemed weighted with less of years
than might have been guessed in her before. It was
the laugh of a woman "with no harm in her," if ever
there was one ; and on Faucit's listening face there was
an expression which was a sort of silent echo of the
laugh he heard. There was relief in it, and somehow
he looked younger, too. Just before, as the lady was
rattling on, he had muttered to himself, " How
changed ! " Now his face had even something of a
smile to answer to her laughter. And so quick, so

singular was the observation of Lestrange that he did not fail to catch the look, as he turned his head in a moment from the knoll where the one stood, to glance at the corner where the other was hidden. Meantime the skirts were more daintily gathered up in the' left hand, and the right waved a laughing farewell.

"In five minutes!" she said; and with the spring of elastic youth the pleasant figure had vanished from the knoll, and was gone, before the echo of that silver laugh had quite died under the moss-grown eaves. Even Frisco had raised his head to acknowledge it, with an indication of a wag of the tail. An odd silence between the two men, with whom such intervals were growing common, followed for a time before either moved or spoke. Lestrange was still leaning over the parapet, and looking after the figure that had just left them, watching her, perhaps, at some little distance, swung lightly to the saddle at the mere touch of a helping hand, and with strange thoughts in his mind, which gave no outward sign other than an expression of greater impenetrableness on the secretive face. Slowly he lighted another cigar, while the other man, full of his strange thoughts too, was coming as slowly to himself. Frisco, coming close to him and whining for notice, and at last taking the unusual step of tattooing Faucit's chest with his fore-paws, first produced a change of attitude. Guy patted him kindly on the head, then stooping, bestowed a welcome caress on his neck, and coming back to the table where he had been sitting when Lestrange appeared, he too immediately consulted the Delphic oracle of modern days, and held fiery communion with his pipe.

"What is she?" presently he said, shortly, and without further prelude, not looking away from the table.

"Mrs. Brent; a social celebrity, and the flower of Lady Luscombe's party," answered Lestrange, not turning his head either, but keeping it fixed upon the road beyond.

"Married?—or a widow?" And the reply, which was a little time coming, was waited for between two whiffs, the pipe showing no sign of life.

"Married."

"Ah." The head sank a little forward as the suspended whiff came. "Where's her husband?"— abruptly.

"Where husbands should be—in India."

"Who is he?"

"Mr. Brent," said Lestrange; and he turned away from the road and left the parapet, the impenetrable look seeming to deepen as he did so, and seated himself once more at the table opposite to the recluse. Then he went on sentence by sentence, dropping them with the same crystal clearness and deliberation, but apparent absence of any marked intention, as before. "A bad husband—he treats her abominably. He was rich, and lost his fortune in speculation. She lives with Lady Pepperharrow as a kind of ward—and stays a good deal at Luscombe Abbey. She is not well off."

The last sentence was more deliberate than the rest, and marked by a quiet disentangling of the ashes of the cigar.

"Has she no relations to take care of her?"

"One—a brother."

"In the army, I think?"

"In the army." Lestrange took no notice of the knowledge of facts implied.

"Isn't he with her?"

"No; he is with his regiment. I don't think he's a very attentive brother." And the two smoked on.

Presently Guy rose and walked down the quadrangle.

"Count Lestrange, I'll join the picnic," he said.

"That's right," answered the other pleasantly. "I am glad to see that you fall in with my views, as I thought you would. Hermitry must be such a bore if persevered in, the essence of life being variety. It is only useful to digest experiences; for when they are assimilated we want to swallow fresh ones. But, by the way, don't call me Count Lestrange. Nobody does except my man Chaffers, and I don't like it."

"What am I to call you?"

"Lestrange, of course. The sooner we get upon the familiar terms agreed upon, the better for the prospects of our meditated fellowship. I can accept my mentorship upon no condition but that of absolute equality."

"Very well," said Guy, who was scarcely listening, as the Count was well aware as he talked on.

He left Guy to his reverie for a short time, watching him in silence, or making some trivial remark, not wanting an answer, till, looking out from the quadrangle again, he saw the figure of a man on the road, to whom he beckoned quietly. Then he went up to Guy Faucit and brought him back to reality.

"Faucit," he said.

"Yes?"

"Are you going to picnic like that?"

"How else?" answered Guy. But as he spoke his eye turned to his rough and uncourtier-like dress and appearance, and he shrugged his shoulders. "I am not very fit for fashion, I suppose."

"Well, the fashions have no doubt changed to a certain extent since those clothes were made. Have you no others?"

"Yes, at my cottage."

"Suppose you go and put them on."

"Eh?"

"It's as well to do yourself justice, isn't it? As mentor, may I venture on a further piece of advice?"

"Certainly. What? After all this dress suits my shaggy personality better than any other."

"Exactly. Don't adapt the dress to the personality —but the personality to the dress."

"What do you mean?"

"There is nothing like a first impression. Of course you know none of this picnic-party; but after the news

I have given you this morning, and one thing or the other, wouldn't you like to be more like the rest of the men of the party, for the benefit of the women? Some one of the women might even attract you, you know."

"And I shouldn't attract them, you mean," said Guy, laughing rather uncomfortably. "I am afraid they must take me for what I am worth. Perhaps there are some of them who ought to know."

"Many people, women especially, are slow to look behind appearances. As I said," added Lestrange cheerily, "there's nothing like a first impression. Now forget the old man, for you're no more of that than I am. Cut off that beard, which doesn't really become you, and come out as the Faucit you were."

"The Faucit I was?" said Guy, very sadly, even through the nervous excitement and restlessness which had taken possession of his whole being and manner since the episode of the rider. "The past is the past, and I don't know how."

"I do," was the reassuring answer; "or if I don't, my man Chaffers will. He's a treasure. I give him no wages to speak of, and he lives on the fat of the land, and is quite content. I ask no questions, and so am I. He never takes my clothes, that I know of, and is always dressed exactly like me. There he is," he concluded, beckoning again with a sign of the head to the man he had noticed in the road, who had passed on, with some picnic properties of which he was in charge, to the entrance by the old arch.

"Chaffers!" called Lestrange in that direction; and the man so summoned came in.

Even in the pre-occupation of his mind Guy Faucit was struck, and rather uncomfortably, by his curious appearance. Not only was he dressed like his master, but "made up at him," as the players say, in every available particular, presenting just the outward and inward difference between an original masterpiece and a careful copy, in which the form is so deftly imitated, that it is difficult to say why the expression is so entirely gone. The height and figure of the man appeared to have been trained upon his master's tailor's measure; the gestures were almost the same, yet gave exactly the opposite effect—servility instead of masterfulness; the dress, as Lestrange said, was identical; and the colouring of the face looked as if stage-pigments had reproduced the other's in a waxier shape. The voice had attained by practice to the same pitch without the same music: and the whole effect was appreciably theatrical, and suggested one of those "doubles" of an actor who are introduced upon the stage, worked up through the footlight medium to what becomes for the first moment quite a startling illusion. Lestrange contemplated him with an amused gravity. He walked furtively into the middle of the quadrangle, keeping a wary eye on Frisco, whose appearance seemed rather to disconcert him.

"Yes, Count Lestrange," he said, in a voice which sounded, after the Count's, like an echo in a decline.

"Leave the hampers for a moment," said the Count. "Chaffers has a soul above hampers," he added to Guy; "but he condescends. This is my friend, Mr. Faucit, Chaffers. You have my little dressing-case with you?"

"Yes, Count Lestrange."

"Quite right. I never, my dear Faucit, travel without Chaffers, or he without my little case. One never knows. It is outside, Chaffers? Bring it."

"Yes, Count Lestrange." And the singular shadow effaced itself with an apologetic bow.

"What an odd-looking servant!" said Guy, as he went out. "Is he pleasant to have about you?"

"He knows my ways, which is essential to me in the wandering life I lead. I never know to-day where I may be to-morrow, and at Trouville or San Francisco Chaffers is equally at home. He is my courier, valet, confidential servant, secretary, everything; and his personal attachment to me is above suspicion. I secured that from the first in a way of my own—quite an amusing story."

But Faucit was paying no especial attention again, and, keenly watching the play of his face, Lestrange left him to his thoughts for a minute or two till the man Chaffers returned with the little case of which Lestrange had spoken. The Count beckoned him, and spoke to him in a low voice before the absorbed Faucit was aware of his presence.

"I want you to wait on Mr. Faucit, Chaffers, as if it were on myself."

Chaffers bowed.

"He will show you to his house, and tell you what he wants. A sweep or two of the razor will get rid of that beard, and—I want him to look his youngest, which should be young. The moustache is a little grey—and — you understand?" he added, with a gesture of the hand towards the jet-black facing of his own lip.

"Yes, Count Lestrange," was again the reply.

"Faucit," said the Count, looking down the road, "I see sign of carriages and horsemen in the distance. My lady's coachmen are too well fed, and feed their cattle too well, to vie with Jehu. But they will be here before long — the Pepperharrows, Pentonvilles, Brents, and all. Some of the party have been 'doing' something in the neighbourhood, and want righteous refreshment after their labours. Had not you better make your escape with Chaffers at once? You will soon be ready to face Society in its own uniform."

Faucit seemed to have gathered himself together again when Lestrange, with a slight emphasis, threw in the name of Brent, and he too walked rapidly up to the road and threw a glance along it. Then he turned to Lestrange with a manner entirely changed from the sad self-possession which had marked him before, for his face and voice had in them something of a boy's eagerness, mixed with a singular kind of man's determination.

"Send your man with me, Lestrange," he said. "I don't know what fancy it can have been that made me provide myself with decent clothes, even in this out-of-the-way place. But you see," he added, with a nervous laugh, "one never knows what may happen."

"Never," said Lestrange, laughing. "Even the hermits of old probably put their Sunday best away in clover somewhere, in the driest part of the cell. No man burns the bridges which connect him with common sense till he can't help himself. Make haste."

"Come with me, Chaffers," said Guy Faucit, quickly; and he led the way through the disused path among the laurels by which Lestrange had entered, followed by the shadowy man-servant, between whom and his master another glance of intelligence passed. Frisco bounded after them.

Leaning against the ruin, with one foot crossed over the ankle of the other, Lestrange watched the pair, as with one hand he put the laurels aside, still with the look on his face, and still smoking.

"Just so," he said. "So far, so good."

CHAPTER VII.

THE PICNIC.

IT would have needed something more of a knowledge of character, more of the power of reading the thoughts in the book of the features than was possessed even by the magician of Edgar Poe's curious fancy, to gather, either from the face or manner of the Count, when he was left alone, anything whatever of the thoughts that were passing in his mind. Perhaps there was something of visible relief when he found himself in his own companionship, as if it were more to his taste than that of any other man. But there was

nothing to suggest to Asmodeus himself, whose part
the chronicler may be taken to play, the smallest key
to the schemes and purposes that were working in that
subtle brain.

There are men among the mask-wearers who have
been caught without their mask when alone; but this
might have been the historic prisoner in the vizard
of iron. The same singular smile—the same restless,
piercing look—the same inscrutable expression—the
same rapid observation of all about him, given now to
things instead of men, were the characteristics of Lestrange by himself, as of Lestrange with others. When
the two who had just left him had gone out of his
sight, he began by taking a rapid survey of the place
about him, more close than he had done when with
Guy. He noted all the bearings of the ruin, paced the
length and breadth from side to side, and made himself
generally acquainted with all the details of the scene.
Then he seated himself where Guy had sate, and took
up the book which Guy had left behind. He glanced
at the title, and turned the pages over, making some
close study, as if with a purpose, of some of the things
he read. Then he let the book fall open on his knee,
and thoughtfully caressed with his hand the short,
pointed beard. More and more he became self-involved,
as one puzzled with some mysterious problem. After a
time his eye glanced quickly towards the laurels, then
quickly towards the road, and something of impatience
might have been suspected from his manner, even in
spite of the impassive face.

But the suspicion could not last long, for after once
more walking up to the parapet and leaning over it, he
took out a telegram, and read it over to himself with a
slight smile. Asmodeus is privileged with telegrams,
and this one came from Scotland. "Foster has had
another stroke, and died last night." Lestrange laughed
quietly to himself as he read it, and tearing it into
minute pieces, let them float away, to adhere together
no more. He began whistling softly between his teeth,

and slowly paced the quadrangle, with his hands crossed under his coat behind, and his eyes thoughtfully reading the ground, in the attitude so much associated with Napoleon the Third, to those who have seen him taking his walks in the garden of the Tuilleries.

No thoughts of the Count Lestrange ever took form upon his lips when he was alone. But Asmodeus may in this instance steal from his heart the peroration of his long soliloquy. "Oh, there must be a Providence somewhere—a Providence which I command—I. Why do they call me 'Satan Lestrange,' I wonder?"

He lifted his head and left his own company at this crisis in his thoughts, as the same clear voice which had heralded the vision on the knoll broke in upon the silence again, this time in a burst of music, carolling like a bird or a bell the opening bars of the waltz from "Faust." In another second the owner of the voice came in through the lancet arch, followed by a goodly company of gilded youth and age, in their fashions more or less elastic or more or less leisurely.

It was obvious at once, however, that the queen of all the revels was Daisy Brent, and obvious that no other woman in the company could hold her own in looks or in grace with this winsome Diana. If distance lent an enchantment of its own to the picture on the knoll, the enchantment of proximity was only greater. The sweet face bore traces of hidden care and of hidden sorrow, and something that had the impress of a passionate regret. Recklessness, too, and a touch of defiance, had striven to set upon it an indelible seal. But the seal, though set, was not indelible. The eyes and mouth and whole expression carried too strongly for that the tokens of a very lovable womanhood, from which neither sorrow nor trouble nor evil had been able to efface the "springtime of her childish years."

To see Daisy Brent was to like her; to know her was to love her; and the many who did know her availed themselves of the last privilege very largely. Nobody ever thought of disputing her royalty anywhere, and the most careless of the careless set in which she lived and moved and had her frivolous being felt a sort of uneasy wish that she were less careless and less frivolous than they. But if any such feeling ever troubled herself, she resolutely and immediately set it down.

The extent of the influence of Daisy Brent over the society assembled at Luscombe Abbey may be measured by the fact that she had insisted on a picnic in the height of the shooting-season, and that the most obstinate male creature had not attempted to dispute her will. For it was trying, certainly, to men of the mental constitution of the Duke of Surbiton and the Marquis of Norbiton, or of the unimpeachable social consistency of Sir Brummel Coates, to be called upon to agree to anything so irregular. All very well in the season, when it is well known that there is nothing for anybody to do, to make holiday of that kind on some popular cricket-ground or race-course, or somewhere in the vague country known as "up the river." But the serious business of life begins with autumn, and it is possible that the men's objections to sacrificing a working day to the caprice of a pretty woman had something of conscience about them. The Honourable Jem Gosling, perhaps, was the solitary exception; for to him the world in all its aspects bore the pleasant face of butterflydom, and though he had placed it on record that, "bar the Brent, he would rather be out in the turnip-fields," he troubled himself about the weighty matter very little indeed.

> " A picnic by tne river's brim
> Another picnic was to him."

Be these things as they may, the will of Daisy Brent was law; and so it came to pass that the rank and fashion of Luscombe Abbey, a social institution of great importance in a certain world, were assembled together for an anachronistic picnic in the grey and old-world ruins of the Owl's Nest, on that sunny and memorable September afternoon.

Daisy's cheek was flushed to its most becoming shade with the spirit and excitement of the ride, and her eyes sparkling with genuine enjoyment. In a moment her quick sight took in the picturesqueness of the whole scene, and the sward of living green which carpeted it.

"How delicious!" she exclaimed. "What a day for a ride, and what a carpet for a waltz! Why can't one waltz in a riding-habit, and combine the two jolliest things in the world? Jemmy, take me round the waist and see if it's possible. Trà, là, làla, lalà, la, làla!"

"Awfully possible to take you round the waist," answered Jem Gosling, who had pushed into the place nearest to the divinity, and was ready to justify against all comers his position as one of Daisy's prime favourites. "Always feel as if I ought to take it between my thumb and finger, as if it were a pen."

"Tight-lacing," observed apart Miss Caroline Beaufort to her bosom friend, Miss Emily Challoner. "I do think she might let Jemmy alone."

"Why don't you take him away from her, dear?" was the sleepy answer.

Emily Challoner was tall and pale and slight, and affected a West Indian kind of manner, as of one who had suffered from the tropics. Carrie Beaufort was plump and small and merry, with twinkling eyes, and one of the most audacious little noses in the world. It always looked, with the rest of her face, as if it had been intended to be classical,—which indeed was a characteristic of all other Beaufort noses,—but had suddenly broken down at the bridge. It was reported in the family that a brother Beaufort had sat upon it once for a continuous time in the nursery, and that all the little Beauforts had afterwards combined to sit on or otherwise put it back again whenever it showed signs of growing, like a Chinese woman's foot. When it resisted such gentle methods too obstinately, they had even been known to tie it round the back of her head with tape.

Then another voice, thick and doubtful, but exceedingly deliberate, took up the tale of Jemmy Gosling's complimentary speech.

"I don't like haw waltzing," said Sir Brummel Coates, baronet of old date, and the best dressed man in London; "in fact, I can't hum waltz. But hum pleasure of your waist haw—in fact, I wish I could."

There was this peculiarity in Sir Brummel's use of the two great monosyllables which serve so large a purpose with the blameless type which he adorned, that they never served with him for interjections, but were embodied, stopless, in the main current of his speech.

"How beautiful!" sighed Daisy, with a tender look at her second cavalier, who had secured the place on the other side of her. "What I like about Brum's compliments is their suggestiveness. They leave so much to the imagination."

"Haw," said Brum, looking red and awkward, and inwardly cogitating what the last remark might imply.

"Poor Brum," said Gosling; "you're going to catch it, old man."

"No, now," remonstrated Coates, "no. 'Pon my soul you're not fair."

Daisy turned to Lady Luscombe with an appealing look, where her hostess was standing close by, superintending arrangements, and in close converse with Lestrange, who had drawn quietly near her.

"Oh, Lady Luscombe, protect me! Here's Sir Brummel says I'm dark, and pledges his salvation that I dye my complexion!"

"Haw come!" said Sir Brummel, with an animal-like protest against a conclusion he entirely failed to follow, amidst the laughter of the party round.

"How much do you get on your salvation when you pledge it, Sir Brummel?" said Count Lestrange, drily. An unpleasant current ran down several spines as he spoke.

"Haw," muttered Coates between the hairs of his moustache, looking at the Count uncomfortably; "when

'the foreign fellow's down on one—where's the hum
.sherry and bitters ?"

He turned aside to a congenial basket, and became
engaged in a discussion of the relative merits of Orange
and Angostura with the Duke of Surbiton and the
Marquis of Norbiton. Both the Duke and the Marquis preferred orange, which seemed to them in some
way intertwined with the constitution, hereditary legislation, and the rights of property. There was a
democratic sound of innovation attached to the younger
form of bitters, which struck them as not quite safe.

"Never liked those things from America, Nor," said
his Grace of Surbiton. "Never quite know where you
are with them."

"Never," agreed the Marquis, emphatically. "All
those sort of things are bad form."

If Nor had decided in favour of Angostura, Sur
would have been equally convinced in his reasoning
powers of the justice of the conclusion. The three
men shook their heads sedately, for Coates had a
preference for Angostura in spite of any political
suspicion that might attach to it, and gravely had a
drink together.

"Have a cigarette, Daisy," said Jemmy Gosling, as
he fluttered fancy free among the hampers, lending a
hand here, bestowing a good-natured word there, and
generally in the best of tempers with himself and with
mankind.

"Thanks awfully," answered his companion, carelessly, as she too helped in the spiriting. "I won't
smoke before lunch."

They began to laugh and chat familiarly together,
much to the inward vexation of a tidy little figure in
another part of the scene, with a pair of bright eyes
and an enquiring nose between them.

"Jemmy," suddenly said Carrie Beaufort, with a
little tap of a very dainty little foot, "come and help
me to unpack this hamper."

She looked temptingly helpless over the task she

x

had undertaken, and Jemmy Gosling would have found it difficult to decline the invitation, even if Daisy Brent had not released her votary by a nod and a smile. Beauty made his way to Carrie Beaufort's side, and they became very pleasantly engaged without loss of time.

The white cloths were laid in picturesque disorder about the strange old quadrangle, more accustomed to rougher and readier festivities from the big trade-town, than to the refined feast of Lucullus which did duty for a picnic to-day. I must leave it to pens more accustomed to the apotheosis of "menus" than mine to enter into detailed descriptions of what there was to eat and drink. And indeed the powers of cookery on these occasions, whatever their possibilities upon paper, always seem in practice rather limited.

The placid and solitary observer who strolls round Lord's Ground during the Eton and Harrow match, and, if he knows nobody to beg a luncheon from, contents himself with a plate of sandwiches and a glass of beer at the tavern, remaining none the worse for either, finds much to speculate on in the absolute sameness of all the fare provided on the different carriages. The same pies seem to do duty all round; the galantine seems to have been turned out by machinery to go round the ground; the cold joints and ducks and fruits to be supplied by one universal purveyor, and even the cups to be compounded of the same receipt. The vintage of Champagne is, of course, the basis of the whole thing from Dan in the gate to Beersheba at the scoring-tent, and suggests sometimes a sort of helpless wonder where it all comes from, or how it is that the supply of the popular drink keeps such effective pace with the de-mand. No wonder Frenchmen drink so little cham-pagne: there can be so little for them. What would be done to anybody in England who ventured to give a luncheon at Lord's or on the river without it? Would he be brought up before Spiers and Pond, or Bertram and Roberts? The historian of these events is at times haunted by the thought that the time will come when we all shall be contracted for in the gross by some one of these enterprising culinary firms, and nationally "found" at so much a mouth, according to our stations in life, from the duke to the man between the sandwich-boards.

There was no lack of champagne in the feast provided by Lady Luscombe, and no lack of enjoyment of a certain kind among the guests who sate down to it. It was no very full-flavoured enjoyment, perhaps, and gave a certain impression of not having been earned, which sometimes tinges such meetings with satiety; and it decidedly rose with the champagne. But one exception, at all events, to any possible rule of non-enjoyment was to be found in worthy Lady Pepperharrow. The soap-boiler's widow was in her glory on the occasion, and beamed, upon everybody round her, reflections of her own harvest-moon-like content.

"The Bird," said Gosling, "was in first-class feather."

"This is really perfectly delightful," she murmured, between two large forkfuls of lobster, to the Duke of Surbiton, upon her right. "Such eavenly scenery to eat in quite sheds an alo about the appetite. Doesn't your Grace think so?" she added.

The Duke looked rather puzzled, but thought it did.

"And lobsters I always find such olesome eating. There are people who find they disagree, but I never ad cause to complain in that way. And I have eaten," she continued, "a large number of them."

Surbiton watched the speaker with quiet admiration; and, without waiting to be asked, transferred a fresh supply of the luxury to her plate.

"Don't," whispered Norbiton, who was on the other side of his friend as usual. "She can't do it."

"She can," answered the other in the same tone. "I'll bet you five to one that she can, and another on that."

"Done," said Norbiton, in a business-like tone. And with a new and personal interest in the result, silently now that the matter was one of earnest, they watched the lobster disappear. The Duke won.

Meanwhile the good understanding between Gosling and his pretty neighbour was destined to be rudely disturbed. The Lord Viscount Pentonville was on the alert. He had taken the deepest interest from the first in the arrangement of the proceedings. He trotted from place to place in all the pride of office, interfered unexpectedly with everybody at the wrong moment, marshalled the servants invariably wrong, and was followed by smothered execrations from their well-drilled ranks as he suddenly descended in his little tight boots upon the toes of one or another of them, and followed it up by knocking up against a second, and profusely apologizing to a third. Assiduously he uncorked mistaken bottles, and nearly made even Lady Pepperharrow ill by pouring her out a seltzer-and-salad-oil, under an impression of hock.

"It didn't taste like ock at all, your Grace," her ladyship said, when recovered in time to save the wager.

And when he had done all the mischief he could in that direction, the Lord Pentonville proceeded to inspect the various groups of two which might be found in different places, sheltered behind favouring joints, or pursuing the universal pastime under cover of popping champagne corks.

"D—do you see," he confided to Lady Luscombe, who was watching with uneasy interest the face of Count Lestrange, "how close G—Gosling and your niece are?"

Recalled to the duties of an aunt and a careful chaperon, Lady Luscombe looked round and spoke to the Beauty. "Mr. Gosling," she said quietly, "I want you here, please."

"What a shame!" muttered poor Carrie, as her hard-won prize escaped her.

To do him justice, he had no wish at all to escape; and made his way to his hostess with what for him was but a bad grace, throwing regretful looks at his pretty companion.

Daisy Brent's eyes twinkled with amusement where she sate enthroned, and engaged in demolishing the intellect of the hapless Coates.

"How delightful to be in such request, Jemmy!" she said to Gosling as he passed her.

"Awfully," answered he.

"Never mind, dear!" purred Emily to her friend, whose bright little face showed obvious signs of her discontent, while Sir Brummel Coates, finding the play of Daisy's small sword too keen for the rather loose joints of his mental armour, by some means or another transferred himself to Emily Challoner's side.

"You won't sit on a fellow, Miss Challoner, will you?" he said.

"No; but I don't mind sitting next him."

"Haw."

The new move in the cards soon attracted the watchful Pentonville.

"C—C—Coates," he whispered in delight to Lady Luscombe, "is spooning Emily Ch—Challoner. Here, I say, the fellows have forgotten the pep—pep—pep—"

"Pepper, Pen?" asked Gosling, offering the article.

"No, salt!"

The serious business of refection and flirtation proceeded on its immemorial way. Some there were playing the game in unconscious earnest, and others in conscious sport, careless enough what the other player might be hoping or feeling. The Count Lestrange alone, self-involved and unusually silent, seemed to have little to add either to the festivity or the purposes of the scene. He had held some talk with Lady Luscombe in the old ironic vein, but not much, and his manner infected her with more and more of a strange uneasiness.

"Where is your promised guest?" she said.

"Wait," he answered.

The furtive and restless eyes were making a close study of the face of Daisy Brent, who, holding her own, first with one admirer and then with another, distributing glances here and fancy there, bright and laughing and careless, yet still with a tone of effort underlying and in an odd way harmonizing it all, moulted no feather of her royalty as queen of the feast.

CHAPTER VIII.

FACE TO FACE.

"And this is the Owl's Nest," said Daisy, looking round her again, "where the Hermit dwells."

"Hangs out," suggested Gosling.

"Hangs out, if you prefer it. What a lovely old place! Just the sort of thing for a scene in a novel."

"Yes," answered Lestrange; "for an unexpected meeting between two old lovers."

He spoke the words carelessly, and a look of pain came over Daisy's face. She turned her head away from the table with a sort of sigh, and began absently to pluck and throw aside some of the wandering wildflowers which clustered about in rich luxuriance, evolved out of some new and unconscious phase of the protoplasm.

"Quite too deliciously romantic!" sighed Carrie Beaufort contentedly, as Jemmy Gosling had made his way back to her side.

"Carrie!" said her aunt, whose attention was called by the rash exclamation, beckoning her niece to her. "How often," she whispered to her in a severe tone, "have I told you not to be so much with Mr. Gosling!"

Poor Carrie's face fell an inch or two, and the

sprightly nose lost some of its curl. "Bother!" was all she had to say to herself.

"Oh, romance!" Daisy exclaimed with impatience, as she left the place where she had been sitting. "Nobody cares for that now; the days, of romance are over."

"Are you sure?" said Lestrange, in a low voice.

He was close at her elbow as he spoke in that soft, mocking tone of his, into which he threw a touch of personal interest.

Lady Luscombe's eyes, which followed the Count very often, followed him now with an ill-pleased expression, which seemed to bode no good. Lady Pepperharrow, at her side, was eating still, under the guardianship of her two peers, who were now seriously engaged in testing her singular capacities in that way to the uttermost. She had distanced the original wager a long way by this time.

"Are you sure?" then said Lestrange.

Daisy shrank from him a little as he addressed her; and then broke into a short, hard laugh.

"Come, you don't mean to say you believe in it?" she said.

"It depends. It's wonderful how long some women will indulge in it, in spite of all disillusion."

"I don't," said Daisy, with an impatient flourish of the little whip she had taken up again. "I care for nobody, no, not I, and everybody cares for me!" She designated the army of courtiers round with a rather contemptuous sweep of her whip.

"You care for—nobody? and are quite sure of it?" asked Lestrange, quietly as before. She looked at him sharp and straight, and the furtive eyes beat a crafty retreat from hers. Daisy always said that she never felt sure of their colour.

"Except my husband, of course!" she answered, with a harder laugh than before.

"No doubt. He's bad enough for any woman to be fond of."

"Let's drop the subject, then," Daisy said, with a hasty shrug of her shoulders, a sort of shudder which passed over at the malice with which the last words were said. She turned away from Lestrange and surveyed the company, like a general looking out for the place to make his most telling attack. "Now, Brum!" she called out cheerily,—"when you and Emily have quite done with the sherry and bitters!"

Brum blushed between the hairs of his beard, detected in a clandestine flirtation in the wrong quarter.

"I say haw," he began, coming up to Daisy apologetically.

"You always do say so, dear Brum," she answered, and dallied with the victim in the toils again.

"I wish she wouldn't," languidly confided Emily to Carrie, with a decided spice of venom in the languor. "We were getting on so nicely." And the two Ariadnes applied themselves to mutual consolation.

"Half-an-hour," said Lestrange to himself, looking at his watch, as he turned away from the place where he had been standing with Daisy, and looked steadily down the road. "He must be here directly."

Lady Luscombe saw the direction of his look, and took the cue it gave her.

"Talking of romance," she said, "you shall see this hermit, the mysterious Mr. Fraser we heard about."

"By Jove!" said Gosling to the knot of men he was discoursing with; "is he coming, after all? How awfully jolly! Who can have drawn the old beggar?"

"A most romantic-looking man," contributed Lady Pepperharrow. "Quite the idea of an ermit about him, and looks as if he ate nothing but erbs and wild oney, like poor dear John the Baptist. I don't think I could be an ermit on only that. Now if I could ave—"

"Lobsters?" suggested Surbiton.

"Lobsters," she said, accepting the suggestion, "it might be done. Yet not, I think, quite to live on." Norbiton poured her out a glass of champagne.

"Thank you; so kind of you to take care of me. All ermits are old, and I ave eard mostly dirty. This one is not dirty; but he is old—about sixty, I should think."

"How awfully stupid!" said Carrie. "Who wants romantic people of sixty?"

"The Clipper sixty!" laughed Gosling to himself. "You wait till you see him," he said to Carrie, who tried to take advantage of the opportunity to get him back to her side. But Master Jemmy had gravitated back to the yet more attractive metal; and even Norbiton and Surbiton showed signs of weariness of the Pepperharrow's appetite, and a, wish to join the circle now gathering round the queen.

Sir Brummel Coates was now in the foremost place, and his mind travelled for some time round the situation last suggested before it arrived at a terminus. Having come to his conclusion he published its results.

"Must be an awful hum bore to be sixty," he said reflectively.

The Lord Viscount Pentonville then put in his oar.

"Nothing when you are u—u—u—"

"Used to it, Pen?"

"No—sound! Is the h—hermit really coming here?"

"He said he would," said Lestrange, still leaning over the parapet, and looking down the road, every now and then taking in the attitude of Daisy, who had formed her court under the shadow of the south-west tower, right opposite the laurels. The eating and the drinking still went on at intervals, the pies and the joints stranded as wrecks of what they were, and the laughter and the talk seasoning the fruits and wine.

"A hermit!" lisped Emily Challoner; "what a peculiar idea! How is it that we have not seen him before, Lady Luscombe?"

"My dear, there are no hermits in our set."

"By Jove, no!" said Gosling, emphatically.

"Jemmy, don't be light," commented Daisy. "Now, everybody, what's to be done next?"

It was a picturesque sight, the grouping of the brightly-dressed party with that sombre background of other days. The old world and the new seemed brought into a violent but harmonious collision, like a drawing-room bravely furnished, in defiance of South Kensington law,—which prescribes a period for every different room or house,—by some unconscious and instinctive taste which picks up everything pretty of its kind by turns, and combines them all together in a restful whole. But Daisy was more and more the centre of the company, attracted by her bright sallies and her ready talk to take part in the skirmishing. Lestrange alone did not seem inclined to add his quota to the general talk, where usually he was foremost in the battle; but restless, impatient, watchful, seemed for once a little unlike himself, and not the master of his usual serenity. Only a close observer would have noted it; and where he was concerned Lady Luscombe seemed a close observer. She looked at him, and she looked at Daisy Brent, and was evidently trying in her mind to find the solution of some problem which was puzzling her.

"Jemmy, come and sit here!" suddenly said Carrie Beaufort, shaken out of the proprieties by impatience, and evidently rather tired of the undivided society of her intimate friend.

"Carrie!" said Lady Luscombe, in a low voice of rebuke.

"Thanks, I'm awfully comfortable!" answered Jem. Gosling, reclined at his full length at Daisy's feet, like a cherubic Hamlet before his Ophelia, shutting his eyes for the full enjoyment of the cigarette which, with his cup of black coffee, he considered that his exertions at luncheon had fully earned him.

"I'm afraid you're à bad boy, Jemmy!" said Daisy, shaking her head at him, and half reclining on her side in an attitude of perfect and unstudied grace, which threw out in bold outline every curve of the lithe and perfect figure. Seen there and so, it was no wonder that all the men raved about her, and only some of the women.

"Come here, Lord Pentonville, there's plenty of room!" murmured poor little Carrie, who had a strong sense that her own advantages were well worth notice, and felt inwardly resentful of the attractions of Daisy, whom she nevertheless liked and admired with all her honest heart.

The small viscount was playing his game of puss in the corner too, and vainly trying to edge his little person into the circle round Daisy.

"I hate these married women, Emily," suddenly added Carrie to her companion, in a burst of involuntary wrath.

"So do I, dear," assented the other with more warmth than usual. "But I wish I was one."

The aftermath of repose was upon everybody, and a general drowsiness seemed to be coming on in the warm and slanting rays of the September sun, travelling slowly on in his never-ending migration, to the far-off lands and waters which were waiting, dark and cold, for his return. The beautiful autumnal shades, nowhere more beautiful than among all this moorland growth, added their subtle influence to the spirit of the scene, and brought into the circle gathered in the grey old quadrangle some magnetic breath from the Island of Proserpine. There was a general and sleepy lull throughout the whole company, and the innumerable small-talk of the insect world made a modest assertion of itself in the interval of sound, like, as George Eliot has finely said of it, "tiniest bells upon the garment of silence." Nobody noted the cat-like figure of the man Chaffers, as he glided in noiselessly through the archway; nobody except Lestrange. A look passed between them as he came up to speak in his master's ear, and Lestrange nodded, while Chaffers as quietly joined the other servants, who were now making up their own picnic in some comfortable housekeeper's room outside, furnished and provided by the care of good Dame Nature, time out of mind the merry-maker's architect.

"How restless you seem, Lestrange," said the

watchful Lady Luscombe, as again the Count paced up and down the quadrangle in a fashion which rather added to the silence than took from it.

"Wait," he answered.

"You must find that coat pretty warm to take exercise in. Unbutton it," suggested Gosling, lazily looking up from his cigarette. He seemed very much of Fox's way of thinking—Why the book?

"Thank you, no," answered the other. "I have a horror of cold."

"Why don't you warm yourself in an honest way then, like the rest of us?" said Daisy. "How I hate a man who doesn't eat lunch, and won't even take a glass of wine in the middle of the day."

"To oblige you, I will, on this occasion only," Lestrange said. And as he said so he stood in the centre of the quadrangle, where a bottle of champagne was near Lady Pepperharrow's hand, as she sate by Lady Luscombe, and poured himself out a glass, looking towards Daisy. "And I think, ladies and gentlemen, that we ought to drink the health of the 'Hermit of the Owl's Nest,' who will be with us directly, I hope, and in his proper place."

"Hear, hear!" was the answering chorus. Daisy Brent held out her glass for Jem Gosling to fill, and the others followed suit all round.

"Hang the foreign fellow," muttered Coates. "He's going to make a confounded haw speech."

"Shut up, Brum," said Daisy. "He won't ask you to return thanks."

"Haw." And the Baronet collapsed.

"Can't you imagine him," said Count Lestrange, in a strange tone of seriousness, "with the help of Lady Pepperharrow's eyes? I know nothing of his story, mind, so only guess. An old man, grey, weary, broken, brought for the first time, under the bright September daylight, face to face with a world which he has forgotten, which has forgotten him—waking, it may be, from a long dream of sorrow and regret, to find that the waking only gives reality to the phantoms that haunted that troubled rest—the phantoms of broken faith, false love, cruel desertion—"

"Count Lestrange!" Daisy said, leaning forward.

One by one, with that strange emphasis of which he was the master, the strong and quiet words fell from him, and with some rapid certainty she felt that, spoken to all there, they were addressed straight to her. A dread and a wonder were upon her spirit, and a sudden forecast of a something that was to come. Was it quite sudden, or had the dread and the wonder sent out some ominous forerunners before them, when first she set foot in that enchanted circle, or stood upon the knoll behind?

"Will he find the world changed, do you think?" motionless in the middle of the circle, like the enchanter who might have drawn it, Lestrange went on.

There was the movement of a step behind the laurels in the tower-angle, and the next moment a man's hand was pushing them aside. "Here he comes, to see—" and with a free and sudden gesture the left arm of Lestrange was directed to the spot.

Upon that spot every eye was riveted, as to every person present the force of that strange preamble had gone home. Above all the eyes of Daisy, which under the sense of sudden expectation, half of hope and all of fear, had dilated to a size unnaturally wide.

Straight through the laurels, and into the middle of the ground, Guy Faucit came. He came like a new presence; handsome, well-dressed, trim, and young. There was no beard upon the manly face, strong in its most perfect prime. The hair was cut and combed and short, fitting compactly to the fine head so firmly set upon the broad athletic shoulders, and the steady eyes looked straight and honestly before him.

Straight to her feet rose Daisy Brent, pale as the cloth behind her, at which she clutched with a crisped and nervous hand, looking full, full at the upright figure before her, and into the eyes which met hers

without a quiver in either, like the crossing of two
blades before the duel may begin.

"Aunt!" cried Carrie Beaufort.

"Good Heavens!" said Lady Luscombe, startled
and wondering. "This is not Mr. Fraser!"

"There is a slight mistake," observed Lestrange,
who had fallen a step back, to watch his effect. And
he took the new-comer by the arm and led him a little
more forward. "Let me introduce my friend—"

Daisy Brent's interruption was like a wailing cry.
"Guy Faucit!"

The Count Lestrange only heard her.

"Just so," he said.

CHAPTER IX.

TRAVELLERS' TALES.

In this strange world of meetings and of partings,
on the vexed borderland of rapture and of pain, no two
ever came together with a greater stirring of the heart
than these. Nothing more utterly unexpected—more
utterly undreamed of—by both of them but a short
space before, who had buried each the other's image
deep in the inner corner, where the most cherished
memories lie unacknowledged, with their petals folded
from the light. Then the light breaks in, and draws
out all the added richness of hue and texture which
have been gathering unawares in the long and wintry
sleep.

Lestrange had prepared his surprise with the art of
a skilful hand when he brought Guy and Daisy together
in that whirl of memories. The weird speech, addressed
directly to her, with which he had suddenly heralded
Guy's entrance on the scene for the girl—girl still, to
the core of her, with all the added lustre of womanhood

and grace of custom—had raised in her mind a strange
anticipation, which the romance of the surroundings,
and the mysterious prescience which touches a spirit of
fine issues,—who knows whence or how?—on the verge
of supreme moments such as these, had unconsciously
begun.

For Guy, whose stronger fibre would bear stronger
tests, the situation was more trying even than for her.
The years which Daisy had devoted to the purchase of
worldly wisdom—which so often turns out to be shoddy
after the largest of prices has been paid for the genuine
manufacture—he had spent in pursuit of a wider but
less conventional experience, which was not so likely to
stand him here in stead. A poor recluse and self-
proscribed outcast from his fellows but an hour or two
before, he came out into the full glare of social day, by
right of wealth and of nurture a leader amongst men, to
take his command up in her presence, for whom once
he had so thirsted to command. Yet round the head
he knew so well, which he longed to press to his heart
with a sort of fiery longing, in the moment when it met
his eyes, was written the most terrible sentence which
can be passed upon hearts as upon souls—" *Lasciate
ogni speranza.*" Yet to all hearts, as to all souls, we
pray, rises even in extremity the undying hope of
appeal, of judgment reversed, and of sentence set aside.
Who shall set a limit to the eternal possibilities, on this
side death or upon the other?

So then they met. With all a good woman's
instinct, and all a good woman's power, Daisy stood the
awful test of that first moment with only the first
moment's sign. Only Lestrange heard the cry she
strangled in her throat; only Lestrange saw the rush
of blood full to the forehead, and the deathly paleness
which instantly followed, to give place almost as
instantly to a perfect self-possession. If the Count had
hoped for a more general effect, he was wrong. Not in
that place and in that company, let the self-conquest
cost her what it might when she should be alone, would

Daisy Brent give way.   All the passionate love of her
life, all the innocent trust and promise of her girlhood,
all the delicious story of the few months of pride and
happiness which had preluded the long and weary
blank of years, were lived and told again in that first
instant of time.   The eyes of all the others, except
Lestrange, were for that instant and more, of course,
fixed upon Faucit, and averted from her; and before
they had time to turn back her course was taken, the
instantaneous and mortal struggle was past and the
"*hysterica passio*" mastered, and the Daisy Fairfield of
a moment was Daisy Brent again.   More—before any
one had spoken, she spoke; for she came frankly forward
with her hand held out, and said,

"Mr. Faucit, is it you?   I am really glad to meet
you again."

Lestrange could admire a strong player, if he could
admire nothing else.

"By G—," he muttered to himself, "that's a great
woman, after all."

"Mrs. Brent, I think?" was Guy Faucit's commonplace answer, spoken in mere uncertainty what he
should say, and guiltless of all intention to wound.
But the name struck her like a wound, from him.

"Yes," she said.

"Now where in the world can you two have known
each other?" asked Jem Gosling, delighted with his
favourite hero's changed appearance, and delighted to
find him an old acquaintance of his favourite heroine.
"It's awfully like old times, Clipper, you know; but
where did you meet Mrs. Brent?"

"Mrs. Brent and I knew each other at Oxford," he
answered.

"At Oxford! nonsense! when I was up there
too?"

"Yes, Mr. Gosling," said Daisy.   "I was really at
Oxford once when you were, and did not know it at the
time.   Think what neglect on my part, and how much
I lost!"

She spoke to him in the old bright tone. But why didn't she call him "Jemmy," as usual?

The position might have been perilously near to tragedy but for Jem Gosling's intervention; and might have fallen into it yet if the muse of comedy, always on the watch when her sister is readiest with the dagger and bowl, had not introduced another personage into the conversation with timely effect.

"Who ever would have thought of it, Mr. Faucit?" said Lady Pepperharrow, warmly renewing acquaintance with her friend of past years. "And yet I don't know why not. It is in romantic scenes of this kind that one would naturally expect to meet a man of your power; though indeed I hardly know why. Only to think of it, Daisy! Do you remember how kind and careful Mr. Faucit was when the Oxford boys ad a rebellion, . and wanted to pull the ouse down?"

This sweeping description of a Commemoration set everybody laughing, and relaxed the strain on the nerves both of Guy and Daisy, even though the associations which the words revived swept over both of them with a wave of pain. Jemmy Gosling, infinitely amused, brought it down to a question of dates, and established the fact that he must have himself been one of the insurgents on the occasion, with Bones of Balliol and Tompkins of Trinity, and many of like thew and sinew.

"Did you know Mr. Bones?" her ladyship asked, mindful of that youth's juvenile attentions.

"I should think I did," said Gosling. "Marrowbones we used to call him."

"Marrowbones!" interposed Carrie Beaufort, whose pert little nose had taken great interest in the new arrival. "Why?"

"Haven't a notion," answered Jemmy. "Cos it runs well, I suppose. Never knew any particular reason for nicknames; we made 'em anyhow. There was a fellow at Eton called Bernard, and we christened him Washpot, and got one name out of the other. How do you think we did it?"

Norbiton and Surbiton showed signs of interest, and wondered if there was a bet in it. And Sir Brummel Coates opined to his languid neighbour, whose long eyelashes were drooping in a very becoming manner, that "there was some queer haw catch in it, Miss Challoner."

"First we called him St. Bernard," ,expounded Gosling, "then Dog, then Doeg, then the Edomite, then Edom, then Moab, and then Washpot. Took about five years to get at it, and then he left."

"What a very silly joke," murmured Emily, in the notes of an Eolian harp. She affected to trivialities the attitude of Hippolyta.

"Stoopid hum bosh," remarked Sir Brummel.

Carrie Beaufort's simpler soul was much delighted with Gosling's playful wit, and she inferred that Eton must have been very great fun, which introduced fresh matter, and started her and Jemmie off on one of their conversational rambles. Grateful enough for the diversion were Guy and Daisy, narrowly watched by the keen eyes of Lestrange. Lady Luscombe the while was intent upon him.

"When did those two know each other, and where?" she asked him. "And who and what is your striking-looking friend, whom you played off in that masquerade? I am sure that I have seen him somewhere."

"I have told you all that there is to know about him; and the romance of his large fortune," answered the Count. "He will be a great addition to our party at the Abbey. You can ask him there before we go home."

"Poor old Bones!" said Faucit, meanwhile, as the old memories began to assert their sway. "Good little fellow he was. I wonder what has become of him."

"Took orders, don't you know?" said Gosling. "He always meant to."

"I never thought he would," was the other's answer.

"Did, though; and came out strong in the extreme

low line. Quite down at the bottom, you know, Lady Pepperharrow—on a seesaw with your friend Mr. Birmingham Pope."

"I'm afraid e must be a very dangerous man," sighed her ladyship.

"Well, he thinks Pope is, you know, and pitches into him every week on a text about charity. Pope uses the same text to pitch into Bones with, so it cuts both ways, and comes to the same in the end. He is very sound in the low line, Bones is, and they call him Grilled Bones now-a-days. Doosid thirsty work this; let's have a split soda, Clipper."

Guy Faucit fitted into his new place soon enough, as we are all of us apt to do when the time comes. There is a sense of unreality mixed up with our lives even at their gravest moments, which stands us in good stead at a crisis, and carries us, calm in all outward seeming, and sometimes even inwardly so, through trials and difficulties which look impossible on paper. That second self, which is a shadowy presence to all men, most realized where the fibre is finest, is ready at such times to step forward and relegate self the first to the background, and make us feel that all that is happening is happening to somebody else. Subtle men have explained this strange double existence by the geography of the brain, and its division into separate thinking parts. But then what explains that? What if that second self, with the half-formed suggestions which at times it makes, escaped before we can grasp them—of having been something else, of being something else, of having done all this before—be the immortal part of us, the thing called the soul? It projects us into another world very often, even here, and makes a world of visions out of this.

Daisy Brent could have told no one afterwards how she lived through that first meeting as she did, with the hero of her solitary love-story in flesh and blood again before her eyes. She looked at him furtively now and again, and saw upon the face that mark of the lasting

Y 2

sorrow which was not to be mistaken. He was alone then, was he? Had he remained unmarried all those years, with everything about him that might charm any woman that might have cared to win him? Or was the wife in the background somewhere, waiting to claim him when he joined her again? A thrill of something which might have been jealousy crossed Daisy's mind. Nonsense! what was this to her? what could it be? No; the second self came to the rescue, and the picnic ended in a dream for Daisy, who felt herself a kind of spirit for the nonce, her gross and earthly counterpart being somewhere else. Like the rest, she soon found herself listening with deep interest to Faucit. With instinctive courtesy, after the first minute or two he began to talk especially to Lady Luscombe, his hostess at the feast to which he had been so unexpectedly bidden, and to Lestrange, who was at her side. The Count, suppressing himself with quiet tact and art, led Faucit on to shine. He brought him, backward and reserved at first, to talk of himself and his travels and adventures, his camp-fire experiences, his moving accidents by flood and field, his

> " Portance in his travel's history,
> Wherein of antres vast, and deserts idle,
> Rough quarries, rocks, and hills whose heads touch heaven,
> It was his hint to speak."

Upon which hint he spoke well, warming to his work as he went on. The things he had to talk about have an interest for everybody, and even Coates and Pentonville felt the better for listening.

Lady Luscombe was fairly fascinated by her new acquaintance, whose whole style of tone and thought, apart even from the experiences he had to tell of, came upon her like a spell of mountain-air, and reminded her of the days when conversation for Marian Vavasour had meant something more than gossip and frivolity. And if she felt this, what did Daisy Brent feel? Every word Guy spoke, every expression he used, brought back the days when she had lived upon the fruit of his ripe and scholarly mind. He was not really changed, she thought. The same vivid observation, the same power of combination and reflection upon what he either saw or read, the same original use of all his materials, marked his talk as of old; while it was the richer for the materials' newer stores of wealth, and for the growth of the mind to its maturest power. And the great education of sorrow had chastened and rounded off the whole. Not Desdemona, listening to Othello, more seriously and more delightedly inclined to hear. Mocking, cynical, devilish,—but himself thoroughly interested in Faucit's adventures,—Iago was on the watch.

Guy Faucit, meanwhile, was surprised at himself, and surprised to find, in spite of the hopelessness of the hope he had once lived for, the pleasure it was to him to be once more talking and talked with, listened to and appreciated. Lestrange was right. He was tired of playing the hermit, after all; and he felt a keen pleasure as he went on in a sense of his own graphic power. Probably there is no keener pleasure that a man can feel than the conscious exercise—the ἐνέργεια as old Aristotle hath it—of a power like that. He had not lost the old trick of fence, then, in all his years of silent self-suppression, in which he had probably not used as many words as came from him now in an hour. "The Man in the Mask" he had been called out in the West; but the mask was off now, and he breathed freely in his native air of culture.

Daisy's presence, perhaps, had more than a little to do with the eloquence which possessed his tongue, as it is just possible that while those horrid house-affairs of hers had drawn Desdemona thence, Senator Brabantio may have found the Moor of Venice a dull dog enough. Well did Guy know how closely Daisy Brent was listening, and though in the circle which had gathered round in the old quadrangle she was the farthest from him of all, he knew that he was talking to and for her. He knew, or he thought, that she alone of all there was aware of the reason of those years of travel and exile whose varied experiences he was depicting. He noted every turn of the graceful head, every change of the mobile face, and he saw with an especial pleasure how, with a playful gentleness, she caressed and made much of Frisco the dog.

The noble fellow had followed on his master's heels when he joined the party, and at once made a house-to-house visitation, sniff-wise, of all the members of it. He was pleasant to Carrie Beaufort, mistrustful of Coates, contemptuous of Pentonville as of Nor and Sur, and generally perceptive and reflective in his views. But he took Daisy into his highest favour, moved by some odd dog-impulse, at once, and she relished her conquest of him more than many of her human victories. He deposited himself at her side, put his cold nose on her lap, and examined her features with close and fearless scrutiny, wagging his tail the while to and fro with a movement as slow and as regular as that of the pendulum of a kitchen clock. And she on her side welcomed this new friend with a curious warmth which had more than matter in it, patted the velvet head, and played with the silken ears, as she listened to his master's story of his purchase of the dog, in all the overpowering destructiveness of puppyhood, in the City of the golden gates.

"Where did you get this fine old fellow, Mr. Faucit?" she had asked.

"At San Francisco, his birthplace and his godmother in one," Faucit said. "It was three years ago, and Frisco has been my one confidant ever since. He knows everything about me."

"Yes?" she said.

It was the only time they addressed each other directly that afternoon.

The afternoon grew steadily to evening, rapt through many a rosy change. The tea went its homely round, by way of stirrup-cup, for those—something of a minority—who preferred it to the attractions of *B.* and *S.*

Guy Faucit took a cup from Daisy's hand, which trembled just a little, for the spoon gave a tiny tell-tale click. The teas in Portland Place rushed back to the thoughts of both of them, through the opened flood-gates of memory. Guy thought it all over—all—in a moment, as he had thought it out to weariness, over and over again, in half the latitudes of the world. Yet, strange to say, for the first time he brought it to a new conclusion.

"It is impossible, impossible!" he thought; "there was some miserable mistake at the bottom of the whole thing."

Was it the magic of her presence which led him to that conclusion? Impassive and quiet under his strong English manner, the man had felt that presence all the time, in the quiver and the tingle of every subject nerve.

Evening; and the horses and carriages were ready. A pretty sight enough, as the animals stood champing the bits and pawing the ground, watched by the well-kemped grooms, on the picturesque old road, as the lengthening shadows fell.

Lady Luscombe, fairly pleased herself into a temporary forgetfulness of Lestrange's leadership, asked Guy Faucit very frankly if he would not come over to the Abbey the next day, and stay there for a time. Count Lestrange had told her about his change of fortunes, she said; and in words which were an echo of Lestrange's, she told him that he must play at hermit no more.

"You are too valuable an addition to society for that," she said.

He fenced with the invitation for some time, till it was repeated with even greater warmth, just as the party was breaking up.

"Do come, Mr. Faucit," Lady Luscombe insisted. "Won't you?"

He hesitated once more; and something made him look straight at Daisy, whose head was turned gracefully and carelessly away, while with her riding-whip

she traced idle forms upon the ground. There was
something in her attitude which spoke to him of an
attention others could not see, unless it was the Count
Lestrange, watching sideways. One moment's pause:
then Guy spoke slowly.

"Thank you, Lady Luscombe. You are very kind.
Yes, I will."

Daisy drew a long breath, and went towards the
gate.

"Will you come to-morrow?" said Lady Luscombe.

"The day after, if you will receive me," he answered.
"I have a few things to arrange here, and then I am
free."

In a few minutes more the good nights had been
said to the newly-elected member, and the cavalcade of
carriages and horse passed fitfully away.

Long after the old ruin had fallen back again under
the great dominion of solitude—long—long—till the
stars had shone out one by one into their soothing
harmony of splendour, and the invisible army of
groundlings was chirping its loudest and merriest to
welcome the march of night, Guy Faucit stood, deep
in thought and deep in dreaming, leaning upon the
parapet above the road, motionless almost as the dog
that watched beside him, awe-stricken, groping his way
in the mazes of a new and startling future. What was
it to be?

CHAPTER X.

GUY AND FRISCO.

THE formal communication from Faucit's lawyer, of
the news which Count Lestrange had anticipated by a
day, reached him the next morning, when he was half
convincing himself that the singular events which had

happened to him were a dream of delusion. Now there was no mistake about it. He had it in black and white under his eyes, written in the well-known hand of the copying clerk of Dryman, Rolls, and Dryman, of Gray's Inn Square, that he, Guy Faucit, was the free and uncontrolled owner of one of those vast properties which now-a-days accumulate, one hardly knows how, from small beginnings. James Foster had probably found the truth of the answer made by some one like him, when asked if he had not had great difficulty in making his large fortune.

"In making my large one, none," he said. "In making the small one it began with, a great deal."

And so the chronicler of this history, who finds himself dealing with colossal fortunes made and lost, with a sense somewhat like his who turns over the sovereigns at the Mint, and dreams of what he would do with them, solaces himself with his humble pint of the ninepence-a-gallon brew, and wonders why Foster shouldn't die worth ten millions instead of one while he is about it. Yet another nought, and the trick is done. Ninepence a gallon, by-the-bye, as has been proved in the course of our housekeeping by Mrs. Balbus and myself,—and she is, I am thankful for it, cunning at the work,—is the right sum to pay, in a well-conducted neighbourhood, for the beer of ordinary life. As it is the cheapest, so is it the purest and the best. Even so doth the philosophic sage, agog among foreign *table-d'hôtes* and the gorgeous ceremonials of the modern pilgrim's progress, divert his eye from high-priced champagne, from generous reds and luscious whites, and quietly order to himself the *ordinaire* of the locality, at three-fourths of a franc, regardless of the name that it may bear. Mark and perpend. A close and silent observation, extending over some years, has convinced the narrator that, in most cases, whatever wine you order *is* that *ordinaire*. Reader, it is *the same, touched up.* Otherwise, why should the Château St. Héliogabale (1801) of one district have a flavour so entirely different from his fellow of the same name of the next?

There is as much humbug about among the wine-fanciers as amongst other men, which is saying a good deal now-a-days. When a man rolls his wine round and round in his glass, passes it under his nose, and then just to his lips, smacks them, holds the wine to the light and looks through it with one eye, then rolls it back again and puts it down and says "Ah!" (having, be it observed, hardly tasted it at all during the ceremony), I mistrust that man.

I remember a jovial friend of mine who was of a hospitable turn, but was wont to buy his wine just as he wanted it, at the nearest vendor's, and startle his family by bringing home bottles of fearful and wonderful vintages—from Australia, California, Honolulu, any-where — about half-an-hour before dinner-time, in his pocket. In fairness it must be admitted, that he did poison his friends sometimes. Once he had a fancier at dinner, who was great on wine, and discussed very learnedly. His host's eye twinkled oddly as he went on.

"Wilkins, my boy," he said, "my cellar, as you know, is small. But I'll give you a glass of port after dinner which—ha, well, I shall be glad of your opinion."

Wilkins acquiesced, and the port came. I remember that it struck my uneducated palate as rather heavy, but I said nothing. Wilkins submitted it, strenuously, to the process I have described.

"Good," he said, "very good, Ned. Now how long have you had that in your cellar?"

"How long should you think now, Wilkins? I thought you'd like it."

"Well, let me see. Seven years?"

"No, my boy. Exactly three quarters of an hour."

I shall never forget the roar which greeted Wilkins's discomfiture.

One story leads to another; and I have a second in my quiver which I must let off here, while Guy Faucit is deep in speculation upon Dryman's letter. One of

these tyrant wine-fanciers—one of the few, I think,
who may really have known what he was about, though
when I once dined with the man himself his sherry was
as bad as any I ever tasted—was entertained, upon
being honoured with some municipal dignity, by the
mayor of the locality, who was nervously anxious for
his opinions upon some particularly old wine of which
he was very proud. It *was* old, no doubt, and seemed
to me as if every vestige of flavour had long died out
of it. The magnate was civil and apologetic, and fought
off offering any opinion. But the luckless host was
urgent and importunate, and would not be put off. At
last the oracle spoke—enforcedly—slowly—cruelly.

"There are some wines," he said, "which you can
tell at a taste have once been good. *I will not undertake to say if this is one of them.*"

Faucit had read his letter. The copying-clerk had
as usual written at the younger Dryman's dictation,
as he did upon all matters, being evidently a man who
must be deeply versed in the private histories and
differences of clients, and probably regarded them all
as a monotonous and wearisome race, who would care
less for law and correspondences if they knew as much
about them as he did. Dryman the elder was an old
friend of Faucit's parents, and had a warm regard for
Guy, for whose recent eccentricities he had been unfeignedly sorry. Dryman the younger was a go-ahead
and bright young fellow, fond of sport and a good
dinner, and the comforts which moneyed clients may
bring, and he saw elysiums in the future as Guy's man
of business, besides the professional delight which might
be taken in manipulating the Foster million, with much
intricacy of conveyance, and of act and deed. The
money was all safely and solidly invested, in house-
property here and in sound mortgage there, all first
charges; but much of it still remained in the business
which had made it, which Guy would not of course
carry on. There would be plenty of scope for consideration what should be done with it; and Dryman, Rolls,

and Dryman, in a letter which seasoned the old tone of easy friendliness with a flavour of deferential admiration, hoped that Mr. Guy Faucit would at his earliest convenience favour them with a personal interview.

Faucit sate and thought over the letter. One million of money! How in the world had his uncle been able to put such a sum together? It is difficult for a layman, certainly, to understand how these things are done, and done every day. Not long ago, the world was speculating on the different sums left behind them, as recorded in a single number of the "Times," by three hard-working and able judges. One left forty thousand, I think, another sixty, and another eighty. And people said, some of them, as the nice people will say, that these men of brains, which they had given to hard public work, had feathered their nests well. Underneath these personalities I saw the humble and remarked notice of another, that of an auctioneer unknown even to auctioneering fame, who, dying younger than any of these pampered justices, left just twenty thousand more than the three put together. Peace be to his ashes! he must have auctioned well, in his modest manner. Nobody seemed to think but that his nest was worthily lined. If money be the end of life, why brains? especially if it is wrong even to use them to line a nest withal.

Of what he was to do with this mass of money which had so suddenly fallen into his hands, Faucit could as yet form to himself no idea. Even with Daisy's image deep in his heart, and the strange encounter of yesterday still thrilling through him, he would have been more or less than man if he had not felt that, after all, life must have some possibilities for him now. Daisy's loss had robbed him of all the energy and all the desire to work for money, but with the money made for him and there in his hands while he was in the fullest and best of his prime, and for some years would be, the matter was different. His old ambitions of the Union at Oxford, and interest in public matters, came back to his mind, and he began to dream of Parliament, even while still dreaming of Daisy. Failing that, if he bought some estate and settled down, there was much to be done by an English squire, a position Guy had often envied for its possible activities. His heart—as the reader knows—had never been in what is called professional work, which only allows of other work as a second string, when the profession itself has grown into a second nature. That is why he had been willing to accept the literary and academic position which Oxford offered, which seemed to him the highest to which a man under his circumstances should wish to attain. Daisy Fairfield came and spoiled the plan. And now when his destinies called upon him to form another,—his fourth scheme of life already, he thought with some disgusted reflections upon rolling stones,— Daisy Brent crossed his path again, like some beautiful and inexorable Fate. Was she his Parca, then, winding her fairy skein round his life at every turn, and was she to shape and to mould his destiny yet again, in some undivined way ?

> " My thread is small, my thread is fine ;
> But he must be a stronger than thee,
> Who shall break this thread of mine."

In some unacknowledged, uncertain, un-understanding way Daisy Brent was in the background of his vision. Brent was her name, was it ?—it was not a pretty name, to his mind.

He would bestow upon Dryman, Rolls, and Dryman the favour of an interview at his earliest convenience, and that convenience should be very soon. But he would go to Luscombe Abbey first, and he would have some talk with the singular man called Lestrange, whose methods of speech and action had considerably impressed him. This Count was a man of the world, and his advice at so curious a crisis would be of great value to him. Meanwhile, there was no hurry to do anything in particular; he could float with the stream

of Pactolus, which had suddenly sprung up in his life.
Its first earnest was in a cheque for a thousand pounds,
which Dryman, Rolls, and Dryman apologetically en-
closed, in the event of immediate needs, informing him,
at the same time, that one of the leading firms of
bankers, in the great city near, had been advised of the
transaction, and would be ready to cash it for him in
the most convenient form.   Faucit smiled to himself as
he studied the bit of paper with the four figures, one of
those documents which drop like the gentle rain from
Heaven upon the place beneath, sometimes just when
we are nearest to parching.

    " Father," a youngster of my acquaintance said
when his future profession was being discussed at an
early age, " I think when I grow up I should like to
become an annuitant.   I've heard it's a very comfortable
profession."

    Mrs. Balbus and I, living by the hand-to-mouth
delights of literature, which knows not certainties,
regard those missives, when they make their appearance,
as telegrams from a better land.

    After thinking the letter over, and smoking many
and meditative pipes, Guy Faucit made his mind up,
for the first and only time since he had occupied his
cottage, to make his way over to the big city and back,
deposit his cheque in the bank, and provide himself
with money for his immediate needs, as well as fit
himself out appropriately for his new voyage, for which
he was booked as a saloon-passenger of the most
comfortable order.   So early in the morning he
shouldered his stick, and strode townwards over the
springy moorland with Frisco at his heels.   The air was
fresh and keen and autumnal ; and the bright lining of
the " fall " wore its newest gloss upon everything, as
Faucit's trained observation noted with delight.   There
was a sense of youth and battle in his pulse which he
had nearly taught them to forget, as far as his healthy
frame and elastic spirit would allow.   He would not
own to himself—he could not—how much the meeting

with Daisy had fired and kindled him. He, who had
never since they parted been "on with a new love,"
could never, in despite of him, be "off with the old;"
and the radiant beauty, which in Oxford days had spoken
straight to his heart, spoke to it as with a trumpet-
call at once again. He did not think he was "in love"
any more; flattered himself that he was cured of that,
and need have no fear of himself with Daisy Brent,
from his memories of Daisy Fairfield. But he was
glad to see her, very glad; and he hoped that she
might be able to prove to him, perhaps, that her conduct
towards him had not been so light as it seemed.

I fancy that, with his fortune and its uses, and the
revolution in his plans of life, and everything else
together in his mind, the fact that he was going to stay
in the same house with Daisy Brent was the foreground
of its picture. He would not have allowed it at all;
and persuaded himself that his anxiety to get to
Luscombe Abbey as soon as possible rose from his
desire to hold counsel with the worldly wisdom of the
Count Lestrange.

He whistled as he went upon his way, while Frisco
made endless sallies on his own account about the heather,
rolled himself over and over on his back when he found
tempting rolling grounds, and treated himself judiciously
for indigestion with periodical doses of grass; then trotted
back to his master's side and sniffed him enquiringly.
He was rather puzzled by the best clothes, to which he
was unaccustomed; which Faucit, by some instinct of
coquetry,—an instinct which is not strictly feminine, as
a matter of fact, but partakes at times of the nature of
the epicene, or common gender,—had dressed himself
withal for his visit to the town. He did not wish to
impress the bankers or any one else with any notion of
eccentricity. Frisco missed the beard too; which it was
his habit to bite occasionally, aiming at particular hairs
as the object of a jump. But he accepted the new
condition of things philosophically, if not, as is probable,
with a canine pride and pleasure. He had often told

his master by eloquent barks, as his manner was, that he might be a very seemly-looking man if he tried. So man and dog went on their way rejoicing.

Guy Faucit wandered curiously about the busy town, like one awaking from a magic sleep of years upon the Catskill mountains. Abroad, he had avoided cities; and he had rushed through London without a pause, to take possession of his northern solitude. A quiet observation of shops and shoppers, and of the throbbing life of trade, was new to him.

The sun which had shone out in all its glory on the moor was dimly visible through the listless pall of smoke, like a diseased ball of gloomy red. It seemed to have neither warmth nor spirit in it, but to be blinking dubiously at the perversities of city-loving men, who like living in their own smoke better than consuming it; build for themselves a world of uniform blacks and greys, with never a contrast of colour unconsciously to enliven their sense and intelligence, and quicken their nerve and spirit; and then find fault with the English climate, and rush abroad, abusing Providence for having cast their lives in a land where the sun never rises. Poor old much-abused and patient orb, the same yesterday, to-day, and for ever. On their own coasts and downs, within an hour or two of them, upon which citydom has not yet encroached, they may find effects which Turner might yet paint, and Ruskin write about, where the sun is as golden and the sky as blue, kissing the sea to its own sweet colouring, and the air as soft and pure and perfumed, as on the slopes and bays of the much-berhymed Riviera.

Everybody looked in a great hurry to make money, and very sick of making it. A glimpse of curiosity was the most they had to bestow upon the man of leisure, who looked so strong and capable, but evidently had no office to go to, wherein to be stowed for the better part of his life. He took a leisurely luncheon at a pretentious coffee-house, where, at his little table, he outsate some three or four relays of dyspeptic neighbours, who hurled scalding soup down their throats, bolted a glass of burning sherry to mix up with it, and hurried off again.

Frisco, in a state of amazed curiosity, kept quietly at his master's heels, and showed his teeth with a suppressed snarl to one or two suspicious persons, who seemed interested in him, in a manner which prevented their advancing any tangible signs of the interest. Contentedly he partook of his master's luncheon, Guy being one who abhorred dog-biscuits and latter-day horrors of the kind, holding that his dog's feelings were best consulted by letting him share on the old principle. He had tried the dog-biscuit regimen once, for two or three days; but the mute reproach of the animal's eyes, with the obvious internal suffering inflicted, cured him of the plan. Frisco scraped a sniffing acquaintance with one or two of the first town-dogs he met, but didn't think much of them, and gave it up. Guy had an odd feeling that the test was a good one, and felt minded to try it himself, upon some of the uncongenial-looking city mice he elbowed, suspecting a like result.

Luncheon over, he presented himself at the bank, where he gave his name, and was received with looks and words of much deference. He presented his cheque as well as himself, opened a temporary account for present purposes, and with a store of crisp bank-notes of sufficient value, departed. Then he made some purchases in the town, ordered some things to be addressed to him at Luscombe Abbey, resulting in more bows and testimonies of respect; and as evening threw its shadows over the moorland, walked back to the cottage again. He breathed the air like a liberated prisoner as he left the smoke behind.

"I shall never make much of town now," he thought.

One or two of his nomad pensioners called at the cottage in the evening, and departed wondering, gazing at some coins in their hands as a curiosity-hunter makes discovery of an unknown mintage.

The next evening Guy was dining at Luscombe Abbey, and Frisco was making acquaintance with a select circle of highly-bred fellows, and narrating to them, in very choice canine, his experiences of Western life.

CHAPTER XI.

LUSCOMBE ABBEY.

LUSCOMBE ABBEY was a noble example of its class, so rich in decorative and architectural beauty. Picturesque and old, and time out of mind the capital of the Vavasours, the late Lord had enlarged and improved it in every direction, as his rent roll grew and prospered, a careful taste presiding over its fortunes, and preventing the symmetry and the order from being in any way marred.

Lestrange used to look at it with bitter and concealed pangs, thinking how much he had had to do with the amassing of the fortune, and with the development of the building and the beautiful pleasure-grounds which girt it round. The gross ingratitude of the owner, whom he had helped to all this with his brains, gave him a just disgust at the vice and littleness of mankind, and a longing to spoil and to punish the Philistines with the confident conscience of one engaged in a Holy War. All this would have been his—all—but for John Brent. Well, he might have his revenge yet, and his modest rent-charge on the property. He was not sorry that he had preserved his title-deeds.

It was a beautiful sight which met Guy Faucit's eyes, as, in a carriage chartered from the town, he drove up through a long winding avenue of elms to Luscombe Abbey, where

"In morning splendour, full and fair,
The massive fortress shone."

It stood clear and strong upon a broad plateau, spreading out at mid-ascent of a sloping westward hill, rich in the luxuriant wealth of English verdure. The hills' further slope, clothed with pine woods and hanging gardens, which further from the house broke and blended into a great park dappled with deer, protected the Abbey from the keen easterly winds, while the north-westward sweep of the hill-range, further on, sheltered it from the other rough point of the compass also. The beautiful valley, rippling with little dots of silver stream and pool, grey village spires pointing lazily heavenward, for the behoof of the small villages clustered round them, and a few stray old-fashioned factories, for some industry of paper or of curious glass, looking just alive enough to support their modest tale of hands, made up the landscape, on which, in all its infinite variety, unstaled of custom, a lover of Nature could never grow tired of gazing from the broad and noble terrace which lay at the Abbey door. Upwards, again, on the western side of the valley, surged the wave of land, crested there with sunny cornfields, lacing with their dead-gold patterns the carpet of emerald turf, giving glimpses of some neighbour's rival turrets and pleasaunces, bosomed in a nest of trees, or landmarked by some quaint obelisk, erected by an admiring neighbourhood to the memory of some local worthy who had made for himself a national name in arms or gown, and was thus fitly monumented in the smiling scenes from which he sprang.

Luscombe Abbey was a cameo worthy of this lustrous setting. The old monastic chapel, which first gave to the place its monastic name, still remained as the north-eastern spur of the building, where the ground rose so suddenly as to make its upper windows level with the path above, from which a quaint bridge gave entrance to a gallery of oak, where a fine old mellow organ still discoursed music under a cunning hand. The chapel had been carefully restored and preserved, inside and out, and for many years in old days had been open for services to the neighbourhood, the Vavasours' chaplain having been an institution of the place. Audley Vavasour had himself kept the tradition up to the last; and, after his death it continued for a short time. But the old-fashioned chaplain did not like Lady Luscombe's new ways and Lady Luscombe's new guests; and, it was said, spoke once or twice to her ladyship in a way of which she did not approve. One day it was announced that he had accepted a piece of college preferment in another part of the country; and his place was not filled up. The services ceased, and silence fell upon the chapel, which, however, though only as a curiosity of architecture, was still carefully tended. Sometimes some guest, skilled in music, would hold quiet converse with the old organ; but that was all. The place was Lady Luscombe's for her life, as it was to have been hers altogether, no Vavasour surviving within the limits of heirship and entail. Now, at her death it was to pass to some distant connexion, whom this story knoweth not, a poor working clergyman somewhere in the west, whom Lord Luscombe had equally declined to know, who was to take up the Vavasour threads with the Vavasour name. The change had been made when the codicil was made, and was very bitter to Lady Luscombe. Was it not she who, for her husband's sake, had done so much for Luscombe Abbey?

The character of the architecture had been carefully preserved throughout the house, now of noble proportions. The entrance-hall, with its richly-tiled floor, was the full height of the house, spanned by oaken girders which recalled in miniature Rufus's famous timber in Westminster Hall. Over the door a Norman window let in, through glass chastened in colour, the flood of southern light, to play upon the gallery which occupied three sides of the hall, led up to by a solid staircase facing the door. Each wing of the gallery was in itself spacious enough to be furnished as a room, and one of them was devoted to the sacred mysteries of the billiard-table. Rooms of infinite comfort opened in all directions upon the hall and gallery—small snuggeries and large state-rooms pleasantly interdotted below, and dressing-rooms and bed-rooms above, furnished with all the most luxurious accessories of the great court of sleep. Noble statuary and pictures of durable pigment; great bookcases filling the regular spaces of the long library, built section-wise after the old attractive fashion, and filled in their turn with generations of volumes which made a chronology in themselves, from the earliest illustrations of the Luscombe friars to the latest and most unilluminated of feminine high-pressure stories; sober wall-papers which seemed graven on the wall; and conservatories glowing with Nature's richest audacities of form and colour, made up a palace of Armida which, after his long seclusion and oblivion of the very existence of such things, fell upon Guy Faucit's spirit like a sudden charm.

He was welcomed by a chorus of lazy dogs blinking in the sunlight on the lawn, ranging in years over the various ages of dog-kind, from sedate decline to playful babyhood. The old sundial over the porch whispered its pleasant legend—"I number not the hours, except they be sunny," and an array of "gallant gay domestics," as Tennyson sings, bowed before the visitor at the door, from the gallant old butler in the front to the gayest and most youthful of the powdered tribe, at the back of the line of receding heads. Guy's portmanteau and bag —still a very modest kit—were transported to earth by hands as agile as the bodiless ministers of the White Cat's castle; and Faucit was inducted to his room before joining Lady Luscombe's tea-table. All this was accomplished with that luxurious smoothness and absence of friction which is characteristic of these lofty households, and is to the heavy-handed attentions of a lower sphere like the Venetian gondola to the London cab. So polished indeed was the manner of the satellite who showed him to his room, that Faucit might have imagined himself already in intimate relations with the fashionable world, if James, anxious to be polite, had not volunteered the dangerous statement, in excuse of his mistress, that "her Ladyship was taking of a hairing."

The airing gave Faucit time to think again over the strange anticipations which had been filling his thoughts during the drive, to please himself with the lazy luxury of the room made ready for him, and comfortably to assure himself that a small collection of choice books occupied a post of vantage near the head of his bed. His mind had to travel back to his Oxford days, when he had been one of the most popular of guests at a pleasant round of English country-houses, to fit itself to the associations of the scene. The sound of carriage-wheels woke him from a long reverie, and he went over to his window, which commanded the drive. There *she* was at Lady Luscombe's side; and standing back by the curtain he scanned and considered her again, the joy, the sorrow, and the story of his life. Why? What was the magnetism, he thought, and what the law, which had wrought so great a ruin out of so frail a thing? A beautiful and a gracious woman, assuredly; but no, no, Orlando! "Men have died from time to time, and worms have eaten them, but not for love." Was he, Guy Faucit of the strong will and brain, really a weaker man than Troilus, who had his dashed out by the Grecian club, or Leander, that washed him in the Hellespont? He had wasted all these years on this fickle fashionable woman, who had cared no straw for him,—or if she had, had whistled her straw down the wind for very weariness,—and had allowed her to make him rust unburnished, instead of shining in use, for a mere memory! Now here she was again, popular and married, as far removed from him under the same roof as she was when three thousand miles of ocean rolled between the continents which held them. And all the world were her admirers, Lestrange had told him. He was not going to be one of all the world,

not he; or if he was, he would show her that he could
talk the easy language of mock-gallantry as well as he
had once flattered himself that he could plead in another
tone. What a prosy admirer she must have thought
him! He laughed at himself for it, and wondered
why, just when the weight which had hung about his
heart for eight good years ought to have been made ten-
fold heavier by her presence as she lived, he should feel
as if it had all been lifted away by magic. He supposed
it was his new fortune and position, and the sense of
consequence which it must give him in the world's eye
and his own; though he owned to himself that he did
not, as yet, feel at all a different man for that. Or perhaps it was that he had seen her again, and that there
was nothing so very much about her after all. That
must be it, he concluded to his own satisfaction. He
had been hugging a delusion and a mirage all that
time, and was lucky to be brought face to face with the
disappointing reality just at the right moment, when he
most wanted to be cured of idle fretting. Guy Faucit
went down-stairs in high spirits, contented with himself,
and feeling ridiculously young. After all, he was glad
that her husband was not there, though at some future
day he should be pleased to shake hands with him.

The meeting this time was pleasant and easy, for
Daisy too had had her time for reflection, and had used
it. She knew her own ground and her own strength,
she thought, and was not going to deny herself the
pleasure of a free and frank companionship with the
companion whom her heart had once held in such high
honour. She too persuaded herself that it was " over";
that nothing survived of the past but a warm and half-
regretful interest, which might be cherished without
harm. He had never cared for her much, or he would
not have taken her so lightly at her word. So she
let her spirits rise also as she thought of being in the
same house with him, without afterthought. She was
so bright and natural all that morning with her old
friend Lady Pepperharrow, so brisk and laughing, so

full of little impulses and outbursts, and tricks of
playfulness, that it warmed the friend's heart to see and
to be with her. The old lady herself was quite innocent
of all knowledge of any reason for this, and edified
Daisy and herself by much speculation upon Faucit's
conduct and proceedings.

"Why he should have done all those dreadful
things out among the savages, my dear; and then
come ome and turned ermit without letting anybody
know, and they so dirty, is what I'm sure I shall
never be able to understand. But then, to be sure,
genius is always so eccentric." And then she gave a
deep sigh, as of one whose own innate sympathies with
genius gave to her also the right of eccentricity. She
welcomed Guy Faucit with a motherly interest, and was
for engaging him, upon her return to London, to give a
lecture upon savage life in the tents, at Glycerine House.
Upon reflection, she thought it would be better to
substitute a recital in costume, with a moving panorama
and living figures, painted and posed by the first artists
of the day. The notion was heartily welcomed by the
company assembled, and Jem Gosling and Carrie Beaufort got into a corner to discuss it, whence they were
promptly expelled by Lady Luscombe.

Guy expanded again in the new sunshine, and had
hardly been in the house a day before he found himself
installed in the old post of leadership among the
younger men, which seemed by old tradition to fall to
him of right. It was the man's nature, and there was
an end of it; and with Jem Gosling as an admiring
first lieutenant, to inculcate Clipper-worship as the first
law of conduct, he ruled as he had ruled on the dear
old river, or at the college-meetings of Balliol. With
the Count Lestrange he contracted a more serious
intimacy, fitted to the older side of his life of experience.
Lestrange laid himself out to please him, and did not
fail. He suppressed for Guy's benefit the cynicisms
and hard sayings which rose so naturally to his lips, and
assumed a certain geniality which sate on him very

well, as every manner did which he chose to affect.
Like Faucit, he had travelled far and wide, and they
had in common all the traveller's talk of strange
countries which men find such a bond. The many-
creeded East, with all its experiences and peculiarities
which stay-at-home readers fail to understand or to
realize from all the books in the world, was known
ground to both of them; and the peculations and persecutions of Turkish rule they could discuss from their
own points of view. They could tell of the Druses,
whose religion mainly consists in abstinence from
tobacco; and could assure their own fair countrywomen
that woman's world-wide rule may be as despotic in a
Turkish harem as in an English home. Guy could tell
indeed of a personal experience of his own, which would
suggest that the Turks are more advanced in their
views of matrimonial justice than a class of Englishmen
are. For he had known of a Turk who beat his wife,
who thereupon took counsel with all the wives of the
street. They considered the matter in all its bearings,
and sent a lusty deputation of their number to beat
him, which they did mercilessly, the other husbands
on their part refusing to interfere in a matter of family
justice. And with stories of desert-travel and sand-
buried cities, Lestrange and Faucit could entertain their
listeners by the hour. So the days went by.

After a week or so Faucit paid his flying visit to
London, and Dryman and Rolls, and by sundry readings
and signings of documents and deeds, he entered in due
form upon his kingdom. He could not tell his anxious
lawyers, as yet, what his plans might be, though he
thought of buying an estate and settling down, unless
Time should show that he was not yet cured of the
wander-fever which leaves such intermittent fits behind.
As for Daisy and him, they rather avoided each other
at first, as by some tacit mutual compact. Guy, as we
know, had never been a man particular in his attentions to women; but if anything he seemed at first
something attracted to Miss Challoner's placid and

reposeful ways. That young lady seemed in no wise
ill-disposed to encourage an admirer of so desirable a
kind, and inflicted pangs upon the ruminating spirit of
Sir Brummel Coates, from which his well-made waist-
coat only partially defended him. The attraction did
not seem to last, though; and gradually but surely the
two, who in old times had been such united lovers,
drew more and more together upon a new footing. The
courtiers who fluttered round Daisy Brent could not
but feel and see that her royal favour seemed more
directed to a special object than had been her wont of
old. They had so much in common: for in spite of all
the external frivolities and dissipations of Daisy's life,
she had succeeded in keeping green her interest in
larger things. Unconsciously to both of them, they
began to talk together again, with the old interchange
of thoughts and of ideas. Unconsciously to both of
them, the spirit of confidence and intimacy grew into
the talk. Unconsciously to both of them, Guy Faucit's
mind began to assert its old mastery over Daisy's.
And unconsciously to both of them the Count Lestrange,
throwing them together with undetected art, and by a
careless remark dropped here and there even leading
others to do so too, watched and waited for his own
purposes; while with the growth of an uneasy feeling
unacknowledged to herself, the mistress of the Abbey
watched and considered him.

CHAPTER XII.

CARRIE'S LOVE-TALE.

The Count Lestrange was in his room at the
Abbey, brooding and anxious, as Chaffers moved about
it on his ministrations.

"This telegram only arrived this morning?"
he said.

"That is all, Count Lestrange."

"You are quite sure there was nothing else from the same quarter?"

Chaffers assented.

"Now you are to be very careful," his master went on. "Keep a stricter watch on the letter-bag than ever, and if you see anything whatever from India, you are to bring it straight to me. If there were a letter, it would probably be addressed to Mrs. Brent. And you are to be especially careful about telegrams. You can contrive to keep an eye on them?"

"Yes, Count Lestrange."

"That's right. Chaffers, you are invaluable; and most for showing no surprise when you are asked to do unusual things. But there's good precedent. The Government opens private letters. Why shouldn't I? Now, what other letters have you for me? Let me look at them."

Chaffers handed a packet of letters to his master, who ran his eye quickly through them.

"Invitations, invitations, invitations. Take them and answer them as usual, Chaffers, except those I shall want to accept. You know my arrangements in that way as well as I do. What next? From Dick Melton, the jockey. Rides Golden Rein at Doncaster, and has reason to know—hem—hem—hem. Chaffers, anything going on down-stairs, in your part of the house, on the Leger?"

"Yes, Count Lestrange."

"Golden Rein in much favour?"

"Yes, Count Lestrange."

"Lay against him as much as you can."

"Thank you, Count Lestrange."

"From my broker," the Count went on. "I don't like this. Money wanted at once. Of course it is. When isn't it? Where am I to find a thousand pounds for the moment? Through Faucit, no doubt. Why all that money should fall from the clouds into the hands of a drone who has done nothing for it, but nurse an idiotic sentiment out in the diggings, while I toil for my daily bread like a ploughboy, I can't imagine. But so it is. Chaffers," he added aloud, "what's that letter?"

"Will you see it, Count Lestrange?"

"How can I tell till you give me a chance? Is it one of those I told you never to give me? Of course; I see. From little Rose Palmer; the old story. Chaffers, how often have I told you not to annoy me with these things? Tear it up."

"If you could see her, Count Lestrange—"

"I shan't, you know," said Lestrange, coolly. "Have you an interest in the matter?"

"The poor young woman was so anxious—"

"Chaffers! Did I detect something like an expression of sympathy? You are going beyond me altogether. Human weaknesses forbidden. Perhaps you are tenderly inclined in that direction yourself?"

"Oh, Count Lestrange!"

"Why not?" said the Count. "I shan't interfere. Have you seen Mr. Faucit about?" he added, putting the letters aside and walking to the window. "With this news from India," he thought to himself, "I must push matters on."

"Mr. Faucit is in the garden, Count Lestrange, with Mrs. Brent."

"Ah!"

The man Chaffers was arranging his master's clothes in the wardrobe with an air of furtiveness which managed to belong to everything he did, even of the simplest kind. As stealthily almost as he, Lestrange went out of the room in his customary suit of solemn black, and left him there, and putting on his hat, wandered into the garden, which in the northern and western direction lay about the house. Two or three croquet-lawns, neatly shaven for the game of the day, were scattered among the trees, and on one of them Lestrange saw the man he had asked for, leaning on his mallet by a hoop, and talking earnestly with a companion whose immediate interest in the game seemed as small as his. The looped-up petticoat and the shapely foot which peeped out of it, doing much honour to the boot it was cased in, might be accepted in proof that she was there for croquet purposes, but her manner seemed to belie it. Whatever it was of which the two were talking that morning had a deep interest for them both, and neither of them saw Lestrange coming towards them. He did not go far upon the way, for he looked at them and smiled to himself, then turned up towards the glass door which opened into one of the rooms of the house, and for a moment looked in.

"Pairing-time this is," he said to himself, as he caught sight of another pair of fresh and curly young heads very close together, and strolled away just as the two heads started apart, like guilty things upon a sudden summons, at the intrusion of Lord Pentonville through a side-door.

The little lord was in all the freshness of adorn-ment, swathed like a mummy in his little tight clothes, which seemed to keep him together; and he trotted towards the young couple he had interrupted, with evident satisfaction in the keenness of his vision in discovering their presence.

"I—I saw you.!" he said, delighted.

"There wasn't much to see," said Carrie Beaufort, poutingly, for that young lady it was. "Only Jem Gosling arranging a bouquet."

"Of course," chuckled the other. "For yo—yo—"

"For her, Pen?" suggested Jem Gosling.

"No!" snapped his lordship; "for Daisy Brent;" and he said it with a malicious chuckle, which made Carrie set her teeth and shake her head at his back.

"I'm afraid it was," she said, looking at Gosling rather ruefully.

"But it's n—no good, you know," proceeded Pentonville, triumphantly. "You're quite cut out since that he—hermit came."

If the remark was intended to provoke the honourable Jem, it failed in its object entirely. His worship for his college idol was quite above proof.

"He ain't much of a hermit now, the Clipper ain't," he declared, enthusiastically. "Isn't he an awfully splendid fellow?"

"He's very big," assented Carrie, with equanimity not yet recovered, "which I suppose means awful splendour."

"I—I—see them there," called out Pentonville in ecstasy, having jammed his nose and his eye-glass against the glass-door. "Out in the ga—ga—ga—"

"In the garden?"

"No, the shrubbery. He n—never leaves her. They're l—leaving the ground. I w—wonder which way they're going."

"What odds can it make to you?" asked Gosling, rather disgustedly, as Pentonville trotted up to him.

"J—just seven to four," he confided to Gosling's ear. "I took those odds from L—Lestrange; he gave me seven to four in hundreds against their running away in three months. I th—think they're all right."

"You mean they won't run away?" said Gosling, with an expression of anything but admiration on his honest face, and looking round lest Carrie should hear.

"N—no," chuckled the other again, like an inferior satyr; "I mean they will. There's C—Coates in the garden too," he added, breaking out in a new direction, "w—with the Ch—Challoner; they're always together now. I'll g—go and dis—dis—dis—"

"Disturb them, Lord Pentonville?" asked Carrie, shrugging her pretty shoulders.

"No; amuse them."

And on his benevolent schemes intent, the Lord Viscount Pentonville trotted out into the garden, and attached himself to the second couple whom he had had the opportunity of discomposing that morning.

Poor Carrie had felt that she might be on the verge of a moment of real interest when he broke in upon her romance, which had been taking quite a delightful shape of late days, since Daisy had seemed desirous to abdicate her throne, and to play Queen of the Revels no longer. It was not that Daisy was exactly changed, certainly not to any of her friends; but her manner had grown more serious and reticent, and she seemed to be putting on something of "the weeds of Dominic." So Carrie Beaufort profited—the more so as her aunt, who seemed prepossessed and absent, had kept less watch over her doings of late, for some reason or another.

"Horrid old mischief-maker!" she said, therefore, with a will, as Pentonville disappeared, knowing how difficult it is to resume tender relations exactly as they were before an awkward interruption.

"Poor old Pen," laughed Gosling, his universal good-will towards everybody getting the upper hand as usual, "rum 'un he is; but not a bad sort when you know him, you know. Did you ever hear how he became a swell by winning a battle in India?"

"Never," answered Carrie, apparently with no great interest in Pentonville's deeds of daring.

"Well, a lot of niggers came down on him when he wasn't looking out for them, and he wanted to give the word to run away, you know; but he stammered so awfully he couldn't. 'Ret—ret—ret—' says he. 'Retreat?' says the aide-de-camp. 'No,' says he; 'charge!' and they did charge, and cut the niggers to bits; and old Hard Labour was made a K.C.B. for it. I say, Carrie," said the honest fellow suddenly, resuming more personal questions without prelude, "how nice you look this morning."

Very nice indeed Carrie looked when he said so, with a very becoming promise of a blush in her plump cheeks, and the pert nose assuming for the nonce quite a sedate air. Less interested observers than Jem Gosling might have thought her an attractive picture of a maiden enough.

"As nice as Daisy Brent?" she asked, slyly and shyly.

"Well, I have hardly seen her to speak to·for the last day or two," said Jem, very frankly. "She does carry on with the Clipper, doesn't she?" he added, with a moralizing air. "She's always pretty good at carrying on,"—this with a tone of conviction;—"but this licks the lot."

"I suppose that makes you feel awfully bad?" suggested his companion, demure as before.

"'Pon my soul, no, I don't think it does," said he of the ingenuous countenance and the ingenuous modesty. "Any fellow might be proud to be cut out by the Clipper, you know. And they were old spoons too when they were young, so Lestrange says."

"Jemmy, your language is confused," said Carrie, decidedly.

"Can't help it," he answered. "You're quite enough to confuse anybody."

More discreet or less malign than Pentonville, the chronicler refrains from emphasizing what may have happened at this interesting point. Enough that it was what a stage-manager would call, in contra-distinction to dialogue, "business."

"What would my aunt say?" was Carrie's next articulate remark, the interval of sound having been filled with something more expressive.

"That she wished I was Gander," said the youth. "I don't. I shouldn't," he continued reflectively, "make half such a good Gander as Gander makes. I say, Carrie," he said, suddenly changing the subject on the suggestion of the train of thought, "your aunt and Lestrange are as thick as ever."

"Don't talk about him," said Carrie, liking neither the change nor its character. "I hate him."

"I don't love him either," admitted Gosling, unwillingly. "Extrorny beggar; I wonder how he lives!"

"He seems to live very well," Carrie answered. "They do say, Jemmy" (confidingly), "that he writes for the 'Saturday Review.'"

"Oh, ah!" said the other, disrespectfully; "I know lots of fellows they say that of. I wrote for it once, but they wouldn't put it in. If they put in all the fellows who say they write for it, the world wouldn't contain the Saturday Reviews that should be written."

"And what a very dreadful thing that would be."

"Awful."

The idea was so serious that it wanted a brief period of serious contemplation before Jemmy went on with the subject.

"Still," he said, "Lestrange is just the man for that sort of thing; quite the fellow to cut up everybody for the fun of hurting them, you know, and not say who he is. Never could see the odds between an anonymous cut-up and an anonymous letter, though one's caddish and the other's the dignity of the press. When a fellow's got anything ill-natured to say of another fellow, he does like old Weller, and puts it down with a 'we.' However, I don't know much about it. Shouldn't wonder if Lestrange put us in an article next week. He's always prowling about somewhere."

Even as he spoke the figure of a man in black was by the glass-door again.

"Just when you least expect him," shuddered Carrie Beaufort, nervously.

"Can't make out why the Clipper's so fond of him," resumed Gosling, who was constantly wanting to make things out, and failing.

Wiser in his generation than persons of greater mark, when he found that he couldn't make them out, he let them alone.

"Carrie," he added, suddenly, shifting his ground with the inconsequence of his nature.

"Yes?"

"What makes people fond of other people?"

"Is that a conundrum?" she asked, looking down with a funny little dimpling smile.

"No; a question."

"I don't know," she said, after a pause, in a voice low

A A

and pleasant. "Pique?" then she asked, looking up, the dimples about the mouth growing very provoking indeed.

I do not know, nor did she, exactly what might have come next; but a shock of cold water down an unexpectant spine does not come with a more sudden chill than the quiet—"Your aunt is asking for you, Miss Beaufort," which followed.

The speaker was Lestrange, who had come in through the glass door as if nothing had happened. Poor Carrie! twice within a short half-hour.!

"Talk of the—" muttered Gosling, fairly disgusted this time. Carrie Beaufort had looked so irresistibly pretty just then.

"The devil, eh?" supplied the quick-eared Count. "Were you talking of love, then?"

The cold water was icing now.

"Talking of love! no!" said Carrie. "It was something very different."

"Really!" he said, scanning the pair with a smile. "Marriage, I suppose?"

Ice—all over.

"Unpleasant beggar!" muttered Jem to his pretty companion, as their two spines gave responsive shivers. "Always sneering at something."

"Yes," she answered, "and at the best things—marriage and all."

"Ah," considered Gosling, "I don't quite know about best."

The Count had brought into his Arcadia a whiff of worldly wisdom.

"What will you give me," said the Count, in a low voice to him, with the well-known mockery in his tones which men were so afraid of, "for coming in when I did? I am very sorry to have interrupted you, Miss Beaufort."

"Oh, don't mention it!" said she, who would have liked to cry.

"But you know your aunt," he added, in a paternal

tone, as if to a naughty child; "you will get yourself into trouble."

"Thank you," she said, bridling. "I can take care of myself."

She turned away indignantly.

"Then why," said Lestrange again to Gosling, "does she want you to do it for her? Have you forgotten Daisy Brent already?"

The Count had the art of changing the whole current of a man's thoughts with a syllable or two, and nothing amused him more than the exercise of this power.

"Oh! she has thrown me over!" said Jem Gosling.

"Are you sure?" said Lestrange, reflectively. "From what she said to me yesterday—yet I don't know. Women are so clever in disguising their feelings; at least," he added, with a look of slight but perceptible depreciation towards poor Carrie, "some of them."

"Gad!" ejaculated the Honourable Jem, the ever-ready vanity of mankind being prompt to rise to the bait; "if I thought that the lovely Brent—"

"Are you coming, Mr. Gosling?" tapped out an impatient little foot at the door; "you promised to arrange these flowers in the drawing-room."

"All right," said Gosling. "Hang it," thought he to himself, as he followed, in his especial vernacular, "she's an awfully good little girl, and I like her. But by Jove! I quite too awfully near put my foot in it!"

The Count Lestrange laughed silently to himself when the two had left him alone, the pleasure of so spoiling sport being in itself a delight to him. As usual with him, he reflected complacently on the high character of his motives, even in so small a matter. It was his clear duty to keep such a pair of moths out of the flame as long as possible, and to fulfil a promise to Lady Luscombe to do his best to avert premature combustion. It might do all very well a little later; but much depended on the constitution of the reigning Gander, which was ruined, but tenacious.

The entire absence of cerebral action, reflected Lestrange, always retards decay in that family. It was known that Gander was very ill, but worse even than he had been known to disappoint everybody, and to marry and beget heirs. Miss Beaufort must not be allowed to throw herself away on the Honourable James yet; but as she was clearly prepared to do so at any moment, the Honourable James must be kept judiciously in hand. But this was trifling, and the Count had his reasons now for not trifling too much.

"How goes the other flame," he thought within himself, "which I must kindle and not quench? Where are my Hercules and my grass-widow, I wonder? They looked in very close confidence just now."

He looked through the glass-door again.

"Yes, there they are. What a pretty innocent picture. Adam and Eve in the garden of Paradise. A subject worthy of a painter—of a poet—a subject worthy of me. So entirely conscious of the rectitude of their motives, too, that they are not afraid of the windows of the house. There's Pentonville at one of them. Ha, ha! The thing of all others to help one in a complicated matter is conscious rectitude on all sides. We all mean well. I do. So does Pentonville. He means to have four hundred pounds of mine. And so he shall. It isn't a bad hedge to help me to the ten thousand; for a more useful agent of mischief I don't know. What a pity he stammers; he might do so much more harm. I don't like the news from India at all. John Brent is dangerously ill, confound him, and I must keep it from his wife. She would be going out to nurse him, or something silly. When people once get certain conceptions of what they call duty into their heads, there is no telling when or where they may start up. And if Brent were to die—oh no: that would spoil my book, so it won't happen. But I must quicken my athlete's stroke, now that I have him well in training.

Nearly a month here, and not up to the mark yet. How slow he is," his thoughts ran on as he looked again from the window. "Go on, Hercules, go on! Muscles and scruples ought never to go together. Nothing but indigestion makes a conscience excusable. I must have another talk with Faucit, and—yes; my Lady Luscombe shall talk to Daisy. There will really be a scandal in the house, I am afraid, if things continue as they are. I'll go and find Lady Luscombe— particularly," he thought, "as I don't think I am wanted here."

The two whom he had been watching were approaching the glass-door. Close to that door, the room in which this scene had passed,—a sort of outer sitting-room,—opened upon a long conservatory, in the centre of which a thick and flowering row of tropical plants and ferns divided two passages which ran down either side of it, communicating at the other end with the main part of the house beyond. Up one of these passages, the further from the door, the Count Lestrange withdrew a little, and busied himself unnoted with a close examination of some of the thickest of the plants, as the two entered the room.

CHAPTER XIII.

THE CONSERVATORY.

"WHY are you so anxious to come in?" said Guy.

"Was I anxious?" she asked.

Her face was very thoughtful, and his too; and there was a strange constraint on both of them.

"You seemed so," he answered.

"It's so awfully wet."

"Wet doesn't hurt Daisies," he said with a smile.

A slight smile crossed her face too as she answered, "You mustn't call me by my Christian name."

He did not disclaim the intention, but he asked, "Why not?"

"Because it's awfully wrong."

"It's not so wrong as your surname," he said in a low voice.

"Oh don't say that; you mustn't," she said very quickly, flushing and wincing as from a pain.

"Why not, if I feel it?"

There was no mistaking the deep earnestness which spoke in Faucit's voice. Lestrange, watchful, smiled to himself, and for a moment looked at the two from the cover of a flowering palm. Then noiselessly and rapidly he moved down the conservatory, and was gone by the other side.

"Who was that?" Daisy asked, her ear catching the sound.

"No one," said Guy. "You haven't answered my last question."

"Why not, if you feel it—wasn't it?" she said.

She had taken her place in an American rocking-chair by a handsome flower-stand in the room, which itself preserved some of the attributes of the conservatory. And her hand was playing with a lily, and her eyes were full as of a deep spring of thought.

"We mustn't say all that we feel," she added, looking straight before her, the lily at her lips.

"No," he said. And he leaned his arm upon the flower-stand at her side, and there was a pause between them. Something, that day, seemed to make it difficult to speak. "Are you glad I came here?" he abruptly asked, without apparent reason.

"No. Yes. Awfully."

"I wish you wouldn't use that word about everything," he said, in a provoked and impatient tone. Womanlike, she at once looked mischievous, and laughed a little, a mere touch on a silver bell.

"What, awfully?" she asked. "It has been the

most expressive word in the language ever since it got into it. It's an awfully good word."

"There it is again!" said Guy. "How can a word be awful?"

"I didn't say it was an awful word," was her answer, given with a spice of good-humoured mimicry of his tone. "I said it was an awfully good word. Ha, ha, ha! Isn't that logic?"

"Complete and unanswerable," he said, shrugging his shoulders, not too willing to fall in, perhaps, with the light and careless manner which Daisy had now assumed. But she would not let it go.

"You see how fast young women are getting educated in these days," she said, laughing.

"I am afraid you are rather a fast young woman," was his comment.

"Why that's a pun!" she exclaimed, "absolutely and positively a pun. Not a good one, but still a pun. Mr. Faucit, I didn't think you had it in you. You will write a burlesque yet, and win the heart of Jem Gosling entirely. How fond he seems of you."

"Good little fellow," answered Guy. "Yes, I think he is. I wish he would make haste and marry that nice little girl, Miss Beaufort. It would be the making of him."

"Marriage is not always our making," answered Daisy. "It is a miserable imposture in some worlds, at all events."

"Not always, anywhere, I hope," he said. "Why do you talk in that way? It doesn't suit you, any more than fastness does."

"There again!" she said. "How can you call me by wrong names?"

"Well, you won't let me call you by the right one," answered Guy, recurring to the old point. "But it frets me sometimes to see you play as you do at a character which is not your own."

"How do you know that?" she said. "Our characters change sometimes. Men change them for us, or circumstance, or anything."

"Was it a man who changed you, then?" asked he. "Somehow I don't believe it. Your heart doesn't seem to me in this butterfly life, the least."

"My heart!" she said, with a laugh. "What can make you suppose that I have one?"

"Or ever had?"

She looked at him for a moment. "Or ever had, if you wish it. It is a thing, from all I have heard of it, one is much better without. Of course I have no personal experience; and you see how well we all get on here without such a thing. I don't think we boast one between us at Luscombe Abbey, except dear old Lady Pepperharrow; so we all laugh at her, of course."

"It's a worldly set enough, certainly, this of yours," answered Guy, shunning any direct issue. "And I hate the familiarity," he suddenly said, with some vehemence, "with which you let everybody in the house treat you."

"Do you?" she said in a low voice. There had been no mistaking the feeling with which Guy Faucit spoke, and in spite of herself it thrilled through Daisy's nerve. "Why do you want the same privilege, then?" she asked with a smile, not swerving from her careless tone, or letting him read anything of what she might think or feel.

"That's different," he shortly answered.

"Of course!" she said. "How grave we are!" continued she in a bantering manner, which had in it, notwithstanding, an odd mixture of expression if it might have been read; something of respect, something of pleading, something of yearning. "You are just what you were eight years ago,"—with a frank and brave allusion to past times which brought an answering look into his eyes,—"the same awful old don as ever! 'Awful' is quite correct there, you know," she hastened to stipulate, in answer to the initiate protest of his lips. "Do you think that everybody is to be as particular as yourself?"

"I think," he said, gravely, "that married women should be more careful."

"Should they?" she thoughtfully answered. "Then"—with a smile playing about her mouth—"you had better go."

Not for the world would Daisy Brent have forfeited the new friendship which was springing up upon the ruins of the old building. For it was friendship, oh ye cynics; and it is possible under such conditions, and true. Daisy knew her heart, and knew herself, her strength, and her weaknesses, and trusted herself out of that knowledge with a deep and fearless trust. She did not disguise from herself that she loved Guy Faucit, and had always loved him, with a love never to be given by her to any one beside in this world. Had she known and cherished it for a safeguard, all those desolate years, to shrink from it now? Might she not rather—did she not rather—thank God upon her knees night and morning for bringing back the old lover, to give him to her for a steadfast friend, just when her life, and heart, and value were going to rack and ruin upon the reefs of circumstance? He could and would save her from herself, she felt, and in his time and way show her what yet to do with her life for good, whose beacon-light had never quite been sunk in all her storms. She felt it all the more because to her heart's core she knew, as she had known in those happy days of the might-have-been, that he whom her heart honoured was thoroughly akin to her. What she felt he felt, what she meant he meant, and his heart and purpose were as steady and as loyal as her own. He showed it to her in a hundred self-controlled ways; and as she had trusted him as a lover, as she would have trusted him as a husband, she could trust him as a friend. Dangerous, would you call it? oh small-thinking and small-speaking world, dangerous—to such souls of choice as these? This was one of the tragedies of life, it may be; and none so well as Daisy felt what she had lost. But it was a tragedy of high and noble mould, which neither she nor he would turn to common melodrama. She bowed her head as within herself she owned the justice of the punishment which separated their lives in the higher sense of union, for that she could not pass safely through the vulgar trial which she had succumbed to, and read her simple duty before her in the bright letters of her love. It seemed so easy and so paltry now! Had she not owned to herself over and over again, that she had expected Guy to remonstrate, to make some sign? If she had expected that, why had she allowed anything to tempt her to give him cause? And as she looked at him now, strong and straightforward, and single of purpose, she wondered how she could ever have dreamed of any other result? Hers had been a hard trial, true; but are not the hard trials sent for the strong and favoured souls? and how had she dared, with such a love in her, to play it false for all the best conventions of the world?

So Daisy Brent judged herself, and recognized the justice of her sentence, while reading there the mercy which tempers justice, and had given her back at last the friendship which was better than all loves beside. What had it given her more? The instinctive knowledge that, as she had loved Guy, so Guy had loved her, and that to the mirage she had made of that love he had been, and would be, true for evermore. Could woman's wound have better balm than that? No. There was no danger. Here was no story of common duplicities, to end in any commonplace of Ill. And so she said to him, with that smile playing about her mouth,

"Then you had better go."

"I am your friend," said Guy. "I can be nothing more now."

He did not mean to shrink, nor she, from such allusions to the past. They were not to be avoided, and were better met.

"Yes; they always begin by that," answered Daisy, whose new fashions still hung about her, though in truth as garments they were but a poor fit. "But your prejudices are so curiously old-fashioned. Look at our hostess, Lady Luscombe."

"What is it about her?" asked Faucit, rather roughly.

"*Who* is it about her, you mean," said Daisy. "Count Lestrange always, except when he's making fun of Lady Pepperharrow. Can't you see that?"

"I haven't looked," said the other, with indifference. "You don't mean that they are beginning by being friends?"

"No; they're ending by it. Don't you know the story? Have you never heard why Lord Luscombe left it in his will, that if his widow should marry again, she was to lose every penny?"

"No," Guy answered. "What were his reasons?"

"Only one. Count Lestrange. Everybody knows it, and nobody minds it. You have lived in the deserts, Mr. Faucit; you do not know our world as at present constructed."

There was scorn in her voice, of herself as of others.

"Was anything known?" asked Guy, whose tone caught hers.

"Oh, no. Then it would have become wrong."

She was playing with the flower with her fingers, absently; and its leaves were falling to the ground. A whole unwritten history of regrets and possibilities seemed locked in the two hearts.

"He is a strange man, this Count Lestrange," said Guy.

"Yes; a strange man, and they say a dangerous one. But I never quite understand what people mean by talking so much of danger. Our dangers come from ourselves, and the Count has always things to say out of the ordinary run of gossip and commonplace. I like his company for that reason."

"So do I, Mrs. Brent. One can always discount a man's conversation from one's ideas of his character, and make the best one can out of it without being afraid of being contaminated. The eternal suspicion of 'something wrong' is a perfect pest of the day, and of every day, I suppose. I often feel disposed to parody the old text, for the benefit of the Bowdlerized edition of mankind so much circulated now-a-days—'To the proper all things are proper.'"

She laughed and answered, "Your text would not be a very welcome one, and would rob many people of their bread. What would become of society, and of morality, and of all sorts of things?"

Inconsistency is an attribute of life; and it is impossible to say why Guy Faucit's next remark was this, with something of a frown:

"Do you live very much with this Lady Luscombe?"

"Yes," said Daisy, "a good deal; though, as you know, my home is with Lady Pepperharrow. Lady Luscombe is not unkind, though hard."

"Hard enough," said Guy.

'I don't mind that," Daisy said, sadly, with a sigh which, for the moment, she could not help. Aimless, loveless, disappointed life that hers was, so full of purpose and of affection and of promise that it had been, it was a weird at times. "God knows," she added, rising from her chair, and throwing from her with an impatient gesture the stalk of the dispetalled flower, "I am hard enough myself!"

She walked to the conservatory, and toyed with some of the rich leaves which clustered there. He followed her with a look, and a very sad one, which she did not see. He did not wish that she should.

"You are not just what you were eight years ago!" he said. "You are bitterly changed!"

The whole frame quivered, the whole scene grew misty, the whole brave heart seemed for a moment to be dissolved in tears. But there was no outward sign but of a graceful woman, bending over a graceful plant.

"Yes, bitterly," she answered, and put the question by as not of much moment. "Come and look at this. What a lovely fern!"

He joined her, and they strolled up the conservatory together, on the opposite side to that where Lestrange had gone.

   *   *   *   *   *

"There they are, you see," said the Count Lestrange.

As the other two drew away, he entered the room from the other side of the conservatory, with Lady Luscombe. They had come in at the further end of it some minutes before, and had been loitering in the way close to the room. To anybody who had seen them together as they stood, with' their unspoken thoughts between them, under the canopy of climbing tendrils, the picture might have recalled the Count of Monte Cristo and Mercédés, when she offered him the grapes in the château of Morcerf her husband.

"Yes, I see," said Lady Luscombe, looking after Guy and Daisy, as in close converse they passed out of sight together. "I wish that I had never brought him here."

"Why ?" the Count asked.

"To win you this infamous wager," answered she.

Her worn face looked more worn than ever, and the hair seemed even to have been whitened under a fresh fall of the snow of age. Her eyes looked harassed, eager, miserable ; and the pity of her life, there among all the rich surroundings which were hers, and not hers, was written in her whole expression and bearing in a way which might have appealed to any man. Count Lestrange, who looked placid and unperturbed as ever, did not appear to be moved by it, or to notice it in any way.

"Are you really beginning to be afraid of your paragon, then ?" he said. "And why do you talk about infamous ? What nonsense ! Exaggerated expressions are such a mistake."

"If I, had known the story of those two at the time," said Lady Luscombe, "I would never have lent myself to your schemes."

"Oh, yes, you would ; but not so readily. That's why I didn't tell you till afterwards."

"And it is really true !" exclaimed Lady Luscombe, seating herself impatiently in the chair which Daisy had left, and tapping the ground with her foot in a restless fashion. "For a bet—for a mere bet—you, who by means of your own can always get money when you want it, will deliberately ruin two people who have never harmed you. There is something more than a bet in this—some revenge. What is it ?"

"I assure you there is not," answered Lestrange. "I respect revenge very much in others, but never practise it myself. It's so very human. I've made a bet, and I mean to win it; that's all."

"By this abominable action ?"

"I think it is a benevolent action—so benevolent that I feel quite pleased with myself. Faucit will make his new start in life with a real reputation. As for the young lady, she has two passions, money and notoriety, and I shall secure her both. She will be the talk, and consequently the envy, of her sex. She will change one husband—bad, old, and poor—for another, good, young, and rich."

"How can they marry," Lady Luscombe answered, "when you have ruined her ?"

"It won't be ruin, only bankruptcy. She can start fresh, after going through the Court."

There was a more open sneer in the last words than was usual with the speaker, who even with Lady Luscombe generally veiled his cynicisms decorously, and seemed unconscious of their point. His manner seemed to sting her, and she turned round upon him with an unrepressed shudder, and looked him straight in the face. His eyes wandered away at once, and he played with the ring upon his right hand.

"Count Lestrange," she said suddenly, "had you ever a mother ?"

"No, I fancy not," he answered with indifference.

The two figures that they had watched down the

conservatory were approaching the room again together as before. Lady Luscombe heard their voices speaking in subdued tones, and she rose to her feet.

"They are coming back. I shall warn them," she said.

The Count had heard them too, and quietly gone over to the other side of the conservatory, where he stood in the archway of it.

"On the contrary," he said, "you will come this way."

"I will not."

"You will come this way."

There was the old tone of quiet and magnetic command, and with it a certain cold glitter in the eye, which enforced obedience as usual.

"What do you mean to do?" Lady Luscombe asked, going up to the Count.

"I will tell you, and what you must do," he answered. "Perhaps I am not so bent upon this bet of mine as you think, and wish, after all, to save things from going too far. You have seen in the last few days how far they are going. Come this way, and I'll explain myself."

They went down the conservatory again together.

CHAPTER XIV.

DUOLOGUES.

"So you are a very rich man now?" Daisy was saying.

"Yes, I suppose so," was the answer.

"And you mean to be a very great one?"

"No."

He spoke wearily and with indifference, and, without meaning it perhaps, he threw into his tone a despond-

ency which struck painfully on his companion's ear, and
gripped her about the heart with a sadness like his own.
It could not but come to them both at times, steady
of purpose as they were.   That same heartwholedness
on which Guy had congratulated himself on the day of
his coming to Luscombe Abbey had been exposed to
some dangerous siege-work in the days which had
passed lazily by since then.

"Are you so changed then, after all," said Daisy,
after a pause, in a voice which had in it a real and
gentle sympathy, "since the old. days when you were
so ambitious of a name in the world?"

The old days!   What a phrase of pregnant meaning
is there, and what a burden, only too often, of an unutterable pain!   The very words seemed to strike a
new note of music on Daisy's peerless voice, and to be
echoed in the man's deeper modulations.

"I am not selfish," he said.   "I was only ambitious
of a name which I might share."

"With others?" she asked.   And both, unconsciously to themselves, spoke very low.

"With one other.   With a wife."

She turned her head away from him as he spoke
the words, that he might not see what she too surely
felt, how the soft colour which had tinged her cheek
deserted it in a moment, and left the blue veins traced
more clearly than was their wont upon the pure
marbled complexion which was one of Daisy's prides.
It was not marble now, but white.   Marble has hue.
She fought with herself, and felt hot tears pressing
behind her eyes.

"Why have you never found one?" she said,
bending over a flower, but with a voice which she made
natural by a strong effort.   Though there was interest
in it, too, the naturalness wounded Guy.

"Don't you know?" he said, shortly, and with a
feeling which on his side he was not at such pains
to conceal.   "I was poor."

"But you are rich," she answered, bravely preserving the same tone, though the sad heart faltered as she did it. "Now you will be able to choose for yourself."

"I suppose so."

"Shall you do it?"

"Do you wish it?"

"I—suppose so."

There was hesitation there, or Daisy Brent had never been Daisy Fairfield, or a true-hearted woman. His wakeful ear caught the slight change of intonation, and he welcomed it with another pause. Then he came closer to her side than he had been standing before, and she shrank, involuntarily, just a very little. And he spoke quickly and thickly, with a feeling almost hoarse in its suppression.

"Do you advise it?" were his words; "from your experience of women? Yes, I am rich; and I might ask some girl to marry me to-morrow, not knowing that she was engaged, perhaps, to some poor devil who cared for her, and for whom she was supposed to care, more or less. She might say 'yes,' and forget to mention the other. That would be a chance for happiness, would it not?"

The laugh in which the words ended was not very genuine, or very pleasant to hear. Daisy shrank from it, but gave no sign he saw.

"She might learn to love you," she said, biting her lip.

"Yes; unless I lost my money."

Guy Faucit was losing his steady tone, and his head was leaving him a little. He said the hard words with intention, and they pierced. But she pressed her hand to her heart, and again she staunched the wound. She did not justify herself in her own eyes, and if she could help it she would not rebel. How could he know that he was wronging her?

"Rich or poor," she said, deliberately, and in a calm voice, "you would be a good husband to her."

If Daisy Brent could avoid it, she would not stand

B B

between Guy Faucit and a happiness which might be his. Yet for the first time, the very first since they had met again, she felt at this moment in the soul of her, that what he had been to her that had she been to him. Yet between him and happiness she would not stand, with the help of God. And herein I think Daisy was doing a brave thing indeed.

He did not see beneath the surface, though, for men do not, any more than they can with as much resolution as women, in time of need, cover the surface over. He saw in her words only their outward seeming, and he grew more and more indignant as in that light he read them. A flirt! a deceiver! and a heartless one, after all. Was her last scheme to affect a friendly interest in his prospects of marriage, then? He could have borne anything but that.

"A good husband!" he said, very bitterly indeed this time, and with an unconcealed scorn. "What? if I found out that she had been so utterly base as to marry me for my money, liking somebody else better, as far as she had it in her to like anybody, and throwing him over without a scruple? I am not quite sure."

There was absolute evil in the sneer which Guy threw into the last words, and threw at her as with an insult. She could not bear it, and it could not be, for the wound of those savage words this time went too deep, though it carried with it a strange balm, for she felt the love in them as she felt the misunderstanding. But the misunderstanding was too terrible to be borne, and her shield fell from her unnerved hand at last. She turned round upon Guy with a look he started from, for the hot tears had welled into her eyes, the red flush had covered neck and brow with a very glow of modesty and honour, and lip and nerve and fibre quivered like an appealing child's.

"But if the terms of the bargain were plain!" she cried, for it was as with a cry that she spoke, and in the force of the feeling which she suddenly unloosed she clasped her hands together as she faced him, and the

words rushed hotly from her lips without break or
stay; "if the girl told you of that other love, and
prayed you to be generous, and you would not! if the
fortune, the subsistence, yes, and the honour of her
father and mother depended upon her saying 'yes' to
the offer to which her very heart and soul said 'no'
with loathing! if she told you all this, and you claimed
her in spite of it! if she sacrificed herself to you, body
and soul,—and in all the world there is no sacrifice so
horrible as that,—and then you broke your bargain! if
your fortune proved as hollow as your love! if you
taunted her, day by day and hour by hour, with the
true friend and true man whose life she had laid waste
for you! if you were bitter, cruel, violent! if—if—
you *beat* her, Guy, what then?"

"Did your husband do that?" said Guy.

"Yes."

"Damn him."

The silence fell between them like a death; and the
beating of their two hearts filled the void of words.
There was no shadow of need for further explanation;
for her sudden and passionate outburst had told him
everything, and he did not disbelieve or doubt her
for a moment more. The statue was restored to its
pedestal in all its gracious perfectness, and he might
lay all the garnered memories at its feet again. What
had she borne before she yielded to this? and what had
her life been since? God help them! What had his?
And a whole concentrated force of anger and of scorn
Guy Faucit threw into that savage curse, not loud but
deep, which haply cast its shadow over John Brent's
unlovely sick-bed, thousands of miles away.

As for Daisy, she shrank from its passion for a
moment, and then it recalled her to herself, though she
would not attempt disguise again just then.

"Oh hush!" she said, "we mustn't talk like this.
What does it matter now?" and the smile upon her
face was sad unutterably. "Only, if I'm fast, Guy,"
she added, earnestly, and with a depreciation of herself

which had more of frank self-pity than self-scorn, "if I talk slang and scandal, and chaff, and flirt, and play, and smoke a cigarette, don't be surprised, and don't be savage, there's a good fellow. It's terribly hard work. I'm so lonely—so wretched! Be my friend, won't you? and don't make love to me—at least," she added, with another smile which struggled to be bright, yet had little brightness beyond the tear which glistened in her eye—"at least, not too much."

"You don't care about other men doing it," he said, very sadly, though in a voice from which all the hardness was gone.

"I don't care—about other men."

*   *   *   *   *

"It is shameful—cruel—wicked!" Lady Luscombe declared, as her whole frame shook with excitement, and her eyes flashed as they had not done that many a day. The Count Lestrange was watching the effect with quite a pronounced interest. "You wish me," she added, as if she couldn't believe her own words, "to compromise Daisy Brent, to turn her out of my house, to drive her to extremities by insulting her,—and all to secure you £10,000!"

"I wish it was more, with all my heart," Lestrange answered. "You may make it double or quits if you like. But you really must remember, Marian, the large fortune which your imprudence lost me—for you must have been most imprudent. If you had been more careful, your husband would never have made that most improper will."

"He might have punished me worse," Lady Luscombe said, a sort of fascinated calmness taking the place of the excitement, as it always did under the hand of the imperturbable adventurer.

"How?" he asked.

"He might have let me marry you."

The silence which Guy and Daisy had left behind them in the room seemed to cling about it still, when the two who had taken their places there had watched the victims of this strange experiment wander away again among the flowers together.

Things had advanced, Lestrange had thought as he saw them. He had heard enough and observed enough now to risk his grand *coup.* He only watched Lady Luscombe with a certain curiosity, which had something of satiety in it. He had come to the end of her long ago, to his notion; and she was but a pipe to his finger, to sound what stops he pleased. He was trying the pipe this time, he knew; but it would bear it, and respond. Very likely the effort would crack it; but what was that to him? He had worn out many pipes in his time in the same way, and thrown them away when they were past work without wasting more time over them.

"I should have made you a very good husband," he said with perfect good humour and an imperceptible shrug of the shoulders, unmoved by her shrinking and repellent tone. "I've an excellent temper, and you never would have thwarted me. You will not thwart me now," he added, with an additional infusion of softness into his voice. He spoke meditatively, and was much interested in his ring.

"I will cut my right hand off before I will help you in this," Lady Luscombe muttered, rather than said, through her closed teeth, tapping the floor with the old impatient action. Lestrange only lifted his eyebrows a little.

"You would scarcely miss it if you did," he said. "Am not I your right hand?" She shrank away from him as he approached her and looked at her hand, then taking it in his added, "It would be a pity though. Such a pretty little hand!"

"A compliment from you!" she said, bitterly. "That is late in the day. You must be forgetting how long it is since you cared to pay one to me."

"Is it?" he said, carelessly. "You must know the value I have set upon the little hand. To think that I could not claim it!"

"You could have done so if you had chosen," Lady Luscombe said.

"You mean," said Lestrange, "that you would have given up your husband's fortune to marry me?"

"You know that I would—then."

"How handsome you are!" exclaimed the Count suddenly, looking at her with an air of new attention. "Marian," he added, almost under his breath, and throwing into his tone an expression which she had not heard in it since her husband died, "would you marry me now?"

She started and looked up at him, and the fragrance of the flowers in the conservatory seemed heavy in the room.

"What!" she said, "give you the little hand empty? What greeting would it have from the penniless adventurer, the Count Lestrange?"

She emphasized the epithet scornfully enough, but it did not affect him in any way.

"Now that is unhandsome," he merely said. "If I am penniless, you should cultivate charity, and be anxious to help me to ten thousand pounds. But— perhaps I am not—altogether. What would you say, Marian," he went on in quite a pleading voice, stooping over her, and a hand resting on the back of her chair, "if I were to tell you that I am making a fortune, not for myself—for you know that I don't care about it,— but for you?"

She started at first—but only for a moment.

"I should say," she answered, hardly and scornfully, "that I did not believe you."

She remembered scenes and days which his manner brought back to her, only too well, and the bitterness of her tone, which was something like contempt, should have moved her companion if he remembered them too. But it did not, apparently. He only threw into his manner a more marked meaning, which looked like devotion, associated with those times when, whoever was in the room and to whomever he was speaking, he conveyed to her that he was conscious of her only.

"But if it were so?" he pleaded. "If I had never forgotten the past? if I can never forget it? If it had been my dream to be able to say to you one day, 'I have always loved you! I could not bring you, rich and high-placed as you are, to poverty and obscurity. Even now I must ask you to sacrifice much—'"

"Lestrange!" she said, in a hesitating, wondering, wistful tone, which sounded to her like an echo of a voice which had once been hers. Were the words suddenly coming, now at this eleventh hour, which after her husband's death her ears had once ached to hear? "Lestrange!"

"Let me go on. 'But, at least, I can give you comfort and a home—comfort that you will owe to me, a home that you will share with me!' If it were true, and I said 'Come,' would you follow me?"

Lady Luscombe had risen from the chair, her heart beating stormily against its silken bars.

"To the end of the world!" she whispered. "Is it true?"

"No."

Intolerably cruel; even in him who made a study of moral vivisection, and perhaps persuaded himself, or tried to do so, that the results of his investigations were as good for anthropology as the advocates of the growing and peculiar practice in the animal-world maintain their morbidities to be for "science"—a word which, unless its worthier professors take some early occasion to repudiate them with authority and with disgust, such monstrosities as these will turn for honest men to something worse than foolishness. Intolerably cruel; but Lestrange could no more help himself than, after sufficient indulgence in vivisection, Doctor Domitian could help, if the fancy seized him, vivisecting his favourite dog, if he has such a thing, which is doubtful. And Doctor Domitian would do it with episcopal sanction from the Midland Counties—a fact never to be forgotten in that connexion.

Lestrange at that moment wanted Lady Luscombe's help in that delicate matter of his very much, as the Doctor might at the moment of his supreme pleasure be afraid of burglars. But that sort of relish heightens the enjoyment, as with voluptuaries of old. When Lady Luscombe professed her horror of the idea of being his wife Lestrange felt the necessity of a moral experiment, and he vivisected. Not more would Doctor Domitian gloat over the writhings of his dog, with a sense of pleasure quickened by personal interest, than did Lestrange over the pale flush which mantled to the worn face of Lady Luscombe at that supreme insult. Even then it was but a slight flush ; for the blood in her seemed to have unlearned its office by long starving of the poor heart; but she shook in every limb.

"Ah !" she said, with something of a long low cry, which had in it the ring of many feelings—indignation, astonishment, self-scorn, shame.

Count Lestrange laughed quietly, and spoke with the old placid good humour, as if there had been nothing in his little experiment to offend or to injure anybody.

"Why," he said, "five minutes ago you said that the worst thing your husband could have done would be to let you marry me. What foolish people women are !"

"There is one who shall not be added to the list of folly if I can help it," answered Lady Luscombe, when she had recovered her self-command, and had space to breathe. "I will protect Daisy Brent, and save her from you. Was it wise to insult me, do you think, when you wanted my help? You should have fooled me a little longer, and laughed at me only when you had won your wager."

"Perhaps it might have been wiser," he said ; "but I did not wish to cause you real disappointment."

"You shall never win that wager now. I will unmask you."

"There's nothing to unmask," answered the Count. "I told you at the time, you will remember, that the wager looked like a mere way of doing you a service. You said so yourself. You can't hurt me. Now I can hurt you."

"How?" she asked.

"Your letters, you know."

"Ah!" Lady Luscombe said; "those miserable letters again. What were they? what are they? Whatever they are, I cannot believe that you would stoop to using them publicly against me."

"Did you ever really suppose that I kept them for sentiment?" he said, looking away from her, and consulting the oracle of the ring. "Haven't I told you— I think I have—that I am a man without scruples? I am in earnest; you must act as I tell you; and I must win this wager—to-day."

"To-day!"

She shrank away from him.

"To-day," he repeated, with an emphasis more marked than before, as he looked down the conservatory, from which once more those two other figures were approaching. "Really, it is becoming quite scandalous. Look!"

"I see no harm," said Lady Luscombe. "Suppose Daisy goes at my wish? She will only go with Lady Pepperharrow."

"I think not. But if so, that absolves you. You must come away."

"You are in earnest in this wicked thing, then? God forgive me! Even I didn't know you!"

"Not quite. Come and talk it over."

*　　*　　*　　*　　*

"Is it true that you only threw me over for your parents' sake?" said Guy. "And that you still believed that I should come to you? and that you never received the letter which I wrote to you?"

"Quite true."

"Is it true that you were fond of me?"

"Quite true."

"I want to know one thing more," he said.

And with short rapid steps, and rough and broken utterance, Guy Faucit was restlessly wandering about the room, in the middle of which Daisy stood, quite still. The barrier of ice had been broken down, and there was no reserve between them.

"What?" she asked, as if bound to answer without a fear, to whatever it pleased him to ask her.

"Are you very poor?"

"Yes; and you're very rich. It's curious. Punished for my sins, ain't I? I, who of course never cared for anything but money."

"It's not that," he said, roughly, putting the words aside with a wave of the hand. "Your people——"

"My father and mother are both dead, as I told you. There's only Dick and myself, and Dick doesn't go for much, you know. He's just got wit and money enough to live on, with his pay."

"And you?"

"Oh, whist and horses, and one thing and another," she answered, with a brief return of the off-hand manner which pained him in her more than anything else, knowing as he did its sad affectation. "I live with Lady Pepperharrow, and a great deal with Lady Luscombe. And Mr. Brent is good enough to make me a small allowance. My clothes always excite the admiration of the men and the envy of the women. What more can a woman want?"

"They tell hard stories of you," said Guy, coming up to her side, and looking in her face.

But she raised her head in the old queenly way, and gave him back the look into his eyes.

"I know that," she answered; "but you are to believe me once for all. The worst stories are not true, and they never will be."

"I do believe you," he said, with a choke in his voice. "But," he spoke with infinite hesitation, and

with his eyes on the ground, "as, after all, your oldest
and best friend, wouldn't you let me help you if you
were in a difficulty, rather than whist and horses, and
one thing and another?"

Daisy was almost crying, and didn't quite speak
at first.

"How good and loyal you are!" she said, with a
sort of pride in him, and in herself too, for having
known it of him long ago. "But in your position
and mine—no."

He turned away and he came back again, and he
went to the window over the garden, and then came
again to her, and he said in a low and hurried voice,
as if it came in spite of him—

"I could give you everything; put you above all
this."

Then she flushed again, and then she grew very
pale, and into her eyes and face there came a look
of sadness beyond words. But she spoke very, very
gently.

"*Above* it, Guy?" she said, steadily. "Was I right?
Are you loyal?"

And the sigh was deep with which he answered
after a while—

"Yes, Daisy; I think so."

CHAPTER XV.

FROM GRAVE TO GAY.

THE situation was becoming painfully strained;
and perhaps neither saw the way out of it. But the
beneficent Fate which so often waits on such situations
was at hand, and interrupted the talk in the intrusive
little person of the Lord Viscount Pentonville. He
had been hopping about all the morning in search

of news or of events, like an early sparrow in advance of its species, and regarding everything as within the province of crumbs. In everything he did he was a glutton for information, out of a spirit of downright curiosity worthy of Paul Pry; a character, indeed, in which his friends had been anxious to induce him to appear at one of Lady Pepperharrow's dramatic galas. His refusal, though the proposal had much gratified his innate sense of the proprieties, had been based upon the absolute unsuitableness of the character to his nature and abilities.

"An old f—f—fellow, who's always b—bothering everybody, and c—coming in where he's not wanted. I s—saw Toole do it, and thought it a horrid caricature. N—never was a f—fellow of that kind in real life."

So, in spite of the insistance of his friends, and the persuasions of Lady Pepperharrow,—who was convinced that "Really, my lord, if you only would, you don't know what a talent you might develop, and how much you would surprise all your friends. We never can be sure of aving nothing in us till we have tried everything,"—the Lord Viscount Pentonville remained a stranger to stage-triumphs, and confined his performances of Paul Pry to the theatre of real life. This morning he had been unusually on the alert. He had observed Guy and Daisy at intervals; had satisfactorily convinced himself that the partnership between Jem Gosling and Carrie Beaufort was interrupted for the time; had with much gratification given in a formal report upon that head to Lady Luscombe; had hovered like a shadow about the languid Emily and the ruminating Coates; and had nevertheless found the time to poke his nose into gardens, and stables, and farm-buildings, and to drive the retainers of the Abbey half wild by idiotic remarks about creepers or manure.

"There never was a little man," Gosling said of him, "so inappropriate as that little man."

His morning's labours on this occasion were crowned

with a signal triumph which he had not anticipated. Fluttering about a laurel-walk near the house, he was in a moment of propitious destiny the absolute ear-witness of a declaration, or rather of the confirmation, ocular and oscular, of a compact which had been entered into a day or two before between two of the *personæ minores* of this veracious history. Old Pen, to do him justice, did not intend to overhear; but, whether from purblindness or natural impetuosi'y, or both combined, he was one of those who are a.ways rushing in upon the paths shunned of angels, and unable to extricate himself in time. He was as a bull perpetually making his appearance in china shops, and wearing a countenance of chronic dismay at the break-ages ensuing. One imagines the awkward eagerness with which a bull of that sort, after a few 'esser con-cussions, beats a retreat from an untenable position and rushes with his head down into the rival shop next door. I feel this simile to be Homeric, and cannot but fall into the hexametric tone.

"E'en as a bull in a shop—where Worcester, Sèvres, and
    Dresden,
Shelf over shelf up-piled, in patterns many and wondrous,
Yellow or rose or blue, the cross-swords glistening under,
Shine for æsthetic eyes in a blaze of saucerous glory,
Cups and chimæras dire, or fearful and wonderful fetish,—
All unawares is seen, with nostrils quivering strangely,
Head to the earth bowed down, and pawing with hoof
    bisected;—
Then, with a wondrous roar, and feet earth-shaking the floor-
    cloth,
Butts àt the nearest group which first encounters his bull's
    eye;
Upsets Phyllis the fair, whose lips of daintiest china
Meet with a pout some swain who pouts as daintily her way;
Rushes away once more, with naught but ruin behind him,
Making, alas, too late! his lame apology taurine,
Then, like the wind let loose, which sufferers execrate vainly,
Scatters the self-same way, the neighbour's wares at the
    corner;—
So did the blameless Lord whose misadventures I sing of,
Blind and luckless and rash, from couple to couple proceeding,

Scatter them here and there like leaves tree-severed in autumn,
Nip in a golden prime the promising buds of proposal,
Cut flirtation adrift, and crush the flower of Affection.''

Such was and such did the Lord Viscount Pentonville ; for having ascertained the facts that excited him
with reference to the couple whom he surprised, he
trotted off, trouser-bound, to carry the news to the next
telegraph-post, and trotting in through the door of the
room next the conservatory without note of preparation,
chuckling to himself and incipiently perspiring, he
came like a relief upon Daisy Brent at the moment
when the last chapter closed. He came like Monsieur
le Beau, with his mouth full of news, and seeing two
figures, which at a distance were but as shadows to
him, he made for them instinctively, like a pointer.

"Ah!" he said, in advance, not caring to ascertain
in whom he was going to confide, "wh—what do you
think has happened ?"

Then he trotted up, peered, and discovered; and
was quick enough to see, too, that the discourse which
he had interrupted was an interesting one.

"I b—beg your pardon," said he, inwardly revolving
that bet of his with the Count Lestrange, and angry
with himself for his forwardness, for a wonder. "How
stupid to have interrupted them," he thought.

"Don't mention it," said Daisy with a laugh, which
had relief in it.

The strain on her nerves and heart had been very
great, and the tension relaxed suddenly. The sudden
contrast of life, which at a moment so trying brought
this ridiculous little peerling upon the scene, struck her
sense of humour at once; and she came back to middle
earth more quickly than perhaps under any other circumstances she could have done.

"What's the latest intelligence?" she continued,
with an immediate affectation of deep interest.

"Something delightful, evidently," suggested Guy,
with more of contempt and less of welcome.

The ingredients of the human mixture differ widely,

and he was perhaps not so pleased by the sight of Lord Pentonville as his companion was, in spite of everything.

"Is it a fire—or a sudden death?" Daisy enquired.

"You're full of news. Out with it," added Guy.

"He can't! it's choking him," said Daisy. "Don't keep us in suspense longer than you can help," she added, in a tone of mock entreaty. With all a true woman's quickness and adaptability, she had her usual manner with her courtiers ready for use at once.

"It's d—delicious!" chuckled his lordship. "Gue—gue—"

"Guess?" suggested Guy.

"No! Find out."

"I give it up," Faucit said, turning away with a shrug of his shoulders, as one whom the coming revelation did not deeply interest.

"So do I!" laughed Daisy. "Go on."

"C—C—C—Coates," stammered Lord Pentonville, with such a number of preliminary consonants tumbling over each other in his excitement, that his veins began to swell, and Daisy had vague thoughts of patting him on the back, "Coates is engaged to Emily Challoner!"

"Poor devil!" was all Guy's pregnant comment, as he sate down in a corner of the room with an odd number of a magazine, and played with its pages, upside-down very likely.

It must be some little time before he could bring himself under command again after the sad and strange confidences of the morning.

Daisy's more flexible spirit, more attuned to the gossips and the interests of the world in which she had lived so long, enabled her to welcome the intelligence at once with genuine amusement and delight. She had watched, with a constant and harmless mischief, the fair Emily's patient and undiscourageable angling, and the floundering of the solemn fish for whom the hook had been baited. The baronet's ox-like devotion to herself had been Miss Challoner's chief difficulty, which it had been impossible to Daisy not to stimulate at odd moments,

knowing as she did that the young lady hated her with
a stolid and hearty ill-will, and lost no opportunity of
insinuating the dangers and wickednesses of her lightness of character. When she had time to realize how
cleverly Emily Challoner must have taken advantage
of the lull in Sir Brummel's assiduities towards herself,
she laughed with a real enjoyment which Guy rather·
grudgefully envied her.

"Oh! is that true?" she said, fairly clapping her
hands in an access of the girlishness which never seemed
to desert her, as it rarely does desert well-constituted
woman-souls. "I haven't heard anything so perfectly
lovely for a long time!"

There was a rush of many feet, and the room gradually filled in anticipation of the luncheon-hour, which
was a rather late and an important fixture at Luscombe
Abbey. Lady Luscombe was none of those painfully
punctual hostesses, who make of the breakfast-bell a
burden to the unfettered soul, and rally everybody to
the morning board at a time when half the world is on
its own cares and thoughts intent; when some of it
likes to be in bed and resting, chewing perhaps the cud
of work by the process of placid meditation in the
place most of all favourable to it; and another part of
it, country-trained, loves to be afloat in the morning air,
upon its own researches and pursuits. The breakfast-
tyrant, who ignores the perfect law of liberty, is far too
common, and does not always meet with so ready a
jouster as the town-bred bachelor, who, when a hostess
of this class said to him quietly on the first night of his
visit to her in the country, "Mr. Urban—we always
breakfast at eight o'clock," answered at once, with
politeness as imperturbable, "Do you, madam? I
never do."

No; it is not in one direction only that the
agitation for a "free breakfast-table" is a valuable
thing. Let the early tea or coffee be imbibed in the
separate chamber; and in this country, where the true
luxury of life and safeguard of digestion, the French

midday fork-breakfast, is unknown and practically
impossible, let the best substitute be found in a running meal, with cold meats upon the sideboard, and due
relays of tea and dishes, with cosies and covers warranted
to preserve the heat as long as possible, which shall not
be enforcedly closed before eleven, while compulsory
attendance before ten should at all times be out of the
question. Thus, madam, will you win your guest's confidence and admiration, and grapple him to your soul
with hooks of steel. Thus, too, perhaps, will you be
able to think of him as of a person of equable and
genial disposition, and one not apt to let the small
crosses of life prey upon his mind, and drive him to
unpleasant moroseness and unamiable remarks.

Perchance, when you are speculating why he is
so acidly disposed some morning, he is but meditating
upon that other half-hour which he wanted in bed, to
bring his wits and his good-temper about him. General
laws about digestion are as futile as general laws generally. But I for one hold, that after the first flush of
omnivorous youth mankind is not properly receptive of
a solid repast, when English customs are followed, until
the divine hour of luncheon—most wholesome, most
appetizing, most sociable of British meals. Luncheon
at Luscombe Abbey was an institution, and one so
tempting that it was apt to tempt even the most gun-
loving of guests to find himself in the covers nearest
home a little before two o'clock.

It would seem, on the day of which I am writing,
that Sir Brummel and his Emily had been tempted to
divulge their delicious secret in more than one quarter.
It is doubtful whether the baronet would have felt any
pressing anxiety so to do, and indeed he had resisted in
the matter for a day or two; but his Emily was mildly
pertinacious, being indeed possessed of a conviction that
publicity was a certain guarantee in such matters, with
which it was not always advisable to dispense. There
was also a sense of triumph in her heart over her
intimate friend, Carrie Beaufort, who never had any

secrets from anybody, in that she had been the first of the two to bring her wooer to the point. She was inwardly conscious that, in respect of this running, the betting had been decidedly on Carrie, therefore the triumph was of the more moment. So, over and above the results of Pentonville's enquiring mind, Emily had confided in Carrie; and Sir Brummel, in his laconic fashion, in the Honourable Jem; and the event of the day became the common property of the Abbey.

"Come into court, Brum," Gosling was saying, as he brought up his companion, looking decidedly sheepish, for introduction to Daisy in his new character; "and don't look so jolly down in the mouth, old man! There's nothing to be ashamed of."

Almost at the same moment Carrie Beaufort made her appearance with Emily. Whatever the latter young lady might amiably have expected, there was no feeling of annoyance about Carrie, who was genuinely delighted with the catastrophe, and felt that she shone with a reflected glory.

"Oh Daisy, what do you think?" she said, before Gosling could proceed. "Let me introduce you to Lady Coates!"

"Oh, Brum! Brum!" said Daisy, in a low voice, with an air of sad reproach, and her eyes dancing with fun, after a complimentary salutation to the promised bride.

"'Pon my soul, Daisy, you know," confided Sir Brummel, in a tone of unusual and quite pathetic earnestness, "I haw couldn't help it."

"Poor fellow!" Daisy said, "did she make you do it? I congratulate you with all my heart, dear," she added to Emily.

"Thanks, awfully, dear," said the heroine of the moment, very languidly; "it's so good of you to say so. Isn't she just savage?" whispered the amiable maiden to Carrie Beaufort.

"If she is, dear, she conceals it, don't she?"

answered the young lady addressed. "Do you know, dear," she went on, the chapter of confidence having been embarked upon, "Jemmy has very nearly asked me."

"Really, dear?" this with a superior smile, as of one in safe haven. "What does your aunt say?"

"I don't know what has happened to her, dear; she left us together just now without saying a word."

"Ah! Lord Gander must be bad, dear."

This was the conclusion of that worldly-wise Emily.

"Faithless Brum!" Daisy was saying to her baronet meanwhile, holding him in amused play. "Have I lived to be deserted in this way?"

"'Pon my soul, no!" Coates earnestly assured her. "If you don't hum like it, I'll haw break it off."

"Not on my account, I beg," said Daisy; "I shall get over it in time, but it took me by surprise."

"Haw yes. So it did me."

"I should like to know how you proposed. Would you mind doing it over again?"

"Haw yes, I would. I don't hum think I ever can."

"I'm sure I hope you never may," said Emily, with a pout, a proper jealousy of her swain's attentions having brought her within hearing of the last word or two.

"Fact is, you know," Coates was still able to assure Daisy, "you know you quite haw cut me for the big fellow, and the other day it was too hum wet to shoot."

But Emily removed him before he could enter into further explanations, only to encounter the anxious gaze of the delighted Pentonville.

"H—have you told Lady Luscombe?" he chuckled out, poised on the point of his varnished little toes, about the breadth of a corn in their boots.

"Haw no," said the Baronet.

"Then 1—let me, p—please let me!" entreated his lordship. "I wouldn't let anybody else t—tell her for the world!"

"Oh, yes! oh, yes! this is to give notice!" laughed

Carrie Beaufort, as Pentonville trotted off. The little lady had again attracted the volatile Jemmy to her side upon a tempting sofa, and was purring with much content. "Exit the town-crier!"

"Somebody take care of him!" called out Gosling, in the same tone; "if he gets so excited his pads will work down. He's padded all over, you know, Clipper; I'll take my oath of it. They brought me his coat one night by mistake; and, by Jove, he's all padding, Hard-Labour is."

"Don't speak disrespectfully of padding," said a quiet and cynical voice, which now joined itself to the conversation, though nobody had seen the owner make his way into the room. "It's the motive power of the age; it's the staple of what we read and the bulk of what we eat; it's another name for adulteration. The creed of the statesman and the oratory of the divine—padding. The backbone of Liberal progress and of Conservative reaction—padding. The mushroom millions that grow on the Stock Exchange, and sprout out in West-end palaces—padding. The calves of our servants and the hair of our wives—padding. The liberal display of the female form divine, which delights the Jemmy Goslings of the age, and constitutes the modern British drama—padding!"

"Hear, hear!" said Guy, who looked up from the magazine he had been communing with when Lestrange entered, having recovered his self-command during the preceding scene.

As he gave his approval of the Count's sentiments, he got up from his seat and insensibly found himself again with Daisy. Nor was it long before the two, deep again in talk, though of a less disturbing kind than that which Pentonville had interrupted, strolled out of the room together down the path of flowers.

Lestrange followed them with his furtive eye, and turned to the rest of the assembled party again. His disquisition on padding had been listened to with the reverential silence to which he was accustomed when in the didactic vein. The sentiments of the company on the subject first found a voice in Coates.

"Haw," said the Baronet.

"How the Count talks!" said Carrie to her companion, with much admiration.

"He don't talk more than me," answered Jem, with little grammar, but some jealousy.

"No, Jemmie; but he says so much more."

"How jolly rude! just like the fellows in a comedy."

"Let me add my congratulations, Sir Brummel," said Lestrange.

"How have you heard?" Coates asked.

"I've always heard," answered the Count, quietly.

"He's like a haw damned conjurer," muttered the uncomfortable Coates.

"Don't you hate that man?" asked Carrie of Jem, with a sudden impulse, as Lestrange was saying something to Miss Emily Challoner.

"Awfully," he answered, with conviction.

"Shall I tell your fortune?" said Lestrange, laughing, and turning again to Sir Brummel, "Mr. Benedick, the married man?"

"I don't know why you call me Benedick," said the Baronet, rather gruffly; "but hum no."

"By all means let us hear it," interposed Emily, anticipating something pleasant in honour of the occasion.

"You will marry in a month," said Lestrange, in the same tone of good-humoured laughter, which he could put on like anything else when he chose; "be tired of each other in two, separate in three, and get divorced at the convenience of the Law."

He had taken Sir Brummel's hand in his palm, and affected to study its lines in the true soothsaying fashion.

"Haw I say hang it!" said Coates.

"How absurd!" added the disgusted Emily, laughing not very pleasantly.

"I don't know," muttered the Baronet, under a thick moustache, which allowed the charitable to suppose that his mouth might be expressive. "It seems so awfully possible."

"What did you say?" demanded Emily, in a rather imperious tone which boded storms on the other side, when the point of matrimony should have been safely weathered.

"Nothing to matter," answered the victim of her spear.

And from her experience Emily believed him.

"You're like the gipsies at Epsom," said Gosling. "By Jove, I'll have a turn. Have you anything to tell me?"

"Let me see," said Lestrange, appropriating the plump and rosy little hand which the other held out to him. "The lines of wit and wisdom strongly marked. You should be one of our hereditary legislators. I think you soon will be."

"You don't mean that Gander's bad?" said Gosling, with a real anxiety in his voice, which had the effect of raising Lestrange's eyebrows a little. He had always been a little contemptuous of the Arcadian side of the Honourable Jem.

"Didn't I say so, dear?" whispered Emily to Carrie, in a voice of confidence.

"Don't chaff a fellow about that," Gosling went on, verb-mixing. "I'd rather anything happen than lose dear old Gander. But it's all humbug this sort of business. Why don't you tell us something about yourself?" he asked, with an audacity he wondered at. "All anybody knows about you is that the fellows say you come from Greece."

"Greece?" said the Count, the eyebrows lifting again; "I give you my word that it's one of the few countries I never was in in my life."

"Hang it! where were you then?" asked Gosling, vaguely.

"Where was I when? This time last year I was in Pondicherry."

"Oh, I say, Carrie," said Jem to his friend, confidentially, "where the deuce is Pondicherry?"

"I don't know," she said, recklessly; "somewhere in the map. Thank goodness, there's luncheon," she added, as a mellow gong rang its summons from the hall. "Jemmy, take me in; I don't half like it."

"Haw yes, lunch," murmured Coates, to himself, his eyes visibly brightening for the first time since he had been promoted to the post of hero of the hour. "Proposing makes one awfully hum hungry. Come in, Emily, I'm doosidly afraid of that man."

CHAPTER XVI.

THE WISDOM OF THE SERPENT.

"You are thoughtful, Faucit. What are your tnoughts?" said the Count Lestrange.

A day or two had passed since the events recorded in the last chapter, and a shadow as of something to come seemed to settle down upon Luscombe Abbey. Changes had taken place in the personages of the scene. Jem Gosling had been called away by the serious illness of his elder brother, and Carrie Beaufort was left for the time disconsolate. Lady Pepperharrow, too, had taken her departure for abroad, somewhere for the winter-quarters of the south, which her ladyship had of late affected. Daisy had at one time arranged to go with her, but they had parted. Daisy was growing restless, strange, not herself, and for the first time in her life had something like a scene with her kind old friend, who, to her astonishment and anger, had one day taken her to task about her friendship with Guy Faucit.

"I always thought, my dear, that the young man was very fond of you," Lady Pepperharrow said; "and indeed I never knew how anybody could elp it. And it disappointed me very much when he didn't come forward, and you married that odious Mr. Brent. I'm sure I'd have done anything I could to prevent it, and to bring you and Mr. Faucit together; and now everybody says that, after all, you were engaged, though you never said anything to me about it, and that you didn't beave at all well to im, and—"

"Lady Pepperharrow, I wish everybody would let me alone. Nobody does such mischief as everybody; and I can't understand how you speak to me like that."

"Well, my dear, I'm sure—"

But we need not follow too closely the story of the difference between two firm friends. Lady Pepperharrow herself could give no account of the manner in which she had been brought to take notice of the growing intimacy between Daisy Brent and Guy Faucit as something singular and to be discouraged. She could not have told—for it had been carefully concealed from herself—how it was that the Count Lestrange had insinuated the first suspicions of something wrong, and had sown the seeds of distrust of her favourite in Lady Pepperharrow's mind. Always laughing with Lady Pepperharrow, and covertly laughing at her, he paid her mock-gallant attentions which from "a man of such powerful intellect, you know," delighted the worthy lady's soul and quite won her confidence.

Count Lestrange had established the absolute influence over her mind, which was desirable in the high priest of the mysteries of Glycerine House, to which post the accomplished Count had been exalted. He was certainly the man for the place. A trained painter and musician, he better than any one could select the subjects and organize the groups for a series of *tableaux vivants*, or superintend the details of a concert or amateur opera. London rang with the fame of a certain performance of the 'Barbiere,' in which the Count's Figaro was a masterpiece of subtlety and

tunefulness, and Daisy Brent warbled the bird-notes
of Rosine like one of the feathered tribe hired and
tutored for the occasion. Young Kensington South
of the Colonial Office brought his cultivated æsthetic
taste to bear on the character of Almaviva, and was
seen to much advantage in the Spanish grandee's
costume, while his mouth was observed, by the initiated,
to open and shut in good time to the accompaniments.
To the πολλοὶ among his audience he gave much of
the gratification which the page-boy derived from the
efforts of a great preacher whom his master sent him
to hear in the neighbouring cathedral. "Well, James,
did you hear him?" he asked, when the boy returned
with a broad grin. "Oh no, sir, I didn't hear him.
But I seed him a hollering." And so young South
of the Æsthetics ("isn't that one of the gentlemen they
call the Aztecs?" asked an enquiring railway-porter
who saw him get out of the train) warbled "Ecco
ridente il cielo" so articulately that the whole of the
front row very nearly heard him. Patti and Nilsson
themselves were among the listeners to the opera,
and Lady Pepperharrow was in the seventh heaven.
She had been with difficulty dissuaded from herself
appearing in the duenna's part, but was gratified by
the appearance of Norbiton and Surbiton as two guards
(*personæ mutæ*) in the scene of the arrest, where they
occupied the opposite corners of the stage like two
loving strawberries moulded on one stem. The performance was a talk; and not less so the amateur
comedies, which put the Prince of Wales's and the
Haymarket to shame, under the skilful guidance of
Lestrange. I attended some of them with Binks, who
growled a good deal, and deplored the absence of professional training. Binks had himself begun stage life
as an amateur, and the ill-natured professed to detect
a flavour of the origin in his most pronounced feats.
But Binks's wigs stood the test of the severest criticism.
    "I feel that I never could have been strong-minded,
Count Lestrange," Lady Pepperharrow said to her

Philostrate, when recruiting herself after her exertions on one of these occasions, and regretting her inability to take a leading part in a thinking movement which was then agitating society. "But I adore art and science, and their charming professors. You see how many of them come to my ouse, and are good enough to say that I am naturally artful — I mean artistic. My life is such a busy one!"

"You take too much out of yourself, dear Lady Pepperharrow, indeed you do," said the Count.

"Do you think so? I am afraid I do. You can't think what a correspondence I ave, Count Lestrange. It was only this morning that I was begged for another subscription for the conversion of the poor dear Jews. I ave so many friends among them that I naturally long to see them converted, though indeed they seem to do very well as they are. You really must elp me, Count, indeed you must, to see about the conversion of the dear Jews."

So in small things and great Lady Pepperharrow learned to lean upon the Count Lestrange, who had a way of keeping all the threads in his hands when he had some especial object in view. Neither Lady Pepperharrow nor Daisy, nor any one else, could have laid a finger on the moment in which he succeeded in working the old lady up to a sense of the impropriety of her favourite's alliance with Guy Faucit at Luscombe Abbey, and inducing her to remonstrate at the most inadvisable time and in the most inappropriate way. She was a safeguard for Daisy of the most invaluable kind; and no sooner had she left the Abbey, as she did, on bad terms with the sore-tried woman for the first time in their lives, than Daisy felt an utter sense of friendlessness descend upon her which had had no parallel before. She had nobody, then, to care for her, nobody but Guy. All communication from her husband, direct and indirect, had suddenly ceased, and even in that she felt a fresh blank of isolation. More—the last payment of her allowance had fallen due, and for the first time had not been made to the day. If it were to cease, what was to become of her ?

Meantime, during the few days which passed after the engagement of Coates and Emily had been announced at the Abbey, the Count Lestrange had seized every opportunity of being much with Guy, especially at night in the quiet smoking-room, when Daisy had left the place vacant. From the first he had not forgotten the promised mentorship, and his dubious moralities and masterful cynicisms had made their way through the outworks of Guy's mental citadel, carelessly insinuated, ceaselessly suggested, web-woven with a skill in dialectics which the Count might have learned from a close study of old state-crafts, and old mediæval habits of thought.

There are two guiding-stars in life, of which one must needs follow one—truth and expediency. The first is cloud-hidden and storm-racked now and again, and not absolutely patent to the clearest vision. But it is as steady as a pole-star behind cloud and storm, and he whose course is steered by it knows always in what quarter of the heaven it lies, if he carry a conscience in good repair by way of compass about him. Once leave it, as an *ignis fatuus,* and fall into Pilate's questioning habit of what truth is, and expediency alone remains to steer by. Woe to those who try the course ! for it sets in one quarter and rises in another by no general laws that man's wit has discovered, and he is apt to fix its latitude and longitude after the last caprice of his own changeful desire. Hence many moral wrecks, and goodly lives cast away. There are always a dozen expediences to choose between in a difficulty, each equally defensible by argument. With a little trouble at times in fixing it, there is always but one truth. Guy's perceptions of truth were getting shaken.

He was watching the new-betrothed pair as, with rather a semi-attached air of devotion, at all events on Sir Brummel Coates' part, they were strolling down one of the garden-paths together, when Lestrange touched him on the shoulder, as told at the opening of this chapter.

"You are thoughtful, Faucit. What are your thoughts?"

They were in the same room as that described in the last chapter—the room off the conservatory.

"If you are Satan, you should be able to read them," Faucit answered, rather doubtfully, and with sadness in his voice. The wound in his heart might not be as wide as a church-door, but it served.

The nickname which men had sometimes given to Lestrange was in his mind as he looked at him, and some one of those timely storm-signals which are set up in our tossing hearts seemed suddenly to speak of danger. Guy was struck with a nameless feeling of the evil in his companion's face. The companion, however, did not wince under the epithet, which indeed he rather took as a compliment, with an amused sense of appropriateness. He was inwardly revelling in a certain jubilant feeling of his own power as he thought of the desert he had made round Daisy Brent. And he was full of a sense of anticipation; for—Lady Pepperharrow gone, and not fixable anywhere for the moment, as she was on travel bent—he had just come from Lady Luscombe, whom he had left crushed and beaten, after a wrestle and a victory.

"I will try," he said, in answer to Faucit's remark, seating himself comfortably in a chair, a cigarette between his lips. Tobacco was free of entrance in all the outer rooms of the Abbey. "You were moralizing on that promising couple, and thinking that marriage is a serious thing."

"You are right—as usual," said Guy, shortly. "I expect it will prove so—to them."

"That depends upon how they take it," Lestrange said lightly; "and by such people marriage is not taken seriously."

"But it must be—by all of us."

"Why?"

"Well—a woman might answer, because it must."

"And I answer as I should answer the woman—why? again. If you wish to simplify the world's problems, Faucit, it is easily done. Most arguments are assertions. Every one of them should be met not by counter-assertion or counter-argument (which are troublesome to oneself—always leave the other side to argue, the standard sign of inferiority), but by one of two questions—'Why?' or 'Why not?' You have no idea how that will bring men to their bearings. Why should marriage be serious,·except on scriptural grounds, which when fairly examined, admit of much debate?"

"Do they know anything of each other?" asked Guy abruptly, ignoring the issue.

Lestrange laughed as he did so.

"Precisely. That is the way in which 'why' and 'why not' are always evaded; the only way of meeting them—the *ignoratio elenchi.* I can answer your question, however. No, they don't know anything of each other. If they did, neither would marry the other."

"I don't understand it," said Guy, impatient of the sneer. "My creed is Mrs. Browning's—

> 'Learn to win a lady's faith
>   Nobly, as the thing is high;
> Bravely, as for life and death,
>   With a loyal gravity.'"

"Sir Brummel has not read Mrs. Browning," said Lestrange, drily. "The motto of his school is an old proverb—modified. Marry in haste, and—divorce at leisure."

"It's a new school," said Guy, with the same expression of disturbed feeling, "and I hope a small one."

"At present," Lestrange proceeded, quite undisturbed. "But we live in an age of progress. This is the cream of society, and the cream always turns first. You have heard how a little leaven leavens the whole lump."

"I have heard," said Guy, with an uneasy laugh, "that you can quote Scripture to your purpose. But I hope that these doctrines won't spread, and that you'll prove wrong."

"So do I," Lestrange answered, with a shrug of the shoulders and a cheery laugh on his own side; "and I don't pretend to know. Prophecy was always an uncertain profession, from Isaiah downwards. But drifting is a dangerous process; and we drift, Faucit, we drift."

"Yes, all of us," Guy said, with a deep sigh, his head resting on his hand and his eyes looking out into the vague. "What am I drifting to?"

He spoke more to himself than to the other, who watched him for a moment without taking any notice. Then he said pleasantly,

"You? To a comfortable harbour," he added in a quiet tone, "not often reached. The success of a first love. I promised you, you remember."

He spoke quite naturally, as of the most natural thing in the world.

"A first love!" said Guy, bitterly, and with an unspeakable regret. "I have lost mine."

"Have you? Ask her."

He sent the arrow straight home, and Guy Faucit started as it struck him. He turned upon the Count Lestrange almost fiercely.

"Do you think," he said, "that I would ruin Daisy Brent?"

"I think that you might save her," said the other, unmoved.

"By robbing her of her good name?"

This was not the first time, perhaps, that the subject had been approached between them; but it had not been before broached so openly.

"Her name is a bad one," Lestrange said, in a tone rather quietly argumentative than anything else, as if a point of business were under discussion,—"getting worse. If you don't run away with her somebody else will. How should you like that?"

The very tone in which the Count spoke seemed to carry the subject out of the region of anger, even of reality. Insensibly Guy Faucit fell into something of the same manner, though his head and heart were in a whirl. Good God! how in the last few days Daisy had taken possession of every fibre and component of his being, with the added strength and tenacity which had sprung of the iron self-repression of the eight long years.

"It is impossible," he said.

"It's a mathematical certainty. Given the premises, —a husband like hers, a nature like hers, a society like hers,—the conclusion follows—elopement. You have the first chance. Take it; if you don't, I think I shall." Quietly and more quietly still, with the venom distilling in every subtle word.

"You!" exclaimed Guy Faucit with a laugh, as if the last suggestion had been intended to remove the whole matter into the region of the absurd—"what have you in your favour?"

"Modestly speaking," said Lestrange, deprecating all personal merit in himself, "the same advantage as other men, of course leaving you out of the question. I am not her husband."

And the Count contrived to throw into the last words such an immeasurable expression of contempt for good, and disbelief in all its possibilities in the conventional world about them, that Faucit fairly shuddered as the iron went deeper into him. He shrank from Lestrange with an uneasy and a formless fear for the man, something of the feeling of vague dread which a great German writer has said always possessed him when he met with a man who professed himself an atheist.

"Lestrange!" he said, after a moment's pause, almost as if he were driven to make a personal appeal to the man for his own sake, "are you afraid of nothing in another world, that you venture so to play with evil in this?"

"Nothing," answered the other, with a look of quite an innocent surprise. "Why should I be?"

"You may learn some day," Guy said, after another moment's interval. "I begin to think that you are right," he added, looking steadily and thoughtfully at the Count, whose eyes beat their usual retreat at once, —it was a habit which annoyed their owner, but he had never been able to cure them of it,—"it would be to save Daisy Brent, to take her out of the reach of such men as you!"

The Count Lestrange smiled as the other said it, with a smile that was almost an inward one—a cruel, imperceptible, victorious smile.

"I told you so," he said.

A very fever of feeling was burning in Guy Faucit's brain. All that he could do for Daisy—all that ought to be done for her—all the bitter sorrow of her broken life, and the blank isolation of his own, from which all the ambitions and schemes he had begun to form when first his change of fortune came to him had vanished into space and nothingness again in the spell of her constant presence, were a torture and a tempest in his mind. How lightly men spoke to her! how lightly they spoke of her! and what right or room had he to resent? The Count's light words, which he caught, with the deep purpose which he missed, stirred all this gathered feeling to a cry.

"Oh Daisy! Daisy!" he called out, forgetting where he was and with whom, "that any man living should dare to talk of you so!"

More than once Lestrange's eyes had wandered to the door before this burst of passion came. Even as it came the door had opened, and Daisy herself had flashed into the room, erect, red to the brow, and quivering with anger, reckless of whom she met, reckless of who was there. Without concert or warning her passion answered Guy's.

"It's cruel, and I'll not bear it!" she said, as if to any one who cared to hear. "What right has any one to speak so to me?"

"Daisy! what is it?" Guy appealed, as the two

vexed spirits came together with a clang; for he was at her side in a moment.

"Thank you, my lady!" muttered to himself Lestrange; effacing himself at once without note of warning. "The flint is hot—and the steel. Strike!"

Unnoticed and unmissed he had opened the glass door leading into the garden, and was gone—not far.

CHAPTER XVII.

THE CRISIS.

"Is that you, Guy?" Daisy Brent said. "Do you know what Lady Luscombe has said to me?" The words came thick and fast and warm, and the indignation in her struggled for expression.

"What?"

"That I shall have to leave this house—because of you."

"By what right has she dared—" Guy began.

"By the right of every woman, I suppose," interrupted Daisy in an infinite scorn, "to think and to say the worst of another. She has insulted me, Guy, that wicked woman, whose name has been Scandal's plaything, to be broken and patched up at will. Oh! why did I ever come here? But I will go now—and at once."

"Child! where can you go?" Guy said, with pity, and tenderness, and self-reproach, and a world of feeling blended in his tone.

"I don't know!" she almost sobbed, for the tried heart was failing. "My brother is abroad, and so is my kind husband, and Lady Pepperharrow even. Oh, what shall I do?"

The woman was very desolate and very weak; and

D D

Guy Faucit had been less than man had not Lestrange's words come back upon him with a strong temptation, and shaken him from head to foot. He loved that priceless woman so deeply; she had been so sorely, so mysteriously, so consistently tried; and he had been faithful to a dream so long. What should she do? The answer seemed to be knocking at his lips for utterance, but he would not yield. He walked away from Daisy and he put himself under a strong constraint; then with a set purpose he turned back again.

"You must not go," he said, hurriedly. "You need not. I will."

She started and looked up at him, and her face grew very pale. Then the tears which she had still held back came welling up into her eyes.

"You will go?" she said, in a voice so dreamily sweet that it lingered in music on his ear—"for me?"

Suddenly he sate down by her, and he took her hand in his, and she left it there, and in its soft, involuntary, clinging caress all the story of her helplessness seemed told.

"I will go for you," Guy said, in a voice into which in its deep repression passion seemed to have concentrated all its notes in one, "as I would stay for you. I will do that hard thing for you, as I would do the easy things; as I would work for you, live for you, die for you! If I can leave you, Daisy, judge how I love you! But you can't guess that."

For the moment—and who should grudge it her?— she yielded herself up to the influence of the charm, and as her hand lay in his she listened with closed eyes.

"I think I can," she answered.

"Not quite."

"Yes," she said. "I know what I shall feel—when you have left me."

He started up and was standing at her side.

"Do you mean that you love me again?" he asked.

She held her breath for a space before she answered

him, and then spoke, fearless of disguise, as to one towards whom now concealment could be but as another wrong.

"I mean that I have loved you always," said she—very simply and trustfully.

"Thank God!" Guy said, very fervently. "I have felt it all the time. I did not know the feeling was there; but it must have been that that I lived on. You—love—me?" he added, thinking out the words, and dwelling on their meaning.

She had confessed it then.

"Hush! let me think," Daisy said. "I have told you this, I think, because you are good and brave. If you were not I would have died first. Yes, Guy, you must go."

Once more there was a pause between them, and each communed with grave and overpowering thought, as two such spirits would commune. The tragedy of the situation told itself—told itself in that frank avowal more than it could have done in concealment. Mark that in her it was very frank; for she had told her love to Faucit without questioning him of his, or feigning womanly uncertainties where she felt none. The position, one towards the other, in which Providence or Fate had thrown them—and it was difficult enough for either to read any ways of Providence for the moment there—taxed human weakness nearly to its uttermost, so far as man might judge of what temptations are, or of the strength they are allowed to carry. Go—then? go—so? go, with the music of that confession fresh upon his ear! Guy Faucit had a new struggle with himself, and spoke as much to himself as to Daisy.

"Oh, but it is hard!" he said, "when I can give you all the things for whose want I lost you. What will you do?" he asked.

"Nothing," Daisy calmly answered, as one who had chosen her part, "that can make me less worthy of you when you are gone."

Silence! silence! silence! Silence in the room and about it—silence in the air and in the flowers—silence and a void almost, in the two hearts so full of thoughts and so incapable of words. The silence which seems to speak, sometimes, from all the objects in the room, which choose such moments to fix themselves upon the unconscious memory as part and parcel of some memorable scene. The mind, unobservant of them before, takes note of insignificant details which had before escaped it, and recalls them afterwards, always—the arrangement of some books or furniture, the aspect of some ornaments, the expression of some pictured face. Such a silence wraps us round in the supreme trials of life, when the sense of their true bearings and deepest realities seems to desert us for the time, and leave us at the mercy of any commonplace distraction or wandering thought, to save us from ourselves and from the overstrain.

There was no one near either, but the stealthy figure of one man which might have been occasionally seen to linger near the garden-door.

"But," said Guy at last—"but"—and his voice began to take a new tone of pleading which seemed half ashamed—"if we laughed at the world that has been so hard on us? Your husband is no husband to you, your home no home. Have we not the right to say to each other, 'Let your life be mine?'"

Yes; he spoke as one pleading, and pleading as much with his own better reason as with hers. She pretended no offence, and she thought a moment before she answered, in a tone as of reasoning, like his own.

"I think that we should have. I know—that we have not."

"But," and his eyes were on the ground and his words scarcely made head-way—"if I were to plead how well I have deserved you? If I were to ask you," at last he added, in one yearning, faltering plea, "to give up everything for me?"

The blood flowed back and ebbed away in her face,

and the parched tears burned behind her eyes, and the brave heart stood still in love and longing. But she raised those eyes to his with never a quiver or a fear in them, and she spoke gently, tenderly, pleadingly, without reproach; but firmly—as she stood.

"Guy!" she said, "dare you ask me?"

You were wrong in your calculations, Count Lestrange! And it was with a singular sense of pride and pleasure, mixed with a miserable feeling that they must part for evermore,—for theirs must be one union or disunion only,—that Guy Faucit knew it.

"I will never ask you, Daisy dear," he said—the last monosyllable unconsciously and lingeringly prolonged upon a note of immeasurable sorrow. He suddenly took her head in both his hands, and she bowed that graceful head to meet the embrace, as he left upon her forehead one protecting kiss, which had a blessing in it. "God bless you, and good-bye!"

He turned straight away, not to look at her again, and walked with a steady step to the glass-door leading to the garden. His plan was formed at once, for it brooked no faltering or delay. He would find Lady Luscombe and make some instant excuse, without allusion of any kind to anything that had passed; and without good-byes or wasted words to any one else in the house, he would pack his things at once, and make his way straight to London. What lay beyond was formless in his mind; but his thoughts were already travelling beyond the seas again.

As we propose we act not, if it be not so written. At the glass-door, even as he opened it, Guy Faucit met the Count Lestrange. In a moment the Count's quick glance took in the state of matters, and there was a slight curl upon his lip, and a fitful glitter in his eyes, which went in and out again like a glowworm's lantern.

"Are you going away, Faucit?" he said.

"I am," said the other, quickly.

The Count Lestrange laid his hand lightly on Guy's shoulder.

"You fool," he said, rather impatiently. "Look there."

Guy turned his head round, forgetting Lot's wife. Daisy Brent had turned deadly pale, and was swaying to and fro upon her feet. He saw her falling, looked at her for a moment, and with one cry, "My darling!" he was at her side. Even as he reached her she fell forward in a dead faint, and he caught her in his arms. At something which might or might not have been a sign from the Count Lestrange,—nobody could say it was,—two curious faces besides his, who seemed to make room for them, peered in at the garden-door. They were those of Miss Emily Challoner and the Lord Viscount Pentonville.

"Just so," muttered the Count Lestrange.

CHAPTER XVIII.

DAISY'S FLIGHT.

DAISY BRENT left Luscombe Abbey before the night had fallen. Before the night had fallen there were whisperings in the fine ladies' rooms and the men's smoking-corners, and battlings of much vehemence in the servants' hall, where Miss So-and-So's maid had never thought much of Mrs. Brent's conduct, chiefly because the Abigail attached to Lady What's-her-name considered her a very charming lady. Calumny ran its course unrebuked everywhere, when the little episode witnessed by Lord Pentonville and the fair Miss Challoner had leaked out in the utmost confidence to everybody, in the course of a well-employed half-hour.

The hostess pleaded a bad headache and shut herself up in her own room; the Count Lestrange had about him an air of deprecatory wonder, whereto was attached a mysterious afflatus of private information in reserve,

which was exceedingly impressive; and when it became
known that Guy Faucit had disappeared too, though by
a different train and at another time, the general excitement grew and prospered exceedingly. When had they
met? how had they met? how had the arrangements
been concluded?—all the surmises of a far-reaching
charity had room wherein to disport themselves at
will.

Miss Emily Challoner was in the rosiest flush of an
uncompromising virtue, and pointed stern morals to Sir
Brummel, which at first elicited from the baronet the
improper reply that Daisy Brent was a good little
haw soul, with no harm in her, and her husband was a
hum brute, who deserved all he got—except his wife,
Jem Gosling added.

Carrie Beaufort stood up for her friend, on the other
hand, right loyally. Daisy had been very kind and
considerate to her in the last few weeks, and had been
giving much unobtrusive help to her romance with the
Honourable Jem. She didn't believe a word about
Daisy, who had left because she had been insulted, and
quite right too, and she held her aunt's conduct—
for the whole story got about in all sorts of forms—to
have been very cruel and disgraceful; and she didn't
know how Mr. Gosling could even venture to suppose
that Daisy had gone away with that great big clumsy
Mr. Faucit, who ought to have known better than to
get her into a scrape. Indeed, she lighted up so angrily,
and looked so wonderfully pretty and tempting in the
lighting-up of her anger, that the Honourable Jem felt
his piece of mind quite seriously threatened, and confided to Norbiton and Surbiton that the girl was a
downright little trump, and no mistake at all about it,
quite too good for her aunt's set, and she ought to be
got out of it.

If Norbiton and Surbiton acquiesced, it was without
emotion. They confined themselves more exclusively
than ever to each other's company, but seemed but
negatively interested in the crisis. A new book of

cloth specimens from Poole's was for the moment absorbing them, and they were men who had learned the practical value of the maxim about attending to one thing at a time. Though he had been at first convinced that Guy Faucit and Daisy Brent had concerted their departure together, Carrie's indignant expostulations induced Gosling to send a message at once to an address which Guy had given him in London, telling him of what was being said, and to come back if he wished to disprove it.

Guy did come back, and immediately, and he came back in a tempest of trouble and of feeling. He had left Luscombe Abbey in loyal agreement with his promise to Daisy, and he had no knowledge of her having gone : so he assured Jem Gosling, with whom he was open in the matter, as with some one he must be. Daisy had had a fainting-fit when he was by, but after she had come to herself he had not spoken with her again. Where was she ? where had she gone ? he knew of no one to whom she could go, for they had been speaking of it in the morning. At the Abbey no one seemed to know; but Count Lestrange insinuated London, and that Mrs. Brent meant to find herself some employment there. She had spoken of the stage, but she was anxious to avoid publicity; and, at least in going, she had left no sign behind.

The world at Luscombe Abbey received the reappearance of Guy Faucit sceptically. Brave little Carrie was triumphant, but found no response in Emily Challoner, who knew that people always arrange these things with some care, and Mrs. Brent was such an adept in intrigue. The evil tongues were comfortably loosed, and there was no chaining them again in a hurry. A few uneasy days went by, and a constraint and discomfort which infected the whole place increased and grew; and no news came of Daisy; and in the cruel position which was his in the matter, Guy Faucit could make no open sign of all he felt, and of the dread and anxiety which were mastering him; and Lady

Luscombe pleaded illness, and hardly showed herself to her guests; and the circle broke itself up in an unadmired disorder.

Jem Gosling was called away by a serious crisis in his brother's health, and Carrie and he had a parting which was something like a pledge; Sir Brummel Coates departed to make preparations at the ancestral home of all the Coateses for the reception of a blooming bride,—he did not seem quite easy in his mind as the time drew near, and hawed more copiously than ever; but his fate was in the hands of one of no vacillating nature, and she thought delay in the nuptials unadvisable;—the Lord Viscount Pentonville was all anxiety to know whether or not he had won that bet of his with the Count Lestrange, which the Count Lestrange himself, with all his omniscience, seemed unable or unwilling to decide; the Count was mysterious and self-involved, but was a great deal with Guy Faucit.

September had been with them in its many-coloured harvest robes when the recluse of the ruins turned his face to the Abbey; and when he left it—sad, hopeless, weary, as he had been in days of old, though with a name at his feet and a fortune at his back—chill October was just coming in with the hectic on her cheek, and, to the sad autumn music of the falling leaves, Nature was drawing back the curtains of Summer from many a far-off view which they had folded from the sight. The fields were bare of grass and crops, and not three full months remained to the time when Lestrange must win or lose his wager: for he knew well enough that Faucit spoke the truth, and that he had not won it yet. But he had not lost it, either. And Guy Faucit and the Count Lestrange, in the early days of October, went to London on a quest together.

Yet the Count Lestrange knew, and he knew all the while, what had become of Daisy Brent. When she fainted away in the arms of Guy, the Count was comfortably persuaded that his wager was safe and sure.

She could never let the lover go now, he thought; poor human nature must be too strong for that; and when he had brought Guy back from the door to his lady's side, and summoned those two convenient witnesses of his to see what looked like an impassioned embrace, he was gone.

When Daisy came to herself again, she saw no one but Guy. She reproached him in the first rush of feeling, the poor, tortured heart, and asked him why he had not kept his word, and gone at once. Then in an outburst of tears, which she could hold back no further, she tore herself from him and rushed to her own room. Even as she did so she met Emily Challoner, and from a few pointed remarks from that virtuous maiden, who already considered the proprieties and dignities of married life under her special protection, she learned that the cruel though hesitating words with which Lady Luscombe had addressed her—she saw the cruelty but not the hesitation—had been but the beginning of a storm that was to assail her. A bitter disdain and anger took possession of her whole soul and spirit, and she was on the point of going straight to Guy Faucit, and trusting her life to him; but in the quiet of her room, even in the whirl of all the passion which possessed her, she soon saw clear before her the purpose of a steady soul. Not for her own sake—not for his— would she allow fancy pictures to tempt her of a happiness which could not be. She had seen an instance before her own eyes not very long before, of a young and frivolous friend of hers, who had taken the desperate step to which she was so sorely tempted now, under circumstances which, as in her own case, seemed to make the transgression venial; and she, who in a large-hearted charity had befriended the poor desolate girl when the world—which had encouraged her to the mistake and given her every opportunity for and incitement to it—turned its back upon her and cast her out, had seen with her eyes the misery which followed, and the rapid deterioration of character and loss of self-respect, which she recognized as the inevitable consequences. Was not Daisy rewarded for her courage, for which the world had, as she knew, after its fashion, blamed her and held her cheaply, by the warning it had given her of her own danger? She would and could blind herself with no sophisms, nor believe that Guy and herself could be the solitary exception to the law which says that the happiness of two souls which "love on through all ills, and love on till they die," is not to be won in that way. But she knew that Emily Challoner's words and Lady Luscombe's made the Abbey an impossible place for her, whether Guy kept his promise of going or not. How she honoured and loved him for the promise! She would not sleep under that roof one other night; but without a word of farewell to anybody, she would make her way to London with what money and jewels she had, and find herself some employment. In the life which she had been leading for the last few years she had often thought of turning some of her many talents and accomplishments to account in the way of work, which seemed to her the one road to forgetfulness and healthy occupation of the mind, for one in her false and unhappy position. She felt within herself high capacities of mind and soul unkilled, and though her trial seemed to her cruelly hard, yet she believed in her way that the harder trials are for the stronger souls, and began to brace herself to the thought of an entirely new life, which should be severed completely from every link with the old. And as her thoughts began to assume form and purpose, she knelt down and prayed for help to resist all recurrence of the terrible temptation which beset her, out of the depth of her love for the man who was ready to give his fate into her hands for good or evil, with a career before him which she could but mar. No—not that. She would not, ever. So she prayed as she had not often prayed of late, poor girl; and rose from her knees with the strange but very real sense of strength and comfort, which follows so often and so close upon real and earnest prayer.

There was a knock at the door of the little ante-room which was set apart in the luxurious Abbey for a private boudoir of her own. By the time that knock was heard, Daisy had entirely conquered her self-posses-sion, and was quietly resolved. She wondered for a moment who was come to disturb or to notice her; then solved the doubt by admitting the visitor. It was the Count Lestrange. She looked at him with unfeigned surprise and mistrust, to which he gave neither attention nor encouragement.

"You here!" she said.

"Yes, Mrs. Brent," he answered. "What are you going to do?"

For his glance had travelled quickly round the room, and taken in all the signs of departure.

"I am going away," she said.

"Alone?"

"Alone."

Her brow contracted, and she spoke with a serious emphasis.

"Hem!" was his answer, or rather the inarticulate sound of which that inadequate monosyllable is the recognized expression in print. His mind canvassed the situation, and he felt that he had failed again. "Confound the woman!" he thought to himself, "is she ice then, after all?"

He could only have made a mistake in tempera-ment, he thought. Principle did not enter into his views of the matter at all as a possible factor. But to one of his mind, the latter would have seemed far the less awkward obstacle to encounter.

If Daisy were, as he now began to believe, strong enough and bold enough to hold her own till the Indian climate, or the course of Nature, or the spirit of per-versity, or anything, were to deprive her of Mr. Brent's valuable husbandship, the result would be to the last degree enraging; and not only for the loss of the bet, which, in the face of certain awkward complications which had been taking place in the Count's finances, was becoming with him a very pressing consideration indeed. What was he going to do? Provoking! Here were these two in the house, avowed lovers, who had gone so far as to fall into each other's arms before witnesses, with everything in the world to tempt and encourage them to defy conventionality with a clear conscience, and nothing to prevent it but either the most ridiculous scruples or the most Machiavellian calculation on the lady's part. She must have heard of John Brent's illness in spite of his precautions, he concluded.

"I am very sorry for you, Mrs. Brent," he said, with a grave air of protecting friendship, having sketched the next move in his campaign at once.

"Yes?" she answered, in no very responsive tone.

"Of course I have heard the things which are being said, and have been said to you."

She might have been stone for any sign of being moved by this.

"I suppose so," she answered.

"And of that unlucky fainting-fit—" he went on.

"Why unlucky, Count Lestrange?" she interrupted him. "It is a thing women are always liable to. If what you call the ill-luck of it refers to Mr. Faucit, I suppose he did what you or anybody would have done. The things which are being said, as you put it, are very foolish and very unworthy. But as I don't choose to give the many countenance, I am going."

"Where?" asked the Count, who watched the proud face with an irritated admiration.

She baffled him, and he hated to be baffled.

"I really hardly know," she answered, with an admirable indifference. "Like most people, I suppose, to London."

"Not to India?"

"Count Lestrange!"

"I beg your pardon. I thought you might perhaps have had some news from Mr. Brent." He spoke hesitatingly.

She looked at him.

"We don't speak of him, you know," she said. "No, I have had none whatever."

The Count indulged in what, if he had given it outward expression, would have been a sigh of relief.

"Excuse me," he said, "but you know that I have been, in a certain sense, his banker here for you for the payment of the allowance he made you."

"Which I have not forgotten that you secured for me," she answered. "I have not found so many friends in life that I should wish to forget that." She looked frankly at him, and held out her hand. He did not seem to notice the action, and the furtive eyes wandered away from her. There was a hesitation in his manner which might have been even more, or more meaning, than was warranted by what he had to say. She anticipated him before he said it. "The last quarter was due a few days ago, and I have not had it," she said. "You told me there was a delay, but only a momentary one. Can you let me have it now ? I really want it."

He walked away from her to the window, and seemed to consider with himself. Perhaps it was another wrestle of the good angel yet. But it did not last very long. The throws had been too many and too rude.

"I am very much afraid," he said, in a low voice of sympathy, "that the delay may be a more serious one than I had hoped. I half feared it, but did not like to say so : your husband has got into difficulties again, Mrs. Brent, and his remittances have for some time past been very irregular."

"For some time past !" she said, very pale, folding her hands upon her lap. What new difficulty had she to meet now ? Was the world to be begun indeed, from the lowest rung of the ladder, by one so little used or trained to climb ? "Yet I have been paid to the day till this last time."

"Yes," he said.

"How, then ? By whom ?" Then in a flash of thought—"By you ?"

"Yes," he said again, in a tone of considerate unwillingness.

She looked at him wonderingly, doubtfully, for she could not help it. Almost to her lips rose the question, "With what object?" But she kept the question down. If he had really done this thing in kindness, it would be too ungrateful. Surely, surely he could hope nothing from her again.

"You have paid the allowance yourself?" she asked.

"I hope you will forgive it," said he, in a tone of deprecation. "It was so much simpler than alarming you unnecessarily; and I really thought the obligation —but don't think there is any—would be of the most temporary kind." Why didn't he repeat it just once more, she thought, in spite of herself again, rather than confess the truth at such a moment as this? He seemed to read the thought perhaps, for he went on— "I would have concealed the real state of things from you still, if I had not been convinced at last that it is for the present desperate, and that I should be wrong indeed in allowing you to take such a resolution as that you spoke of just now, when home and friends are most of all necessary to you."

He is right, she thought, and again mentally begged his pardon. In a moment she had resolved to beg it openly, and she did.

"You have been, and you are, very kind and considerate, Count Lestrange," she said, "and you must allow me to express all my thanks for what you have done. I am sure that I have misunderstood you in mistrusting you, as we both know I have done, and I beg your pardon. But if what you tell me means ruin, it can make no difference now, for here I have neither home nor friends, and never shall have."

"Mr. Faucit?" he suggested, with no sign of disrespect, but as if with genuine interest in Daisy.

She flushed, but only a little, and her sad, grave tone varied not a sound.

"Count Lestrange, I know that you have heard

the story of my old engagement to Mr. Faucit, I know that you all have here; and I was foolish to think that it might not be known. Friends I hope that he and I shall always be, but I must fight my fight for myself without help from him, for both our sakes. I do not despise help, though, for indeed I want it very much. You know London well. Will you give me yours, and say nothing to anybody of what you may be able to do for me, or of what I am doing?"

Daisy Brent never showed her fearlessness more; for this was to place herself in Lestrange's power, and she knew it. But it mattered nothing in her new scheme of life, and she did not wish, from her ignorance of the world's ways, to founder and to sink at the outset. She was in her own power in the first instance, and she knew its value. Lestrange felt the significance of her confidence as well as she, and felt a thrill of satisfied surprise, though he had played for it. Once more the idea of abandoning other pursuits, and using the confidence for himself, came across his mind; and once more he put it aside for the colder and more practical purpose of his matured scheme. "And for three months—well?" he thought within himself in Shylock's words. His face showed a sort of pleased emotion when he answered Daisy.

"I am much touched by your confidence in me, and will try to deserve it," he said. "What is it you wish to try?"

"The stage, if I can find an opening in no other way," answered she. "I have some jewels, which will serve me at first, though not much."

"You might have had a fortune in them by this time."

"In presents, you mean? Yes; I never cared about that. Better than the stage I should like teaching, in which I think I might, after a short practice, succeed. I would rather have quiet than publicity."

"It's dreary work."

"That I don't mind. But it is difficult to find, I know."

"For an English-woman, yes. If you could pass yourself off for a German it would be easy; and I know a Duchess or two who would take you up at once. You speak German perfectly; why not try?"

"Under false colours?" she said with a smile. "No, I must stand or fall on my own merits."

Lestrange was deep in thought, and he was pacing the room. Events seemed to play into his hands, yet neither events nor he could bend the spirit of Daisy. He risked the next card.

"If you want quiet," he asked, "why do you mean to try London?"

"Because everything that is to be found, is to be found there," she said.

"Not always. I feel for you very deeply, Mrs. Brent," said the Count, "though in that mistrust you spoke of, which I know I brought upon myself, you cannot yet quite bring yourself to believe me. I take your confidence as a proof that you are beginning. If you wish it, I can find you a place as a teacher at once, for which you will be accepted on my recommendation. It is quiet enough certainly, and modest; but it will be a beginning, and you will be safe from the most passing annoyance."

"Tell me about it," she said.

"It is a school-teaching place, in the care of a clergyman near here, who is a friend of mine; and there would be lessons to give in his family too."

"Near here! that would be impossible."

"If it is Luscombe Abbey whose observation you want to shun for the present, you could find no safer place. Mould-on-the-Moss is right away in the heart of the moors, and no breath of its politics would ever reach the fashionable Abbey. Half-an-hour's train and an hour's drive, and you are there."

Rapid and clear was the course of Daisy's thought, and she answered almost at once—

" When can I go ? "

" To-day, if you like.   I can telegraph to the clergyman, and no one here but myself need have trace or
knowledge of you."

*   *   *   *   *

There was some little more talk between them, and
within an hour or two, as has been told, Daisy Brent
was gone—gone out of the life and circle which had
been so entirely hers, of which she had been the centre,
without a sign.

In his own room Lestrange examined his hand of
cards, and felt that his ace of trumps was there yet.

" Three months of that, Mrs. Brent, and I can
hardly fail again.   Mr. Brent's remittance must be kept
back for the present.   Not a bad stroke that; and I
can still play the generous cashier.   I shan't be out
of pocket by it either.   Let me see—' The Rev. Miles
Bickers, The Parsonage, Mould-on-the-Moss.'   Chaffers,
this telegram to the office at once."

" Yes, Count Lestrange."

CHAPTER XIX.

MOULD-ON-THE-MOSS.

MOULD-ON-THE-MOSS was the highest inhabited
village in the county, some said in England.   In winter
it was generally inaccessible, and in the best seasons
of the year the springs of the carriages which made
their way to it groaned under the infliction': for the
roads were as unmade as the famous ones which General
Wade took in hand, and were little more than rough
tracks struggling over moorland between walls of stone.
The main road of the world of civilization was severed
from Mould-on-the-Moss by two miles of desolation,
over which distance these enrutted tracks made their

uneasy way. Between main road and village there were no signs of habitation, and the two miles to it were a long climb. When it was reached, the wonder was why or how it had ever got there, or what in the world could have induced the rude forefathers of such a hamlet to sleep or to eat there, or to cast anchor for a day. The village was one straggling street of white homesteads, which the original designer had carefully picked out with pounds and pig-styes, strewn about in the orderliness of disorder. On a small scale, the arrangements of next-door-neighbourdom were of so casual a kind, that they recalled the city of magnificent distances, called Washington, where an imposing row of public offices rubs elbows with a pawnbroker's shop, or a brand-new hotel and a stately private mansion are separated by an unsightly piece of waste-land, devoted apparently to a spontaneous growth of vegetable. As you turned your back on the church, which was the apex of the village, and wandered down this street, the houses grew gradually fewer and more far between, and the melancholy waste-lands more and more patent to the eye, the acrid odours of pighood being the more diffused withal. Purely agricultural were the poverty-stricken population of this child of the sleepy hollow. Eyes with as much of rumination and as little of thought behind them as those of the animals which made so large a part of the community; the fixed gaze of vacant curiosity, which is of all human problems the most perplexing to the μέροπες ἀνθρώποι who have their senses for use, and can only speculate darkly upon the way in which men can live through twenty-four hours as long as our own, absolutely thinking about nothing. If we are bored sometimes, what must they be? Yet no aspiration beyond seems to stir them; no Mould-on-the-Mossian was ever heard of who tempted fame and fortune in a wider sphere, or was other than content to marry and beget children after his own ancestral type, and then to sleep with his fathers after the orthodox but rather irritating form of

monotonous succession so insisted upon—surely in a
vein of quiet irony upon the recurring decimalities
which make our scene of life—in the chronicles of
their majesties of Judah and Israel. The only living
inhabitant who had ever been in London at the time
we are writing of had been so oppressed by the movement and the unrest which were there about him,
that on his return he took to his bed to make up for
it, and left it no more. The inquiries of neighbours, so
far as sine-mental organization permitted them to be
made, as to the things which he had seen and heard,
resulted in little that could be held more articulate
than a shake of the head or a moan. In this strange
colony of agricoles life was as an English edition of that
led by the wandering shepherds of Central Asia, com-
memorated in the finest strain of pure human tedium
ever set to lyric shape, by the cripple-poet, Giacomo
Leopardi. His 'Canto Notturno' has to me always
seemed like the reverse of the shield to Wordsworth's
'Ode to Immortality,' even as between the two poets
there is a certain strange community of expression.

> " Thou silent orb of Night,
> What dost thou in the Heaven?
> Thou risest up at even,
> And o'er the deserts throw'st thy light,
> To sink at day:
> Answer—and say,
> Hast thou not yet too weary found
> The grey hills' everlasting round?
> Iiks it thee not for aye
> On the broad plains' monotony to gaze?
> How like to thine pass the poor shepherd's days!
> He rises with the sun,
> Drives to the field his flocks, and sees
> Fountains, and flocks, and trees;
> Then, his task done,
> Lies wearily down at eventide,
> And asks for naught beside.
> Oh, tell me, of what use may be
> His life to him, or thine to thee?
> Oh, tell me, whither tend,
> And to what end,

These our brief pilgrimages,
Or thine eternal course throughout the changeless ages ?

*　　*　　*　　*

Happy, my flocks, are ye,
That know not your own misery !
How do I envy you your lot !
　Nor only so,
　Because ye sorrow not,
And that all terror, pain, distress,
Are in a moment's time forgot,—
But that ye never chanced to know
　Life's utter weariness :
Lapped in the soft shade, on the growing grasses,
Ye cheat the time in indolent repose ;
But, though for me as peacefully it passes,
　No peace my spirit knows ;
　Verdure and shade invite in vain,
Some strange spur goads me with an aching pain ;
The more I rest, the more upon me grows
　This dull unrest of brain.
Yet have I naught to ask, naught to lament ;
As idle as your joy my discontent !—
But, though I cannot measure
Whence or how great your pleasure,
　Happy, my flocks, are ye !
　Would ye could find a voice
　To tell why ye rejoice,
And that which gladdens you so wearies me ! " *

It may be doubted if the speculations of Mould-on-the-Moss ever rose consciously to this poetic vein of enquiry, or exceeded a general wonder what it was all about. That question strikes so home to many of us in altogether different forms of life. Where did I read of the actress who, in the middle of a passionate scene upon the stage, stopped by a sudden impulse, and whispered to her companion, "What nonsense all this is ; suppose we don't go on with it ? " The story has been quoted in depreciation of the actor's art ; but surely it has a much wider moral, and is pointed equally against all the pursuits of life.

---

* The translation (by the present author) of the 'Canto Notturno,' from which these passages are taken, appeared in 'Blackwood's Magazine' for September, 1878.

For myself, Balbus, who write this chronicle, I should be sorry to say how often during its progress the same reflection has silently obtruded itself. Does a politician never feel it in the middle of some passionate burst of patriotism about the honour of England, which, especially of late years, is always suffering the rudest shock it ever received since the Conquest, in the hands of the other side? Does the barrister never feel it during an appeal to the jury? Perhaps not so often, because of the fees. Above all,—I ask the question with fear and trembling,—does the man of science never feel it, he that for some occult reason is presumed now-a-days to monopolize what is called "information," and propounds amazing and uncomfortable riddles, to be answered perhaps "in our next world" in cases where the continuous circulation is admitted? Does he never say, suppose he didn't go on with it? I am sure his readers do. Yet it is just because the mysterious δαίμων insists upon answering us all in the same way,—"But you must go on,"—that the actors and the politicians and the scientific (or knowing) ones, all set their heads at each other, such as in their different ways they are, to keep this jaded old world wagging. Even therefore the herds of Central Asia, and the agricoles of Mould-on-the-Moss, give in all round to the remorseless law, and I, Balbus, swayed as by a resistless Nemesis, resume the diagnosis of the sleepy Yorkshire village, after indulging in a digression towards which five minutes ago I had not the vaguest disposition. Perhaps it arose from a strong and sudden desire to "do nothing;" to which immediately quoth the δαίμων—"But you must. You needn't do this; but you must do something, whether you like it or not." Even so said the judge to the jury, in the old days, at twelve o'clock at night, when they were rather tired of it,—"After all, gentlemen, we must be somewhere."

So we are at Mould-on-the-Moss, watching with the expectation of the rustic by the brawling little brook which gives the place its name, and gliding and to glide in its eternal roll, goes plunging down the meadows and fields which lie behind and parallel to the village-street, to mingle somewhere with a larger stream before its baby-waters are salted in the sea. No wonder that the rustic does watch. There is something so infinitely tempting, when once the practice has been indulged in, in the aimless contemplation of running or falling water. The chirrup of the brook, and the call of the waterfall, and the roar of the cataract, have all such wonderful languages and burdens of their own, to which one seems bound to listen, as in the hope of gathering from them some definite meaning. They seem to make very sentences in their flow, in a tongue which is strange but should not be, and holds out a promise of being understood some day, when the mighty waters shall be "rolling evermore" on the shores of the immortal sea. It seems to me as if we "in a moment travelled thither," now and again, in the murmur of that gracious message. Lie for an hour on the Canadian verge alone; give yourself up to the spirit of the place, and consult the oracle of Niagara.

Very, very often did Daisy Brent commune in this way with the whisper of the Moss, when she had fixed her quarters, lost but not yet forgotten, in this 'Ultima Thule' of the moor. Clear and bright and sparkling, always a well-fed little bantling of a brook, nurtured by a generous mother-spring which flowed from a tarn upon the hills, the Moss became quite self-important when it was swollen by a burst of rain, of which the district was by no means sparing. Then it became brown and insolent, and discontent with the proportions of its bed, and went about with a head on it, like the tawny mane which Father Tiber tossed at the Etruscans when Horatius cut the bridge down.

"Carry my messages to Guy, little brook," sometimes she whispered to it, "when you have joined the big river which runs at the foot of the Abbey hill. Will you whisper to him sometimes, even through the louder message which the big river carries, of the unforgetting

heart which I know he is thinking of now? You will
not always think of it, Guy. If I went to London, and
you heard of me or found me, you would be fretting
still, and unable to take up the work and the name
which are waiting for you, my fine old noble Guy. You
will be anxious and miserable about me at first now, I
know; but you have grown accustomed to that in all
these weary years; and in time you will think that I
have passed out of your life. If you do not—if you
will not—you shall think that I am dead, Guy; and
whispers from the world without shall reach me of your
new career, and of the fame that I know you are bound
to win. And I will watch you quietly through the
world which will be no longer mine, and think how it
might have been with us if that dream of ours had but
turned to a reality—the dream we dreamed together so
long ago. And so it would have, Guy, if I had had
more of courage, and more of patience, and more of
faith. We never should have met again, dear; and yet
I hardly know. It may have been good for us both,
after all, to know how much we could love, how much
we did love, and how impossible—how utterly impossible
—is the lesser feeling we both thought we could live
upon, after the old! Tell him all this, little brook, tell
him all this! and tell him too, when one day he takes a
wife to his heart to help him in his life and in his home,
that the first love who prays for him has sent him her
blessing by you—in a tear!"

For even as she thought out these things, Daisy
Brent was bending over the long green grasses which
wind and stream were brushing and laving where they
grew by the water's edge, and she felt something warm
fall from her eyes and mix with the waterdrops, of
which she had been unconscious till it fell. Then she
looked with a sad smile downwards towards the valley,
and followed her tear in fancy, as we follow some stick
or leaf that we have cast upon the stream, till her fancy
lost it to the sight.

She took up her burden and she went back up the

village street again, after she had been thinking these
things one day, some weeks after her flight from Luscombe Abbey. The lips of autumn and winter were
just meeting now in their long kiss of yearly welcome,
warm and rich in this season of which we are telling,
and full of the charm which the popular phrase associates with an Indian climate. The season was an
abnormal one altogether; and Dame Nature was in
one of her contradictory moods with the calendar, interfering with the calculations of farmers, disposing of the
auguries of prophets, and giving all the hints in her
power to the irrepressible American to let her alone.

Daisy Brent looked very tired. She was changed
from the brightly dressed beauty whom we have known,
and wore nothing better than the modest gear of a
village school-mistress, which became her quite as well.
She was like Perdita in the eyes of Florizel, looking
and doing her best whatever she looked or did. But
the tired appearance was marked and sad. It had
always been there during her years of London queen-
hood, and her looking-glass knew it well. But it was
kept out of sight of the world, who being no longer at
hand to keep it in check, it had its way. Time might
come, when the rest and tranquillity of the village on
the moor should bring something of their own repose to
Daisy's spirit; but that time was not yet. The teaching
in the very primitive school where the youth of Mould-
on-the-Moss acquired as little education as they liked
to get, for schoolboards were in the infancy of their
development, was not perhaps very restful to her; and
she liked as little the monotonous piano-strumming of
the Misses Bickers, which she superintended for a
small stipend. For poverty, in its grim reality, was in
good sooth knocking hard at Daisy's door.

She had secured for herself, with the help of
Lestrange, a small but sufficient room in one of the
cottages of the aristocratic quarter of the village, which
belonged to the old village sexton, Delves. A crabbed
but very honest specimen of humanity was he, holding

up his head at the Bells Inn, in the sanded parlour which is vanishing before the bar of civilization, on the strength of the varied experience of mankind, which he considered that his official position towards all classes of them gave him. He realized his position all the more because he had for a better half the midwife of the locality, and between them he considered that they represented the sum of human life. They "assisted at his birth, and attended at his death," like the letter "h" in the old riddle, and had the right to feel that but for them there could be in a manner neither living nor dying in the village of Mould-on-the-Moss. He had prospered as times went in that part of the world, had Delves the sexton, and was respected as a warm man and a well-informed, with a touch of scholarship acquired by a large experience of epitaphs, and a dash of political wisdom even upon extra-parochial matters.

The daughter who had shared the house and hearts of the worthy couple had married and taken wing : and they were glad of the opportunity to add to their modest income by taking a lodger to supply Keziah Delves's room.

Lestrange, who had ferreted out Mould-on-the-Moss in the course of his many solitary researches in the vicinity of Luscombe Abbey, and made an amused study of the sexton's peculiarities, came to the conclusion that this was just the place for Daisy to instal herself at the outset of this new career of hers.

The catastrophe pleased the Count's sense of humour very much, and the grim contrast of life which Daisy's new experiences presented, added quite a new chapter to the book of his studies in the see-saw of circum-stance. The fact that he had himself been riding the whirlwind and directing the storm, and that after ingeniously compassing Daisy's flight he was installed in her confidence as the one person to be trusted, of course gave a considerable zest to his satisfaction. He recommended his charge warmly to the parental care of the Delveses, inwardly resolving that one month of

the *régime* would be quite enough for the fashionable
Mrs. Brent's patience; and he introduced her to the
Rev. Miles Bickers, widower and incumbent, as a young
lady anxious for quiet occupation, and exactly suited to
the requirements of his school, and also of the Misses
Bickers' musical development. And Daisy on her side
took up her new part with a quiet seriousness which
astonished Lestrange, who confessed to himself that he
never came to the end of his surprises in the matter
of this young lady, though that the seriousness would
last he never supposed for a moment.

Daisy meant what she was doing, though. She
believed that she possessed in herself a strong capacity
for teaching, and teaching well, and for earning her
livelihood in more ways than one; and she did not care
how low on the ladder she began, if by that means she
might acquire the elements of a profession in which she
might make an interest for her life, failing the great
interest of all, which was denied to her. She had confidence in herself; and dreary as the surroundings were
in which she began this new battle in the campaign of
life,—in which she had lost, unhappily, so much,—she
felt in it something of the pleasure which earning your
own bread, and living a useful, however humble, member of the working community, produces in every mind
above the lowest capacity of the drone. She started on
her forlorn hope gallantly.

The Reverend Miles Bickers was charmed with his
new school-mistress. He was a reserved student of
the old classic school, whose place is apparently to be
usurped before long by the more litigious followers of
science.

Bickers, who had a dry humour of his own, was once
remonstrated with for confining all his excursions outside the domain of theology to the districts of the
Athenian republic, on which he was a great authority.

"My dear fellow," he said, "if you knew the comfort
of sticking to a nation which is dead and done with,
about which nobody can contradict you to any purpose!"

' But that was some time ago, before the humour and the Hellenism had faded out of Bickers's life, being, as he was, one of those who have a certain alacrity of sinking in this world, without any apparent reason for it, to be compensated mayhap by some mystic buoyancy in another. He was to have ended in a Bishop's see, it used to be said for him, if only for that treatise on the Anapæstic Tetrameter Acatalectic form, which recalled the best thoughts of Porson.

But Miles Bickers was growing old, and he wore a very threadbare coat of cloth instead of the sleeves of spotless lawn, and the Bishop's see had subsided into the highest and loneliest and poorest benefice in England—the perpetual incumbency of Mould-on-the-Moss. He had loved his wife very dearly, and he had lost her young; and the absent student found in the two colourless and depressed maidens, who grew up as her legacy at his side, but poor consolation for the woman who had lighted up a short passage of his life, and had been leading him into the ways of other men, as the best and earliest methods of access to that preferment for which alone her Miles was fitted.

It is hard to say, and at this period of our story unnecessary, how the sad decadence came about in the career of the widowed solitary, who seemed to have taken root in Mould-on-the-Moss, and to be falling day by day to the level of those around him. He spent most of his time, sometimes with a Horace, sometimes with a New Testament in his pocket, in hanging about his own churchyard or his own church, in which he took the deepest interest. Sometimes—rare and precious chance!—some intelligent stranger would penetrate to the place; and looking haply into the old tumbledown temple, lingered.to examine the curious monuments and strange complexities of mediæval architecture, which did their best to peep through the detestable whitewash which neutralizes so many treasures of old ecclesiastic work. The shambling and seedily-dressed man, who would address him with some shy remark of half-apology, and at first be taken for a decayed verger, would presently make it clear to the visitor that he was a cultivated gentleman of rare attainment, and hold him charmed, if his own mind was open to it, with discourse historic and archæological, which would send the other wondering away, perhaps to fall into the hands of Delves the sexton, who, having long sate at Mr. Bickers's feet, would favour the stranger with a second-hand edition of the same argument from a popular point of view, many years in bottle.

On the memory of more than one casual pilgrim the church and the clergyman and the aspects of Mould-on-the-Moss left a curiously deep impression. It was by some such traveller's accident that Lestrange hit upon the place; and with his adaptability and variety of mind, he came back more than once to study his fossil reverend, whom he helped in a variety of small ways, and moved to such admiration and gratitude, that his praise of the Count addressed to Daisy went far to increase her growing confidence in him.

As for the answer which Lestrange sent him, to his querulous wonder where he was to find a school-mistress for the young flock of Mould-on-the-Moss, Mr. Bickers found her a revelation. Her sweet face and gentle manner soothed and softened him; and the sympathy which attracts two sorrowers in a great sorrow, drew them much together. She helped to refine and raise the minds of the two unattractive girls, whose lines of education had fallen on so hard a place, and before the two or three months had passed which were to bring about the close of the year, had made herself quite an influence in the village upon all connected with it.

It was on that day of which we have been speaking at the opening of this chapter, that Daisy returned from sending her fairy-messages down the little Moss, to have tea at the vicarage. How oddly she looked round the bare walls of the poor room, sometimes; how strange she felt as the rough country loaf and the metal teapot went their rounds, and thought of

—how many weeks ago? Surely not weeks—but lives: —worlds — anything! Was she really Daisy Brent, that had been Daisy Fairfield, and was she acting a, part in some private play, whose catastrophe was not yet? Or was she indeed that same Daisy turned into another woman, seriously and humbly labouring to make her own bread? That evening Mr. Bickers's odd and slow, but rather pleasant, voice woke her out of a dream she was falling into over the bread-and-butter.

"Yes, Mrs. Fairbank, I assure you. Count Le-- strange is not the only man of intellect and of cultivation who has consorted with us of late. Another of the true καλοὶ κάγαθοὶ honoured us more than once not many months ago, who had drunk of the true Castalian at the same source as I. Balliol, Mrs. Fairbank, classic Balliol—"

"You were at Balliol, Mr. Bickers?"

"Yes, indeed, and I am proud to say so. Do you know the place?"

"Yes, I have seen it."

"He too came from Balliol, this scholar of whom I am speaking, and made himself most attentive to Mary and to Martha here—eh, Mary? eh, Martha?"

"Lor, Papa," from Martha and from Mary.

"A singular and delightful man, who had taken up his quarters upon the moor some miles away yonder, and liked to walk over here sometimes with his big dog."

"Poor old Frisco!" volunteered Martha or Mary.

"Frisco!" said the school-mistress, as she turned her head aside.

Mr. Bickers and daughters dilated on the merits of the dog's owner, and told Daisy how often he had sate in that same seat of hers. Her heart beat very fast and her eyes were full of tears. Should she go? should she stay? might he not come there again?

But the days passed by and he did not; and a warm and heavy Christmastide, with a sense almost of uncanniness in the air, and some roses in bloom looking rather ashamed of themselves, found Daisy Brent still teaching in the lonely moorland village, while yet but a few days remained for the winning or the losing of the Count Lestrange's wag

---

CHAPTER XX.

A NEW TEST.

LONDON! London! London! Reeking away in an atmosphere of impossible fog, filth above and grease below, everybody cursing the English climate, and nobody putting in force the act to compel the money-spinners to consume their own smoke, as by law provided. ("Oh useful and wonderful English law!" quoth the Count Lestrange. "Any two sham doctors and a selfish person or two may make a man mad in law; and if he 'goes to law' afterwards about it, it takes half the bench and half the faculty to decide whether he was ever mad or not, and unless twelve people of no faculty at all agree one way or the other, it's a moot point till the day of judgment. Meanwhile the manufacturers are poisoning half England for their own profit, and the law can stop them, but doesn't. Oh useful and wonderful English law! one half evil and the other half useless! *Cosas d'Inglaterra!* What does anything matter?") Britons in general, and Londoners in particular, make their own climate and then abuse it; and they were abusing it more than usual in the early winter-months of the year of grace of which we are writing.

It was hot, muggy, murky; comforting and welcome, it is true, to tens of thousands of unimportant units who found life in warmth, and were apt to die off like flies in fine old seasonable winters, but annoying to the curled darlings who associate fixed months with fixed pastimes, and are put out when they don't get them.

There was the consolation of talking about the weather,
certainly; in comparing all the notes of all the oldest
inhabitants to show that there never within human
memory had been such a winter as that, so late on into
the year.

November came and went with a procession of fogs
as long and as depressing as her own Lord Mayor's;
December took up the tale and crept on towards Christmas, and still no sign of winter.   The human passage-
birds who take flight at these times for Egypt or the
Riviera put off their flittings, and talked of Torquay or
even of Brighton: for was not the western watering-
place reported to be too hot? the botanists went crazy
over their flora, and the men of science over their
phenomena; and good people apocalyptically given
shook their heads in corners about the end of the world,
and held meetings to deprecate the tendencies of the
times, which tend, as most times do, to the talking of
much nonsense upon matters not so insoluble as they
are made out to be, and to the setting up of sundry
claims to genius and to thought, on the score of
obscurity, and the gift of confusion of tongues.

Men and women get into print so much more easily
and generally than they used, that all the little doubters
come and buzz out their little doubts in ink, whereas of old
only the grave and serious spirits, on whom the calamity
of unfaith had fallen, were allowed to make their public
profession of it.   It is not that more men doubt—but
that so many more talk about it; and surely the smart
doubter, who haunts the skirts of 'Nineteenth Centuries'
and 'Fortnightlies,' is of all men the most wearisome.   He
is always great on "the processes of the mind:" as if there
was such a thing as "*the* mind," or any two minds
processed in the same way.   If my processes were as
those of Impey of St. Nil's, I should arrive at the same
conclusions as his.   But they ain't; and I don't.   The
impossibility of getting much further in mere human
philosophy than king Solomon meets one at every
point.   Though indeed the old gentleman is like to be

revised before long, and to be shown to have meant
something entirely different.

Guy Faucit, during those two or three months which
followed the flight from Luscombe Abbey, spent his
time in London, in close and constant association with
his chosen mentor, the Count Lestrange.

Lestrange made periodical disappearances into the
country for some twenty-four hours or more, which
might have been shown to be coincident with certain
flying visits to the cottage of Delves the sexton, or the
parsonage of the Reverend Miles Bickers.

For the main part of the time Faucit and he were
inseparable, penetrating and examining together into
strange and obscure corners of London life, the thought
ever present in Faucit's mind that somewhere and some
day he must come across, in the great city desert, the
woman who was now more than ever the world to
him; without whom money, position, ambition, health,
everything, seemed as the ashes of the Dead Sea. He
loved her more than ever since that parting at Luscombe Abbey. The idea of her having lost home and
friends for him—perhaps being in poverty for his sake
—wrought upon the generous spirit with an overpowering charm, and left room for no other thought but one
Strangely enough, as happens, however, with many men,
this great trial and crisis of his life proved the turning-
point in his mental history. He was up to that time,
as I think I have told of him before, one of the many
men perplexed by the buzzings of the doubters, and
half inclined to throw in his lot, and his trained literary
skill, with the speculative literature of the time. But his
Pegasus turned restive, and wouldn't obey him, arguing
with him in a fashion almost as articulate as Balaam's
donkey, and proving to him that on subjects which started
from the thesis that they couldn't be known, there must
assuredly be nothing to be said. And in the middle of
his doubts and fears and troubles, even among London
clubs and London talk, and with the cynical presence of
Lestrange at his elbow, conviction came home to him—

comes as it does come home—in a moment, as in some flash lighting up the dark corners of doubt, in which the searcher's mind has been blindly but prayerfully searching,—setting his mind at rest for ever, victorious over the after-struggles, the after-troubles, and the after-pain. The paradise such a man so attains to may be but a fool's paradise; but it is one for all that, and even on the dreary showing of those who think so, he has clearly the best of it.

So it was that in the time of his hardest trial and his greatest sorrow, and through and out of that very sorrow and trial, Guy Faucit became in one sense a happier man than he had ever been in his life, even with the one thought of Daisy otherwise uppermost and alone in his mind, and the Count Lestrange discoursing to him of the philosophies of life.

The Count, very much to his astonishment, found himself to a certain extent the confidant of this new phase of Faucit's thoughts, though indeed the other was but shy and reticent upon the matter, as men who partake of this singular good fortune are apt to be. When first Faucit's views became clear to him, he was fairly staggered by the presence of a phenomenon so entirely out of his sphere of calculation. Wide as that was, and widened every day by the active self-cultivation which after his manner he followed, it beat him. He understood worldly motives, and was as able to use the good sides of worldliness as the bad; and he thoroughly understood the use of religion as professed and practised by many excellent persons, and the practical ends it might be made to serve. He even believed in the existence of a genuine religious conviction in a class of people whom he regarded as of no conceivable use in the world, and indeed cut off from it by the very fact. They didn't amuse him and they couldn't serve him, and he kept out of their way. But here was a man of another kind, who would certainly before long, Daisy or no Daisy, be likely to fill a considerable space in the world's eye,—for Lestrange knew a man very well when he saw him,—suddenly going off upon a tack which might turn the boat's head none knew whither.

" Good Heavens ! " he said, startled so far out of his ordinary placidity as to drop his cigarette and sit bolt upright in his arm-chair, when first Faucit broached his new theories to him—" you don't mean to say that you are going to believe in that sort of thing ? "

" What sort of thing ? " asked the other, quietly.

" Well, that sort of thing—illumination and supernatural conversion, and all that."

" Why not ? "

" Why not ? " Here was one of the Count's own favourite weapons of logical destructiveness turned against himself. " Well, I'm sure I don't know. But —my dear fellow—nobody does now-a-days."

" Oh yes, a great many do; more than we think or know, I suspect. It is an active agent in more lives than you can guess at."

" Horatio's philosophy, and that kind of thing ? " said the Count. " How very odd." The Count began to laugh to himself and to twist about his ring. " Are you going in for a conviction of sin ? " then he asked abruptly.

" No. I don't think I shall ever talk cant, or even what may sound like it. I'm not aware that I've been more sinful than my neighbours—at all events, towards them. But my life wanted a purpose, apart from the one you know of; and I think it has found one."

" Dear me ! I don't quite understand. Isn't wealth like yours, with what it may find for brains like yours, a purpose in itself ? "

" None whatever, to my thinking."

" Are you going to turn monk then ? " said Lestrange, " or preacher, or what ? Or are you going to turn hermit again ? "

" No. I'm not going to turn anything. I shall find work to do in the world presently, as you say, I suppose; and I shall know better how to do it. That's all."

The conversation did not go much further. But

Lestrange, after much smoking at home, and much meditation, and much uneasy examination of his financial condition, which a series of unlucky circumstances was rapidly bringing to a crisis, which he didn't at all like to contemplate, began to consider whether he might not be able after all to utilize, as his manner was, even so new and awkward a factor in the problem before him, which had to be solved, now, in so inconveniently short a time.

"Upon my soul," he said to himself, "I believe the man will turn philanthropist. The philanthrope in earnest is the most unaccountable type in the whole Chinese puzzle of mental anatomies. The idea of loving man, of all things in the world, except for what you can get out of him! What on earth am I to do with my athlete now, if he goes in for this entirely new form of training? Religious exaltation, eh? Wait a bit."

Then with an infinite tact, and in a manner quite his own, Lestrange set himself to play upon the chord in Faucit's mind which answered to such new and subtle music.

If Guy expected, as he did, that the Count would laugh at him, he found himself wrong. On the contrary, Lestrange contrived to show himself curious and interested in the state of Faucit's mind; to insinuate a deep sympathy with the phase upon which it had entered, and to profess himself only too willing and anxious to arrive at a similar solution of the hard ways of life. He neither did nor said anything to undermine or to shake the faith that had entered into his pupil, for, as he said with conviction to himself, he hadn't the time. That if he had, the thing could be easily done, he entertained no doubt at all. Much shallower arguments and duller sophistries than he could use were enough to demolish such crazy old fabrics as Faucit's excited frame of mind had raised. But time was required to knock such fabrics down. These fervid phases, which he admitted were new to his personal experience in men of his pupil's calibre, had to run their course like the small-pox, or any other dangerous malady, whose infection was carried by some subtle particles floating about in the air.

If Lestrange had ever looked upon Guy as a likely subject for such an ailment, he would have provided against the danger by a process of mental inoculation. But he never had; and had so contented himself with saturating him with purely worldly maxims and safe-guards, that he had left the other ground untrodden. His first feeling, when he understood the change which had so suddenly taken place in Guy's feelings and convictions, was that his wager was lost. Armed with his new faith and purpose, Guy would be for defending his mistress against harm with the armour of the red-cross knight, rather than doing her any.

Ah! but what was harm? Might it not be possible to persuade Faucit, that to one so newly and miraculously convinced of a higher law, the laws of the world were but a delusion and a snare? that a pure love like his and Daisy's, tried and tested through flame after flame, was in itself too sacred for the world's foolish restrictions to meddle with? He would try. And to this, about the worst and most devilish task which the man had yet set himself to do, the Count Lestrange bent all the power of his magnetic mind. He did his work wonderfully, and found Guy more apt for it than he had hoped. Side by side with these higher convictions, especially at first, is apt to run a dangerous proclivity to tamper with what seem to be lower laws. For a man who has never, in real earnest, however well-principled in purpose and in life, done otherwise than live the life of those about him inwardly as well as outwardly, the reaction against the gods which he has ignorantly worshipped runs into dangerous extremes. It needs time, and the quiet settling down into the world's work and the world's ways, which is the only alternative to the life of a cloister (where, mayhap moreover, there is like to be as much world about as anywhere else), before the man who has set his hope upon another world can realize the very necessary and salutary influence of the rules of this.

It was not difficult for Guy, exalted as he was, to persuade himself, or unconsciously to allow Lestrange to persuade him, that such an unblest marriage as the Brents' was a breaking and not a fulfilling of the Divine law; that it was one of those cases where the verdict of divorce has been emphatically pronounced by the higher tribunal; and that it might be Guy's highest and truest duty to take bravely upon himself the consequence of his own doings—for it was he, after all, who had brought about poor Daisy's flight from Luscombe Abbey, and condemned her to the life of struggle which she might now be leading.

In spite of himself Guy's excited fancy caught the fire; and when he was growing most evidently warped towards Lestrange's purpose, the latter threw in an ingenious suggestion, no more than insinuated, that he might be able to lay his hand on Daisy. He would do no more than hint at it; and with it at his own absolute obligation of secrecy. And much to his infinite satisfaction and cynical delight, he began to feel that in Guy's new phase of thought he might have found his best ally instead of his most dangerous enemy, and that what worldly wisdom would, in spite of all his versions of it, have prevented, an unworldlier wisdom would abet.

Lestrange was delighted beyond measure. In all his manipulations of mankind he had never been able to congratulate himself on such a success as this, and the audacity and defiance of his intellectual pride rose to their culminating height. The man had a new spirit in him, which gave him a certain grandeur. With his friends and intimates he took a higher and more masterful tone than before, and among the circles he frequented was at his most brilliant and his best. The sayings and doings of Lestrange during the early months of that curious winter were not soon forgotten in London.

It was late in December, when Christmas was close at hand, that the Count Lestrange paid another of his visits to Mould-on-the-Moss. The supplies which Daisy had been receiving had been, by his contrivance, running shorter and more short, and the pinch of genuine distress was making itself clearly visible in the face and figure, and in the brave, uncomplaining voice, of the old sexton's lodger. He and his wife consulted, and said it wouldn't do; and conferred with Mr. Bickers, who couldn't see it through his old gold-rimmed spectacles, which had stuck to him as his one piece of personal adornment, being himself too well accustomed to the effect of chronic short-commons to observe it much in others.

Lestrange marked it sharply enough; and marked too how the unutterable weariness of the whole thing was beginning to tell upon Daisy's mind.

"If it would only freeze," he said to himself as he looked at her, and calculated what cold might be like in a cottage at Mould-on-the-Moss. When he saw her he talked about old haunts and old comforts, with the professed intention of cheering her spirits; and sketched for her Tantalic pictures of wealthy homes and luxurious rest. He told her how provoked he felt with Lady Pepperharrow, to whom he had written. She was terribly indignant, and believed, as half the world did—what?—why, that Daisy had really gone away with Guy, and was living somewhere in retirement under his charge.

Daisy's pale cheek fired up for a moment, though she said bitterly enough that it didn't much matter now. She would write herself to Lady Pepperharrow, though; though she would not let her know from where. It would be no use now, Lestrange feared, after the way in which the old lady had expressed herself of Daisy's conduct to her.

"A friend lost, then!" said Daisy. "Very well.

As a matter of fact, poor Lady Pepperharrow had been half-distracted by the news of her favourite's disappearance, had come home to find her, and had various conferences with Faucit on the subject, thoroughly believing his positive denial of all knowledge of Daisy's whereabouts—about which, owing to odd circumstances and the peculiar remarks of Lestrange, on none of which could anybody lay an absolute finger, the world was divided in opinion, according to its various proclivities in the matter of charity.

So the world wore on, till Lestrange had paid that last visit of his to the village on the moor. And when Christmas-tide came, it came about that once again, as if by the craft of some practised stage-manager, a merry-making party was met at Luscombe Abbey.

In a suit of sables, and under a new title, Lord Viscount Gander, once Jemmy Gosling, had been induced to pay a quiet visit to the house of a certain young lady's aunt, who regarded him now with different eyes, giving Lestrange the opportunity for many pleasant insinuations both about aunt and niece; Miss Carrie of course not being absent upon the occasion.

Sir Brummel and Lady Coates supplied another kind of interest, paying their first visit after their wedding-tour, which had been by mutual consent brought to a rapid end. And round the whole party trotted Pentonville, busy and anxious as ever.

Guy Faucit and the Count completed the party. The former had at first refused to come, feeling himself but little in cue for it; but Lestrange let fall one strange and vivid hint upon the subject he had been plying so hard; and eager, excited, his mind full of his new ideas working upon the sad story of the past, Guy Faucit came.

As for the Count, he stood at his open window one night at the Abbey when the rest had gone to bed, and the unnatural warmth of the atmosphere seemed to charge it with a summer's electricity.

"Phew," he muttered to himself. " I wish weather would be always like this, as far as I'm concerned."

Then he paced the room anxiously and with a set face, turning over a telegram which he held in his hand. "Good-heavens!" he thought, "what a narrow escape! To-morrow makes me or mars me, schemes and all. If I win, the news of this bit of paper will be known too late to hurt me; and if I lose—well, nothing matters, and I throw up the game. I shall have to leave England; and to-morrow night I shall be out of it. Nonsense. There's no such thing as losing in a fight like this. Chaffers! lay my hunting-suit out to-morrow morning; and good-night."

CHAPTER XXI.

THE MEET ON THE MOOR.

THE morning was closer than the previous night. A heavy damp, which felt like August, was steaming up from the moorland slopes, and there was a sort of summer-hush upon the world that Christmas-tide. It was a week-day in the Christmas week, when holiday is still made far and wide by thousands who treat but as a myth the name they still make it in. The holiday-makers of that year made merry with the welcome warmth, and dotted the sea and country-side like flies, to an extent which made the faces of railway directors to beam, but failed to induce them to show any gratitude by making more comfortable the customers they fattened on. On the contrary, they treated them with even more contempt than usual; disregarded their contracts with the magnificent indifference to the elements of morality which has characterized corporations (railway especially), from Sidney Smith's time upwards and downwards; inveigled unwary tourists into first-class tickets, and then jammed their laps into pancakes with third-class passengers unlimited, carrying birdcages and

sandwiches free of charge (subsequently suing some of
the latter for travelling first-class with third-class tickets,
albeit thereunto not incited only, but compelled by the
company's own guards); treated the time-tables as a
myth, and time itself as a delusion; shunted their
victims into sidings, and played pitch-and-toss with
them at level crossings; tortured their limbs and mad-
dened their tempers, causing improper expressions to
fly about like flakes in a snow-storm, and every description of execration and remonstrance to descend upon
the devoted heads of innocent guards and porters, who
bore them, as a rule, as only angels and railway-men
can, in the vicarious cause of superiors who don't
overpay them for it. Oh, that on some excursion
day these rank and file of the railway army might
pocket the receipts, and the directors be condemned
to run the gauntlet of abuse from their miserable
victims! But then, what a number of accidents there
would be.

It would be difficult, I admit, to re-introduce Mould-
on-the-Moss by a less appropriate opening. The village
on the moor knew nothing of railway-trains, or even of
any definite communication with them. Its part in
the Christmas season would have been as usual one of
undisturbed placidity, but that on the special morning I
am writing of there were singular signs of life about
the place. The rustics were all agape at their porches,
to gaze on an army of gentlefolk who invaded the
village from all sides at once, in uniforms of red, black,
and velveteen, a picturesque regiment of irregular horse
with camp-followers of an attractive kind in the shape
of brightly-dressed dames and damoselles in pony-
carriages of coquettish build, rattling up over the moor
to the pleasant music of merry laughter, as the wheels
cleared some sudden obstruction with an unexpected
leap, or the ponies shied at some barricade left casually
in the middle of a turn of the road, like a relic of
the Deluge.

Behind and about the pony-carriages, and in close

and admiring proximity to the heels of the horses, provoking sundry get-out-of-the-ways and hoarse remonstrances of a more inarticulate kind, were a horde of savage infantry collected from the stray cottages and homesteads, apparently even the burrows, of the moor, rushing out to see anything that might be to be seen, deserting the plough at least as willingly as Cincinnatus took to it, and hob-nailing the neighbourhood in a state of unreasoning felicity. There were the hounds too, bred out of the Spartan kind, and matched in mouth like bells, answering name by name, like the boys at a school roll-call, to the huntsman's mellow cry, and providing a dappled variety of colour for the many-coloured scene. For there was a novelty afoot in the world-forgotten village, and there was a meet by Mould-on-the-Moss.

The bell-music of the dogs was answered by a different peal of bells, which sounded from the cranky-looking old church-tower upon a series of discords quite as cranky. And as it sounded, the figure of old Delves the sexton, shuffling in a crab-like fashion begotten of rheumatic years, might be seen making its way through the open place which still called itself the market-place, where a rude stone cross with an inscription which might have been Runic upon it, for all chance a casual reader might have of deciphering its meaning, marked the centre of gravity of Mould-on-the-Moss. An old village fountain gurgled at its foot, and the moss-grown pavement, rough and uneven, sloped and straggled up or down from it to the best cottage homesteads of the place, amongst which the sexton's house was conspicuous on the upper side, its door opening upon the market-place, and side-wall abutting upon the mournful and overgrown, but picturesque, churchyard, whose uncared-for turf ، and thickly-scattered, nameless mounds of sepulchral earth matched the pavement of the place in unevenness of grain.

The sexton's house flanked one side of the churchyard, and the church itself the other, its quaintly carved

porch and door opening upon the market-place westward, to which a flight of steps also led down from the
middle of the churchyard, raised a little height above it.
To the north side the place contracted itself into the
straggling street, if street it might be called, which constituted the village, which to the south came to an
abrupt end at the church, save only for the unpretend-
ing parsonage, which hid itself in the fields beyond,
communicating by a foot-path and a stile with the
market-place. Delves had it to himself that morning,
the entire population being bent upon the gathering in
the fields beyond, which had drawn even the Reverend
Mr. Bickers and the fair Martha and Mary from their
trivial round and common tasks, to see what was going on.

"All right, mum, all right," the old sexton was
saying as he came out of his cottage, speaking in a tone
at once respectful and parental. "You stay where you
are, and keep quiet. You couldn't be asked not to feel
more out o' spirits than ever, this being Christmas
time." And Delves threw into the word an indescribable
effect of grumble. "Oh yes, go on!" he added to himself, apostrophizing the church bells; "there's the bells
makin' believe to be merry, and bustin' theirselves over
it, for all the world like the live folk that runs to
turkeys. Merry indeed! who's a goin' to be merry at
the end of December? If you've troubles on the mind
or rheumatics on the body, that's when they finds yer out.
And when you puts the summer 'eat on the top of it,
and makes as if you meant to fling in a dash of thunder
and lightning, what's to become of you? Hallo, sir, that
you?" the old man proceeded, not varying his grumbling
tone a whit, for indeed it was part and parcel of him.

The man whom he addressed was leaning over the
stile, and had been watching the sexton with the quiet
observation of one accustomed to watch everybody, for
a few seconds before he was discovered. Picturesque
enough the Count Lestrange, for he it was, looked in
the shapely hunting-dress he wore, which set off the
slight figure to advantage.

· "Good morning, Delves," he said. "Is your young lady lodger at home?"

He came into the place as he asked the question, raising his hat from his head and wiping his forehead with his handkerchief, as he felt the stifling closeness which was in the air.

"Yes, sir," answered Delves. "Do you wish to see her?"

"Not immediately," said the Count.

He said it with an odd smile on his lips, and a look at his watch. It was not yet mid-day, and the start from Luscombe Abbey had been made very early.

"She's expectin' of yer," said the old sexton, contemplating the Count admiringly; "but not in them gorgeous togs. That's for the huntin', is it? We don't see much of that up this way."

"You owe it to my suggestion that the hounds meet near here. I look well in red and black, don't I?"

"Born to it," answered Delves.

"Exactly. This is the only opportunity which the age affords me of coming out in my true colours."

"Eh?" asked the sexton. "I don't foller."

"It's as well you shouldn't," said Lestrange, with an amused smile and a look of mastery on his face, "it might make you uncomfortable. Ouf! it's close enough. What's in the air now, in this eccentric climate?"

"Thunder an' lightnin' 's in the air," growled Delves, "and it don't mean to stop there. We shall have a big storm before we've done with it."

Even as he spoke there were one or two drops falling, but they ceased again for the time.

"A thunderstorm at Christmas!" said Lestrange. "That would be a curiosity."

"Ay," added the sexton, seating himself on the old market-stone by which stood the cross. "It don't happen often, but it does sometimes. It's thirty years ago and more come this Christmas-tide when the winter lightnin' struck the old tower yonder, and twisted it all o' one side, just as you see it now. We don't run to repairs much up 'ere."

"Ah! struck by lightning, was it?" asked the Count, curiously. "I haven't heard that before. A heavy storm, I suppose?"

"Ah, I believe you it was heavy. And it wasn't content with dumb things like church-towers, neither; for the same flash that did that mischief struck a man down just where you're standin', a black blatherin' scoundrel who was never no good to anybody. It knocked him clean out of time though, and he blathered no more."

"Dead?" asked the Count, with a slight shudder.

"Dead."

"Ah! Has there been much more doing in that way lately? in your way, I mean."

"What should there be doin'?" answered Delves. "Nobody can't be expected to die 'ere when nobody don't live 'ere. Drat the musty old place! What's the good of my telling them as I show over the church, —which it represents a hincome of about arf-a-crown every other year,—that it dates from the reign of William the Conqueror? What's the good of that, I asks you, when there's nobody in it in the time of Wictoria?"

"It's the thin end of the wedge, Delves," said Lestrange, laughing.

He was leaning against the stone cross at the foot of which the old sexton was sitting, being to the latter personage a kind of rostrum from which he was wont to discourse social and political wisdom to the rustic senate of Mould-on-the-Moss.

"Is it now?" said Delves, looking at his companion with a face indicative of no comprehension whatever of his meaning, but much conviction of its depth. "What wedge?"

"Disestablishment of the national Church," laughed the Count, carelessly. "You look disestablished enough here to please anybody. What are your political views on that point?"

"I don't rightly know as I has any—not to speak on. I goes for adwance, I does. That's where it is— adwance. And there's no doubt that we wants it bad down here."

"Well, we shall educate your successor," said Lestrange, "and dispose of your place by competitive examination. But cheer up; you shall show your church this morning to a party of fine folk from Luscombe Abbey, which you may have heard of. They'll be over here directly for the meet, and will have some little time to spare."

"Fine folk in these parts!" answered the sexton. "Well, it's a sight o' time since I seen that. Darn me if I harn't forgotten what cent'ry that there roof was restored in; it worn't in this, I know. I can't be expected to remember my history when I gets no practice. Howsumdever, I knows arf-a-crown's worth, I reckon."

"I want you to forget another half-crown's worth," was the quiet remark which followed, as the Count put the coin in the other's hand.

"Eh?" asked Delves, puzzled again.

"You'll forget my visits here during the last three months," said the Count, "and you'll forget to mention anything about your young lady lodger."

"About her, pretty lamb?" answered the other, quite a touch of tenderness coming over his rough and grumbling voice, which indeed was no uncommon matter where that young lady was concerned. "That's right enough. I promised her I'd never say anything about 'er; nor I wouldn't, without takin' o' your money, which I'll keep notwithstanding."

"Excellent philosopher!" laughed Lestrange.

"Not much of that," growled back the other; "which I'm told it's one as don't mind other folk's troubles, and werry much minds his own. Now her pale face goes to my heart; she's troubles enough of her own, whatever they are, let alone a jolly Christmas."

An infinite emphasis of disgust the sexton managed

to throw into the last adjective, expressive of a contempt for the festive season which might have made·
the calendar blush. The season, however, being not
only a jolly but an assertive season, wont to insist upon
its historical position and traditions, responded at once
to Delves's challenge by a fresh peal from the old
church-bells, whose ringers had free license from time
immemorial to discourse December music to the moor
when the spirit moved them. They found the spirit
move them mightily that morning when they saw the
number of groups of unusual visitors, from whom sundry
half-crowns might surely be expected. The Count
Lestrange didn't seem likely to be of the number of
contributors, however, for the bells of Mould-on-the-
Moss seemed in no way to commend themselves to his
sense of harmony. Certainly their notes were none of
the soundest, portending that the little rifts within the
metal had been slowly widening for many years past,
possibly even before the oldest Mould-on-the-Mossian
had worn the semblance of the tiniest of the trots now
sucking their dirty little fingers with their dirtier little
mouths at the door of some friendly pig-stye, or mud-
built hovel scarcely distinguishable therefrom. If that
same rift had carried the poet's process further, and
slowly silenced all, Lestrange for one would have had
no objection. His face bore the expression of pain
which defiance of tune wrings from involuntary muscles,
and he put his hands to his ears and drew up his legs·
with that octopedal contraction which is part of the
same expression of suffering. Delves's face presented
a pleasant contrast to the Count's, as of one who regarded the divagations of these charges of his with a
certain humorous parental pride.

"Confound those bells of yours! how cracked they
are!" said the Count Lestrange.

"So'd you be, if you'd stopped here so long as they
'ave," was the answer.

The *tête-à-tête* between the strangely-assorted pair·
was at an end, for the rattle of the wheels of a pony-

carriage was heard on the south side of the market-place, and it discharged its contents at the door of the Bells Inn, which occupied (of course) the angle of the market-place opposite the church, nestling in confiding proximity thereto.

It was part of the same good old Church-and-State system, and the progress which Delves desiderated for the village had certainly spared it so far. Its convenient position with reference to the church, and the churchyard, and the sexton's own house, was very welcome to him in his advancing years, and he rarely stirred outside this three-cornered kingdom of his, which he had as it were in a ring fence under his hand. Under some protest, but with some curiosity, he shuffled up to help the smart tiger-groom (specimen of the genus hippo-anthropoid not formally tabulated) in his ministrations by the pony-carriage, from which the Count Lestrange, his hat raised in old-fashioned and punctilious courtesy, assisted Lady Luscombe, Carrie Beaufort, and Lady Coates, *née* Challoner, to descend.

CHAPTER XXII.

THE WHIP-HAND.

"WHAT a picturesque old place!" said Miss Caroline Beaufort, fairly delighted with the oddities of the scene, and taking it all in with a lively and pleasant curiosity. She looked a very agreeable figure in her well-fitted driving-dress, and the neat little Swedish gloves, with buttons which had apparently neither end nor beginning, but disappeared from view in the direction of the elbow. "How strange that we should never have been here before, aunt."

"Not at all," Lady Luscombe said, languidly and

absently. She looked even more hunted and worn about the eyes than of old, and with a restless movement they continually sought Lestrange, who avoided meeting them with his. "It's a great distance, and there's nothing to see," she added. "How singularly close it is." And she seated herself upon the sexton's stone with unconsciousness, moving the venerable gentleman, who had in it a sense of proprietorship or of tenant-right acquired by long usage, to a look of distracted uneasiness, as if he opined that the lady meant to take it away with her.

"There never is anything to see in this sort of place," observed Lady Coates, in a voice more distinctly unappreciative of things as they are than had been characteristic even of Miss Challoner. "Why did you organize the meet in such an out-of-the-way corner, Count Lestrange?"

"A meet is always the best of reasons for coming anywhere," said the cheery Carrie. "Nothing like hunting to wake a place up."

"Why ain't you hunting yourself to-day, then?" asked Emily.

"So I am, in a pony-carriage," answered Carrie, examining the Runic inscription, and trying to scratch the dust upon it into some intelligible form with the help of her parasol.

"The new Lord Gander doesn't like young ladies to hunt," said Lestrange, sententiously, producing a grimace from Carrie, unremarked.

"No, of course," said Emily, with an added touch of verjuice in her well-bred voice. "Only married ones, like that Daisy Brent. No news of her, I suppose, Lady Luscombe?"

"None," said Lady Luscombe, slightly flushing, wearily and with a sigh. "How fearfully hot it is," she said again. "The place is like a grave."

"It is warm," said Lestrange. "I like it."

"Don't talk in that way," Lady Luscombe answered hurriedly, and in a low voice. "It sounds like an omen."

"Poor Daisy!" Carrie said, with regret and sadness in her voice. "What can have become of her?" And as she looked very hard at the inscription, there were tears in the kind eyes which looked. "Ah, well! Why don't you hunt, dear, by the bye?" she added, abruptly, to Emily, to change the subject.

"Sir Brummel," observed the Count as before, but with a rather more pronounced sneer than he generally permitted himself (Lady Coates was one of his favourite studies in womanhood), "wishes that his wife *would* hunt."

"Sir Brummel is not interested in anything I do," Emily said, in a tone of profound indifference which seemed destitute even of pique; "let us find a more agreeable subject. Is this the church which is supposed to be so curious?"

She moved across the market-place as she spoke, and with a pair of double eye-glasses, which she had assumed by right of fashionable matrimony rather than of short sight, proceeded to survey the old temple without any superfluity of reverence. She looked it up and down as if it had been a young person of the middle classes, speaking to her without an introduction. Her inquiry, however, was Delves's opportunity. The old sexton, having satisfied himself that the unceremonious lady who sate down upon his stone had no designs upon it, but was merely in a state of ignorance of his claims and character in the village, for which she was rather to be pitied than blamed, had transferred his observation to the two younger ladies, having still his share in the universal weakness of male humanity, which finds the attractiveness of the opposite sex in provokingly inverse proportion to its age. Delves, who had an eye, as he thought, for everything, would have been sorry indeed not to possess one for beauty. He bestowed inward approval on the outward appearance of both the young women, with a decided preference for Carrie Beaufort.

"A stuck-up sort t'other one," he thought to himself.

"The little one's nose does all the sticking-up for her, and she's a good little filly."

Such were his reflections when they were interrupted by Lady Coates's question, which brought him back at once to meditations on half-crowns and the main chance. He would not allow any shadowy preferences of his own to distract him from that primary object, and bestowed his gracious patronage upon Emily at once.

"Built in the early Norman," he said with much promptness, as he came forward from the back, where he had .been suppressing himself by the churchyard steps, and taking up the cue—"as is observed in the lancet window of the north hisle. The roof was erected in the twelfth cent'ry, and till the time of Holiver Crummles——"

"Thank you, yes," lisped Emily, with an infinite impertinence which took no account of beings of that clay; wounding the old gentleman's feelings with as much compunction as she might show in treading on a disabled wasp—less, as a display of sentiment on the latter head might be interesting.

"*Appelez-vous celà un homme?*" she might have answered if any one had suggested that any such result could follow her words. To do her justice, it would have astonished her considerably. She did not even focus Delves with her glasses for a passing moment, but continued to patronize the church with them. "What a tumble-down old hovel!"

"And what a tumble-down old man!" whispered the delighted Carrie, careful with her very different instincts that the sexton should not hear her; "and what tumble-down everything! And oh, Emily, what awfully jolly poetry! Look here," she said, as in the course of her perquisition she had mounted the churchyard stairs and was applying herself to an examination of those wonderful "tales of the tombstones" which play such an odd part in the literature of the country :—

    "'TOBIAS TROTTER—AGED 91.
     He were the righteousest of men,
      As there is few of such :
     We ne'er no more shan't see again
      One good for half so much.'

Now what's that out of ? "

"Out of the heads of his sorrowing relations," said the Count Lestrange, laughing. "Probably he was one of the worst characters in the parish, eh, Delves ? "

"Which he certainly were, sir," answered the sexton, scratching his head over his internal reminiscences, like a famous member of his guild moralizing over the skull of Yorick. "Beat all his wives, as there was three of 'em, and starved all his childern, as there was sixteen, exceptin' those as he boiled. And only died hisself when there was none left to keep him alive through bullyin' on 'em. He were a rare 'un, he were. And I was main fond of him."

"And perhaps wrote his epitaph ? " suggested the Count.

"Well, sir," said Delves, with much self-respecting modesty, scratching the other side of his head with an indescribable grin, "I allus had rather a turn in the way of verse."

"I thought so," commented Lestrange, while the young ladies received the intelligence after their respective manners. "What you might have been had there been an Education Act in your time ! "

"A local poet," exclaimed Carrie. "How awfully lovely ! "

"How excessively silly ! " was the observation of her more refined friend.

Carrie Beaufort, however, proceeded on the strength of his lyric gift to cultivate an acquaintance with Delves, who responded willingly to the young lady's attention, and proceeded to bring to her notice the flowers of the Mould-on-the-Moss anthology one by one. All the virtues seemed, from the touching records by descendants provided, to have flourished garden-wise in the ancient village, and anything like vice to have been unknown in its Arcadian precincts.

Where are the bad people buried? is a question which will exercise the mind as much as the fate of postboys did Dickens's hero. Carrie went from mound to mound and stone to stone, and delighted herself with an examination of the old sexton's individuality, while the other three still lingered in the market-place.

Ominous signs began to gather in the sky, which seemed to threaten but a wet and soaking day's sport to the Nimrods, and suggested uncomfortable reflections to the tenants of the pony-carriages. Darker and heavier grew that strange, unseasonable atmosphere, and the ominous stillness which precedes an exceptional storm was sensible everywhere.

"If there is anything to see inside the church," said Emily, drawing her shawl closer round her in spite of the warmth, "come and show it to us. The rain will be upon us in a moment, and at least it will be a shelter."

"Yes, ma'am," said Delves, who had by this time made the circuit of the churchyard with his pretty charge, and felt in nowise disposed to change her for the other. "Will you come in too, miss? The kneelin' figger to the right, as you enter, represents the ——."

And followed by Emily, producing his history by the yard as he went, the sexton opened the stout old door with an immense key of an antiquity as venerable, and disappeared from the scene.

"Lady Coates is a good deal changed in the last few weeks," said Lestrange to Carrie, who was following.

"Yes," answered she from the old porch, which framed a very pretty figure; "she's not too jolly."

"Marriage is not good for young ladies."

"Think so?" Carrie said, off-handedly. "But what's come over my aunt?" she went on, as she noticed Lady Luscombe tracing idle figures on the ground, still seated on the market-stone, and unconscious apparently, alone with the painful thoughts which seemed to have possession of her, of all that was going on around her. " Ain't you coming to see the kneeling figure to the right, aunt ? " Carrie Beaufort added, with a funny imitation of the old sexton's manner of speech.

" Directly," said Lady Luscombe, absently, as her niece followed the others into the church. Then she raised her eyes straight to Lestrange's, now that she was left alone with him, and spoke without parley. " What have you brought us here for ? "

" For the meet."

" And then ? "

" To see the church."

" You are not so fond of churches."

" As an outsider, yes," said the Count.

" You have some new scheme," Lady Luscombe said, speaking rapidly and clearly, and with a nervous emphasis upon the words. " I have not forgotten that the time for winning or losing that wicked wager of yours is nearly gone by. Have you won it ? The world believes that when Daisy Brent left my house suddenly, after that scene three or four months ago, it was with the help and knowledge of Guy Faucit ; that he knows where she is now, though he denies it. Is the world right ? "

" I am not a court of appeal from the world's judgments," answered the Count, undisturbed. " Why refer to such an old scandal as that ? "

" Old ! " echoed Lady Luscombe.

" Surely. Three months are a great age for a scandal with us. There have been several since. Let us hope," the Count proceeded, in his best sub-acid manner, " that Lady Coates will soon provide us with another."

" I don't want fencing," said Lady Luscombe, impatiently. " Where's Daisy Brent ? "

" Nor do I. She's here."

The Count riposted with the vividness of a swordsman, and he leaned upon the cross by the stone, from which Lady Luscombe rose at once to her feet at the answer.

"In this village!" she exclaimed.

"Yes."

"I guessed it! I guessed it!" Lady Luscombe said. "I guessed it from your manner about this meet. She is in the charge of Guy Faucit."

"No," said Lestrange, composedly. "He knows nothing about her."

"In whose then?" Lady Luscombe asked.

"In mine."

"Yours!"

The Count's softest and best-pleased laugh answered her. "Are you jealous?" he said. "Don't be alarmed; I only take a friend's interest in the poor girl."

"Your friendship is only less dangerous than your love," said Lady Luscombe, with a deep and scornful bitterness.

"Well, you ought to know," said Lestrange, carelessly, with a shrug of the shoulders and a turn of the ring. "You're nervous and excited; sit down while I explain."

Nervous and excited Lady Luscombe was, so much so that her hand shook with the agitation of her thought, as she wondered and speculated what this scheme might mean, which she had so rightly suspected and feared. She sate down again upon the old stone, and her face took a hard, set expression as she looked straight before her, to listen to what the impassive Count might have to say.

"I repented," he went on placidly, leaning on the cross close by her in a familiar attitude, "what you justly call my wicked wager" (no expression in his voice denoted anything much more than amusement), "and provided this refuge for Daisy Brent, to save her from Faucit and from herself."

Lady Luscombe looked at him eagerly, with a quick, inquiring glance, then gave a merely contemptuous ejaculation.

"I don't believe you," she said.

"You're quite right," with the same quick parry.

Then his voice and manner took a sterner mould, and all vestige of banter left them. He spoke with grave and unusual seriousness, and Lady Luscombe's face flushed deeper than before. She knew of old what might be likely to happen when the Count Lestrange was in earnest.

"You prefer the truth, and you shall have it," he said. "I meant to win my bet four months ago, and thought I had secured my lovers. I was wrong. I meant the lady to run away with the gentleman, and she ran away from him."

"Good girl!" Lady Luscombe said, with a genuine gladness and even pride in her voice. "You had miscalculated one thing, you see: a brave woman's power of resistance."

"Yes," said Lestrange, relapsing for a moment into his wonted cynicism. "My excuse must be my want of experience in that respect. For the time I had failed," he went on, serious again. "But I found Mrs. Brent at her wit's end where to turn, and offered to find a home for her, though I could only find a humble one. She was too proud even for that, but accepted my help so far as to take work which I found for her. She is living in this village."

"Where?" asked Lady Luscombe after a pause, as the Count said no more.

She was trying to puzzle out the problem.

"All in good time," he said.

"You still dare to think that you will win that wager?"

"Yes," he said, "I do; to-day. I shall not fail this time."

"How?" said Lady Luscombe, shortly.

"As before, with your help."

She bit her lip till the blood came.

"Again!" she said. "What am I to do?"

She had the old appearance of watching him, but something with it of a new purpose slowly rising in her mind.

"You will meet Daisy Brent presently," Lestrange answered, with his dangerous seriousness, "and you will be careful to receive her as one woman loves to receive another when she is under a cloud, especially when—"

"When what?" asked Lady Luscombe, as he did not go on.

He shrugged his shoulders.

"Never mind. Not a word of this, of course," he added; "I can trust Lady Coates to follow suit."

"Is that all?" presently Lady Luscombe asked again, with the same air of increasing purpose, but no definite expression in her voice either of submission or of dissent. Lestrange's keen observation did not miss the new phase, and he looked at her, this time with no shifting of the eyes at all. This time her eyes did not meet his.

"At present, that's all," then said the Count.

Lady Luscombe waited as if she expected him to say more. As he did not, she spoke again; her eyes turned away from him, but as if from some concentrated thought.

"Daisy will not be without a defender," she said. "Her brother has come home."

If she anticipated making some impression, she was wrong.

"I know that," was all the Count said.

"You know it?"

"Yes. You know I always know everything. He will probably be at the Abbey this morning, find a line which I left there for him, and follow us here."

Lady Luscombe's singular self-possession failed her again, and she left the seat where through all this conversation she had been sitting as quietly as if she had been chained to it. She began to walk about the grey market-place, which might have been a desert left to the two, for any soul that interrupted them. Still the omens hung heavy in the air; but the clouds did not break, and the storm-god held his hand.

"To thwart you!" then she said, looking at him.

"To help me," was again the quiet answer. "He has a violent temper. I am so much obliged to you for making no objection." And with a graceful air of courtesy he raised her hand to his lips and kissed it.

She did not wince; but she looked at him again, as Portia may have looked at Shylock across the table in the court, when she saw the man who was bent upon a purpose as diabolical as ever crossed a human brain. And there are people who want to represent Shylock as a suffering martyr! the savage usurer, whose best and only plea is that he believed in his religion, which he gave up in a moment to save half his cash! Shylock was merely a terrible specimen of a perverted brute; and Lady Luscombe remembered how they had spoken of him on that day the wager was made.

"Did you think that I might make objections?" she asked, quite gently.

If the womanly touch in her voice was meant to disarm him, Portia's plea for mercy was never more misplaced.

"None that I shouldn't silence," said Lestrange, with an unmistakable contempt from which sometimes he could not refrain. It was not always wise.

"If it ruins me, I will save her if I can," was the thought passing through Lady Luscombe's mind. "I wonder that you can trust me," was what she said.

"I can't help myself," answered Lestrange, with his habitual tone of good-humour. "Now-a-days even Satan cannot work without instruments. It takes two now to make the devil, of whom one—at least—must be a woman. Phew! how hot and dark it is! The proverbial season for me—a green Yule!"

As he spoke Count Lestrange turned away from the cross by which he had been so long standing, and took his handkerchief from his pocket to wipe his forehead. Intenser and more intense grew that pressure in the air. His back was turned to Lady Luscombe, and as he drew the handkerchief out, a paper fell from his pocket on the ground. She saw it, and instinctively leant forward to pick it up and give it him, for he did not see it fall. "You—" she began. Then the words upon that paper caught her eyes, and she started as if she had been stung. Then she looked at the paper for a moment close, close, and crushed it up in her hand.

"What did you say?" Lestrange asked, turning.

"Nothing." With more than Portia's interest she was looking at him now, and her heart beat almost audibly under her dress, and her hand crushed the piece of paper tightly away. Portia had no interest in Antonio, as so many critics feign. Why should she have? she knew that he was safe. Portia was wrestling with Shylock, for Shylock's soul. But Lestrange's face, as Lady Luscombe looked at him, wore nothing but its usual mask of well-bred indifference. "Have you heard anything of John Brent lately?" suddenly she asked, and without preamble.

The Count Lestrange looked at her very sharply.

"Why do you ask?" he said.

"Have you?" again she asked, weighing her words, and pleading. "By the last news he was seriously ill."

His eyebrows went up in the old familiar way—the way which she knew so well.

"I have heard nothing since," he said on his side as deliberately.

"Ah," she said. What was the sound she used? A word, a whisper, or a sigh? She made as if to shake her head, and puzzled him. She looked at him once more, with a look in her eyes which was a dumb appeal, but found no answer in his. "I must go into the church," then she said. "They will be wondering what has become of me."

"Very well," said Lestrange. "You understand me?"

"About what? Oh, yes. I understand you very well."

She did indeed. There was a crucifix in the porch of the church, which met her eyes as she entered it, and her lips seemed to move. On the threshold she turned back once more, with one more earnest look at her companion. He seemed to have forgotten her, and was absorbed in his ring. She made a half-step towards him, which he either would not or did not notice.

"Will you take those ten thousand pounds from me —as a gift?" she said.

"No," he answered. "But as a debt I will, to-day."

So she drew back again, and was gone. The sun had been trying to struggle through the clouds just then; bnt the clouds closed over the sun, and the darkness seemed almost to speak.

CHAPTER XXIII.

DAISY'S BROTHER.

"I DON'T quite like her manner," thought Lestrange. "She wouldn't play me false: oh, no, she daren't. Can I have made any mistake this time? I think not. Only a few days left to win in, and I must have that money. Give it me, will she? Well, that's a comfortable hedge. So she shall if I lose it, and I needn't leave the country after all. I've run it fine; but not too fine, I think. Unless I'm much deceived, my Samson's last scruples have disappeared before his new gospel. What an odd ally! And as for the lady, she has had more than enough of poverty and Bickers by this time. With the women's tongues to stab, and the men by to sharpen them, and that idiot of a brother, if I've timed him rightly, fresh from the first news of the scandal, and the longed-for lover on the spot, if they don't fall right into each other's arms— well, I'd better go to school again, that's all. That's awkward news from India, though, which she must hear in a day or two; but not just yet, I fancy. It upset me for a moment, but I can keep it back just long enough. How it will sweeten my triumph when it comes! It's very exciting. It will be a 'meet' with a vengeance. I'm glad I'm dressed for the occasion, to be in at the death."

A sound of many feet and many voices made itself heard in the street, where the pony-carriage had landed its company before, and Lestrange drew back as he saw them coming.

"More of my puppets dancing to my tune," he said to himself; "that's right. Now for my pretty penitent."

He knocked gently at the door of Delves's cottage, turned the handle, and went in. Quietly he went upstairs to a room above, where Daisy Brent, with books and account-books and papers before her, and unconscious of the excitement which was agitating Mould-on-the-Moss, was making ready for her village-school. Worn and pale and thin she looked, the brilliant beauty of a former day, and it passed through Lestrange's mind, for a moment, that her changed appearance might have the wrong effect upon Guy, and repel instead of interesting him.

"It would me," the Count thought. "But Faucit is on the high ropes, and the thing will be all the sweeter."

For a moment he glanced from the window of the room down upon the place below.

"Did you hear any noise in the market-place?" he said, after exchanging a morning greeting.

"No," she answered; "I was very, very tired, and have been asleep. I am not strong now."

He drew the blind down upon some excuse, and sate down to talk to Daisy for a time, consulting his watch at intervals, and every now and then looking out from under the blind. Just as he entered the cottage, a group of four riders made their appearance in the market-place, and dismounted for the moment to leave their horses at the inn, while the inspection of the church took place, as agreed upon. They were old friends of ours all of them, and as they proceeded to examine the market-cross, and other dilapidated lions, were engaged in an animated discussion;—all but one, who was occupied with his own thoughts, and seemed at first to pay no attention to what the others were saying.

"It's t—too bad, Gander, too bad," observed his lordship of Pentonville with emphasis and conviction, trotting about the while, though sensibly weaker in the knees than when we first made his acquaintance. In the head he seemed to remain stationary. "You ought to come to the p—point with the Beaufort girl. I b—betted that you'd propose to her directly; you came down to the Abbey this C-Christmas, and now you're going to th—th—"

"Throw her over?" supplied Coates.

"No! Back out."

"I don't want to say anything indelicate, Pen," said he whom we have known as Jem Gosling, dressed in quiet and appropriate mourning; "but mind your own business."

"It *is* m—my business," screamed the little lord, emphatically; "I've got my money in it."

"He's haw quite right, Jemmy," quoth Sir Brummel Coates, with the air of one now qualified as a moralist. "You ought to hum marry that little girl."

"Awfully disinterested, old boy, aren't you?" answered Jem. "Marrying little girls seems to have paid so well with you."

"That's a haw doosid different thing," said Coates.

"Well, it may be; but suppose it wasn't?" said Gosling, with a marked irreverence which nettled the accomplished baronet.

"Fact is," he said, rather angrily, "you're too great a hum swell since your brother's death."

"The fact is nothing of the kind," answered Jem, taking the challenge up. "Look here, you fellows! why can't you let a fellow alone? I've had an awful

lot to think about since I lost my poor old brother;
and I'd give all I've got, and lots more, if I could only
get him back again. The mum says I'm no good at
all after him, and she's right."

There was genuine regret in the tone, which
there was no mistaking. The new Lord Gander's two
companions looked at each other with undisguised
astonishment.

"I d—do believe he's r—really cut up!" confided
Pentonville to Coates, crescendo.

"Must be haw putting it on," said the worthy
baronet with much conviction.

"You're a good fellow, Jemmy," said Guy Faucit
in his deep, grave voice, joining for the first time in
the conversation, and laying his hand affectionately
on the younger man's shoulder; "and I'll tell you
another thing. Carrie Beaufort's a good girl; marry
her."

Lord Gander's face fell. "I suppose," he said,
"that, like most girls, she'd take me now."

"Like few girls," said Guy with warmth, "she'd
have taken you when you hadn't a penny."

"Perhaps," Jemmy said. "But she knew how bad
my brother was." Faucit looked at him wonderingly.
"Lestrange says—" the other went on.

"Ah! he's been talking to you?" said Guy.

"Yes; he's been awfully kind."

"The less you listen to Lestrange, my boy," Faucit
said kindly, "the better for you."

Jemmy shook his head.

"Clipper, old man, you don't practise what you
preach."

"Lestrange can do me no harm," Guy answered,
with a sad and singular smile. "In the world's sense,
my life was broken long ago."

"I hate to hear you talk like that," said his friend
impatiently. "You're awfully changed by all this.
That Daisy Brent business has been a bad one for
you."

"Hush!" said Guy.

"Oh, I know you won't let a soul speak to you about it," Jemmy went on. "But it's awfully strange. On your honour, Faucit," he said, gravely, "you don't know where the poor girl is?"

"On my honour, no, indeed," Faucit answered. "I don't know to what I've brought her. My old pupil," he went on, very earnestly, "listen to me, and not to Lestrange, whose unfaith in everything is well enough for him, but isn't to be shared. Few men are so lucky as you; don't let your luck go by you. You know in your heart that a good woman loves you for your own sake; marry her, and you'll be a good man."

Jem's cynicism could not have gone very deep, seeing how easily Faucit's words moved him. His face had a pleasant smile upon it, and his voice an expression of much relief.

"Thanks, old fellow," he said. "I'm awfully glad we've met again down here. Yes, I suppose Carrie's in the church. Time about thinking of looking at the monuments, isn't it? Good-bye!"

And reconciled to his conscience with extreme rapidity by a verdict upon Carrie Beaufort's merits, which coincided completely with his private convictions, pronounced by the man whom he had always regarded as approaching infallibility upon all subjects, the young senator proceeded to make his way into the old church, to join the ladies in their discourse with Delves. Guy watched and nodded to his old pupil kindly as he went, then returned to his own reflections, not caring to interpose in the conversation in which the other two men were engaged.

"Y—yes, you must go in for po—politics," Pentonville was observing, in answer to something Coates had let drop which might not have been in favour of domestic life. "It's the best dodge when you're unc—comfortable at home. I b—bet you two to one you'll g—get in for the county if you stand."

"Yes," said Coates, reflectively. "I've haw stood

twice; once as a Liberal and once as a Conservative. Got licked both times. I'm sure I don't know why; I must have been right once. But politics are such very rum things."

"Aw—awful!" said the other. "C—come into the church; they must be wondering where we are "

"Lady haw Coates never wonders at my being anywhere," observed the baronet, "except when I'm hum with her. But I suppose we've got to do it."

"Q—queer shop altogether," said Pentonville, peering about the porch. "I n—never before was in—in —in—"

"Inside a church, Pen?"

"No; asked to see one!"

And resenting assistance as usual, the Viscount trotted into the church with his oddly assorted companion, to favour Delves and the ladies with his views of architecture and antiquarianism. Only Guy Faucit remained in the old market-place of this grass-grown village of the dead, dreaming. He was sitting on the old stone as Lady Luscombe had, like her infringing upon the vested interests of the old sexton, and wondering, wondering. Taking up the burden of his thought, through which, now, two strains ran ever side by side, he dreamed at once of the new purpose which had come into his life, and of her who seemed to have vanished out of it altogether. Where was she? where could she be? what had been the meaning of Lestrange's mysterious hints, which without assuming any definite form, had been enough to bring him down again to the scenes so closely connected with the last chapter of their ill-starred story? Where could she be? And as he sighed over the last thought, he rose listlessly to follow into the church. Even as he turned his head, his eyes met a man's angry look fixed upon him. The man had rapidly come up the road, and as rapidly come upon the place.

"Ah!" he said, when he saw the other, and he stopped him as he turned.

" One word, Mr. Faucit ! " he said.

" Captain Fairfield ! " Guy exclaimed.

" At your service," said the soldier.

Dick Fairfield looked like a man, Guy saw at once—more like one than he had ever thought before. And he looked thoroughly in earnest, and spoke in suppressed and passionate tones ; while he was white about the lips, and dangerous about the eyes. Guy did not take much note of this for the moment, for he saw nothing before him but Daisy's brother.

" Have you heard anything of your sister ? " he asked, eagerly.

" A good deal—just now—at the Abbey," Fairfield answered, the voice quivering now with new passion at the question. " I have come to ask you for an account of her."

Guy Faucit was not a man often addressed in that fashion. He drew himself up in a moment at Fairfield's tone, and looked him in the face. He saw the white heat there, and wondered what was coming. But he was not in a hurry to resent anything from Daisy's brother, and he only answered, very shortly, " I have none to give."

No one else would have had so much concession. But Fairfield began to lose himself more. He had blood in him, after all, and it was up.

" By God, you have though, and a heavy one ! " he said. " Where is she ? "

His hand would have gripped Guy's shoulder in a moment, but Guy drew back.

" I don't know."

" Have you thrown her off already, then ? "

Guy started, and stood a step back. His eyes and face began to look very dangerous too.

" Thrown her off ! " he cried, his old scorn of the man before him coming into his voice, as he looked him up and down. " By what right do you talk like this to me ? "

" By the best right. I am her brother."

H H 2

"And a careful one!" said Guy, breaking into a contemptuous laugh. "You remember it to-day, do you, for the first time? The child whom you helped first to sell—the woman whom you neglected afterwards, whom you left among all the dangers of a dangerous life; whom you left—"

"Not to you!" answered back Fairfield, as both voices rose now, high in anger. "I know my own faults—answer for yours, you—blackguard!"

"Ah!"

No human being ever spoke to Guy Faucit like that, and none ever saw his face look as it looked then. The fist was clenched at once for the blow which would have followed, and would have left Fairfield but small chance of returning it, full of fight as at that moment he was. It was an even chance, for a second, which man struck first. Fairfield raised his arm, but Guy caught it in a vice, even as for Daisy's sake he held himself in still.

"Take care!" he said, "take care! I can't stand that, though you are her brother!"

But Fairfield shook himself free.

"Again—where is she?"

"Again—I don't know!"

The voices had risen to the height of the argument, and the two men found each other under that leaden sky, brimful of deadly mischief and of deadly harm. But a hand had put aside a curtain above, in the cottage near to whose door they were standing, and a voice which startled both of them gave a cry. In another moment Daisy Brent herself flashed right in between them, just as Fairfield was once more on the point of striking full at the other man—flashed between them like a vision, with a cry of "Dick! what are you doing?"—and the two men fell back instinctively; Fairfield to burst into a laugh which was bad to hear, and Guy Faucit to say only, in a voice in which an infinite variety of shades and expressions were blended all together,

"Daisy here!"

"And now, Mr. Guy Faucit?" said Fairfield be-tween his teeth.

They had a full audience now. The tones of quarrel had reached the church, just as the party inside were finishing their round, and all the actors in this strange scene were gathered to witness its climax. They came out of the church, and they all saw Daisy—Daisy with her pale face, paler than ever now, and in the modest dress which might have given the lie to suspicion. At the back of them all, having quietly followed Daisy Brent out of the cottage, was the man whose wakeful ingenuity had planned his effects so well. He watched the group from the church steps, resting one foot on the lowest step of them, with an approving and appre-ciative eye. He had contrived to dismiss Delves.

"Neat—and well-timed—very!" he said to himself.

* * * * * *

"And again, now, Mr. Guy Faucit!" said Dick Fairfield. "Surprised, are you not?"

"At nothing you can say or do, sir," answered Guy, with more of the mischief in him than before. For Dick Fairfield had put his sister roughly away from him, and she was standing aside for the moment alone.

The excited group were talking together, not know-ing what to do, and the buzz of voices might have drawn all Mould-on-the-Moss together in a few more minutes. Only a few gaping rustics, however, who kept at a respectful distance from the "quality," sup-plied the local contingent for the occasion. The Count Lestrange it was who came to the rescue of propriety, seriously endangered in the hands of the two men.

"My good fellows," he said, very gently and per-suasively, indicating with a gesture the publicity of the place, "remember that this is the nineteenth century, when civilized emotions mustn't rise above drawing-room level. Never forget that you are civil-ized, and that there are ladies present."

Whether he meant to succeed in his pacific purpose or not, he failed with Fairfield, though not with Guy. The latter's bow was calm and courteous to all outward seeming, but Captain Fairfield was less scrupulous.

"I won't forget it!" he said. "Listen, all of you. This was my sister, Daisy Brent: she is no sister of mine now."

"Dick! you don't know—" Daisy appealed.

"Don't I?" answered the brother. "Let me alone."

"Shall I stop him, Daisy?" whispered Guy, with his teeth set.

"No, Guy!" she said, proudly. "Let him go on."

The scene was passing like a whirlwind, and took its own course. Moved by a strong impulse, Lady Luscombe moved a step forward.

"Daisy!—" she began.

"Remember!" said Lestrange to her very low, and with just enough force he held her back.

She looked at him again with the strange look of appeal, and again he let it go.

"You have disgraced yourself and me," Fairfield went on, "who should have known you better than to have trusted you. But I never expected this. You came to this place with your lover. Curse you—leave it with him!"

A shudder went through all there, even the coldest of them, except the Count, who merely made an amused observation of Fairfield, whose scratches revealed the Tartar.

"Hair about the heels," muttered the Count to himself.

Daisy turned upon her brother like an outraged goddess.

"My lover!" Then to Guy,—"Say that it isn't true!"

"It's a cowardly lie," Guy answered, "and everybody here knows it. Speak out, some of you!"

Carrie Beaufort (who had a new brightness of her

own in her eyes) was at Daisy's side, and had taken her hand.

"I'm sure it is!" she said. But she met with no response there.

"It looks awfully bad, you know," said Sir Brummel Coates.

"You doubt my word, then?" said Guy. "Lestrange!——"

"What can I say, my dear fellow? I know nothing about it," said the Count.

"Lady Luscombe, speak for me!" Daisy cried.

Lady Luscombe was looking at the Count, and the Count only. Still with that look in her eyes, and a paper crushed unseen in her hand.

"I have nothing to say," she answered, with mechanical coldness. "Won't he speak?" was her inward whisper.

"Emily!" Daisy said.

"Sir Brummel," said her ladyship, with a sweep of her garments, and even the eye-glass in requisition, "hadn't we better go?"

"Excellent Lady Coates!" muttered Lestrange; approvingly. "You see what you have brought her to," he said to Guy.

"What can I do?" Guy said, distracted.

The suddenness of the whole thing seemed to daze him.

"You have only one course," Lestrange said to him, in a matter-of-fact way. "Console her. You speak to the poor girl, Lady Luscombe," he whispered, with a cruel emphasis on the words.

"I am sorry—that you should have come to this," Lady Luscombe said, with the same passionless deliberation, and the same direction in her look.

"Oh, oh!" Daisy cried, pressing her hands to her head, as if the words were wrung from her with physical pain. "But where am I? What does all this mean? I don't even understand of what I am accused. I left your house alone, Lady Luscombe, driven out of it by you. I have lived here alone, worked here alone, to be safe from the shadow of a danger; and you all come here like this, my brother and all, to insult Guy and me with your wretched suspicions. And you know, Count Lestrange, you know! It was you who brought me here—say so! For shame, all of you, for shame!"

"Brought you here, I?" said Lestrange, with an air of sympathetic interest. "She's wandering. Didn't I tell you that I never forgave?" he whispered to her in a pitiless undertone.

"Oh!" Daisy said. "Oh! I see now. How cowardly —how cruel!"

"As bold as brass," said Lady Coates, in a voice of vinegar. "It's quite shocking. But it is just what I always expected of her. Lady Luscombe, it's time to be going, at all events from here."

"Yes," said Lady Luscombe. "Let us go."

There was some purpose in her face which might not be understood, and something in her manner which affected Lestrange strangely; but only for a moment.

The chattering group was clustered about the place, and Carrie alone seemed to wish to remain at Daisy's side. Daisy was unconscious of her presence, unconscious of everything, for the stabs of her brother's tongue and all the others had gone home.

In another minute the party had broken up under the influence of this sudden catastrophe—some to their horses, others to their pony-carriage, none for the moment with any definite aim in view: for all thoughts of meets and commonplaces of that kind had disappeared before this unexpected incident. The hunt at Mould-on-the-Moss, on the day of the great storm, though it left its memories on many a drenched skin, was to be innocent of the attendance of the party from Luscombe Abbey. Gossiping, tattling, wondering, shrugging their heads,—even Lord Gander was not quite proof against suspicion, and a brief argument with Miss Carrie ended in a pitched battle, in which he had humbly to own himself worsted,—the Abbey guests dispersed from the market-place. As they were scattering, the church-bells took up their Christmas tale once more.

"Peace on earth! good-will towards men!" said Daisy with a sad smile. She was too proud to try to justify herself one step further just then, had she the wish or the presence of mind. Guy Faucit knew the truth. What cared she for the opinion of any one else now? Captain Fairfield was still fuming, and again tried to escape from the quiet remonstrances of Lestrange.

"Now, Mr. Faucit!" he said once more.

"Not now, Captain Fairfield," the Count urged. "I am pained that I should have brought you here for this. You are naturally excited—not yourself. But I have some things to tell you which may be worth your hearing. You will see your sister again."

"I leave her in safe hands," answered the other, for Daisy had sunk down, rather than seated herself, upon the market-stone, and Guy Faucit, thinking, was by the church steps. The others were all gone, and the storm-clouds, which had looked like dispersing, were gathering more ominously again.

Daisy's attention was attracted by her brother's voice, and she made one more appeal.

"Dick!"—

"Don't speak to me!" was the answer.

Count Lestrange placed his arm in Fairfield's, and led him away. As he passed Faucit the soldier breathed quick and short, then suddenly said to him—"You will have to cross the Channel with me, sir."

Faucit scarcely took the pains to look at him.

"Wherever and whenever you please," he said.

Once more Lestrange spoke to Guy, a few words heard by him only.

"Don't desert her this time," he said, with an accent of grave interest. "As a man, you can't."

Guy shook from head to foot.

And once more, in the vicissitudes of their lives, these two hard-tried lovers were alone together.

CHAPTER XXIV.

THE COUNT LESTRANGE MEETS HIS MATCH.

"It is I who have brought these insults upon you," Guy said after a time.

He was leaning against the wall in the church-porch, and looked away from Daisy rather than at her.

"No," she said, like him looking away. Looking straight before her where she sate upon the market-stone, as if out into a future which she tried to read. The crisis of their lives, forced apparently upon them in spite of their own brave efforts, had really come upon them at last. "No, it was no fault of yours."

"But a few words will clear you," said Faucit, not leaving the porch, but turning round towards Daisy. "All this was so sudden that there was no time to think. And I don't understand, myself. Where have you been living all this time?"

Daisy turned her head, and looked at him with a sad sweet smile. The pale face, the worn appearance, the infinite look of weariness and suffering in the eyes, struck him like a wound. Disenchant him, Count Lestrange?—no fear of that. Guy Faucit felt a rush of passion and of tenderness come over him, which seemed to rob his very eyes of sight.

"Good God!" he thought, "in a few more months she would have been dead!"

She made a sign with her head towards the sexton's cottage.

"Where have I been living? In that house," she said, answering his question.

Guy looked at it, wondered, walked from the church across to it to look more closely, and then turned again to look at her, the lady of his honour. He could not realize the contrast.

"Here?" he said, with incredulous emphasis. "Here? in this wretched place?"

· "It's a peaceful place enough," she said, with a sigh; "and I have learned to love the old mounds under the window, where so many generations of trouble and sorrow have found one rest together.

> 'The city's golden spire it was;
>> When hope and health were strongest;
> But now it is the churchyard grass
>> We look upon the longest.'

I remember your favourite poet, you see. I came here to escape from my old self, but these people have brought it back with them."

The tone in which she spoke choked Guy. He felt the rising in the throat, the dimness in the eyes, which are the unspoken utterance of heartache, when a sharp and sudden sympathy strikes on the sensitive chord.

"Daisy," he said, with what voice he could find, and his head was turned away again, as he seemed to be examining the sexton's cottage, "I would not lose the old self."

"Would you not?" answered she. Then suddenly she said, "Guy, come here."

She turned to him, and he came—came to the market-cross, and leaned over her, and took her hand in his. She was very still and very serious, and left it there without pressure, but without withdrawal. Grave thoughts were passing through her mind, and she looked up in his face with the expression of a deep trust.

"I'm glad to see you again," she said.

"And I—and I—" he managed to stammer out in his choked voice. "But—" and the words followed with a cry, and broke the barrier down—"how changed the old self is! how changed you look! Oh, Daisy, Daisy! poor little Daisy!"

It was too much for her. She burst out crying, and sobbed her heart out for a while. The tears were rolling down his cheeks too, in one of those fits of silent weeping which seem to shake the fibre of a strong man's frame. The frame gave no outward sign of it, and he never looked stronger than when he stood upright by Daisy there. But the tears fell, literally, in big hot drops upon the ground. At last she began to grow quieter, as he held her hand soothingly but restfully in his. The tempest passed in waves which seemed almost to shatter the weakened breast and nerves, and she looked up at Guy with the piteous appeal of a little child, asking for protection and caress.

"This has stunned me, I think, Guy," she said, half sobbing through the lingering tears, and with her handkerchief wiping them away. "I never could, you know. I suppose that all this has changed me. I have tried to pray, too."

"You won't be without your answer some day," he said gravely, growing calmer too as she recovered calmness. "But you only see the world answer—as it does answer prayers."

"Yes," she said. "What am I to do now, after this?" added she suddenly, and clasping her head with her hands, bewildered. "I can't die. Where am I to go?"

The appeal was absolute and submissive, and Guy Faucit felt it. He had one short and sharp inward struggle, one last wonder where the true right lay, one last petition for light that he might know. Then he said abruptly, roughly almost, "You must come with me."

She showed no sign this time of resentment or of confusion. She received what he said as he said it, as a commonplace, and her eyes alone seemed to be puzzling out the riddle. She fixed them straight on his, and they filled with tears again. She was weak and ill and shaken, and the old self-command was gone. For a moment he wondered if he was taking an unmanly advantage of her; but he thought—no.

"You do care for me, don't you, and you don't think me very bad?" she said, with a trust, weakness, pathos, desolation, which seemed to pull at his very heart-strings. He had never seen her at all like this, he who thought he knew all the chords of the beautiful lute so well.

"Care for you? think you bad?" he repeated, with an emphasis which nothing can describe. "Don't ask me these things. Let me show you."

The unstrung nerves gave way again at the touch of the intense tenderness which spoke in his voice, and the deep respect which found expression there. It was too hard! too hard! their love had been, and was, so true, so pure, so high, their fate so unutterably perverse, so incredibly cruel. They had strolled away together from the market-place, and had found a corner of the old churchyard where they thought themselves safe from all possibility of an intrusive eye or ear. Nature was holding her breath as before some strange convulsion, at this terrible crisis in two lives. Neither of them noticed, absorbed and over-strung, how close and closer grew the unnatural warmth of the day.

"I don't think I should have been tried like this— I don't—I don't!" Daisy Brent sobbed out, growing almost hysterical as she went on, and Guy tried to soothe her with what gentle and re-assuring words he could find. "It is my punishment for treating you as I once did; but I wasn't so bad as to deserve this. You told me that you had been a long time forgiving me. God has been longer."

"You'll break my heart, Daisy mine," was all he could answer.

This time it had gone too far with him for even outward calmness, and the deep, strong sobs through which he drew his breath shook him from head to foot, and struck full upon her ear. She looked at him suddenly, tearfully, bravely, at the startling sight of a strong man broken down; and the sobs and the plea— the most powerful, if he could have known it, which he could possibly have used—calmed her on her side by magic, and dried her tears up at their source. She put her hand upon his shoulder with a sudden effort of will, and in the spirit of a brave and, to her even then, a terrible self-sacrifice, she said to him, in a voice into which all the gathered love of years threw every tone in which love can weave its harmonies—

"No, I will never do that. I can't think; I can't decide. Decide for me, Guy. Do with me what you like."

He loved her as few men have ever loved a woman; and it was written that, the shadow past, his love should, growing day by day, be yet more nobly anchored in his growing reverence. But never, to the final parting, did he love her half so well for any words she spoke to him as for those in which, that day, she gave herself with a fearless grandeur up into his hands. Would she have gone with him if it had come to the test? He was never sure; nor she.

The test did not come. They had thought the scene unwitnessed, and they were wrong. Witnesses there were two, out of whose mouths that scene might be established.

"She is lost!" said to himself, but half aloud, a man concealed behind a buttress of the church, to which he had made, as he thought, his unobserved way. Low as he spoke, there was in those three words of the Count Lestrange an inimitable triumph, which gauged the measure of his infamous success. But even as he spoke them the limit was reached, and the check was to come. Another figure, and that a woman's, stepped from under the church-wall also in front of his, and the woman held a crushed paper in her hand. As she passed Lestrange she heard his words, and answered them.

"She is saved!" Lady Luscombe said. "Daisy, you are a free woman. Your husband's dead."

"Dead!"

From every one there it was almost a cry. Lady Luscombe held out to Guy Faucit the paper which she had taken—the telegram which, the night before, had brought to the Count Lestrange from India the

news that all was over for John Brent, and that the bad
and harmful life had gone out for ever. The Count
Lestrange had known it all the time. When he saw the
paper in Lady Luscombe's hand, he tried to stay it, but
too late. It was secure in Guy Faucit's strong grasp,
and when Lestrange sprang forward, it was to read
defeat and ruin in the other's look.

Then it was that the Count Lestrange lost before
others the mask that he had worn, and that the awful
evil of his face was written there in letters as of fire.
He seemed to have aged twenty years in a moment, and
a positive distortion of rage and disappointment made
every feature look as if it changed its very shape and
mould. He gripped hard at one of the old tombstones
which gave their silent testimony to the strange scene,
and for a minute he seemed absolutely dumb, and
incapable of articulate sound. He looked at Lady
Luscombe, and she looked back at him, with more of
wonder than of anything else in her eyes. The prophet
of Khorassan could have startled her no more. Great
God! what a wicked face! And darker and heavier
and hotter grew the lurid day.

Guy and Daisy were busy with the telegram
together, not able yet to realize the strange thing which
had befallen.

"My husband dead!" exclaimed Daisy. "What
does it mean?"

"It means that the storm is over," said Guy with
a great tenderness and reverence, "and that we can
wait now."

"It means," muttered Lestrange between his teeth,
as he began to find his voice again, "that I am ruined,
but that the storm is to come!"

He looked upwards savagely at the thick and murky
clouds, which carried for him neither warning nor omen.
Lady Luscombe looked at him steadily—steadily—as in
that perfect revelation she saw at last the nature of the
idol which she had set up and framed, with the head of
brass and the feet of clay. If she could have seen, even

then—if any one could have seen—a trace of repentance or regret! But neither she nor any one could, for no such trace was there. If the outward change was visible, inward change there was none. The man's heart was seared with a red-hot iron, and there was no place found there for any feeling but a baffled and a fruitless rage. Lady Luscombe spoke next, and though she spoke to Guy and Daisy, she accented her words for him.

"It means," she said, "that I would not stain my soul and his with such a wanton sin! It means that he tried hard, step by step, to bring about your ruin. It means, Daisy, that he failed once because you are a good woman; and that he has failed again, because I am not so bad as he thought me. It means that I will not be his instrument; and that I defy him!"

Daisy shrank back from the presence of this defiant evil, and from Lestrange's vindictive look. What had she done to him?

"And it means one thing more, my Lady Luscombe," hissed Lestrange, "that you shall pay to the uttermost farthing for this day's work! Failed, have I, then, and through you? No—not failed. Marry your pretty piece of goods, Mr. Guy Faucit, and learn one day what you have done! Your scandal has become too open, even if I had not heard what I have heard to-day! I defy all your money and all your love to wash her name white again. And then for your turn, Daisy Brent! The pretty baby eyes have never cried such tears yet, as shall dim them then. I should have liked to see you brought to open shame before those fair-weather friends of yours, though! Why, I have made you all my playthings and my sport—the tools I worked with—the ladder by which I rose! And I have lost, have I?—lost everything—curse it all! Bah!" suddenly the Count said with a desperate effort at self-mastery, after the one passionate outburst any one living had ever witnessed from him—it fairly petrified the three who heard it,—"I always did lose in the dark ages—it's traditional."

So for the last time he assumed that Mephisto-phelean fancy of his, and then he turned on Lady Luscombe with a concentration of hatred which was horrible to see. It was the man all over—that in her he always saw and remembered the destruction of his favourite scheme, for which he had toiled more than for anything else in his life.

"Good-bye for the present, Lady Luscombe," he said, "I am going to fetch your letters—and to use them."

The threat came home to Lady Luscombe with the shock of a blow, even after all the emotion which had been roused by this stormy scene. In the strength of her anxiety to save Lestrange from the sin he had been so coldly contemplating, she had fairly forgotten her fears for herself—the fears to which the Count's evil ingenuity had given such vague but threatening shape. In the tempest of the moment she had no room for thought, and the formless fear of ruin and disgrace— more even, for she had an indescribable terror of Le-strange's power, and believed in it still as in a fate— suddenly assumed meaning and presence in her eyes. She turned suddenly to Guy as if for refuge.

"Oh, Mr. Faucit—Guy—can you save me?"

"From what?" he said, as the Count's threat had conveyed no meaning to him, and his savage tirade little but disgust.

"From ruin!" Lady Luscombe answered. "He has letters of mine which he will use to ruin me. Oh, get them from him! Daisy, help me!"

And she clung to Daisy Brent with a womanly gesture. The Count Lestrange laughed.

"Guy! she has saved us," said Daisy. "Save her!"

The Count laughed again, and turned upon his heel. Just in the path and under the shadow of the church Guy Faucit stopped him, and laid the strong arm upon his shoulder. The two women who saw it never forgot the picture. The Count Lestrange had recovered that mask of his again, but for the mocking cruel devil in

I I

his eyes, and, slight as he looked by the side of the other man, his overweening pride of brain gave him, in spite of it, again the look of mastery which all men felt in him. He seemed to heed Faucit's arrest not a whit, secure, even in defeat, of his own consciousness of power.

"You shall not pass, Count Lestrange!" Guy Faucit said, careless for the moment what might come of it.

"Nonsense, my athlete! Who ever stopped me? Who's to stop me now?"

Sudden and terrible, out of the heart of the storm-cloud, the man's only answer came. Even as the strange scene above described was passing, the actors in it all felt the gathering of the dread invisible presence which charged the clouds in the air. Heavier and heavier and heavier, till every leaf and weed, every life and organism, seemed panting as for want of breath, the portent gathered, till the very principle of Life seemed stayed. Then the clouds themselves first broke in upon the awful silence in one livid flash, full upon Lestrange's words. And even as the flash came the clouds crashed together, and broke the silence itself to pieces in one stupendous roar, followed by a horror of great darkness, and a sudden waterspout of rain dashing down upon roof and tree. In the churchyard there rang out one unearthly cry as of a man in pain, but in a voice which no one there knew, and so thick was the momentary darkness, that in the shadow of the church-wall what had passed was hidden. Daisy Brent broke the silence first.

"What has happened?" she called out. "What is it, Guy? Are you hurt?"

"No, Daisy—not a hair."

"The Count!" whispered Lady Luscombe, in the tones of an unutterable fear. "Is he dead?"

Guy Faucit was kneeling by a prostrate—powerless—insensible figure, and his hand was laid upon the heart.

"No," he said, after an almost intolerable pause.

" But powerless for further harm, poor fellow, I think—and always: He will live to repent, Lady Luscombe; but, unless the old leech-craft of my wandering-days deceives me, it will be a very death in life."

Lady Luscombe was kneeling by him too, now, and she only said, " Thank God. It will be better so. I loved him, you know;" then she added with a very simple dignity, " I may take care of him now."

" Oh, Guy, this is terrible," Daisy said, as she clung to Faucit's arm by the fallen man's side.

" Hush, dear!" he answered, raising his hat,—very reverently and very low — " let the justice of God pass by."

And all unknowing of what had happened at their feet, the old bells rang out again the comfort of the Christmas chime.

CHAPTER XXV.

LAST WORDS.

THE chronicler takes up his pen once more, but for a few minutes, hoping that his tale may need but little epilogue. For what more is there to tell that an acute and kindly reader will not guess? If I tell any-thing, will not many a reader wish that I had let it alone, and given him scope for his own imagination? But then there is that trying person—the *enfant terrible* of literature—who will insist upon asking how it all ended, and jibs at a ' t ' uncrossed, or at an undotted 'i.' For his benefit, then, let me supply something which had happened in the old church of Mould-on-the-Moss, which may be that the more intelligent reader will have divined from that brightness we spoke of, in Carrie Beaufort's eyes. When the youthful Gander joined her after Guy Faucit's admonition, what need to follow him ?

"A touch of her hand, and a word in her ear," under the shadow of some fantastic gargoyle, grinning on them with an air of protection; and the pink blush rose in Miss Carrie Beaufort's pretty face, and the plump hand gave back an answering pressure, and the frank eyes gave a promise which the frank life should keep. Happy be you, little people, in your own honest way; and as age tones down and steadies those frivolities of yours, which are as harmless as the proverbial crop of wild oats when a heart sound at the core underlies them, grow up together with your small Goslings about you, worthy and useful members of the world's motley club-house.

But oh, Sir Brummel and my Lady Coates, what are we to say of you? To say for how many months that loving voyage was victualled, might be to do injustice to the possibility that the term never ran into months at all. Still I am in no mood to turn out the seamy side of things, now that I am winding up the story which has been so long my companion. There is oil to strike in all of us, or nearly all, if the true means be found. The terrible moral of Lestrange's accident, which was the world's wonder for more than nine days, even as he had filled a larger space in it than falls to the lot of many men, may perhaps have carried home reflection and wisdom to the not too harmonious pair, and developed in them, at all events, those capacities of mutual toleration upon which at least a certain negative form of happiness may be grafted. We may be sure, at all events, that if the fair Emily were brought to that way of thinking, she would find her lord's essentially imitative mind ready to receive the necessary impression. He was not a man of quick parts, Sir Brummel.

The Lord Viscount Pentonville trotted on his way rejoicing, peering into everybody's concerns, and especially proclaiming the friendly interest he had taken in Mrs. Brent, and the perfect confidence he had always felt in her. A proclaimed and confirmed bachelor to the last, in spite of his sustained interest in the beauties

of the hour, and in the cotemporary journals of society,
he died at last suddenly, and creating much curiosity as
to the disposal of his very comfortable fortune, when
the world discovered, with a shock which it was long in
recovering, that he had been for upwards of ten years
married to his cook. The Duke of Surbiton and the
Marquess of Norbiton were especially exercised in the
matter, and made several bets upon the source of the
spirit which could have moved him, which they were at
last driven to refer to the widowed and ennobled artist
for decision. She refused with contumely to throw any
light upon the subject, and it was never known with
any certainty in society whether the lady had done the
trick with a *jambon en surprise*, as Norbiton thought,
or, as Surbiton would have it, conquered with a
Mayonnaise.

Good Lady Pepperharrow returned from foreign
parts not much edified with her wanderings, and as she
said after her cruise in the Channel, with one of the
locutions of which her ladyship was occasionally capable,
thankful to set her foot upon *terra cotta* again. It was
a very short time before she learned of the stirring
things which had happened since she left Luscombe
Abbey, and before a warm reconciliation took place
between her and her favourite Daisy, with a full explanation of the dreadful things which that shocking
Count Lestrange had said.

"Quite the most wicked stories, my dear," she said;
"and who could ave believed it of him and he so
distinguished? But we mustn't think anything about
it now, poor dear man, in the state which e's brought to,
when all we have to think of is what Mr. Birmingham
Pope tells us about charity, though indeed he says it's a
word which never ought to have been used, and really
means nothing."

No more welcome and frequent guest sate at Guy
and Daisy's table, than good old Lady Pepperharrow.

One other guest there was of theirs, who came and
stayed often. A woman with hair as white as the

driven snow, and a face which seemed to have out-
grown all human emotion but a gentle sorrow. A
woman quiet and tender and refined, speaking with
kindness and sympathy and allowance of all, and
winning a sort of pitying respect from all who met
her. Much of her time—most of it—she spent in
constant and in watchful nursing of a helpless invalid ;
a man looking old before his time, deprived of speech
and of the use of his limbs, and showing little sign of
remaining life but in a pair of black and restless eyes.
With those, before he died at last a quiet and a
painless death, he learned to watch her every movement with what she could not but believe bore some
appearance of gratitude and affection, bred and cherished
obscurely in the darkened mind. During the early
days of his long illness he had crises which seemed
terrible—moaned and started in his feeble sleeps, and
shrank with those eyes of his, instinctively, from meeting every other eye. From the poor lady who nursed
him he shrank most of all—cried and cursed at times
when she came near him, and looked at her as with
a blending of fear and of mislike. But she held her
own bravely and graciously, and she went on her way
with her sad and self-imposed task, till, as we have told,
she was rewarded in the end. The Count Lestrange
died with his hand confidingly in hers, without a quiver
and without a sigh, looking so young and placid when
he was dead, that it was hard to connect the face with
the perverted brain which had once so schemed and
sinned behind it. With his death, Marian Luscombe's
work in this world was done ; and not long afterwards,
after an affectionate farewell to Guy and Daisy, she
retired into a quiet sisterhood in the county in which
she had been born, to devote the rest of her years and
her own disposable wealth to the tasks of unobtrusive
charity.

Yet one more guest at the table, whom some of our
readers would perhaps not have altogether forgotten.
He has not shown himself much upon the scene of late,

from a wonderful instinct about being in the way. When the sun shone again, and the events of life settled down in their ordinary course, he was as much to the fore again as ever, and so remained till, in extreme old age, laying himself down one day to his toothless but unvexed sleep in the sun, he blinked himself quietly away to the side of his forefathers. His remains rest under a special stone which records the date and place of his birth and of his death, and tells how before he passed away there were two equal candidates for the affection of the famous Guy Faucit's once only friend—Frisco.

And Guy and Daisy—our Daisy—what last of them? Quietly and unostentatiously they were married after the year of formal mourning was past, which Daisy spent with Lady Pepperharrow. I have not seen such love as theirs, which seemed to reward these two chosen souls for all their storms, in an excess of blessing rarely given to men. Could she make him love her more than he did? If he had any feeling that jarred at all, it was a sort of retrospective jealousy of that husband to whom she had once belonged, which he felt as an insult to his flower. One day in wifely love and confidence she told him, with a face rosy red and the deep soft eyes turned down, that he must not even hint at thoughts like those to one who had never really been John Brent's wife. And as Guy Faucit kissed and blessed the mother of the baby-boy who threatened in his tub-days to rival his father's athletic feats of daring, and squared out with his one-year-old fist when any unauthorized person came near during his ablutions, he thought in his heart of all the force and meaning of charity, and had a gentle thought even for the evil and the meanness and the cruelty of John Brent.

Guy Faucit went into parliament, and became all that his college friends had so proudly augured of him. But his successes meant little to him save when those steady eyes beamed their bright and proud approval, and the noble face, chastened by trial and time into a newer and more statuesque beauty, looked down upon him in all the undoubting confidence, given and received, of the perfect law of wifehood. She was not his wife and his love only; but his friend, his confidant, his companion, his "mate" in very deed. Her pursuits were his pursuits, and his thoughts hers— in emulous sympathy rather than in imitation—as his mind insensibly moulded hers again, as it had once begun to do in those early Oxford days. So, blessed and blessing, loving and beloved, they went on hand-in-hand together on a path which was made very happy and smooth for them, when the storm-point had been turned. And with faith and hope bestowed upon them very largely, to make them look upon the happiness here as but the shadow of the bliss beyond, they thanked God night and morning that they had learned from Him according to His Word. that "the greatest of these is Love."

THE END.

BUNGAY: CLAY AND TAYLOR, PRINTERS.

S. & H.

Lightning Source UK Ltd.
Milton Keynes UK
UKHW010318110119
335176UK00010B/728/P